SON OF SEDONIA

SON OF SEDONIA

A NOVEL BY
BEN CHANEY

Cover by Ben Chaney
Design by Erin Campbell
Copy Edit by Abby Workman

First Edition

For information about permission to reproduce selections from this book write to:

TIPS Techincal Publishing, Inc.,
108 E Main St, Suite 4
Carrboro, NC 27510
www.technicalpublishing.com

Library of Congress Cataloging-in-Publication Data
A catalogue record for this book is available from the Library of Congress

eISBN: 978-1-890586-22-5
pISBN: 978-1-890586-23-2

1 2 3 4 5 6 7 8 9 0

For Mom, Dad, and the amazing friends who pushed, supported, and tolerated my excuses along the way.

...

And for anyone with a wall to climb.

Contents

PROLOGUE

JOGUN'S SHOULDER BAG swung wide as one of the grown-ups knocked into it. He stumbled on his scrawny, six-year-old legs in the dusty Falari Market street. Might as well have been invisible. There in the morning crowd, that was a bad and a good thing. Bad because he got treated like shit and people ran him over. Good because they didn't notice his hands darting in and out of their pockets. At least most of the time. Sometimes he had to run.

Jogun steadied himself then shrugged the strap back into the callus on his shoulder. The pinching weight made him smile. It had been a good day. A few jewels made of polished glass and circuit board shards. A whole bottle of aspirin. Two nine millimeter magazines, one regular and one hollow point. Even a small propane tank, half full. All of it clinked heavily in his bag as he made his way through the buzzing market. *No way he's gonna hit me tonight...* He breathed a little easier, but there was one last thing on his list before going home to find out.

He saw it ahead to his right, piled on a high counter. Bread. Long loaves of it, fresh from the cinder block ovens. He waded through the crowd of colorful fabrics and stood at the end of the line to wait his turn. Stealing food was a sin. Prayers didn't come true if you used sinful bread at the Stepstones. The baker called him to the counter.

"Whatchu got?" asked the baker, scowling down at Jogun through dark, black wrinkles. Jogun rifled through his bag and came up with the aspirin. He grabbed the lid and twisted hard, but the cap wouldn't budge. *Not givin' him the whole thing...* He tossed it back in the bag and kept digging.

"Ain't got all day, boy! C'mon!"

Jogun's little fingers closed around one of the jewels. Tiny gold lines glistened in pretty patterns on its shiny green surface. He reached up and handed this one to the frowning baker. The thin, flour-covered man squinted at the jewel, put it in his pocket, then tossed a quarter-loaf down to Jogun.

"Thank you," said Jogun, smelling the loaf. As his stomach growled, a low rumble rolled down through the market. Everyone's head snapped up. The slate gray sky hung heavy above them. Rows of tiny white headlights crept in long straight lines against the clouds. Afternoon aerial traffic from the City. As the crowd whispered rain prayers to God or gods, Jogun frowned up at the distant cars. *I hope you all crash.* He stuffed the bread in his bag and set out west toward the Rasalla River.

The Blue Ladies gathered past the edge of the Stepstones' concrete shore, ankle-deep in the shallow, oily water with hands locked in prayer. Dwellers of all kinds gathered at the water's edge, sending little floating lights downstream. Jogun approached the beached long-boat by the water. The Blue Lady inside smiled up at him and happily showed her lack of teeth in the light from dozens of candles.

"A good day for prayers, young man," she said. "God has shown he's remembered us."

"One, please," Jogun said, passing the quarter-loaf to her.

"Bless you, sweet boy, here you go." With both sand-colored hands, she offered him the flower. Cut soda-can petals splayed out in colorful layers of red, silver, and green. A squat wax candle filled the center. Head bowed, he accepted it. With a long reed, the old priestess passed flame from her candle to his.

"Go on," she smiled warmly and nodded to the River.

Jogun walked carefully down to the edge, found a bare spot by the water, and knelt. He closed his eyes.

"God hear me," he said under his breath. "Please protect Mama, and me, and my new baby brother or sister and make Dad go away. I promise I'll take care of us after. Amen." Jogun stooped, placed the flower gently in the water, and let go. He watched the light float past the Blue Ladies and toward the round mouth of a tunnel. There, it joined the other prayers in a flickering, starry stream. The first drops tapped his shaved head like an answer. He stood and looked up, savoring the damp, earthy smell.

"Thank you."

The rain built to a downpour on his way home. Dwellers danced and sang on the rusted streets, balconies, bridges, and rooftops beside their catch basins. Too many languages to count. Jogun broke into a run through the muddy neighborhoods. He'd be in for it if their basin wasn't flipped...but maybe his prayer had come true.

He was completely drenched by the time he got there. His thin, oversized tank-top clung to his narrow frame. The grey-green freight container apartment sat highest on the Stack, staring down at him. The fight last night had been one of the worst he could remember and the look on his mother's face was fresh in his mind. Sad. Broken. Surrendered. The way she had cradled her swollen belly...

Their plastic front door was cracked open when he reached the top of the rickety stairs. The water basin sat upside-down and unmoved next to the door. Jogun flipped it over to let the rain collect and used some to rinse the mud from his feet. Through the crack in the door, the apartment looked pitch black. He leaned in.

"Dad? Mama?" His voice came out in a squeak. No answer. He strained to hear through the noise inside. Rain on their metal roof sounded like machine-gun fire. *Not home.* He breathed a sigh and walked in. When the door shut, a faint whimper rose above the noise. He tensed as he saw the pale light at the far end of the room.

Jogun's father stood motionless outside the back door on the balcony, facing the shining Sedonia City skyline in the east. Jogun's eyes adjusted to the dimness of the apartment. Signs of both last night's fight and a new one were all around. Overturned crates, boxes, and tables. Their radio smashed to pieces in the corner. Broken bottles and glass lamps shattered and scattered and now...blood. A lot of blood. A spreading puddle of it led to the family mattress and stained the edge. A soaked woolen blanket covered a limp, curvy shape on the bed.

Jogun's heart sank and pounded near his stomach. The fingers on his small hands flexed as one foot crept in front of the other toward the bed. Keeping one eye on Dad, he knelt next to it. Pulled back the blanket.

The wide-open pupils of her blue eyes stared at him. Through him. The color had gone from her light brown skin. Her full lips gray and dry. Jogun dropped the blanket and threw up beside the bed.

"That you, boy?" his father said without turning. "Toss that bag in the corner, I'll look through in a minute. Better be more'n last time." Jogun heard the whimper again, louder now and coming from the balcony door. *The baby!* Shaking and dizzy, Jogun got to his feet, picked up his satchel, and reached inside. Closed his fingers around a pistol grip. Hesitated.

"Ma...Mama—"

"Told the bitch she couldn't have any more. Now I gotta deal with it." It sounded like he was talking about the chores or something. Jogun's hand whipped out of the bag gripping the jet black nine millimeter pistol. It was so heavy he almost dropped it.

The big man turned with a sneer twisting his dark leathery features. A brown-skinned, newborn baby boy lay naked in his arms. It sputtered and coughed between brittle cries in the rain.

"If I gotta take that from you," Jogun's father growled, "you won't get it back." They glared at one another as the room dimmed. Another clap of thunder. *Shoot. Shoot!* Jogun's trigger finger wouldn't obey. His arms drooped under the weight of the pistol. Dad snorted. Turned back into the storm.

Jogun couldn't hear a thing over his throbbing heartbeat. Sobs choked in the back of his throat. Then a sharp wail ripped through the room. His baby brother's. Jogun raised the gun and pushed back the hammer with both thumbs. He squeezed the trigger.

PART ONE
Family

1

Brotherhood

Twelve years later

ON TOP OF a low island chain of concrete apartments, Matteo could almost see everything. Didn't matter that he was short, sick, and weak. Countless hazy miles of the living, breathing Slums surrounded him. The cracked, sun-drenched streets. Tin roofs and awnings sticking out from cheap brick apartments. Gutted spacecraft and hull fragments turned into neighborhoods. And a dizzying network of scaffolding, catwalks, and plank bridges tying it all together. He grumbled at the mess. Squinted further east through the early afternoon heat.

Towering bright and proud above the Slums, Sedonia City glittered in silence. Matteo's big brown eyes traced the ivory skyscrapers at the center and carved each of them into memory. Early rush-hour traffic flew high overhead, to and from the center. *Where do they go?* He saw one ship had a cluster of glowing, blue-green engines on its belly. He watched it shrink into the skyline until his eyes watered. But as his gaze drifted down, his nose crinkled. The Border. A half-mile high, concrete barrier that separated City from Slum. He raised his hand in front of his face, blocking everything under the Border from view. Smiled.

The sting of the soccer ball came without warning, slapping him in the face. It knocked him off his tiptoes, down into the dust of the rooftop. Against the pain, he pushed himself up on shaky, bony arms. Realized he couldn't breathe. Panic flushed through him as he fumbled at the clear plastic tube under his nose and pressed the release. Cool mint air rushed in. The airway relaxed.

A group of kids laughed and pointed at him. Oki, the biggest one, was beside himself. The asshole had hit his growth spurt much earlier than his gang but still swelled with baby fat. Yellow teeth glinted in his big mouth.

"H-HA! Hey Wheezy! Hey uh...you wanna pass that back over here? Gotta finish our game," Oki sneered.

The patchwork, semi-flat ball rolled to Matteo's feet. Head throbbing, he stared at it. Clenched his fists. He wanted to hurl it back at Oki's head. Maybe bust out some of those crooked teeth. But the results of that choice played through his mind like a memory. Oki and the other thugs would chase him until he ran totally out of breath, then put another beating on him. He'd barely survived the last one.

Carefully, Matteo shifted to his skinned knees and pushed himself up.

"Pick it up," Oki said. Matteo shot a glare at them. Softened when he noticed another familiar face in the entourage, peeking from behind Oki like an anxious mouse. *Raia.* The cute neighbor girl that lived a few family-boxes down in his home stack. She never looked at him...at least not for long. Her blue almond eyes always glanced away when he noticed her gawking. *The airtank. The tube... me.* People always looked.

But here on the roof, she didn't look away. She stared hard along with the others, waiting for him to move. Matteo found himself shying away from her. *Her eyes...so blue...*

"PICK IT UP!" Oki shouted, making Matteo jump. They all laughed. All except her. Matteo swallowed bitter hate as he stooped and picked up the ball.

"Now lick it!" Oki said. Matteo stood perfectly still. Swallowed hard as he stared at the stained, worn out ball.

"Go on, bitch! Do it!" one of the others chimed in.

"Yeah! Come on, *Wheezy!*" said another.

"Oki..." Raia's tiny voice broke through the laughing. Matteo looked up to see her place a gentle hand on Oki's shoulder.

"Leave him alone, he's—"

"Shut the *fuck* up, bitch!" Oki jabbed an elbow into her boney chest, knocking her down.

"HEY!" Matteo shouted. The ball left his hand and sailed through the air before he knew what happened. It arced, then hit the ground. Rolled to a harmless stop at Oki's feet. A prickling acid wave crept over Matteo's skull as the situation came back into focus. The gang burst to life behind a still, scowling Oki. Raia sat up, dirt caked to streaks of tears. She wiped them away and continued her jeweled stare.

"Ohhh shit! Wheezy done fucked up now!" one voice called.

POP! Oki stomped the ball flat. Everyone jumped. Six lunging strides and the oversized boy was right on top of Matteo. Inches from his face. Sour breath flowed over Matteo as he looked down and away, staying silent. Oki turned his ear toward him.

"What was that? Speak up, Wheezy, I can't hear you with this shit in your face!" Oki yanked out Matteo's nose tube then shoved him in the chest. The gang behind chuckled nervously as Matteo sputtered and coughed. Oki threw his head back and laughed. They laughed louder.

Tears stinging his eyes, Matteo forced down the fit. The words came to him, crystallizing out of the fog.

"They don't really like you," Matteo said. It had come out in a whisper.

"The fuck did you sa—?"

Matteo struggled to smooth his ragged gasps as he straightened. Looked dead square into Oki's beady, close-set eyes.

"They're *scared* of you. They pretend to be your friend so you won't hurt 'em. But you do anyway. If you don't keep 'em scared, you got nobody. And havin' nobody *scares you*."

Matteo braced himself in the trembling quiet. Watched the thick fist cock back, fly forward, and catch him in the gut. The world went white. He doubled over, distantly aware of the kick that was coming next.

BANG! A gunshot split the moment in two. The kick never came.

"Fuck off. All of you," said an older voice. On the next rooftop stood a fit, broad-faced boy of eighteen with a black nine millimeter pistol in hand. He turned his sleeveless shoulder to them, showing the characters "T99" tattooed in a triangle. Oki and the other kids scattered like roaches. Raia got up, hesitated, then scampered off to follow.

Matteo crumpled into a tight ball. Looked up through throbbing vision to watch where Oki went. *Across those two wood bridges…then through Mr. Ramesh's garden.* He winced as he turned toward the sound of the shot. Scowled when he saw his older brother.

Jogun jumped across the gap in the rooftops and sprinted toward Matteo, holstering the gun in his waistband.

"Can you breathe? Are you okay?" Jogun wasted no time. He refastened the tube under Matteo's nose, sat him up, and felt his rib cage. Matteo coughed hard. Glared at Jo.

"Come on, bro, talk to me!" said Jogun.

"I'm—I'm fine. You just—" Matteo tried to swallow in a dry throat. Pushed against Jogun's grasp.

"I'm fine!" said Matteo, staring hard into his brother's eyes. Jogun hesitated. Released his hands. Matteo rolled and pushed up, head swimming with a sudden rush.

"Nah, you ain't fine, kid! I told you to stay away from them! But here you are, sight-seein' on their turf again…"

Matteo's eyes fell on the gun in Jogun's waistband. Fingernails dug into his sweating palms. *Across those two wood bridges and through Mr. Ramesh's garden…* Tensing his arm in an instant, Matteo reached out. He snatched the pistol and lunged away toward the first bridge. As Jogun reached after him, a noise broke above the midday Slums. Both brothers stopped dead in their tracks.

It rose to a roar, echoing over the rooftops. It got sharper. Louder. They looked up in time to see a white, wedge-shaped object streak overhead. Its blade wings jutted through thrashing engine flames. *A Pulsar HVX! Luxury class!* Matteo's pulse raced. Whoops and cheers sounded throughout the neighborhood. Jogun, without looking, held out his open hand. Matteo placed the gun in it. Jogun got to his feet, then turned.

"Stay. Here." Jogun glared at Matteo, waited for a nod, then took off after the bulging smoke trail. He ran across a narrow catwalk, vaulted over a guard rail, and disappeared behind hanging laundry in an alleyway.

Matteo fidgeted in the excitement. *It was luxury class! I saw it!* His feet begged him to follow. Oki's gang reappeared and ran past. Turned to wave 'goodbye' on their way after the ship. Oki back-pedaled to face Matteo and clutched his chest in a mock coughing fit. That was it. Matteo took three deep breaths from the tube and trotted off after them.

Jogun bounded from rooftop to rooftop, glancing up to keep the smoke trail in sight. Ahead, two young T99s in tank-tops, shorts, and running shoes darted up a fire escape and matched pace with him. Together they scrambled over walls, up ladders, and through the apartments of cowering dwellers. The locals cleared a path without complaint. Everything else in the Slums stopped when the Nines moved in force.

As the smoke thickened, they were joined by one, and then two more guys, all with 'T99' on their left shoulders. The wreck was close. Sour smells of charred carbon fiber and burning coolant confirmed it.

"The H3!" one of them shouted, "gotta make this quick, or it's gonna go off!"

Running up one final stairwell, the group emerged onto a flat, concrete rooftop. The Pulsar HVX sat wrecked at the end of a savage gouge in the concrete. Jogun sprinted up to it, meeting the several other gang members who were already tearing it apart. At the rear of the hull, Jogun recognized the radioactive symbol. He cringed as the Cutters yanked out the canisters of Helium-3 and tossed them to the waiting Runners. Nothing happened. He sighed. *No meltdown today...*

Jogun got to work. He and two others forced open the trunk with a hydraulic hiss. Revealed pay-dirt. Groceries. Laughing and whooping, they rifled through the treasure and filled their satchels. Jogun caught glimpses of detergent, potato chips, soap, shampoo, ground beef, and...*fresh produce!* He took care not to open that bag too wide while he took his cut from it. The others didn't seem to notice. Boomer was too busy stuffing his face with tortilla chips, and Porki chewed on a frowning mouthful of toothpaste. Spat it out in a soggy lump.

The Cutters torched panels from the hull while three senior T99s drew pistols and surrounded the cockpit. Suomo, the ranking member, waved his long lean arm for a Cutter to pop the driver's-side hatch. It swung open with a flick of the crowbar. A spongy, yellow-green material crumbled out the door. Suomo checked inside, then relaxed with a metallic smile.

"All clear!" Suomo called to the group. Jogun took out his crowbar, pulled his satchel drawstring shut, and trotted over. Met Suomo at the door.

"Cheap-ass foam," Suomo said, holstering his pistol, "Did the job for us. Jo, go on and pop the other side." Jo looked inside. Stalled. A family of three sat partially encased in their seats. Hollow stares from the husband and the eleven-year-old boy in the back seat told of instant death. The wife slumped over the dash, her face half-buried in foam.

"Well do it quick, fool! Better believe the Robos gonna be here any time!" Jogun ran around to the other side, pried the door open, and climbed up just in time to see Suomo reach into the foam on the driver's side. The husband's harness straps zipped back into the seat, Suomo grabbed the arm, and yanked the corpse out into a crumbling heap of dry foam. The senior Nine started rifling through compartments without a second thought. Jogun reached in. He grabbed the dead wife by the shoulder and eased her away from the dash.

She gasped and flashed her eyes wide open.

"SHIT!" Jogun stumbled out of the ship. The woman groaned, pulling a shaky hand from the foam to touch the gash on her forehead.

"A live one!" Suomo shouted, "Go ahead wit it, Jo." Only one thing that could mean.

Jogun swallowed hard. His heart raced. All eyes watched him as he pulled out the nine millimeter and climbed back up into the ship. He found the woman struggling to keep her eyes open. Her light-brown hair was stained yellow-green, clinging to her scarred, middle-aged features. *She looks like...like Her...* Twelve years ago, and her face still haunted him clear as yesterday.

"*Today*, Jo!" Suomo said. Burying the memories, Jogun raised the pistol. Looked down the sight at the woman's head. His breathing quickened. His arm trembled. Awareness gathered in the woman as her eyes rolled toward the sound of the clicking hammer. BANG! Red splashed against the sick-colored foam. Her head returned with a thump to the dash. *I'm sorry...* Jo pinched his eyes shut and pulled her out of the cockpit. Cheers and applause erupted outside.

"Yeah!"

"GOT that city-bitch!"

"That's the *shot*, Jo-*Gun!*"

Jogun flicked the safety on his pistol, stuck it in his waistband, and climbed into the Pulsar's backseat. *Just get to business. Don't let 'em see you sweat.* He scooped foam out by the arm-full, digging for the center console. Suomo climbed into the driver's side, leaned over to Jogun, and slapped him on the back. Jogun managed a nod then continued working. He kept his attention fixed on the console and away from the boy's body next to him. He looked away as that corpse was unhooked from its harness and dragged out.

They picked the wreck clean within a matter of minutes. First the factory stereo and speakers, GPS, head-rest monitors, yards of fiber optic cable, and anything with a circuit board. Then the heavy lifting. The seats, undamaged glass, polyurethane interior paneling, and the carbon fiber hull came out in crudely cut sections, tossed into piles on the roof to be carried off by the Runners.

Jogun, with full satchel in tow, stepped out of the skeletal remains in time to see the kids arrive. Despite their long pursuit, they had lost no energy. They pestered the Runners for closer looks at the loot. A few ran to the piles, picked up all they could carry, and followed behind their elders. A tiny kid arrived dead last. His tiny body heaved with each exhausted gasp. *Matteo!* Jogun sprinted to him, and crouched down.

"Dammit Matteo, when I say stay, you *stay!*" said Jogun. He glanced back, scanning behind him for traces of the bodies. Gone. They were carried off too. Jogun tried to block thoughts of what they'd be used for.

"I—I wa—" Matteo struggled.

"Slow down man, like we practiced," Jogun pursed his lips, drew in a long, deep breath, and exhaled. Matteo nodded and obeyed. Jogun pressed a hand to Matteo's stomach and pushed against the pressure of each breath. The boy's breathing slowed, accompanied by shrill wheezing.

"You good?"

"Y—yeah. What'd you get?"

Jogun furrowed his brow.

"Never mind what I got, boy, you need to learn how to listen! This ain't no place for you!"

Matteo frowned at the remark. He looked at the kids with armfuls of cable and hull fragments. He huffed through the wheezing.

"You ain't like them," said Jogun. Matteo shot him a dirty look.

"C'mon, I didn't mean...I just—whatever. Sounds like you need to head down to the Doc for a refill." Jogun tapped the inhaler tank in Matteo's hood, stood up, and dug into his satchel. Pulled out a ripe clementine orange.

"This should be enough...'specially with the seeds," said Jogun. Matteo held the alien object close, studying the texture and shape, "Don't even think about it. Not one bite, understand?"

Matteo rolled his eyes. Nodded. Jogun's ears perked up at a rising sound in the distance. The other T99s did the same. The distant, familiar thrum of hover engines echoed across the slums. Getting louder every second.

"Five-O! Get the fuck out!" shouted Suomo. The gang exploded into a frenzy, holstering cutting torches, bagging remaining scraps, and securing their satchels for escape. Jogun stooped to Matteo.

"Get to the Doc, and be home before dark!"

"Will you—"

"NOW!"

Matteo shuddered at the command, and hobbled to the fire escape. Jogun watched his little brother go as he tightened the satchel straps. *Be safe, little man...* With the gunship seconds away, Jogun broke into a dead sprint across the rooftops.

The IG-6 gunship, a repurposed military relic painted EXO blue, pulled its nose up as it reached the crash site, blasting the rooftop with a breaking thrust. Vet pilots called them FFT's or 'Flying Freight Trains.' The force of the hover engines floored a few T99 stragglers as seven EXO-Cops dropped to the roof like lead weights. Sergeant Kabbard and his men stood tall in the urban camo Augmentor gear on their arms, legs, and partial torsos. Each EXO drew his weapon and formed the first-response perimeter. Through his visor, the Sergeant's steel eyes took a quick survey of the scene.

"Davis! Leitmeyer! Ruiz! Olin! Legs on! Pick up some trails and run 'em down!" The four officers nodded in their tight-fitting helmets, and crouched. Each turned dials on their upper right hip, triggering the crescendo of a high-pitched, electronic whine. Four audible clicks snapped at full charge and each officer bolted in a different direction. Their bounding, inhuman strides cleared rooftops at a time.

"Shima and Mason, you're with me. Switch to spurs." Kabbard pulled the barbed stun pistol from his shoulder holster. Shima and Mason followed suit, converged on the recovering T99s, and fired stun spurs into their backs. Short convulsions followed by deathly stillness. The three fanned out to secure the wreck. Kabbard double-tapped a hotkey on his temple, dousing his vision in electric blue. No movement or body heat signatures appeared inside the wreck.

"Sound off!" Kabbard shouted.

"Clear!"

"Clear!"

Kabbard retracted his visor and glared at the stripped skeleton of the wreck. Ground his teeth. Another failure to add to the list.

"We were dispatched what, six minutes ago?" asked Shima, "How the hell could they have done this so fast?" The mouthy rookie lifted his visor. The sharp, bird-like features gave the kid a shifty look. Kabbard didn't think much of him. Too much of a taste for violence and cool gadgets. Mason, the fatherly elder vet, was all too happy to offer a sagely answer.

"You saw the prelim scans coming in. There were kids up here. They do this kind of thing from the second they can hold a blowtorch," Mason grumbled, squatting to inspect the torch-cuts on the mutilated rear-end. Ahead, Kabbard leaned into the cockpit. *Fucking mess.* He found it difficult to focus on any particular thing in all the twisted metal and shredded plastic. Only a wet, crimson smear on the passenger side caught his eye. His boot nudged a bullet casing on the ground by the frame..

"Sir!" Shima called from the opposite side of the ship, "I got three RFID chips here, minus three civvies! By the look of 'em, they were carved outta the vics' forearms right here...nasty shit! Sir." The rookie pulled out a plastic bag, dropped the bloody, square-inch microchips inside, and handed it to Mason.

"Must be gettin' wise..." said Mason, passing the bag to Kabbard.

"Won't be trackin' 'em that way anymore," said the Sergeant. He studied the chips. Bits of flesh clung to the tight circuits. Dark blood pooled in the bottom of the bag. All that was left of three more innocent lives. *Twenty years on the force... five Governor commendations for valor...two holes in my shoulder, one in my hip, and one in each leg. None of it makes a damn bit of difference...* Anger flickered inside of him, but had scarce little fuel to burn. *Empty.*

"Think they can pull the mem logs?" Shima asked.

Kabbard ignored the question. He pressed two fingers to his throat just beneath the jaw. Felt the familiar pop there.

"Pursuit Team, we've got civilian casualties," he paused, hating the words, "Find me at least *one* of these shitheads, and put the blue octopus on 'em. Can't let this go without a message." He released his fingers and turned from the wreck, walking straight toward one of the unconscious T99s.

"Blue octopus?" Shima raised a thin eyebrow.

"Yeah. Four cops. Eight arms..." Mason buried a fist into his meaty palm. A tight grin stretched over Shima's face.

Kabbard pulled out a stun pistol and pressed a button on the side. A dual-pronged barb flicked out of the grip. He stooped, twisted the T99's head to the right, plunged the barb into the base of the neck, and squeezed the trigger. The skinny gangster seized, shocked out of the stupor. Kabbard waited calmly as the thug shook his head and looked up at the three EXOs.

"The fuck you want, robo?" asked the gangster.

"Oh yeah, we're a *hard ass*, aren't we?!" Kabbard stood with the buzz of servos. Planted the armored toe of his boot in the scumbag's ribcage. Once the coughing died down, Kabbard knelt.

"Names and whereabouts," Kabbard said, "The pain stops when you tell me."

2

Prayers

MATTEO CRADLED THE orange in the belly pocket of his hoodie. The faded-yellow pullover was so baggy on him, no one would see anything bulging from the pocket. Not that anyone would think to find food on a scrawny kid like him anyway. All the same, he kept his head down through this part of Rasalla. So near the Falari Market, the streets swelled with the poor and starving. One whiff of his precious cargo, and they'd swarm him.

Dusk had settled over the Slums, casting scary shadows into the alleys flanking the street. Matteo's heart pounded against his ribcage. Detailed scenarios of desperate, violent thieves came to mind without permission. He shook his head and tried to focus on his route. *Right at the Alati Shuttle House, walk two blocks, and left into the Temple of the Wheel.* The wheezing was getting worse. He freed a hand from the orange and pinched the release on the tube. The medicine trickled in. Starving noses nearby caught something strange as he passed them. Matteo slipped his hand back into the belly pocket and sped up. Hung a tight right around the Alati House, a salvaged medical shuttle turned hospital that signaled the start of the Healer's Quarter.

"Healing" came in many forms. If you had the cash to spend or the goods to trade, you could buy anything here from antibiotics for an infection to the best highs in the Slums. Witch doctors and surgeons worked as neighbors. Lines between pusher and pharmacist blurred. They ignored Matteo, barking over his head to the shuffling crowd. He squeezed unnoticed through the queues of sick and wounded and came out at a T-junction. Took a left. Then the second right.

A twenty foot tall, circular metal gate spanned the path. Strings of lights wrapped around the red painted frame, making it glow like a warm hover coil. Matteo smiled. The Temple's smells of honeyed melon incense and fresh-grown

11

herbs always felt like a greeting. Breathing was easier for a moment. Past the gate, high rafters loomed above him with multicolored prayer flags hung in long, drooping lines. He wondered what each of them said...and if God really listened.

Matteo wove through the silent evening patients to Doctor Utu's clinic. It sat at the bottom of a stack of cinder block apartments. The gray concrete peeked through the ceremonial mural and hand-woven draperies decorating the walls. The evening torches were lit, filling the air with their cinnamon-spiced kerosene. The Doc could afford it. If a T99 or his family needed care, any self-respecting member sent them to Utu.

Matteo approached the front door and brushed a hand over the hanging beads. He loved the sound. Parting them slightly, he peered inside.

"Be with right with you, Mister Matteo!" said the Doctor in his rich, laughing tone. *How can someone sound like they're smiling?* Copper candle-light flickered all throughout the room, interrupted by the cool glow of the exam lamp. Painted prayers in English, Arabic, and Chinese snaked around the entire space, playfully overlapping the shelves. *'Blessed are the poor in spirit, for theirs is the kingdom of heaven.'* Matteo furrowed his brow, thinking. Filing the phrase away for later, he hopped onto a painted stool by the door and turned attention to the Doc.

"Almost..." Utu said, crouched beside the prosthetic leg of a reclining patient. The Doc stroked his round, lightly bearded face. He wore a loose, white linen robe and his natural paunch swayed underneath. He peered at the new leg. A curved strip of homemade carbon-fiber cut to shin length and socketed into a metal cuff below the man's knee. Utu adjusted the cuff with caramel-colored hands then lifted the leg to bend at the knee. Repeated the process.

"There," the Doctor said, "Try to stand." The large man lurched forward and pivoted in his seat to face the doctor. Matteo tensed. It was Raia's dad. The man had lost the leg in the Pits to a falling scaffold...it didn't make him any nicer. Too many good nights' sleep were interrupted by his drugged out screaming.

Utu stretched out his arms and beckoned to the man. Raia's dad planted his real foot, and with a shaky heave, put weight on it. Utu braced him under the left shoulder.

"Now take your time and *shift*," Utu began gradually withdrawing support, "to the new extension of your body." The man dipped and wobbled for a moment before finding balance. He tested the weight.

"Chafing? Discomfort?" the Doctor asked. Raia's dad pursed his lips and shook his head. Utu bowed and turned to the shelf behind him. He plucked a small frond of leaves and held them over a candle, scorching them. White smoke wafted from the crackling leaves.

"What was taken, let it thus be restored...through this joining of flesh and invention," the Doctor intoned, tracing the prosthetic with smoke. He straightened and extinguished the leaves in a bucket of water. A crutch made of welded pipe and sewn bits of upholstery leaned against the wall. Utu picked it up. Handed it to the man.

"Use this for one week as you get used to the balance. After, try walking as often as possible without it. Short periods at first, working your way up to longer ones. The muscles will ache with the new movement, but be sure to come see me if you have trouble. Okay?" the Doctor smiled up at the thick man.

The man grunted, touched his palms together, and bowed his head. Utu mirrored the gesture.

"Namaste," said Utu. The man turned, crutch under his left arm, and hobbled carefully toward the door. Matteo dismounted the stool and held the door beads aside. Though ignored, Matteo lowered his head in respect, then turned to see Utu beaming at him.

"Such a boy from *this* neighborhood...It does my heart good! How may I help you this evening, my friend?" asked Utu.

"Just a refill," Matteo rasped, taking out the orange and handing it to Utu. The Doctor accepted it, but seemed not to notice. His bushy eyebrows arched at the scratchy voice.

"And then some." said Utu, "Come! Have a seat." He wrapped the orange in a cloth and set it aside. Flipping around, he lowered the patient chair, and patted its cracked vinyl seat. Matteo climbed on.

"Let's just take this out and have a listen, hmm?" Utu reached around Matteo's head, gripped the plastic tube between gentle thumbs and forefingers, and removed it. Matteo fidgeted. He remembered Oki ripping the tube from his nose. Everyone laughing. The wheezing started as Utu set the empty canister aside, picked up a tarnished stethoscope, and fixed it to his ears. He exhaled on the metal pad and reached through Matteo's cutoff hoodie sleeve. Placed the pad there. Listened. Moved it and listened again. Utu sighed.

"My friend, what have you been doing?" Utu asked, setting the stethoscope aside. "Let's see..." The Doc scanned the shelves in the room then focused on a door in the corner. "Ah," he said. He crossed the room in a flutter of linen and opened the door, spilling white light into the room. Matteo leaned and squinted to see what was inside. Green plants of so many shapes and sizes. A broad leafed one with gold blossoms. A sparse, spindly one with red berries. The Doctor entered the closet and knelt beside a bushy one barely larger than Matteo's orange. He plucked a few coin-sized leaves from it, exited, and closed the door. It took a moment for Matteo's eyes to readjust to candlelight. The Doctor picked up a wooden mortar and pestle and started grinding the leaves.

"Well?" Utu said.

"Wasn't *doing* anything...just went empty. That's all," said Matteo.

"Mmmm..." Utu nodded slowly. "Hold this under your nose and take ten deep breaths." Matteo slouched in the chair, his small hands cupping the bowl under his nose. A strong menthol wave chilled his nostrils, throat, and lungs. The doctor turned away and hummed a gentle tune as he fetched a fresh canister. Through Matteo's growing buzz, the notes seemed to have their own healing quality.

His thoughts drifted. One breath. *Two. Three.* He was back on the rooftop next to the soccer game, gazing out at the city. *Four. Five.* Memories of countless buildings in the skyline appeared. Every curve and line. Every arrangement and set of windows. Every hazy silhouette rose in his mind and was lovingly examined. *Six. Seven. Eight.* He saw himself climbing over the wall, tunneling under it, blasting through it, or flying a ship—like the one he saw today—over it. The humming tapered off.

"Where are you right now?" Utu asked.

Matteo blinked. Shook his head slightly.

"Oh, I only ask because you certainly aren't here...or *now* for that matter."

"Huh? But I'm—I don't understand," said Matteo

"Yes, your *body* is here, but *you*? You were far away...a place you like to go?"

A snapshot of the city skyline flashed through Matteo's memory.

"Yeah...someday...it's just a stupid dream though."

"Dreams are a gift from God! Keep that one close to you, child, and it can be yours," said Utu, pruning a jagged leaf on a potted plant.

Matteo shrugged.

"Jo doesn't believe in God," said Matteo.

Utu stopped halfway through cutting a stem.

"I know, my boy...I know. Your brother, he...has his reasons," Utu continued cutting, "What do you believe?"

"I don't know," said Matteo, "I guess I've always had this...feeling. Like I'm supposed to be somewhere else. Like I *will* be somewhere else...doing something great. Is that God?"

Utu smiled.

"I don't know either. Do you *need* to call it something?" asked Utu. Matteo shrugged again.

"Then don't," Utu said, "But it is up to *you* to follow it or not."

"I want to..."

"*That*, my young friend, is Step One to achieving anything your heart desires," Utu offered the full canister to him. Matteo looked at it. Frowned as he dropped it in his hood and fed the plastic tube over his ears and under his nose.

"I need to get better," Matteo said, adjusting the nose-piece, "Stronger."

"Now there I think I can help you...*if* you're willing to work," said Utu, mock frowning.

Matteo perked up. Nodded. Utu continued.

"Come over once a week from now on. There's plenty that a kind young soul like yourself can do for me around the Temple. In exchange, I'll give you regular treatments *and* physical therapy. Together we will test this 'Faith' of yours."

Matteo's heart fluttered, making him wheeze a little. He squeezed the release. A fresh tank always felt good. The sweet mint coolness swirled in his chest.

"Thank you," Matteo smiled shyly.

"So! Back to the present moment...feeling better?" asked the Doctor.

"Yes, sir."

"Good man! Now, this fine orange you gave me...it's something *very* special. Maybe too much for my services this evening..." Utu turned and trotted to a shelf. He bent and slid out a lidless cardboard box. Reached inside.

"Your brother's friends get these from time to time. They're not the most... literate lot, so they pass them on to me. Haven't seen a new one in a while though." Utu pulled out a magazine and held it up. 'National...G-e-o...gra—' Matteo squinted to make out the faded letters, but a big worn spot on the cover cut off the end. It didn't matter much though. Here was something new.

"I've read each of them so many times now, I think it's time to pass them along. At least to those who might be interested." said Utu. Matteo fixated on the faded blues, greens, and yellows of the cover photo. He recognized the curved towers and cascading windows. But this... *This was taken from the air!* The words over the top of the picture tugged at his curiosity. 'Sedonia City: The Great More Machine'

"Well!" said the Doctor, "I'll take the vacant expression for a 'yes.' Why don't you go on and take that?"

Matteo's stomach flipped. He reached forward and took a delicate grasp on the magazine's edges. Peering into the photo, he fed these new angles and foreign shapes into memory. They slid into the gaps in his mental models, widening the big picture. The thought of looking inside the book overwhelmed him. He tore his gaze away and looked up at the Doctor.

"You're welcome. Now be careful with that on your way home. The binding isn't what it used to be."

"I will, I promise!" Matteo blurted out. Shyness returned to him. He brushed a hand against the beads on his way out the door.

Utu chuckled with a full heart, watching the boy disappear into the street with the prize. Yet as the room settled, sounds of the early evening drifted in through the swaying beads. Sirens. Drug-induced babbling. Shouting. The muffled tap of distant gunshots. Utu's gentle smile dragged down into a grimace he allowed few to see.

"Be careful, child..." Utu looked up at the ceiling. Beyond it. "*Take care of that one.*"

3

Weight

GOVERNOR ENOTA SATO sat oblivious to the fourth drink he'd poured that evening. Though the kinetic dampeners prevented any sensation of turbulence in the dark limo cabin, melting ice clinked in his glass of bourbon. The vinyl seat shook as his leg bounced. Multi-colored images, news feeds, and mail windows hovered before him, blurred together by the alcohol's effect on his neurotech. The resulting lag made everything linger when he pinched his eyes shut. He rubbed them. Opened them again. Set to mute, an economic reporter raved and thrashed above a cascade of scrolling stock-tickers. *'Full of sound and fury...'*

Sato pinched the bridge of his thick, straight nose. *Ring goddamn it!* His finger itched, ready to dart out and tap the simulated "Accept" button that would appear in his Neural. For now, he stared at the barrage of numbers. One set in particular made him compulsively wet his lips. *'Prescott Resource Group: -10.7, C230/share'*

Text reading *'Incoming Call: PRG'* appeared before him, shattering the monotony. Sato jerked in his seat. He tried to still the pounding in his chest and clear his throat. After two more obligatory rings he tapped 'Encrypt,' then 'Accept,' feeling the false vibration in his fingertips. A conference room materialized. The 3D effect offered by his Neural made him feel as though he sat amongst them. *Surrounded.* Seven people in spartan designer suits sat around a long mahogany table. Three women and four men. Behind them, the Milky Way drifted through an elegant bay window.

"Good evening everyone, I have two minutes before session, so if we could keep this brief—" Sato said.

"Cut the crap, Enota," the throaty vibrato of PRG matron Janice Prescott came in vivid through his inner ear, "We need to know that this...*incident* with the

DOJ is contained." The false youth of her century-old face sent a chill through him. He feigned a casual eye-roll to avoid her piercing stare.

"Of course. Contained *and* isolated. All evidence has disappeared into the Slums and Kabbard's hero cops are catching a few villainous faces for the eleven-o-clock news. Further inquiries into Slum dweller due process might seem a touch...vulgar, given the crimes of those imprisoned. Katheryn Roland's successor is well prepared to be less sympathetic to murderers." Sato internally loosened. The pitch. The tone. All exuded casual control, reassured by the focus augments in his head. *Let them just see how useful I can be.*

"Our concern is not with the plan or the execution. It's with you," Prescott's response was a slap. "All you say may be true, but the method... Anyone skeptical may begin to see a pattern of 'sudden and tragic' crashes in the slums. We need to know you're solid. Four bourbons in one Limo ride make us nervous."

Blood filled Sato's cheeks as he felt the perspiring glass squeak in his hand.

"I'm *fine. Let* them look for patterns. Any crusading investigator will end up chasing the history of every civilian death in the Slums. There are too many dots to connect."

"Kathy Roland connected more than a few...right under your nose, too. What happens when someone digs up Alan Rindal?" Prescott's question hung in the air a moment. Sato swallowed hard. Only one way to conceal the rush of anxiety.

"How dare you even *mention...!*" Sato leaned toward the screen and extended a sharp finger. "Rindal is ancient history. Finished. Buried. Forgotten. You leave him in the past, and that is where he'll stay." He curled the finger back into his fist and reclined. Glared at Prescott's glowing image in front of him.

"This speaks to my point. Making this personal is a mistake. We need you to detect and respond to threats and do so *separate* from emotional bias. There is *too much* at stake to miss a step now. If you can no longer differentiate between assumption and fact—"

"I told you, I'm fine. As of now, all *facts* indicate that the DA died a martyr's death at the hands of those she sought to defend. And with her public investigation suspended, the news and the polls will bounce back to green. Now if you'll excuse me..." Sato moved to press "Disconnect."

"Work on your image, Governor," said Prescott, "And be *careful*.". Her stone expression underscored the final phrase. Meanings within meanings.

"Always," said Sato. His smile weighed a metric ton.

"Thank you for your time," said Prescott. Sato tapped 'Disconnect' and the usual message appeared in front of him. *'Call Ended. Memory Block 081274_510p: Deleted.'* A bitter reminder that he, Enota Sato: Governor of the People, had much to hide from. His Neural flashed back to the muted economic report. He swiped a hand across it, dismissing all feeds from view, then grabbed the watered-down glass of bourbon. Gulped a bitter mouthful.

He traced a clockwise circle on the armrest touchpad. The tinted windows turned clear, brightening the limo cabin with the emerald skyscrapers of the City's Center Ring. He squinted through the migraine as he peered outside. *Almost home.* He reached into his coat pocket, produced a small green capsule, and tossed it into his mouth. Spearmint erased his bourbon breath as he watched the two-hundred story high-rises pass by. The calm flow of traffic drifted in perfect choreography. It soothed him...until the thought of a crash intruded. *Jesus, Kathy... why couldn't you just take the money and keep quiet?*

The limo merged with a climbing slope of traffic and exited into a neighborhood of luxury penthouses. Open-air swimming pools, roof deck patios, and lyrical floor-plans passed underneath. The limo dipped and touched down on the corner pad of a crescent shaped complex. Part of him relaxed, but luxury in this part of town brought with it the sensation of being utterly trapped. It took a moment to stir himself from the leather upholstery when his driver opened the hatch.

"We've arrived, sir," the driver gently reminded him. Sato's posture straightened. Chin raised, he lifted himself out of the hatch, triggering a head-rush. He winced as the ice-pick sharp pain bored into his temples. The driver moved to help. Sato waved him off, then descended the remaining limo steps, put his feet on solid ground, and adjusted his suit.

Walking was harder than he'd guessed. He reigned in his staggering as best he could along the paver-stone walkway. His rooftop villa didn't appear to get any closer. The low arcades of curved window-walls swayed ahead of him, fuzzy against the shining backdrop of the City. The driver trotted ahead and waved a bare forearm over the security plate, triggering a beep. Sato caught up slowly. Nodded a terse 'thank you' and stepped inside the foyer.

His villa was dark and still inside. The main hall windows had all been set to maximum tint and no interior lights were on. Sato paused and swayed.

"Jada?" he called out, straining to hear against the ringing in his ears. Nothing. He cleared his throat.

"Windows thirty percent." he said. The black glass panes cleared, spilling golden light into the main hall. Lacquered Spanish tables, art deco bronzes, and marble tile shone in the glare. Sato squinted.

"Make that sixty-five percent." The hall softened to a rich, honeyed orange and he rubbed his eyes. Crossed the entry hall and turned into the kitchen. Black marble counter-space lined the walls, inset everywhere with stainless steel appliances. The place was spotless. Scrubbed in a way that told Sato she'd been stress-cleaning again. He poured himself a tall glass of water, drank it down, then turned to the right. Stumbled through the dining room. High arched ceilings of glass and ribbed rosewood craned above a long black table.

"Jada?" He listened. A muffled voice carried down the hall from an adjacent room. Sato followed the sound until he made out the words.

"On-scene investigators have said that with so much of the craft having been stripped, the exact cause of the crash could not be determined. However, many owners of the '72 model have issued complaints in past months referring to errors in the navigation system and aerial attitude control. The FAA has issued a statement that formal inquiries will also be made into the impact foam delivery system of the Pulsar HVX..."

A ninety inch screen reflected its grim images off the vaulted glass ceiling. Sato's stomach turned. A GloboMetro Special Report showed HD video of Kathy Roland's family transport, gutted and stripped on a rooftop in the Slums. A series of sharp sniffles and sobs came from the leather sectional couch. He swallowed.

"Jada? What's going on? What happened?" Sato said. Jada pushed upright from her nest of blankets on the couch. The folds of her satin bathrobe wrapped her round, protruding belly. She wiped tears and bleeding mascara from her cheeks.

"Enota! You scared m—it's Kathy... Kathy Roland, her car crashed in the Slums. She's missing...they," Jada's throat tightened, "they say that she and her family have been taken...probably *killed*. She was coming to the shower next week, I..." Her soft features twisted in anguish as she cradled her round belly. Trembled with each heavy sob.

Sato sat next to her, pulled her close, and placed a hand on her stomach. She cried hard into his chest. His mouth opened to say something but the words evaporated when he felt a tiny kick against his hand. Jada's sobbing died down, and she sniffed hard.

"H-have you been drinking?"

"One in the car on the way here, that's all. Rough day."

4

Promises

DUSK CREPT ACROSS the overcast sky toward the horizon. Miles of evening lights flickered on, feeding the dull orange glow of the clouds and the ruddy twilight of the Slums beneath. But the south-western Rasalla district waited quietly in the dark. With the EXOs on the war path and the risk of stray bullets, the locals shut off their lamps and locked themselves indoors.

Jogun felt exposed no matter which corner he ducked into. Word was the EXOs could see in the dark...maybe even through walls. He crouched at the edge of an alley underneath a fire escape. Pouring sweat and out of breath, he struggled to hold still and listen. No engines. No thump-whine-thump-whine of Augmentor boots...at least none that he could tell. He eased a hand into his satchel and searched through the contents. Touched the cool sweat of his water bottle. A few things shifted and clinked in the pack. He winced.

Jogun gulped a mouthful of cloudy water, replaced the cap, and swallowed the urge to clear his throat. He put the bottle back in his pack then pulled the draw-string shut. Settled a moment. His exhausted muscles throbbed in the stillness. *I made it quick for her...it was mercy. Mercy.* He shook his head, cleared the woman's bloody face from his mind, and leaned out of the alley's edge. Scanned the red gloom of the street. Beyond a few meters of open ground, a narrow stairway carved a path upward through a multi-tiered neighborhood of scrap metal shacks and lean-tos. They'd run him all the way to the North-west edge of Rasalla, almost to South Bogi. Jogun stayed still for a few more heartbeats. *All quiet...*

He sucked a breath, ducked low, and sprinted toward the stairs. No more than four strides passed when he heard it over his own footfalls. The rhythmic, violent thumping of an approaching EXO. Panic begged his body to push harder. *Shit!*

He leaped for the stairwell and crashed hard against the mud-brick steps. Pain shot up his right side but fear kept it dull. He pressed his back against a shack wall.

Thump-whine-thump-whine-THUMP. The EXO crouched on the rooftop two buildings down from where Jogun had hidden in the alley. A black silhouette against the dim copper sky. The EXO touched something on his hip then the whine of Augmentor servos died to silence. The ambient roar of the City filled the neighborhood.

Jogun paralyzed himself against the wall. He was out of the cop's line of sight, but that didn't mean much. No way of knowing if they could hear the faintest sound, trace the smallest sign...or even smell fear. Jogun slid a hand behind his back and wrapped his fingers around the pistol grip. He eased the weapon out from his waistband.

Two electronic beeps from the rooftop shattered the moment. Jogun froze.

"No sir, it's all lights-out over here. Sector 7's on lock down—." The EXO's voice, though hushed, echoed against the thin metal walls of the block, bouncing down to Jogun.

"Yes sir, on my way." The EXO's Augmentor gear whirred to life. He straightened, stretched, then loped off East. Jogun slackened. Hearing the thumping foot-falls fade away, he holstered the pistol. Pain flushed through the shoulder that had broken his fall on the steps. He threw the satchel over the less-sore shoulder and limped toward home.

Six, eight, twelve, f-fourteen. Matteo climbed the rickety metal stairs to their apartment two at a time as he'd seen Jogun do. His scrawny thighs burned and trembled by the time he reached twenty-four, and there were forty-two to go. He grumbled and changed to slow single steps. The stairs coiled around the stack of freight container apartments where Jogun had raised him. The ragged, torch-cut window holes were creepier tonight. None of the usual candles, glow lanterns, or day-charged solars. Dark shapes moved around inside, speaking in hushed voices. *Lockdown here too? Robos must be really pissed...*

Dozens of tenants lived in this Stack. He passed a few sitting out on their balcony and a quick glance told me they were stoned. Sway addicts. Red powder caked their noses as they sat and stared up at nothing with giant pupils. Cigarettes smoldered at the filter in their stained hands. Further up, a man and a woman spilled out of a doorway in front of him. The man staggered back on a familiar prosthetic leg. They screamed at one another, punching, kicking, and clawing. Raia's dad, shirtless and missing teeth, slapped the straw-haired woman. Matteo waited, keeping his eyes on his feet.

"Hey, shut the fuck up, up there! The Robos are sweepin,' goddammit!" a hushed, rasping voice called up at them from nowhere. Raia emerged from the house, tugged her mother and father back inside, and grabbed the door. She paused when her glance met Matteo's. A purple bruise surrounded one of her perfect blue eyes.

"Are you okay?" Matteo asked, barely loud enough to hear. She crinkled her nose in a show of disgust.

"Freak!" She yanked the door shut. Tingling upset washed over him as his mind wrestled with the word. Maybe she said it to push him away and protect him from the other kids? Maybe to protect herself from Oki? *Or maybe I AM a freak...* Matteo hung his head, hid his tears, and stomped up the stairs.

He finally arrived at the top apartment, entered, then shut the plastic door behind him. His legs wobbled as staggered to the floor mattress and flopped down. Wincing, he rubbed his thighs just above the knees. *I'll get stronger. I'll do it or die trying.* A fantasy of running with Jogun materialized. Jo ran with his satchel and pistol as he'd done earlier that day, and Matteo carried a fearsome assault rifle with flames painted up the mag, over the bolt, and curling at the butt-stock. The muscles of his body rippled and pulsed as his powerful legs launched him over alleys and up massive flights of stairs...taking steps three, four, or five at a time. Jo fell behind and called ahead, begging Matteo to slow down. But Matteo went faster. Faster. *Faster.* He ran until he reached the Border. Looking up, he flashed a brilliant white smile. No plastic tube in his nose. With the deepest, clearest in-breath he'd ever taken, he crouched and then exploded upward in a soaring arch over the Border. Jo became a spec far below him. He turned away in mid-air to look at the City. Only he was high above it, looking down.—

The book! Matteo wiped his cheeks, reached under his hoodie, and pulled out the magazine. His eyes strained to look at his prize. *Too dark in here...* He reached for the battery lamp then stopped. *Right. EXOs.* Matteo tucked the magazine under his arm, pushed himself up on shaking legs, and almost buckled again. Grunting and fighting to stay up, he crossed to the balcony door. Heaved it open, spilling the fake dawn of a billion City lights across the hard floor. Matteo sighed. He stepped out onto the balcony and willed his aching limbs up the ladder to the roof.

The attempt to sit became an awkward fall onto his hip. He swallowed the pain and pulled his legs to the cross-legged position. Bent over the magazine in his lap. The colors were ruddy and brown in this light, but the shapes on the cover were clear. Drawing in as deep a breath as he could from his airtank, he opened to the first page.

Jogun opened the plastic door of the apartment and limped inside. He lowered the satchel to the floor, then paused in the pitch black. He listened for Matteo while his eyes adjusted, but heard nothing in the close hot air of the apartment. A twinge of worry came over him. He shuffled toward the mattress and crouched beside it. Empty. *Where the hell is he?* The balcony door creaked slightly open and a sliver of dim orange light entered. He hated that Matteo loved that balcony so much.

"'Teo?" A moment passed, then two light knocks clanged through the metal ceiling. Jogun puffed a sigh and walked to the balcony door. He climbed up to find Matteo pouring over pages of a magazine. The boy didn't seem to notice him.

"What? No 'Hey big brother, welcome home! Glad ya didn't get shot'?" said Jogun, walking over and sitting down beside Matteo. His little brother blinked and shook his head as though waking from a Sway trance.

"Huh?"

"Nevermind. Get what you needed from the Doc?" asked Jogun. Matteo nodded and demonstrated with a smooth, deep breath. "Good good. He gave you *that* too I guess... Can I take a look?"

Grudgingly, Matteo held the magazine up. Above chunks of text that Jogun couldn't read, a picture of a giant crane atop a skyscraper spread across two pages.

"Oh...I see." said Jogun. Matteo pulled the magazine back and turned to the next page. Jogun chuckled. "Dammit, Utu...I need to have a talk with him." Jogun stretched and laid back on the tarnished metal roof. Hands behind his head, he stared up at the twinkling flow of traffic. Matteo sighed sharply.

"About *what?*"

"About fillin' your head with all...*this*," Jogun waved a hand at the magazine. Matteo sat motionless, staring at the book. Jogun sat up. Leaned forward to grab eye contact.

"And I know you don't like to hear about it, but maybe one day it'll sink in. Out here, you gotta keep focused on what's in front of you. You starve, catch a bullet, or get locked up if you don't."

"Like Dad did, yeah I know," Matteo snapped.

"Y-yeah... Like him." Both of them went quiet. Jogun dug around in a cargo pocket for the hand-rolled cigarettes there. Hearing Matteo's nasally breath, he released the pack and took his hand back out. Flexed his fingers. Drug addled ravings rose from a few floors below. Matteo fidgeted with the corner of the magazine's frayed binding.

"I wish I could remember *something* about him. Anything," Matteo said.

"Wish I could forget," Jogun stood up. That dark apartment flashed again through his mind. Instinct turned him to look down at the boy. He saw the magazine clutched in the tiny hands, pulling his little brother away. In one quick motion, Jogun crouched and snatched it up. Matteo lunged after it but grasped only air.

"Man, *look at that wall!*" Jogun thrust a pointing finger at the giant concrete barrier in the distance. It loomed high above the shanty towns that clung to its base. Tiny red lights set at wide intervals pulsed along the top edge, and pillbox watch towers punctuated each broad slab of concrete. Everyone in the Slums knew of the big guns stationed in the towers.

"What does that say to you?!" asked Jogun. Matteo blinked back tears and turned away.

"It says 'Don't bother! We don't want you here!'" said Jogun. Seeing tears run down Matteo's cheeks, he buckled. Smoothed his voice.

"Dad wouldn't get with that. Always talkin' about buyin' and killin' his way in. How Mama and me cost too much already and she couldn't have no more... It got him killed, 'Teo, and he took Mama with him. Almost took *us*." Jogun sat again. Leaned toward his little brother.

"This right here is your home. These are your people," Jogun waved a hand over Rasalla, "Smart as you are, you can find a way to help us all out right here... make things better *here*... understand?"

"Y-yeah..." Matteo sniffled.

"And don't ever let me catch you with a gun in your hand again, aight? Bad enough one of us got blood on his soul, ain't no need for you to have it too," Jogun said. Matteo sucked in a sob and nodded.

"Promise me."

"I promise."

"Cool," Jogun said, "Love you, big man..." He wrapped an arm around his little brother and pulled him in close. Matteo hugged him back. Jogun both heard and felt Matteo's stomach growl.

"Boy, you forget to eat *again?* How you expect to get stronger if you don't—" Jogun froze. His eyes rolled down to his left arm. A shiny, jagged barb stuck out below 'T99' on his shoulder. Dead cold spread out from it. His mind screamed as he watched himself slump and topple, sprawling him flat on his back. The sounds of thumping footsteps and whining servos approached from all sides. Matteo threw himself over Jogun's limp body.

"Don't move, kid!" One of four EXOs shouted. They surrounded them, glaring through lifeless black visors.

"Just stick a spur in him!" said another EXO. Behind his back, Jogun felt Matteo's hand close around the pistol grip.

"Stand the fuck down, Shima! Stun this one and his heart could stop. What do you think happens when all of Rasalla learns we killed a sick kid? Just pull him off."

The one they called Shima nodded, then approached the brothers. Matteo started pulling the pistol out from Jogun's waistband.

"D-don't," Jogun rasped through clenched teeth, "No...b-blood..." Jogun's wild eyes met his brother's. Matteo released the pistol as an Augged hand clamped on his shoulder. His bony arms tried to cling, but were easily ripped away. They tossed him to the side.

Jogun tensed as the four officers converged on him. His body was deaf to every plea for movement. They flipped him over like a carcass at the market and cuffed his wrists. The ranking officer stooped low next to him and raised the visor. *Kabbard...* The flat scowl and gray eyes few got away to talk about. The straight, sharp scar from chin to cheek left no doubt.

"You know my face, you piece of shit?" asked Kabbard. Jogun could only stare. "Good." Kabbard turned to his officers.

"So our boy here must know what we *do* to lady-killing scumbags when we catch 'em," said one of the others. An older, deeper voice. Jogun's face contorted as he tried to spit a curse. It came out in a weak hiss. Kabbard shrugged and stood up.

"You heard the man." Kabbard nodded. Shima stepped forward and landed a kick into Jogun's ribs. Two others followed suit, driving carbon-fiber toes into the kidneys and shoulders. Sharp cracks punctuated Jogun's grunts. Through the pain, he saw Matteo crumple in the corner of the roof, hands pressed over his ears with eyes clenched shut.

"Pick him up." Kabbard ordered. The EXOs lifted Jogun by his cuffed wrists. Kabbard touched under Jo's chin. Raised the bloody head.

"Her name was Kathy. She was a District Attorney. A wife and a mother. I'd kill you right here if I weren't already sending you to Hell." Kabbard's dead-eyes glared into him. The Sergeant's finger servos buzzed as they curled into an armored fist. It cracked into Jogun's jaw with a right cross. The world shocked to white, then went black a moment.

Straightening, Kabbard pressed two fingers against his throat.

"Omega-Two ready for pick-up."

The throbbing of hover engines emerged from the background noise of the Slums and grew to a pounding roar as the drop-ship flew in. Jogun watched in horror. The black cockpit glass and pulsing red beacons at the nose formed a gaunt, lifeless face. A demon without mercy. A yawning mouth opened toward the rear of the thirty-foot craft. Dull fluorescent lighting blinked on inside, revealing rows of unconscious, bloody prisoners sat harnessed and bolted into metal flight seats. Two of the EXOs grabbed Jogun under the arms and dragged him toward the hatch. With agonizing effort, Jogun turned his heavy, shaking head. Looked at Matteo through eyes nearly swollen shut.

"M-matteo," his mouth sputtered blood, "Y-you got this..." Something like a smile creased his broken mouth as the EXOs threw him inside. They found an empty seat, hefted Jogun's limp body, and dropped him in. A bulky metal harness locked down on him. Kabbard and the officers stepped inside.

"We're good here, button it up," Kabbard said. The hatch door clamped shut, swallowing all of them. As the thrum of the engines picked up, the drop-ship listed heavily to the right, pulled up, then blasted off into the night sky.

Matteo whimpered. Though unhurt, he struggled to open his eyes. The rooftop was dark and quiet again, and wet black stains glistened on the metal. The magazine sprawled open near Matteo's feet. Its pages flapped in the breeze.

5

Greater Good

SERGEANT KABBARD FELT the landing gear of the IG-6 touch down at last, though tonight he couldn't let the relief of the dying engines fully take him. The worst part of the job waited outside the passenger hatch. He, Mason, and Shima unhooked their harnesses and stood up. Checked each prisoner's restraints. Kathy Roland's killer looked up as Kabbard tugged on the shackles. The swollen eye-pits stared, weeping bloody tears.

"Show time," Kabbard said as he stepped to the door. Keyed his throat mic. "Rear compartment secure, open her up," he said. The hatch hissed open, revealing a legion of reporters, camera men, and bright stinging lights. Their questions overlapped one another in a squabbling din that echoed through the main hangar of EXO Headquarters. Shima, the new kid, grinned and waved. Kabbard slapped the hand down. He felt bile rise in his throat as he prepped the broken, bloody scumbags for transfer. Cuffed at the wrists and ankles, each limp body was un-hooked and placed on a procession of hover gurneys. Kabbard sure as hell didn't feel like a movie star. Covered in dried blood and Rasalla dirt, he stepped out.

"Sergeant! Sergeant!" one of the voices called out from the paparazzi, "Which one killed the District Attorney?"

Kabbard looked at the bodies. Pointed to the boy who had shown up in the last mem-data entry on Mrs. Roland's RFID chip. A skinny, malnourished kid of eighteen covered in bruises, blood, and clear bone breaks. Kabbard knew what was coming next. The GloboMetro press corps wanted a monster. A raging, evil face to justify the fear of the people beyond the Border. This little shit-bird didn't qualify.

"Sergeant, how do you account for the prisoner's condition?"

"Resisting arrest," Kabbard said as he tried to push past the throng. The voices shouted more questions until one cut above the rest.

"Sir, Kathy Roland was a staunch defender of due process and fair treatment of the Dwellers! What do you think she would say about this?"

Kabbard stopped in his tracks. Turned to face the reporter. A jumped up twenty-something metroboy with short, carefully shaped hair and a pound of makeup. An Inner Ring yuppie who'd never known real horror.

"She can't say anything now. This *Dweller* shot her in the face for the contents of her vehicle. Happened plain as day in the mem-feed, so we were able to get the conviction on the way here, now if you'll excuse us..." Kabbard, Shima, and Mason towed the line of prisoners to the acquisitions team while the other officers corralled the press.

"Fuckin' vultures," Mason muttered.

"Just another part of the machine," Kabbard said. He was tired in his bones. The fighting would never stop, outlasting his last breath by centuries. And the City would always demand more. The procession stopped at the acquisitions team and the transfer shuttle. As the bodies started tracking into the cargo hold, most of their eyes were wide open. Scanning the high ceilings of the EXO HQ bay in animal terror. Tears streamed through the dried blood on the murderer's cheeks.

"I could use a drink or twelve," said Mason, "Dive Bar? Kid, you in?"

"Hell yeah!" Shima said, pushing the gurneys along.

"Sergeant!" an unfamiliar voice spoke up, stopping Kabbard before he could decline Mason's invitation. A blonde haired, bug eyed man in his late twenties stood behind the officers. His suit was clean, pressed, and perfect...the kind that screamed 'Government.'

"My name is Andreas," said the young man, "Sedonia Chief of Security. Mister Sato would like to speak with you."

"Look, son, it's been a day and I really don't feel like a long ride up to the Tower, so—"

"Follow me, please," said Andreas.

Kabbard recognized an order when he heard one. He looked at Mason. The old vet snorted a laugh, and nodded toward the Suit.

"Go ahead, we'll finish up," said Mason.

Andreas led the way down the platform and across a skywalk to the main complex. The massive structure of equipment bays, barracks, and office space rose from the sixtieth floor to the hundred-and-twentieth. The angled prow of the building stood sentry over the Outer Ring, the Border, and the twinkling Slums beyond.

From the main lobby, they took the elevator up to the executive level. Commander Gorman's office. *Sato's here? In person?* Kabbard thought to ask, but knew Andreas wouldn't answer. Suits were like that...solid gold rods shoved so far up their ass that they'd never bend over for the 'lower folk.' Andreas swiped his chip arm over a security plate and the elevator doors opened onto a long windowed hall. They turned right through the double doors to the main conference room. Voices inside.

"—for us, we'll of course be in your debt," Governor Enota Sato turned in his chair, "Sergeant Kabbard! Thank you for coming and apologies for the interruption...I'm sure you're ready to clock out for the night. Please, have a seat...care for a drink? This eighteen-year-old Choril Scotch isn't going to drink itself." Sato pulled a fluted crystal bottle from the center of the table and started to pour into a short glass. Commander Gorman sat opposite to Sato with a glass of his own.

"No thank you, sir, I'm still on duty. Water would be fine," said Kabbard. Though polite as he could manage, it still sounded like a rebuke. Not giving much of a damn, he walked to one of the high-backed chairs and took a seat. The bouncy cushions felt strange against his bulky Augmentors.

"Good man. The Commander and I were just discussing what a good job you did this evening. You handled yourself *very* well with the press...not an easy task, I know," Sato said, smiling.

Kabbard frowned. Darkened.

"I told the truth. Katheryn Roland deserved justice," said Kabbard.

"Yes...yes, of course," Sato said, "Which leads me straight to the point. The Commander and I agree that your service to this City has been more than exemplary, but your abilities *far* outstrip your station. John Kabbard, I would be honored to have you for my new Chief of Security." The words seemed to take the wind out of the room. Kabbard instinctively glanced at Andreas. The young Suit seethed in the corner, holding an eerie silence. Kabbard tensed, sensing the kind of rage that could slip so easily to violence. *This kid is a killer...*

"Andreas here has done a great job for us, but it's time for some new blood in this administration," said Sato, "He will assist you in the transition."

Andreas excused himself from the room with a rapid click-click-click of his patent leather shoes. In the silence that followed, Kabbard realized that the Commander and the Governor were waiting.

"I appreciate the offer, sir, but...my place is here with the EXOs," Kabbard said. An assistant entered the room, quietly placed a tall glass of clear water on the table in front of him, and left.

"What, do you think, is the purpose of the EXOs?" Sato asked. The question was almost insulting until Kabbard started thinking of an answer.

"To secure the Border...to protect law, order, and democracy for those on the other side..." Kabbard stopped, interrupted by Sato shaking his head.

"I asked what *you* think," said Sato, "Men like you aren't impressed by the official version, and I know it."

That knocked Kabbard back a step. There might be more to this Suit than the squeaky-clean public persona. Kabbard's true opinion stuck in the back of his throat. He knocked back the glass of water, swallowed, then took a breath. Forced the words out.

"Public opinion and control. Government uses the idea of an Enemy to keep civilians afraid. Scared people are easier to unify. Easier to distract. It's our job to keep the fear fresh and the wheels turning," Kabbard said. Twenty years of accumulated cynicism in a handful of words. Commander Gorman shifted his stocky frame uncomfortably in his seat, and looked at Sato. The Governor blinked. Shook his head as though suddenly disoriented.

"Well...there it is. A surprising view for a civil servant to say the least. Thank you, Sergeant...though the next question is obvious. If that's the case, why stay?" asked Sato.

"Ours is not to reason why," Kabbard said.

"...but to do or die. Tragic and beautiful," Sato said, "But I wonder. Would you be willing to hear a *better* reason?"

Kabbard furrowed his brow, skeptical but suddenly alert.

"The EXOs remind our neighbors beyond the Border of our power and authority, so that they don't even *think* of crossing the wall. You and your men, in effect, keep the desolation of the Slums from infecting the best of Humanity, but that by itself is unsustainable. So what's the solution?" Sato waited for an answer. Kabbard had none to offer. The governor continued.

"We protect our Border so that we can preserve our strength. If we preserve our strength, we can not only grow, but *flourish* again and hasten the day when City and Slum are one and the same. When the Border is dismantled and prosperity returns to all."

Kabbard looked down, staring at his glass of water. *A solution? Peace? Repatriation?* His mind rejected it instantly. A liberal pipe dream, and possibly a dangerous one. Yet his palms slicked with sweat on the cool glass. Sato leaned forward. Continued.

"John, this is impossible without a man like you. I need someone who understands the Slums. Someone who's walked in the rows of Falari Market. Someone who knows the people and someone who the people know...on both sides," Sato leaned back, "It's a lot to take in, I know...especially after the day you've had. Go home and think it over." Sato stood up and extended his open hand. Kabbard did the same and accepted the handshake. He nodded to Gorman, turned, and left the conference room on the way to the lockers. The commute back to his Inner Ring apartment went by in a flash. A blurry, distracted Superway train ride through the dingy high-rises of the lower middle class. *Peace is impossible. The Slums might as well be a separate country. A separate hostile country. They'd never trust us again.*

"Watch your step. Watch your step," said the artificial woman's voice through the Superway speaker. Kabbard looked up, disoriented. Stood and shuffled out with the other red-eye commuters into Seraphim Station. The cavernous commercial hub throbbed with neon advertisements that clawed at his attention. All around, people were absorbed in their Neurals, browsing restaurant menus, ordering clothes, and podcommenting on aggregator blogs. Apps as extensions of their minds and bodies. A few played aug-games, dodging simulated green fireballs they threw at one another. Kabbard's law enforcement Neural allowed him to see through all the privacy-mode blocks. He ground his teeth as he disabled it. No one was watching the news. Or giving a damn about the third world country a shuttle-ride away. They flooded in and out of the segmented Superway cars like blood cells flowing through a vein, gathering at the Commons' hundreds of shops and kiosks. *Consume, rinse, repeat. If they only knew.*

IAfter a half-hour trip over skywalks, up commuter lifts, and into the Alessi Building, Sergeant Kabbard arrived at his single studio box in the wall. Neighbors passed without a glance as he buzzed himself in, shut the door, and plopped down in his beat-up recliner.

He looked around. Cardboard moving boxes stacked in each corner. How long had they been there? Seemed like only last week when he found Shannon's note saying that she couldn't 'take anymore' and was leaving with the kids. Their family pictures sat off in the corner, still encased in thick, green bubble wrap. He'd moved out of their dream apartment in Whitlatch and into this squat. *Must have been, what, four years ago? five?*

The long nights. The endless browsing through her Neu feed, waiting for a message, or worse, a news update. The painful, silent dinners and days off. The nightmares. The outbursts. She'd had enough. He both hated her and understood.

Kabbard got up and stepped outside to the shallow balcony. The City wound down to its midnight humming glow. The soft roar of civilization filled him as his civilian-clothed body tingled and twitched from Augmentor withdrawal. *My City...* he thought. All the sacrifices he'd made for it. Had he really helped at all? No clear answer came.

He looked up. High above the scraper-tops, the hazy spire of Sedonia Tower stabbed into the sky. The red light at its peak blinked silently like a watchful eye. He chuckled to himself.

"Well...it'd be one hell of a paygrade bump."

PART TWO

Choices

6

Savings

Six Years Later

AS ALWAYS, THE long daily pilgrimage to the Pits began in the dark blue haze of the gathering dawn. Bodies streamed out of their hovels to join the march, all in silence. Only the clink and rattle of handmade equipment and the shuffling of feet advertised their passing. Some didn't want to wake their children. Some, the oversleeping T99s. Others kept quiet for no other reason than the fear of what the day might bring.

Matteo stretched in the gloom of the container apartment. His body ached as usual, but the pain had gotten lighter over the years. Already he stood as tall as Jogun ever had, and tight whipcord muscles wrapped his slender frame. It had taken four years of chores with Utu to get to this point. Changing bed-pans, washing soiled linens, bathing the elderly—all worth it. The healthier he got, though, the less he wanted to be around sick people. And there were other kids in need of Utu's help. The old man had smiled. Seemed to understand. 'Go find it,' was all the Doc said.

Still looking. Matteo thought bitterly as he threw his gear into Jogun's old satchel. Blowtorch. Ball cap. Tape-patched sunglasses. Handkerchief. *Airtank.* He didn't need it much anymore, but sometimes... Curling a lip in disgust, he shoved it in the bag.

Breakfast was a hastily-cooked ball of rice. Lunch would be too. He shoveled some uncooked rice into a plastic bag, tossed it in the satchel, and yanked the draw-string shut. He switched off the hot plate and scooped his breakfast out of the pot with a bare, calloused hand. All five scalding mouthfuls were eaten in seconds. His stomach still growled on his way to the door.

Hand on the latch, he paused. Looked at the camouflaged metal plate in the corner by the door. He knew how much was in there. Down to the milligram.

But the urge to check anyway was irresistible, especially at the start of another day in hell. Matteo put his satchel down and crouched in the corner. Uncovered the hidden compartment. Inside were three plastic containers, each no bigger than his palm. He picked one up. Breathlessly pried open the air-tight lid.

Kale seeds. Hundreds of them. He caressed the top of the little pile with a fingertip, feeling each of the pin-head size pellets. The other two boxes housed the tomato and spinach versions. Four years of savings. Enough to keep him fat on rice, chickens, and greens and still have plenty left for months of Utu's advanced treatments and remedies. But they were worth more than that. Nine-point-eight more grams of Kale seed, and he could afford to hire a Lifter.

Matteo felt the rough skin on his left forearm where the jailbroken RFID would go. A new life. A new identity. A ticket across the Border. Word was Lifters could hack a new ID into the chip, square it with the City networks, and arrange for transport over the Border. No one ever came back. Most assumed that meant death. *Plenty of ways to die here, too...without trying...* Starving to death or getting crushed in the Pits among them. The only other option was the Nines. With them, he could make nine-point-eight grams in no time, but what would he have to do to get it? '*No blood.*'

Matteo replaced the cap and returned the box to its hiding place. His stomach growled again as he stood. Pushing out of the front door, he tucked the sensation away for the ten mile trek to the edge of the Slums.

In the wastelands, beyond the fringe, the silhouettes of hulking cargo freighters, hover-liners, and vehicles of all other sizes and descriptions signaled arrival at the Pits. Although the place didn't get its name from the scrapyard. Vast man-made sores yawned open in the ground as far as the eye could see. Deep terraces filled to the brim with garbage. One of Matteo's magazines said they were made by something called 'strip mining' before all Earth's 'industrial resources' ran dry. Flying scows from the City flew over the Pits, dumped their loads, and flew away. Scores of men, women, and children did their best to dodge the incoming trash then converged on it to get first pick of what fell. Watching them belch a few fresh tons, Matteo rubbed at a ragged scar on his shoulder. *A bad day.* A falling chunk of countertop had almost killed him.

His new job, while it paid slightly more, wasn't much better. Few workers survived past the age of eighteen.

Sparks fell from the ship's hulls in the distant scrapyard as the first Cutter crews got to work. Gigantic chunks of scrap metal were already falling to the dirt in violent, ground-shaking crashes.

The mood of the workers lightened when they formed up into their usual crews. Chatter, joking, and singing rose with the sun. Matteo approached a crew of four Cutters.

"I'm tellin' you bro, she can't get enough! We did this one thing last night..." A short, stocky Cutter stopped when he saw Matteo. Matteo smiled.

"'Chu lookin' at, freak? Move on!" said one of the others. Most crews were like that nowadays. Utu had called Matteo a 'savant' when it came to machines. He could strip an engine block down to clean, usable parts in ten minutes. Not normal and not appreciated like he would've thought. Matteo gritted his teeth. Kept walking. He listened to the other conversations while he stewed.

"I'm tellin' you, that's what I heard! They grab you up and shoot you to the damn Moon! Ain't sayin' I believe that shit!"

"—and maybe if you wasn't so lazy, we'd do a decent Cut once in a while!"

"Whatchu know 'bout a *decent Cut?*"

"My cousin! He heard it from Suomo *hisself!* They're payin' *triple salvage* on the shit...some shit about 'parts for the struggle.'"

"Triple salvage?" Matteo blurted out. That kind of seed would go a long way. A crew of three young men no older than seventeen turned angry glares on Matteo.

"*You wanna keep your fuckin' voice down!?*" the shadow-skinned one rasped. "Don't everybody know 'bout this yet!"

Matteo didn't flinch. He stood straight and stared them down.

"If you wanna keep it that way, cut me in. What are they lookin' for?" he asked.

"Oh I'll cut you!" the thin, scrappy one said, pulling out a sharpened metal wedge.

"Ruka, chill," the command from the dark Cutter seemed to slacken Ruka's muscles. "Blood wastes time and attracts attention. 'Sides, an extra hand might work out." The Cutter casually turned back to the third man. The move was subtle, but Matteo saw him mouth a word into Ruka's ear. '*After.*' Good to know.

"I'm Samir. That's Ruka and that's Taliq. Get your gear, follow us, and keep your mouth shut." Matteo pulled up his shoulder strap and followed. The four of them climbed through a ragged tear in the lower hull of a skyliner called 'The Somnium.' Just inside, crews swarmed all over the hover-engine room, grabbing everything that wasn't riveted down and torch-cutting anything that was. The shell of a fusion reactor came down in minutes. The workers' only protection against the radiation: rubber kitchen gloves, thread-bare track suits, and expired re-breathers they'd found on the walls.

Samir wasted no time getting up the metal stairs and through a hatch at the aft end. He led them through the maintenance corridors, a twisting, turning, climbing series of angular, high-ceiling passages. The path grew pitch black as they passed the last of the early crews and their lamps. Samir took out glow sticks, cracked all four, and passed them around. Shaking them bathed the hexagonal tunnel in blue-green twilight. Deep in the aft end, they finally reached an untouched block of engineers' quarters. Two bunk beds per room with all the trimmings intact.

"Okay, we're lookin' for batteries, copper wire, and any kind of switch you can find. Lights, TV, window, A/C, whateva, so long's it turns on an' off. Get the plumbin' pipes too, 'specially PVC. Go," said Samir. All four of them took a room and got to work. Matteo glanced around his first bunk in an instant, mentally marked his targets, then stuck the glow stick between his teeth. Batteries in the emergency floodlights. Copper wiring in the wall sockets, intercom, and light fixtures. Light switches from the door, bathroom, and shower. Panel switches for the wall-mounted monitors. Circuit switches from the climate control box. He squinted behind his sunglasses and handkerchief as he torch-cut PVC pipe from under the sink. All flew into his satchel, and he was on to the next room. And the next. And the next.

With his bag filled to the brim, he pulled it shut and stepped out into the corridor. Glowing light still flickered from the others' first rooms. He grinned, stuffed his glow stick in his waistband, and pulled the hoodie down over it, dousing the light. Their route to this section played back in his head. Reversing it was easy. He stepped carefully past the rooms and turned into the inky darkness of the main corridor. *Bye, Samir.*

Less than halfway down the path, he saw lamplight appear. *More crews headed aft.* He wondered if Ruka would pull a knife on them too. He thought about warning them, but his heart sank when they came into view. A young worker and his younger friend, neither over thirteen. Both lay motionless against the bulkhead. Both burned beyond recognition. The eldest seemed to have tried to carry his friend away from the fire before collapsing there in the tunnel. Matteo tried to wake him. No response. Only a vacant stare.

Hotburst. They were common enough. A Cutter would torch right through a line and trigger a fireball, cooking all inside the compartment until the gas pocket burned away. Smoke gathered in the passage as Matteo crouched beside the boys. He reached into his bag and took out his air canister. The sight of it made the callus under his nose itch. He dropped the tank into his hood, wrapped the tube over his ears, and fastened it under his nose. The air inside tasted stale. Metallic. He put down the rushing flood of memories to focus on finding the way out.

The morning had been difficult, but continuing through the rest of the day drained him. After leaving 'The Somnium,' and the threat of bumping into Samir's crew, he crossed the yard to join a Cutter crew on a Virton Energy bulk-freighter. The afternoon and early evening was spent climbing all over the ship, rappelling from the sides, and cutting massive gashes in the bulkhead so the chains could yank it down in sections. No one was killed. He thanked God for that. But the injuries weren't any easier to see. A crushed leg here. An open gash there. Those always happened.

The sun dipped under the horizon by the time he got in line for the Seed-master. The blue-uniformed, squat City man sat behind a table just inside the open hatch of a City Municipal shuttle. Two armed guards, likewise uniformed, stood silent beside him. One by one, the Cutters, Runners, and Medics took their day's wages. Each hung their head after. A bad sign.

Matteo's turn came.

"Job?" asked the Seedmaster, smacking loudly on a wad behind his lower lip.

"Cutter," Matteo said, "Worked 'The Somnium,' 'Virton JF-145,' 'The Sedonia Queen—'"

"Yeah, yeah, okay." The Seedmaster reached behind the desk. Matteo stood on tiptoes to watch. Five giant duffels of seed sat behind the table. The Seedmaster sunk a plastic scoop in one and brought it to the table over the scales. Matteo got excited. *Gotta be at least an ounce in that scoop!*

The Paymaster tipped it over the scale tray, dropping a trickle of seeds. Stopped. Matteo sank as the tray was emptied into a plastic baggy. He could count the tiny seeds by looking at them.

"Point-oh-eight grams. Next!" shouted the man as he handed over the bag.

Matteo lingered, scowling at the bag. Weak for a Runner. Damn insulting for a Cutter. He did the math in his head. A hundred-twenty-two more days of this to hit the nine-point-eight goal. *A hundred-twenty-two more days to die....IF they don't cut rates again.*

"Move on!" one of the guards snarled, pointing his weapon at Matteo. No use arguing. Matteo pocketed the insult, shouldered his satchel, and made for the road into town. *Triple salvage...Samir, your cousin better not be full of shit.*

7

Risk

POLITE APPLAUSE CRACKLED from the press corps as Governor Sato shook hands with Elias Finley, CEO of Virton Energy, the largest Helium-3 fuel production company in the western hemisphere. Sato's best and last hope to turn the polls stood a full foot shorter than him, squinting through a smile on a pinched, froggish face. To everyone there on the Virton Hub's central landing deck, that hope already seemed dim.

The gray sky and bitter ocean air did nothing to help the mood...or the frizzing in Liani Ray's curly, auburn hair. She struggled to tame it as Sato and Finley waved to the crowd and departed the landing deck for the Hub's Main Office tower. Mr. Kabbard and a compliment of black-suited goons followed behind.

"I look insane, don't I?"

"Of course not, Ms. Ray. You are sanity personified." Corey, her cameraman, panned his camera left to right, tracking Governor and CEO on their path along the catwalk. She would have punched him in the ribs if he wasn't focused on keeping the shot framed in his real-time Neural readout. Instead, she looked into the pin camera on her ring. Her pouting face frowned back at her in a floating video feed.

"Hopeless."

"No kidding. Sato can plead and beg with Finley 'til the sun goes nova, but he'll never get *that* tight-ass to restructure the budget," Corey said. Liani rolled her eyes and switched off her ring-cam.

"Win or lose, a story's a story." She tried to sound confident, but her hands trembled as she smoothed imaginary wrinkles on her tight-fitting blouse. She caught Corey peeking at her curves. Relaxed a bit. Those curves had served her well, gaining the attentions of the station manager and thus a shot at a story that

41

no twenty-three year old rookie had any business covering: The last power-play of the once-great Governor Enota Sato. Yet now, in the moments before her first sound byte, her mind buzzed with all the ways she could fail. Corey pressed a few buttons and lowered the camera. His scruffy, more experienced face smiled at her. *At least he knows what he's doing.*

"Got it. Ready for your big moment?" Corey asked. Liani breathed in sharply, straightened, and nodded.

"What do you think? Over there by that palette of barrels?" she said.

"You mean the one's marked 'Highly Flammable'?" Corey grinned, "I love it! The volatile nature of both the commodity *and* the situation against the back-drop of the Hub. Brilliant, Ms. Ray!" She punched him this time. He grunted and chuckled.

"Wise ass. Let's go before someone else spots the metaphor." She strode across the landing deck, forcing Corey to clumsily collect his equipment and follow. Before she knew it, she was standing in front of that giant, lifeless multi-lens. Her lines waited, paused on her Neural teleprompter app.

"Five...four...three...," Corey completed the countdown with his fingers, then pointed to Liani in silence. She settled her shoulders and did her best to 'smile with the eyes.'

"Thanks, Mitchell. The mood here at the Hub is optimistic as Governor Sato and Virton CEO Elias Finley begin renewed energy negotiations inside. Sato aims to assist Virton Energy in trouble-shooting its year-long slump in production and the resultant spike in the cost of Helium-3 fuel. Governor Sato has cited the spike as the primary cause of the economic downturn, warning that continued price increases could trigger a recession not seen since the construction of the Sedonia City Border nearly three decades ago. Going into this meeting, both men are determined to not only avoid such a crisis, but to ensure many years of growth and prosperity to come." Liani's heart pounded as she paused for a few smiling seconds then gave the 'cut' signal. Corey lowered the camera.

"Beautiful. 'Growth and prosperity,'" Corey snickered. "With the Chinese, Indians, Russians, Japanese, and who-knows-who-else scraping the lunar surface for every last inch of 'growth and prosperity,' Finley's got his work cut out for him."

"A very liberal attitude for such a grateful employee of the most conservative news network in the City," Liani teased.

"Liberal. Conservative. Whatever. Facts are facts, but we don't *deal* in facts, we deal in agendas. That doesn't make you even *slightly* bitter?"

"It makes me have to pee. Start packing up, I'll be back in ten."

"Ten? You sure it's a 'number one'?"

"Ew." She turned and walked off down the catwalk where Sato and Finley had left the platform.

"The porto-cans are right there!" Corey called after her, pointing to the blue plastic pods just below the landing deck. *Porto-cans. Double-Ew.* She stepped daintily down the catwalk steps in her black heels, each stiletto snagging on the metal-grill walkway. As she reached the plastic door of a vacant can, something caught her eye further down the catwalk. A directory hung above the metal hatch at the far end. She read the labels. *'Gate 1A: Storage. Sic Bay. Conference Room 1A.'*

"Conference Room..." she said to herself. The urge to pee, probably caused by camera anxiety, suddenly evaporated. A little initiative could go a long way at the network. It had gotten her this far. *A story's a story.* One of Kabbard's tall, black-suited security guards blocked the hatch door. *Worth a shot.* She settled into her role, adjusted her posture, and trotted daintily down the catwalk toward the guard. Flashed her press badge and attempted to push past him. He didn't budge. Glancing down, Liani saw the RFID security panel by the door.

"Sorry ma'am, no Press allowed inside."

"I'm not *Press-ing* anything right now. I'm just a girl with an emergency!" Liani tried to sound distressed and flirty. It seemed to work. *Or maybe it's just the cleavage.*

"I...uh...I really can't. Mr. Kabbard's orders. Facilities have been provided below the central landing deck. If you'll just proceed to—"

"Are there?" she turned and leaned well over the railing to feign a look for the porto-cans. "You'd have me walk all the way back *there?* I'd never make it!" She looked back in time to catch him staring at her. *Men. It's almost not fair.* The guard's pale complexion blushed, but he furrowed his brow and broke eye contact. Straightened.

"Ma'am, I'm sorry, but you'll have to use the facilities at the landing deck, now please step away from this entrance," said the guard. His tone was final. Liani frowned and retreated. The closed hatch gnawed at her the whole way back down the catwalk. Not only would she have to get past the guard, she'd have to figure a way to buzz open the door. *If only there were some way to—*

The sound of her heels gave her an idea. *'Knock-Knock!'* Sure, it was a cheap prank she'd learned in college, but it just might do the trick. She entered one of the porto-cans and suppressed the need to gag. Brushed her hair aside and tapped her temple. The Neural 'Home' display of semi-transparent 3-D icons greeted her.

"Open VoxBuddy," she said. A full voice recording interface appeared in front of her. She hit the red circle button, shoved her mouth into her elbow pit, and screamed. Stopped recording and played it back. Muffled, but not quite there yet. A few tweaks to some audio filters and the Spatial settings made it sound like it was behind her. Like a voice through plate steel. She grinned. *Perfect.*

"Save and attach to New Local Text," Liani said as she stepped out of the porto-can. She started walking down the catwalk like she was headed back to the platform. Kept an eye on the guard as she entered the code string into the Text. Her roommate in school was a Neural Media major and showed her this cool trick to scare the shit out of their friends. Usually a 'BANG!' or a random screamed word like 'Tallahassee!' Good times. She hit the floating 'Send' button and waited.

The guard jumped about a foot and looked behind him at the hatch. As he keyed his throat mic, Liani stooped. Retracted her heels to form comfy, arch-supported shoes. *Best invention ever...*

"This is Schaefer at 1A, did anybody hear that?" she heard him ask. Schaefer waited for a response Liani couldn't hear, then buzzed the hatch open. *Good boy. Here we go!*

"Stand by, I'm checking it out," Schaefer said. Liani broke into a run, muffling her steps as best she could as the hatch slowly closed. *Shitshitshitshit SHIT!* It was too far away. Liani whipped the purse off her shoulder and chucked it at the door. The strap draped over the hatch frame, stopping it from latching.

"*Yes!*" Liani whispered to herself. She peeked through the door, picked up her purse, and stepped in. Quietly shut it behind her.

The place looked more like a battleship than an office complex. Reinforced plate-steel walls lined the hall with exposed piping and valves running the length. Every door she passed was a heavy slab of metal with hydraulic hinges. *Like a fallout shelter...nervous about explosions, are we?* Hurried footsteps approached. She ducked into a narrow hall and pressed against a wall in time to avoid Schaefer's notice. Waited to hear Gate 1A open and shut.

Two hydraulic double doors capped the end of the corridor. The words 'Conference Room 1A' embossed the surface. She scurried to the end and hung a right into the hall to the lavatories. Entered the ladies room, closed the door, and tapped her temple.

"*Call Corey,*" she whispered. Three beeps later, he picked up.

"You didn't fall in, did you?" he answered.

"*Corey! Corey, hi...I need you to do me a really big favor.*"

"Uh oh...I don't like the sound of that. Are they out of TP or something?"

"*Ha ha, asshole. I was thinking more along the lines of a diversion.*"

"Uhh...come again? What the hell do you mean by 'diversion'?"

"*The kind where you trip and fall into Gate 1A, make a lot of racket, and get into a big argument about 'Freedom of the Press' with any guard who comes your way!*" Moments of static passed.

"Does this mean we're actually after some *real* News?"

"*Yes!*"

"On my way."

"*Awesome! I'm sharing the feed from my ring cam...stay tuned.*" Liani ended the call. She sent Corey the cam invite, straightened her hair, and waited. In a matter of minutes, she heard the deep vibration of the conference room double-doors open and rapid footsteps break off down the hallway. She stepped out of the lavatory and tiptoed to the doors. *Godddd, what the hell are you doing?!* Liani winced as she crouched, placed the ring on the ground, and skated it across the linoleum with a flick of the wrist.

"You fucking fascists are all the same!" Corey's voice echoed down the hall as Liani snuck back to the lavatory. She pulled up the ring cam feed.

It had landed perfectly under a solid oak table, peering out into the posh, circular conference room. The light was much warmer inside, reflecting off of spartan mahogany wall panels, dark cream marble floors, and fluted columns. Finley's characteristic laugh snorted through the chamber.

"Create jobs? That's essentially your answer isn't it? 'Create jobs.' Mister Governor, I fail to see exactly how increasing my workforce by forty percent could possibly lower costs. It may help you curry favor with the electorate, but... heh heh...if you think a spike in overhead will solve *my* problems, you're gravely mistaken, sir," Finley said, theatrical as ever.

"I understand your apprehension, Elias, but more bodies means faster production and more coverage on your lunar holdings. Now a forty percent increase may be extreme, but that's just a rough figure. If we crunch the numbers, I'm sure we can come to a much more reasonable—"

"Reasonable? *'Reasonable'* the man says!" Finley turned to his advisers on his side of the table. They made sure to laugh.

"Sato, do you have any idea what hiring just *one* worker on the Moon costs Virton? Standard medical *plus* cosmic radiation, micro-meteorite, decompression, et cetera! Safety gear, equipment inspections, and every other regulatory fulfillment your liberal friends could dream up! Vacation, sick days, holidays, psych leave...and that's all before the bloody Specialist wages themselves! What you call reasonable, I call ruinous. I'll grant that more bodies *may* be able to secure more real estate, but it would take months. Multi-national corporations have pauperized themselves in shorter times, I assure you." Silence filled the chamber. Sato rubbed at his chin and stared at the floor. He swallowed past a lump in his throat. *No alternative then.*

"Kabbard, would you go check on that thing at the gate? It's been an awfully long time," Sato said. The grumpy Chief of Security gladly excused himself. The man had never developed the stomach for bureaucracy. Once the double-doors closed again, Sato continued.

"What if—what about your prisoner labor programs? No wages, no insurance, no unions, and, as far as I know, no vacations, holidays, or sick leave. Could those be beefed up to off-set gaps in a smaller *paid* workforce?" Sato asked.

Finley scoffed. "Hardly. Inmates can drive forklifts and load freighters, but they're not exactly qualified for advanced surface work. Most are untrained, unskilled, and potentially violent. If that's the best you can come up with, then—." Finley's smirk drooped as Sato took a tiny glass vial out of his pocket and placed it on the coffee table. A bluish-white fluid sparkled inside. Finley shifted in his leather chair.

"And just what is that supposed to be?" asked Finley, poorly feigning ignorance.

"*Our* people in your facilities tell us every new inmate is injected with this. Pretty crude nanotech, Elias, but effective. I'm told it blocks aggression centers in the brain while leaving the host extraordinarily pliable to instruction and training. After a month, the body expels the cheap little buggers, but by that time the effects are permanently imprinted on the mind. Very, *very* illegal, Elias."

Finley's smug veneer cracked, but didn't break.

"Well and good. Not that you could do anything about it. Hang me for this, and Helium-3 production not only suffers, its dead in the water! In effect, *you* are dead in the water!"

"Agreed," Sato put the vial back in his pocket, "along with the City and everyone in it who both trust and pay us to keep things running. But my friend, you mistake me. Remember, I said 'more bodies.' I hoped you would have agreed to employ more of our struggling citizens—and you may yet when you hear what I propose—but what would you say to tripling your illegitimate workforce? Would that gain you the real estate you need?"

Now it was Finley's turn to rub at his chin and stare at the floor.

"Mmmmm...such an increase in population would need more housing, food processing plants, water treatment facilities, CO_2 scrubbers..."

"Easily assembled given the financial aid, regulatory cuts, and *personnel* we are prepared to provide."

"And how, pray tell, will you square this massive acquisition of '*personnel*' with your voting public? Sympathy for the poor, impoverished Slum dwellers has been on the rise of late."

"We say 'terrorists.' The EXOs have, as it turns out, discovered isolated store-houses of explosives all throughout the districts. The right media coverage makes it an imminent threat, and the crackdown begins. A few days of raids should yield more than enough bodies."

"Hmm, yes. That could work. My God, Sato. Amazing that the public thinks you such a timid decision-maker. If they only knew!"

"You *will* give me enough new *legitimate* workers to show to the media, won't you? My soul isn't sold so cheaply."

"Oh, don't be dramatic! Fine, fine. You'll increase Helium-3 production, lower prices, combat the evils lurking in the Slums, and create a handful of jobs while you're at it." A smile curled back on Elias Finley's crooked teeth. "You're as good as re-elected! Not bad for one soul!"

Liani, suddenly sweating and nauseous, took her cue to leave. She stepped out of the lavatory and tensed. John Kabbard and the other two guards stopped at the end, opened the double doors, and stepped inside. They hadn't seen her. Liani puffed a sigh and stepped into the main corridor.

Halfway thinking about the next 'Knock-Knock,' she froze. Looked up. Schaefer stood in the hall, paler than he'd appeared before. He started to key his throat mic. Hesitated.

"Please..." Liani said. Schaefer scowled at her. Stepped aside.

"You're lucky I want to keep my job."

"Oh my God, thank y—"

"Get the fuck out," Schaefer said. Liani trotted past him with tears in her eyes.

Outside, Corey sat on the steps by the landing deck, dabbing a bloody nose. He shot up when he saw her beside the guard.

"Liani! Are you...are you okay?" he asked. Liani felt dizzy. Half-dreaming.

"What the fuck happened in there?!" said Corey. "You said 'news' not...not *this...Li!*" Corey touched her shoulder.

"Huh? What? Oh...I was wondering if you were listening," she took a breath. Made eye contact. "How much did you see?"

"Enough. Had your ring's audio feed up until they wiped my recent History. You know what could happen to us if—"

"*Of course I do!*" she hissed, "and it almost fucking happened to me in there!"

A hush fell over them as they tried to casually walk past the other reporters to their vehicle on the far end of the landing deck. Corey adjusted the strap of his equipment duffel, and leaned slightly over to her

"*So...what do we do with it?*"

"I have *no* idea."

8
Opportunity

LOOKING FOR T99S on a Friday night, you went to Ninetown. *The Palace*. The closest thing to a dance club in the Slums mixed with the protection of a fortress. The bass throbbed through graffiti-laced, reinforced concrete walls. Armed guards kept watch in sheet steel towers and patrolled behind sand-bag walls along the roof-line. The T99s showed up by the hundreds. Some stood in line wearing their best designer clothes, gold necklaces, and assault rifles. Others hung out by the custom bikes and cars parked in rows along the street.

Matteo noticed the girls first. Glistening bodies of tan, brown, and black barely dressed in bright colors. They clung close to the T99s, ignoring any man without the Mark on his shoulder. He smelled their sweet, rich perfumes as they walked by without a glance in his direction. Matteo pictured the seeds back home in their hiding place. He sped up. *Just get this over with.*

He knew the line to get in was off-limits. Instead, he picked out a group of gangsters sitting on their bikes by the main Palace wall. He took in a deep breath, stuck out his chest, and walked toward them. The girls noticed him this time, but their glossy pink and red lips curled at the sight.

"Check out this *nasty* Pitta' Rat comin' up in here!"

"He all covered in dirt an' shit, look!" Their laughs and giggles took some of the wind out of Matteo's chest. He hesitated mid-stride, fighting the urge to turn around and storm off into a dark alley somewhere. Then he heard them say it.

"Oki, maybe he wants to sell you some shit in his ratty ass bag," one of the girls squawked. *Oki. Mother. Fucking. Oki.* The chubby boy who'd ripped the oxygen tube out of Matteo's nose had grown into a much larger T99 thug. He was built like one of those 'gorillas' from an article Matteo had read.

Not extinct after all. To make matters worse, there was a familiar girl perched on Oki's lap. Raia's blue eyes were a dead giveaway, studying Matteo in that same unreadable way. She had grown up. Filled out. Each time she moved, she had to hold her short skirt to keep from exposing herself. Oki's hand kept finding ways to make that difficult.

"Yeah? What's up, Pitta' Rat?" Oki said. He lifted Raia, set her aside, and stood up. "What'chu got for me?"

Matteo turned his face down and away. Hopefully Oki would take it for respect, and wouldn't look too close.

"Don't be shy!" Oki looked back and chuckled to the other T99s. Matteo stayed quiet. His mind raced a hundred miles-an-hour looking for something to say. A way out. Anything. Only anger came to him. Oki shrugged and stepped closer.

"What was that?" Oki leaned forward with a hand cupped by his ear, "you say I can *have* it? For *free*? Ah, thanks Pitta' Rat!" He reached for the bag over Matteo's shoulder. Matteo stepped back.

"I said—THANKS!" Oki's fist rammed into Matteo's stomach. Sickening agony doubled him over on the concrete. The bag was plucked from his back and upended, dumping the contents on the ground. Amidst the switches, wiring, and pipe, an aluminum canister clattered on the ground. Oki squinted at it through close-set eyes. Then opened them wide.

"Naw," he rolled Matteo over with the toe of his high tops and glared at the wincing face.

"HAH! It is! Mother fuckin' *Wheezy*! How you been, kid? Last time I saw you, your baby-sittin' brother pulled a gun on me!" Oki craned his neck and looked around the Friday night crowd in the street.

"Don't see no brother this time!" He crow-hopped and kicked Matteo in the ribs. Under the blinding pain, Matteo felt and heard the crack. Oki crouched beside him.

"Ohhh, now I remember. He got picked up that night, right? Heard they beat him bloody, too," he laughed. Jogun's broken body flashed into Matteo's mind. The smile through the swollen mouth and shattered jaw. For a moment, his pain and Jo's seemed the same. He rolled to see Oki laughing and shouting back at the others. Pain spilled into rage. His hand swept across the concrete and bumped into something round, cold, and metallic. His fingers closed around it, and he rose to his feet.

As Oki turned, the air canister cracked him square in the temple, knocking him off of his heels. The T99s back at the bikes all stood at once, submachine-guns and pistols in hand. Raia scurried back behind them with the other girls. She cupped her hands over her mouth. Turned away. Oki shook his bleeding head and staggered.

"Shoot this mothe—"

A metal door swung open from its graffiti camouflaged place on the wall. All heads spun to see two Black Hoods step out. Black track pants, black shoes, and black sleeveless pullovers with hoods drawn up. 'T99' appeared bold and dark on the right shoulders, surrounded by the triangular outline of a hood. Everyone with a gun in Oki's troupe switched on the safety and lowered it. The Hoods walked straight to Matteo.

"Yeah, take this piece of shit to Suo—"

A backhand from one of the Hoods shut Oki's mouth, splitting his lip. The big Hood's size and chiseled muscles made Oki look scrawny.

"Pick up this brother's belongings and put them back in the bag," the big Hood said in a low and cold voice as his partner lifted Matteo to his feet. Matteo coughed and watched in amazement. Oki wiped blood from his face, stooped, gathered every last bit of scrap on the ground, and put it back in the satchel. The big Hood inspected Oki's work then snatched the bag from him.

"Suomo wants you to know if you beat on a Pit worker again, expect to be dealt with permanently."

Matteo glanced at the fear etched on Oki's broad features. The same look of terror he'd made years ago in front of Jogun's gun. *At least I got to hit him this time.* The thought of laughing made his ribs ache, so he settled for a sideways grin as they led him through the painted door and pulled it shut.

Inside, his grin faded, replaced with a blank stare. Beyond a low, neon graffiti-tagged divider, the Palace interior pulsed with colors, bodies, sweat, and thumping rhythm. The music, while loud outside, seemed to drive through his chest in here with lyrics rhyming in strange, garbled languages. Lights pulsed and swirled around the room, casting neon rays through the hot, wet, smoky air. He could smell the liquor and herb as if he was drinking and smoking. Making sense of the surging crowd took a moment. He saw a girl with her back pressed to a young T99. She traced her hands up her slick, wet sides to her bikini top, reached back, and wrapped them around the T99's head as he leaned in to kiss her neck. Matteo watched the T99's gold rings sparkle on his fingers as they traveled down the girl's stomach and under her low-riding waistband.

A nudge made Matteo jump. He had started sweating. The Black Hoods nodded up toward a catwalk that ringed the club's interior. Matteo stole glances down at the crowd below as he climbed the stairs, drinking in what details he could. The dancing girls in glowing body paint made it hard to watch his step on the catwalk, and he tripped soon enough. The big Hood picked him up. There was something not unlike a smile on the man's concrete face.

"Eyes front, kid." he said into Matteo's ear. They reached a thick hatch door at the far end of the dance hall where two more Black Hoods stood guard. The Hoods nodded to each other and the door opened. Matteo tried to draw in a deep breath but it made him cough. Weak, wheezing memories entered. He clenched his fists.

"Mother fucker, admit it! You messed up!" shouted a voice in the Boss's upper room. "Now you gon' have to pay for *that* shit!" The Black Hoods rushed inside with pistols drawn. Matteo ducked behind the big one.

"Whoa whoa whoa! Y'all some nervous thugs, brother, I'll tell ya that!" the voice said. Both Hoods relaxed, holstered their pistols, and took the drinks that were handed to them. Suomo looked much like Matteo remembered, only now wearing finely-sewn baggy clothes of bright white and navy blue. Gold and silver bracelets clinked on his wrists as he spun a long, smooth stick. He leaned over a thick table topped in green and aimed the stick at the shiny round balls that sat there. Matteo cocked his head at the strangeness of it. The balls clacked as they struck one another, sending two on the far end into corner pockets.

"Hell yes, you gon' pay! Ha HA!" Suomo laughed at another well-dressed T99 seated by the bar, likewise holding a long smooth stick. The man shook his head and took a drink from a brown glass bottle.

"My man, take a seat on the couch over there, I'll be right wit'chu," Suomo said, spotting Matteo in the doorway. Matteo turned to see the L-shaped couch in the corner and the three incredibly hot girls who sat on it. Their tight bodies sank into the soft, shiny red cushions. One of them patted an empty space for him. He tensed. The girls in Oki's gang had made fun of his dirty clothes. He tried his best to brush himself off and summon some courage. At last, he willed one foot in front of the other, turned, and lowered himself between two of the girls. His heart seemed to pound up into the back of his throat. *At least none of them got blue eyes.*

"Ooh, what happened to your poor shoulder?" said one with short raven hair and long smooth legs. She traced the scar tissue with a fingertip. Goosebumps spread down Matteo's shoulder, chest, back, and arm.

"I—I, uh," his voice shook. *It was a counter-top falling from a garbage scow. I was digging through the Pits for food.* The truth sounded ridiculous. Pathetic.

"It was an EXO." The words came out on their own. They seemed to work. All three girls listened now, and the blonde made a show of gasping.

"You're so brave! I dunno what I'd do if I was face-to-face with one of them."

"Yeah...up...*close*," the raven haired girl rubbed her bare leg on his.

"YEAH! THAT'S RIGHT! Pay up, *fool!*"

Matteo jerked at Suomo's victory shout, and his shoulder cracked a girl under the chin. Her teeth made a loud 'clack.'

"Oh shit! Shit, I'm s-so sorry! Are you okay?" Matteo babbled. The raven-haired girl rubbed her chin and moved her jaw side-to-side. The other two girls couldn't stop cackling.

Suomo ignored the noise. He collected his winnings and walked over to the couch.

"Aight, y'all, take a walk. Gotta talk with my man here," said Suomo. All three got up. The two uninjured girls turned and waved a giggling goodbye to Matteo as they walked out the hatch. He wanted to sink into the couch.

"*You* are Jogun's little brother!" said Suomo. Matteo sat upright at the name. Suomo grinned. "Yeah...I thought so. 'Cept *damn*, boy, you grew *up*! Got strong. That's good little brother, real good." Suomo snapped his fingers and the big Hood at the door brought over two short glasses filled with brown-red liquid and ice. *Ice!* Matteo took the glass. Studied it. Felt the coolness of it. He took a sip and swallowed. The burning in his throat shocked him, taking his breath away. He fought down the urge to cough.

"*Jo*, man...miss that motherfucker, I do. Good dude to have at your back. Smart. Honest. *Loyal*. Been what? 6 years since they grabbed him?"

Matteo nodded.

"Damn...but look at'chu, man! He was always so worried about what's gon' happen to you, and here I just saw you knock that fool Oki in his skull *with* his whole dumbass crew watchin'!" Suomo pointed to the monitors on the wall. CCTV footage streamed in from places all over the club, inside and out. Suomo took a swig of his drink.

"Takes stones, kid...big ones. But anyway, yeah. What'chu got for me?"

Matteo leaned up and looked at his bag by the door. Suomo, drink in mouth, waved for it to be brought over. Matteo took it and pulled it open. Switches, copper wire, batteries, and pipe all clattered around. Suomo reached in and took out a light switch.

"Nice work, little brother. Clean strip job. Nothin' bent, twisted, snapped... solid." Suomo tossed the bag to the Black Hood.

"Get a Runner to take that on over to Oki an' his crew tomorrow. Teach that fool some respect."

"Wait—" Matteo stuttered. Suomo raised an eyebrow at him. "The bag... it was Jo's." Matteo's chest tightened. Interrupting a T99 boss was bad enough, but trying to block a command... Suomo just nodded and looked him square in the eyes.

"Yasin."

"Yeah, boss?"

"Get the parts from the bag, tally 'em up, and pack 'em separate for Oki. Make sure all Matteo's belongings are returned to 'em."

Yasin turned and walked to a table to obey.

"Thank you—," said Matteo.

"Uh uh," Suomo said, "No need for that. Jo was family. Still is even if he's dead. That makes you *family*, little brother." He planted a finger in Matteo's chest. Paused. Springing off the couch, Suomo walked over to the green-top table and grabbed the stick he'd set there.

"But Jo must've told you that. Never seen nobody cared more 'bout his family. Which brings me to my next question: why ain't I seen you around 'til now?"

"I—I just...wanted to make good on my own," the half-truth hung in the air a minute. Matteo searched Suomo's expression for doubt. Didn't see any.

"See?!" Suomo shouted around the room for all to hear, "What we have here is a *real* man, gentlemen! Takin' responsibility for hisself! Buildin' his own shit from scratch, now *that's* what I'm talkin' about!" The others smiled and nodded in agreement. "Not like y'all bitches, just hangin' around beggin' for a handout and a pat on the motherfuckin' back!" The smiles faded. Suomo's appeared, full of glinting, shiny metal.

"But all that's different now, little brother. You did your time in the Pits and now you a man, brought home by God to his brothers. You believe in that shit? 'Course you do." Suomo tapped out a line of red powder on the glass table by the couch. Snorted it.

"Jo always bragged 'bout how smart you was. How you could fix anything in the house, remember things told to you once, or even tell what he was thinkin' sometimes. Could use a man like that when I take a crew over the Border."

The words made Matteo's head snap up. His jaw dropped.

"You been there? To the *City?* How'd you get past the Border? What'd you see?" The questions poured out of him. Suomo chuckled.

"Damn, kid, Jo told me 'bout that too: Little Matteo, always goin' on and on about The Big City. We ain't been yet, but we workin' up to it. Plenty of factories and ports to raid on the other side. That somethin' you think you might be interested in?"

A stream of possible events and scenarios streamed through Matteo's imagination. The stealth flight over the Border under a cover of darkness. Stealing into churning factories to dismantle exotic machines. Climbing into a port-yard to hijack containers of treasures from across the world. EXOs hunting him down like a stray dog. Killing him with an Augmentor boot to the skull. The vision soured. Jo's bloody face pleaded with him in his mind's eye. He shook it off. The seeds... *the slow way*...he could die tomorrow chasing a measly nine-point-eight grams.

"My whole life, I wanted to see the other side," Matteo said, half to himself. "Almost saved up enough for a Lifter, too. But I'd rather die tryin' than die in the Pits. If you're goin', take me with you."

"Ha HA! *My* man! Yasin! This man'll be needin' The Mark! We Liftin' all the crews soon for this anyway, so we'll roll you in with that, too."

Here it was in front of him. The ID, the ticket, and the ride. *I'm going.* It didn't hit him like he'd thought. It didn't hit him at all. The idea of actually crossing the Border hovered in front of him like a boldfaced lie. He shoved the thought into place. *Yeah...yeah, this is it!*

Across the room, the Black Hood left the table of scrap and went searching through a stack of drawers. Came up with a bottle of ink and a tattoo gun.

"And," Suomo said reaching behind his back, "you'll need one of these." The Boss took Matteo's hand, opened it, and placed a nine millimeter handgun in his grip. Matteo stared down at it. *The truth of the lie.* The touch of the pistol-grip in his palm...the cold metal...the weight. The night on the roof replayed in full color. The fear he'd felt when gripping the handle behind his paralyzed brother's back. Jogun's plea. *No blood.* He let go of the gun now as he did then.

"I can't..."

"Can't? What'chu mean, 'can't'?"

"I promised."

"Promised Jo? Bullshit, man. Look, if you want in you gotta be *in*. I can't have a Nine wit' me who ain't willin' to pull the trigger when shit goes down! *'Specially* over the Border! What'chu think, they'll just arrest us over there? Send us packin' back on home? Nah, man, they'll shoot you dead on site, sayin' you was a 'Terrorist,' whatever the fuck that means!"

Matteo's eyes stayed fixed on the weapon.

"Listen, man, we just doin' the best we can out here, tryin' to get a piece of somethin' you could call a real life. You gotta keep focused on what's in front of you and make a choice. Tell you what— Yasin!" Suomo snapped his fingers. "Bring me that bag o' his." Yasin obeyed. Suomo held the bag in one hand and the gun in the other. Matteo looked back and forth at the two.

"Seein' as how you family, I'mma give you somethin.'" He dropped the gun in the bag. "One week. Think about it. Come see me." Suomo pulled the drawstring shut and held the satchel out. Matteo hesitated, then took it. Suomo didn't let go right away.

"I'm a businessman, little brother. And that chunk o' metal in your bag? That's just a tool of business." Matteo nodded, stood on shaky legs, and met Yasin at the hatch.

"Oh, one more thing," Suomo said, tossing a small plastic bag to Matteo. The seeds shifted inside. It felt no less than three whole grams. *Maybe three and a half!*

"Triple salvage and then some. Oki got'chu pretty good before you clocked him...go see the Doc."

9

Chivalry

THE TECHNO-ORCHESTRAL MUSIC died at the end of the GloboMetropolitan News eleven-o-clock broadcast. Barking voices of the station technicians carried to Liani's desk where she sat idly, rifling through newsfeeds and blog posts in her Neural, waiting for the call she knew to be coming. The pick-up recording she and Corey had filmed on the Virton Hub landing deck had been a rush job at best. Throwing up in the porto-can had trashed her makeup. Her normally radiant skin had looked pale. *Sick. I looked sick. Like a Sway junkie right outta the damn Rasalla District.* On top of that, Sato's thugs had mag-wiped all Corey's background footage of the Sato-Finley handshaking. She found herself wishing they had been as thorough with her chip as they had with Corey's. First chance she got she had backed it up on an external mem-stick, deleted it from her RFID memory, and cleared out the history.

Her fingers drummed on the desk next to the mem-stick. She picked it up, worrying at the smooth edges with a fingertip. Despite weighing no more than a gram, it felt heavy. A sudden clack-clack-clack of high-heels approached behind her. She palmed the memory stick and put her hands in her lap.

"*Heyyy* Liani!" junior correspondent Melody Stewart smiled at her through perfect white teeth and injected red lips. Liani took a deep inner breath and unsheathed her own smile.

"Melody! Listen, I just *loved* your piece tonight. Who knew that a Pekingese could be trained to do *that* with a parachute?"

"Aww, thanks Li-Li! She was *too cute!* Loved your piece too, by the way... shame what that salty air does to those gorgeous curls of yours, though. And *seasick?* I don't know *what* I would have done in your place!" Melody turned her lips into a pouty frown. *In my place.* Liani's smooth jaw tightened as she thought of a riposte. The bubbly blonde cut her off before anything came.

"Oh! Where is my head? I just came from Mr. Kirnden's office, and he wants to see you right away." Melody chirped. All Liani could do was suck her teeth. She wished she had fangs so she could open the bimbo's scrawny throat. *He sends her? Her?!*

"Really? He could have called...you didn't have to trouble yourself. It's getting late and you should be on your way home. Those rail hoodlums on your route make me so worried for you!" said Liani. Imagining Melody getting pushed off a Superway terminal platform helped revive her smile.

"You're too sweet! But I've gotta burn the midnight helium tonight...no rest for the hungry, right?"

"Right," Liani said. *Maybe you should go eat a sandwich then you skinny—*

"Well I hope it's good news! You deserve it, Ms. Liani Ray!" Melody winked one of her over-sized baby blue eyes then clack-clack-clacked away with a swinging of curvy hips. Male correspondents took poorly hidden glances as she passed. Liani squinted at them, brow furrowed. A low whistle came from behind. She whirled to find Corey leaning on an empty desk.

"I don't guess I can start calling you 'Li-Li' can I?"

"Not if you want to keep breathing."

"Damn. It's kinda cute."

"Is there something you need?" Liani opened her purse and shoved the memory stick in a side pocket. Zippered it shut as hard as she could.

"Kirnden wants to see me too." Corey said. Liani clutched her purse in her lap.

"Could he know?" asked Liani.

"Not sure. I doubt that security guard said anything...would'a cost him his job."

"Yeah, you're probably right." She tried to find the will to stand. Her legs felt frozen. Corey dismounted the desk, walked to her side, and offered her his hand. She accepted and wobbled to her feet.

"Don't worry. Just let me do the talking," said Corey. The urges to both hug and slap him came at once. *Fine line between chauvinism and chivalry.* Though she couldn't deny her relief.

They walked side-by-side through the bullpen to the lofted head-office that loomed above. Its broad incline windows reached out over the room and reflected the cool light from the desks below, making it impossible to see in from the outside. Corey's sudden hand on her shoulder made Liani realize she was shaking.

Awards decorated Kirnden's enormous loft office. A gold obelisk here. An upright glass plate with embossed medallion there. Who knew what they were all for but they had the desired effect on visitors. Them and the inclined windows that overlooked the cityscape beyond. Liani always felt like she could be pushed off the edge and plummet the full 130 stories to god-knows-what below.

Kirnden sat in his supple leather chair watching a curved array of Neural feeds flicker and shift above his desk. To Liani, most were set to the blank gray 'eyes-only' mode. That made her more nervous. He reclined far back in the chair over the slanted glass. *Maybe the fat ass will bust one of the wheels and crash through.*

"Careful, Boss, one of these days you might fall back into that fabulous view of yours," said Corey. Kirnden straightened his bulk in the chair. *I hate you, Corey...*

"Ha ha! That *would* be bad, wouldn't it?" Kirnden's famous squeaking laugh sent shivers up Liani's spine. Everything about the man seemed plastic. Rehearsed.

"Come in! Come in! Have a seat," Kirnden said as he reached chubby hands toward his Neural display. He shuffled the screens around.

"I was just reviewing you guys' story this evening, and, I'm sorry to say, something seems...off. Want to tell me what that is?" He shared permission to view one of the gray screens. Flipped it around and pinch-zoomed it to show them. Liani's seasick, frizzy-haired face stared back at her, mouthing shaky words into a mic.

Helpless, she dug her red fingernails into her palms. Tried to find words behind tight lips. Corey jumped in.

"Yeah, sorry about that, Boss. Had a problem with the video storage on my chip, and lost all my footage of the handshaking. This pick-up shoot was all that we could salvage by the time I could debug it." said Corey. Liani had to admit, it sounded plausible. Thin. But plausible. Kirnden made a show of sighing, curling in his fat lips and shaking his head.

"I'm afraid that doesn't cover all of it, now does it, Corey?" He watched both of them in the silence that followed. *Shit.* Liani's head swam.

"Not only was that footage critical to the Governor's reelection campaign, but I also received a call from Mr. Kabbard, Governor Sato's Chief of Security. He tells me that one of my cameramen attempted to gain entry into a restricted area and got into an 'altercation' with the guards. He also tells me they had to wipe the man's RFID chip as a precaution...this won't do, Corey. Not at all, I'm afraid..." Liani gripped the armrests of her chair.

"Heh, yeah...sorry Boss. I just thought—I thought that if I could get some more shots of the Governor and Mr. Finley then—"

"I understand, Corey, I do...and I appreciate your initiative! But you see, this could have seriously damaged our 'open door relationship,' so to speak, with the Governor. A relationship that has afforded this station top priority in interviews, first questions in press conferences, and more government functions than I care to count. Why, I had to spend *15 minutes* on the phone assuring this Mr. Kabbard that nothing like this would ever happen again!"

"I promise you, Boss, it won't."

"We're going to have to let you go, I'm afraid." Kirnden frowned, doubling his chins. Liani rose in her seat.

"What?! You can't! He didn't—" Liani started.

"I didn't...mean any harm! Thanks, Li-Li, but I've gotta say this myself. I screwed up once. Once! And you fuckin' *can* me for it?!," Corey stood up, "You know what? I take back what I said. Lean back over that fancy window all you like. Maybe your fat ass will bust a wheel, and go careening through it!" Corey spun and stormed off toward the door. Liani suppressed the insane urge to laugh, and stood up.

"Wait!" she shouted with an awkward grin. Corey stopped without turning. His shoulders sank. Liani turned to face Kirnden. The moment felt like an hour as she stood there.

"It—it was all my idea, sir. Corey was just following my lead...it wasn't his fault."

"*Your* idea? Liani, I think you'd better explain," said Kirnden, steepling his fingers. He almost leaned back, but quickly straightened. Shifted uneasily in his seat.

"You're always saying how field reporters need to be more aggressive. I thought I might be able to get a piece of the meeting or something on audio. Corey just distracted the guards while I tried to get in, it wasn't his fault!" She fidgeted in the thick quiet of the room. Kirnden stared at her.

"And did you?" Kirnden asked.

"Sir?"

"Did you 'get a piece of the meeting or something on audio'?" He leaned forward. The purple lips seemed to moisten. For a moment, Liani thought she'd found her way out, but seeing the look on his fat plastic face brought the words back to her. *An 'open-door relationship.' He would rush the recording to Sato for a pat on the head, and they'd toss me over the Border. Or worse.*

"No. No sir...I couldn't get into the meeting hall."

"Ah," Kirnden said. He pivoted in his chair. After a moment, he reached up and touched a panel in his Neural display.

"Security," he said as a uniformed man appeared on screen, "please escort Ms. Ray and Mr. Burrows to their desks to collect their belongings, and see to it that they vacate the premises immediately."

At the Superway platform, Liani sat holding the cardboard box of random desk junk in her lap. A hairbrush, makeup kit, breath mints, and four big bags of Guatemalan dark roast...her prize possession and very tricky to get a hold of. *Better than sucking down that synthetic-tasting shit from the break rooms.*

The other employees' desks were covered in family pictures, non-funny annual calendars, squishy stress reliever balls, and all kinds of other crap. Too much to deal with. Liani had read in an article somewhere that the ambitious should always remain agile, take risks, and pack light. Less than six months at GloboMetro and she'd moved desks three times, all in the upward direction. Now, as then, she had little to carry.

Angry tears streamed down her cheeks. She hated each one. *The weak little girl fucked up and now she's crying. Pathetic.* She cried harder, clenching her perfect teeth. Approaching footsteps flipped a switch and Liani stifled a final sob. She sat up straight and wiped her bleeding mascara. Corey came lumbering up next to her, sweating like a pig as he grappled with the massive box of his belongings. The arms and legs of several action-figures peeked out of the top. He set the load down on the superway bench next to her and nearly collapsed into it.

It wasn't supposed to make her laugh. The look on his face was one of exhaustion, frustration, and suffering...but that clenched it. Her angry tears turned into sobbing, coughing laughter. Corey squinted at her over the top of the box, panting and trying to force words out between gasps.

"S-stop it! It's so creepy when you 'laugh-cry,'" he said, pushing his box on the bench to make room for him to sit. Liani scooted down a bit but was almost pushed off the edge. It set off another giggle-fit as Corey plopped down onto the seat. They made eye contact. Liani's hair had blown up in a ball of frizz and her eye pits were stained blue-gray. Corey was pale and pouring sweat from his buzzed head. They both burst into laughter.

"You—you look—"

"How I feel!"

The two of them could barely breathe. Their throats ached by the time the fit died to exhausted silence. A superway rail train shot past them, leaving its characteristic sour metal odor behind. Its shape disappeared down the track into the ocean of downtown lights. Minutes passed with only the roar of the City in the air. Corey sighed.

"Liani...thanks," he said.

"Thanks? For what? Getting you fired?"

"Not what I meant...but maybe, yeah. It's about time I had an excuse to get outta this pit."

"Well, you're welcome and congratulations," she said, staring at her tiny, highly-portable box.

"I was thanking you, dummy, for speaking up to Kirnden and trying to help me...albeit exactly what I told you *not* to do. Took guts."

"Maybe. Or maybe I couldn't stand the idea of letting you be the hero and having that guilt follow me for the rest of my career. Am I brave for wanting to spare myself? You're Mr. Chivalry, not me." Liani picked at a frayed corner of the box and contemplated walking to the end of the platform to throw it off the edge. Corey sat bent over, rubbing his hands together. He shot a few sideways glances around the area.

"Do you still have it?" he spoke in a hushed tone. She reached into her purse and pulled out a tissue. Wiped her nose with it.

"And if I do?"

"Listen..." he leaned in close, "I've still got friends in some indy circles who might be able to do some good with it. Maybe even—"

"No fucking way, Corey. You saw the look on his face! Kirnden knows I was in there. What do you think happens when a recording of the whole damn thing suddenly surfaces on the Net? I get suicided, is what. Probably in some Sway overdose in my apartment or a 'tragic mechanical failure' that crash-lands me in the Slums to be dragged away for god-knows-what!"

"Liani, it could save *thousands* of lives!"

"Bullshit, Corey. They'll find us, discredit us, kill us, and *bury* the truth. And I've had enough martyrdom for one day."

"Shame," Corey said as he stood up, "so what then? I guess you'll destroy it..."

"I—I will. I just..."

"Why not now? Get rid of the thing and save us both." Corey stared her down as she reached into her purse. Her fingers closed around the memory stick. She withdrew it and looked up at him. In a heartbeat, she stood up on her high-heels and stormed off toward the Superway platform. He trotted after her.

"Li, wait! Please!" She didn't turn or break stride until she reached the edge. The 76-story drop from the GloboMetro Plaza to the ground below made her head swim. She staggered back a step, the memory stick clenched in her fist. Corey caught up and steadied her by the shoulders.

"Christ, Liani! Come on..." Corey said. She trembled in his hands, clutching the chip. It would be so easy to just toss it.. Forget the whole thing. But the plastic stayed glued in her palm. She bit her bottom lip. The low hum of another superway train approached. It rushed up beside them and stopped.

"I'll take it, you don't have to—" he stopped as she jerked out of his grasp.

"No," Liani said, tucking the chip deep in her purse, "No, I have to think about this." She turned as the train doors opened. Stepped inside.

10

Duty

KABBARD FELT LIKE he was on the wrong side of the briefing. He should be sitting out there with the officers, leading one of the squads...not standing up on the platform next to Commander Gorman. But that time had passed. And all the gym memberships in the world hadn't kept Kabbard from losing his edge. *This is my place now.* He took a breath at the silent reminder. The hangar of EXO HQ filled with the nervous chatter of the men as they sat with their squads. Pilots, infantry, medics, and specialists. More than a few leaned to each other in whispers, pointing at the former Sergeant.

He'd had some oversight through the planning stages of the Raid. Basic goals, timing, structure... But the commanding officers had reluctance to listen beyond that, and he didn't blame them. Better that the missions be scoped by the 'boots on the ground' than the 'suits in the Tower.' *I'm a suit in the Tower...* The soft, designer jacket and slacks suddenly chafed him.

"Easy, John," said the Commander, privately, "This is necessary."

Kabbard nodded. The data the Commander had shown him was conclusive. The T99s had been busy, setting up labs all over the Slums. And not the Sway-cooking variety. Bombs big enough to disable Border towers had been confiscated over the past weeks. A clear threat. *So why the fireworks in my gut?* It must have been all the rookies.

The labs were so spread out and so heavily defended that the EXOs didn't have the numbers to pull it off. Not all at once. The only way to fill the ranks had been to fast-track a few hundred kids out of Red Gate Academy. Their young, eager faces filled the crowd, jawing excitedly as they sat equipped in full Aug kit. *It's reckless...they need more time.*

"TEN-HUT!" said one of the acting Sergeants as Commander Gorman crossed to the podium. Kabbard stood up out of conditioned reflex. Noticed that the entire hangar stood too. Vets and rookies in perfect unison. Part of the weight lifted. Discipline was a start, but it had to be proven in the scrap, ashes, and dirt. And blood.

"At ease," said Gorman. Officer Vaughn took his seat with the other recruits. His pale skin throbbed softly beneath the humming Augmentors. He'd worn Full Kit thousands of times back at the Gate, but here, the hyper awareness seemed to spread his heartbeat through every nerve.

At the far end of the hangar, the engineers prepped the IG-8 dropships and A39 fast-mover gunships in a din of noise. Vaughn ran a trembling hand over his fresh head of grunt stubble. Scratched the back of his neck. His grades were never that great, and he was decidedly average in the exit physical. *What am I doing here?* He couldn't help but think it over and over. A sudden tap on his shoulder actuator snapped him out of it.

"*Hey man,*" one of the other recruits whispered behind him. Vaughn turned. An over-caffeinated junior classman. The squad readout in Vaughn's Neural placed the name 'Dreivan' above the kid's ridiculous high-and-tight hair.

"Look! It's him!" Dreivan said, pointing to the stage.

"Him who?" Vaughn whispered back.

"Kabbard! Sergeant John. Fucking. Kabbard!" said the kid. Vaughn squinted at the stage. There he was, alright. The man who basically wrote their textbooks in addition to having been the most notorious EXO on the force since the Border Offensive. A legend in the flesh...though there was more flesh on the man now than in the archive pictures and vids.

"*SHUT THE FUCK UP! BOTH OF YOU!*" hissed Sergeant Shima, whirling in his seat. The man looked like an psychotic jack-o-lantern when he was pissed. Vaughn snapped his eyes front. This vet had a reputation too. A hell of a temper, and a tendency to go just a little nuts on certain missions. Luckily First Sergeant Mason had also been assigned to their squad, presumably to keep things level. Vaughn had ended up in one of the only squads with two vets. The fact soothed his jangling nerves. Sort of.

Vaughn's Neural beeped a notification in his inner ear, and a vast glowing map of the Slums appeared overhead. Big enough to hover over the entire regiment. Vibrating lines of light rendered the topography and major neighborhoods of Rasalla. Commander Gorman cleared his throat.

"This, as you know, is the Rasalla District. The largest single district in the Slums, separated into thirteen major zones. Tonight, we've gotta hit 'em all," Gorman said. One to three sections of each zone were the target areas, highlighted in yellow. Thirty squads for thirty targets. *A 'smash and grab'...on the whole damn District...*

"Each squad," continued Gorman, "will be simultaneously dropped via RaDVert into their GPS designated target area at 0400 hours. Once on the ground, you will have *fifteen minutes* to get into position and wait for the Big Go. By 0430, primary prisoner and ground-force extract should be completed! The longer we stay, the greater the risk of casualties. The name of the game today is *prisoners,* boys. Live, undamaged ones. We go in with spurs, drop the suspects, load 'em up, and get out."

"Sir!" Sergeant Shima raised his hand. The Commander sighed. Nodded.

"Sir, are we to understand that we'll be hitting Rasalla *without* live ammo?" Shima asked. A low muttering wave spread over the men. The lack of respect rubbed Vaughn the wrong way, but he wanted to hear this too.

"Calm down, Shims," said the Commander, "*No one* goes into the Rasalla District without brass jackets, but they are *last resort, End-of-Times only!* This goes ugly if the metal starts flying. 0430 hours. Drill it into your skulls. Now, each target will require specific, dynamic tactics to neutralize, so pay close attention to your vets and squad leaders. God bless you all. Dismissed!"

Vaughn watched Kabbard approach the Commander and immediately start talking. It looked serious.

"Vaughn!" Shima yelled. Vaughn jumped and turned. Realized that the squad was filing out of the rows. He scrambled to pick up his helmet and follow. Shima fell in beside him on the way to the ships.

"There he is, huh? That's what you're thinking? There's the all-wise, all-knowing John Kabbard..." Shima said. Vaughn thought it best to stay quiet. Shima continued. "Forget that fucking sell-out, son, he ain't coming with us. You got your head on straight? Or am I gonna have to worry about you..."

"Sir, no, sir!" Vaughn said what the man wanted to hear. But he wasn't truthfully sure.

"Good. I don't need you rookies comin' loose after your first RaDVert... it ain't exactly like the Neural sims." Shima quickened pace to the front of the squad, making himself the first to enter their IG-8 dropship. Its broad, curved belly shimmered with the light-bending camo that would reflect the sky above in any weather and any time of day. *'Rapid Descent Vertical Insertion...'* It had been a screaming Hell even when it was just a projection into Vaughn's brain. A long ramp led up to the officer compartment, above the 'cargo hold.' Vaughn felt another hand on his shoulder. He turned, expecting the rookie from before. Instead, he met John Kabbard face-to-face. Rumor had it that the scar on the former Sergeant's cheek came from a bullet graze. A T99 punk had Kabbard dead to rights with a gun barrel under his chin...but the Sergeant knocked it aside, discharging it as he ripped the punk's throat out. Without Aug gloves.

"You got a loose seal on your anterior delt plate," Kabbard said. Vaughn flushed pale and reached for the clasp. Kabbard got it for him, bleeding air from the seal. Pushed it closed with a click. The shoulder moved much more freely. "You'll be fine. Just Flip-the-Switch and watch the man next to you." With that, the man left. Walking from squad to squad, sizing things up and talking with the men. Most of the vets didn't seem to appreciate it. Vaughn slipped his helmet on, pressed the seal, and felt it tighten around him. He started up the ramp.

"All in! Lock it down!" First Sergeant Mason said into his throat mic.

"Roger, securing rear hatch and personnel harnesses." The voice of the pilot hummed in Vaughn's inner ear as the rear doors of the IG-8 hissed shut. Bolted. Red light filled the cabin. Carbon-fiber harnesses dropped down, securing each officer in his seat with a click.

"EXOs, check restraints! Visors down!" Shima barked. All nine officers slid their clear visors down and tested the fit of their harnesses. They sounded off down the line, each confirming 'Secure!' One of the rookies added a 'Yeah!'

"Cabin secure! Go for launch!" said Mason. The elder vet saw Vaughn staring. Gave a smile and a nod. The engines picked up, sending vibration through every surface in the cabin as the craft lifted off the deck. Vaughn felt the landing gear retract under his feet and took a deep breath as the ship bobbed, turned and hovered forward.

"Yeah, baby, here we go!" a voice barely shouted above the hum of the engines. Mason pressed and held a finger to a button on his helmet temple. Neural screens materialized in front of Vaughn and each of the other officers. Video feeds from forward, aft, starboard, and port appeared, showing the entire EXO fleet in motion. The hangar doors yawned open, exposing a vast plane of orange lights under a pitch black sky. The cabin went quiet.

One hundred and seven ships flew out of the hangar in formation. Gunships formed an expanding octagonal perimeter around the IGs as the fleet flattened into a slow-moving wave. It crept to within a mile of the Border when the whole fleet went dark.

"Exterior lights off. Beginning my ascent to 7600 meters." the voice said in Vaughn's ear. The ship lurched and climbed straight up. The force pressed the officers down and back into their seats. Silhouettes of the other ships disappeared on the video feed, visible now only by dots on the radar. When the screens went totally black they switched to radar-only. Seconds later, the IG-8 slowed. Stopped.

"Seventy-six hundred meters. Moving over position for RaDVert." the voice said. The blue dots on the radar fanned out over and past the Border, each eventually stopping over a different outlined sector.

Vaughn swallowed hard. He looked across from him and saw Mason's head bowed in the dim, red light. *Praying. Wish I could do that.* He thought about trying, but nothing came to mind. *Side effect of being an atheist.* The dot in the center of each screen, their dot, glided over a section of Southwest Rasalla and froze. As

Vaughn felt the ship come to a hovering stop, everyone's Neural flipped to Tactical Mode. Visible squad IDs, GPS minimap, ammo counters, and a myriad of other combat apps. A chorus of other mechanical buzzes, clicks, and beeps sounded throughout the cabin.

"In position. Awaiting 'Go' at 0400 hours," the pilot said. Everyone took hold of their harness handles and waited in the humming silence. The seconds felt like hours. Vaughn, at the last second, remembered his mouth-guard. He lifted his visor, put the guard in, bit down, and closed the visor again. Gripped the handles.

"We have a 'Go.' Beginning RaDVert in 10. 9. 8. 7," Vaughn tried to breathe evenly past the jackhammer in his chest and think of the mission. All of that disappeared at "3. 2. 1. Drop!" The engines cut and the IG-8 went into free-fall. Vaughn's forearms bulged as he strangled the safety handles. His shoulders dug into the harness padding, pressing harder and harder toward the ceiling. He thought his teeth would bite through the mouth-guard and break his jaw. Terminal velocity gave the officers a short-lived break to look around wide eyed at one another. The roar of rushing air filled the cabin.

"AAAAAHHAHAHAHAHAAAA!" Shima screamed above the noise. Some of the rookies followed his example. Most were laughing when the engines kicked on again full blast, humming smooth and loud. The crushing force shoved them down into their seats and, in seconds, brought the IG-8 to a dead stop. The exterior camera screens appeared again and showed a 360 degree view of an empty Rasalla street in Zone Four. Vaughn shook his head. Collected himself in the moment. The harnesses clicked and lifted off the EXOs. Mason and Shima stood and secured their submachine guns. The rookies managed as the hatch doors hissed open.

"Legs off, weapons hot! On me!" said Mason.

Vaughn willed his shaky legs down the ramp with his squad. They made it about twenty paces from the ship when the sudden smell of sewage raised a lump in the back of his throat...enough to give his stomach the excuse it needed. He doubled over in the street, retracted his visor, and puked. The other officers looked at each other, then nervously at the concrete and scrap-metal buildings around them. Vaughn spat, wiped his mouth and stood. Mason came in close next to him, weapon ready.

"You good?" Mason asked.

"Yes, sir," Vaughn answered. Mason stepped back and pressed his throat mic.

"We're clear. Proceed to recon altitude," said Mason. The IG-8's four hover engines glowed a masked blue as it lifted off and up into the night sky. Mason pinch-zoomed the hovering mini-map of the area and tapped a group of buildings. It became highlighted in each officer's display, and set a waypoint.

"Objective's two blocks west then north through the alley. I'll take point. Shima take the rear. The rest of you stay close and keep it tight," Mason said. Shima dropped to the back, scowling at the stain on Vaughn's flak vest. They stalked through the street. Vaughn felt the eyes on them, peeking down from ragged window holes cut from steel and cinder block. He swore he could see silhouettes darting away in the shadows, off to warn Rasalla.

Mason halted them at the edge of an alley and all pressed against the wall. Broadcast his view to the squad over the Neurals. The target building sat to the right, atop a long stairwell. Mason pressed his throat node three times. Vaughn heard a beep in his inner ear each time. *Hold sign...* They waited in silence.

"Recon altitude reached. Stand by for audio, depth, and thermal data." The pilot's voice buzzed in each officer's inner ear, and a digital task bar appeared in their Neurals. *30%. 67%. 100%.* Vaughn watched blobs of color focus into distinct, outlined figures all around him. People sleeping on the floor by the dozens in several shacks. A woman bathing her baby by candlelight. A couple making love under a lean-to. As if they all lived in houses of blue glass.

In the target area above and to the left, he saw the shapes of nine men. Two sat on buckets outside, dozing with submachine guns on their laps. Four inside sat around a table working on something. The remaining three stood around the room, pacing and talking to one another. A sound-wave readout in Vaughn's Neural tracked and recorded the conversation.

"—need to tell Suomo we got all the tech we need, man! I'm knee-*deep* in switches and pipe, but I ain't got much left to put in 'em!"

"I hear you, I hear you! But I can't keep tellin' him that every time I go back to the Club, man, he'll put a bullet in me just for gettin' on his damn nerves!"

"Well tell him again! And explain if he wants to shoot somebody for bringin' the truth that he'd best shoot me, cuz ain't no way I can keep makin' shit blow up if I ain't got the main ingredient!"

Mason tapped his Neural screen, selecting the two targets outside the house. Marked one '*Mason*' and the other '*Vaughn.*' Vaughn gulped and pushed to the front. They each slung their SMGs back around their shoulders and un-holstered sleek, black pistols. Pressing the mag release, Vaughn double-checked the ammo. Stun spurs. He clicked the mag back into his pistol and chambered a round. A digital countdown started as Mason took aim. Vaughn gulped a bad taste in his mouth. *Okay...just like the range at the Gate...*

One. Two. Three. Vaughn and the First Sergeant leaned out of the alley and fired. The spurs found their marks in the flesh of the guards. Both convulsed, then slumped where they sat. Vaughn exhaled. Mason turned to the officers in the alley. Waved them forward as the scene inside the shack played over audio.

★ ★ ★

"What the fuck you lookin' at? Go! Tell 'em now!" A T99 with the face of a pitbull and build of a silver-back gorilla waved a giant chrome-plated pistol toward the door.

"Oki, come on, man...he's either high, drunk, or sleepin' right now...maybe all three," a fat gangster said. His double-chin wagged as he shrugged. Oki thumbed back the hammer on the gun and waved it again. The fat guy rolled his eyes and turned to leave when his SMG strap caught on the chair of one of the techs. The tech's skilled hands flew up and away from his work in an instant, a metal pipe full of gray putty on the table. Wires stuck out of it on all sides, one of which was connected to a gutted light switch. The tech turned to look at Oki, staring wild-eyed over a dust mask.

"Lopei, don't move...you stupid, fat piece of shit." Oki walked over and gently unhooked the strap from the chair. Lopei backed away, sweat pouring down his face from under his backward ballcap.

"Outside! Now!" Oki pushed him toward the door with the gun barrel. Lopei's huge clumsy legs barely managed to back-pedal.

"Man, Oki, chill!" the lanky T99 in the back said, "You'll push his ass over and he'll—"

They all heard it. Footsteps outside coming up the stairs. Before they could react, two white discs slid under the door and exploded in a blinding flash. EXOs rushed in firing stun spurs. The first two hit Lopei and sent him to the floor in a massive heap. The others sprayed across the techs. Half-blind, Oki squeezed off four ear-shattering rounds at the shapes in the door, pushing them back. It gave him and the lanky T99 time enough to find the window and scramble through it.

"Shit!" Shima yelled, cranked up his Augmentors, and took off after them out the window. Mason reached for the crazy bastard and missed.

"Vaughn with me!" Mason shouted, "Dreivan, take the squad and—"

Vaughn switched on his legs, shoulder, and grip assists then stopped. Turned and looked. Dreivan, the dopey rookie from the briefing, had taken a bullet in the throat. No vital signs appeared in the Neural readout...just three letters. *'KIA.'* It didn't come close to sinking in.

"Officer Babb, take the squad, secure the prisoners, and prep Dreivan for dustoff!" Mason said. The First Sergeant grabbed Vaughn by the flak vest collar and yanked. "MOVE!"

After Mason disappeared through the window, Vaughn stepped back from it. He took a breath, hopped to the window frame, and pushed off. He sailed through the hot, damp Rasalla air. Came down silently on a concrete roof below, muffled by a dampener pulse. Mason was already way ahead, chasing after Shima. Vaughn put everything he had into the Augs to catch up, leaping, diving, and vaulting through the schizophrenic landscape.

A squad cam window popped into his Neural as they reached Shima. Officer Babb's live feed streamed in.

"Uhh, sir, Dreivan's twitching...his RFID may be on the fritz, should we call in the medivac?" asked Babb. In the feed, the other officers struggled to move the fat T99's face-down body. Vaughn could hear them in the background.

"Je-sus! This shit-bird weighs a metric ton!"

"Turn on an Aug boot and kick him over..."

Mason, mid stride, tried to keep his voice down in reply.

"Negative! That man is KIA, now *get off the comms!*" Mason said as the fat T99's body flipped over in the feed...wide awake and clutching something to his chest.

"RASALLA!" the T99 yelled.

The feed cut out. The shockwave slapped Vaughn in the back before he heard the deafening blast. Searing heat filled the air behind him. Ears ringing and bleeding, Vaughn rolled on the dented tin roof where he'd landed. Saw the curling molten cloud rise into the sky.

"NO!" Shima yelled, sprinting past Vaughn and Mason toward the blast. Mason caught up in two strides and grabbed Shima's camelback.

"No, Shims!"

"LET GO! They could be—" Shima protested.

"They're all KIA, and we will be too if we stick around—DEBRIS!" shouted Mason. Flying chunks of cinder-block, scrap metal, and charred whatever fell from the sky, some of it stabbing into the rooftops like throwing knives. Vaughn pushed out of his dent on the roof and stood up.

The three of them ran for cover.

11

Spark

MATTEO AWOKE IN the dark, panting and sweating. The dream images still flickered through his mind, becoming fainter but no less real. Or terrifying. Blaring engines and fire. A dark space with a broad window of fiery light ahead. Everything shaking...screaming and crying. He recognized, and yet didn't recognize, his voice among theirs.

As the vision slowly cleared, he remembered where he was. Utu's recovery ward in the Temple of the Wheel...a long narrow ship hull, gutted to fit two rows of bedrolls. He could have gone back to the family apartment days ago. Back to work in the Pits. But Utu, upon studying Matteo's lost expression, said the same thing every morning.

"Hmm...more rest. Yes. More rest and another day of hot food, and you'll be free to go." He would end with a squinting smile. Something hid behind it, Matteo could tell, but nothing to fear. A soft bed, three meals a day, and no Pits... hard to argue with. Even if he couldn't sleep more than a few hours. The Choice wouldn't let him. In the stagnant darkness, his mind throbbed with possibilities.

I could be Lifted and over the wall in less than a month with the Nines...nothin' would happen...I might not even need the gun. But if I did...Jo... Shit. Might still be able to do it if I hit triple salvage enough times. Yeah...that could work. Unless I die in the Pits trying. Okay. Hm.

He suddenly became aware of the exhausting thought stream. No way he was getting back to sleep. He rose carefully from the bedroll, crouched and lifted his bag. His belongings clinked inside and an elderly man a few beds over shifted in his sleep. Matteo winced and allowed the bag's contents to settle. He tip-toed past the huddled bodies and out the embroidered door-flap.

The cool night air and the spiced smells of the Temple refreshed him. Much better than the faint reek of sickness in the ward. Torchlight licked up into the air from posts in the ground. The same time of night it had been whenever he stirred. After all of the most nocturnal dwellers and gangsters had turned in. *So still. Peaceful.* He'd never realized how loud the Slums were until the volume had been turned down. With a deep breath he walked along the wall and found the ladder to his new favorite spot.

Row upon row of green growing things bloomed out of burlap sacks in the rooftop Temple Garden. Utu gave him a tour two days past, giving names to the shapes and patterns. There was fresh kale, a messy clump of wrinkled leaves that felt weird on the tongue, but tasted good. Spinach with its round, softer leaves. And then the red, round tomatoes. The fruits of a fortune in seeds, and the source of still more. Utu could have lived in a dweller mansion, but instead chose a monastery, clinic, and free kitchen. Yesterday, he had given Matteo a small tomato to try. The sweet, juicy flavor had made Matteo's eyes roll back in his head. He thought about taking another every night since, but never dared.

Instead, he walked among the plants, felt their textures and savored their smells. He sat between two kale bushels and dug through his bag, searching for the slick pages of the new magazine Utu had let him borrow. A curious picture on the cover teased his mind. A spiral shape with a big bright center made up of uncountable dots of light. Utu read the word "Galaxies" on the cover aloud, though he claimed he didn't know what it meant. Something to do with the stars. People could travel to them now, further away from home than Matteo had ever imagined. *Gotta fly at the speed of light for four years to get to the closest one...* He had noticed the ships that flew straight up from the City and into the sky before...always wondered where they went. The City was more than a City. It was a key to the universe. Maybe even God...or whatever the force was that pulled him there.

The sound of a shifting brick yanked him to the present. He whirled, eyes wide and staring into the twilight. *Thieves...* Most left the gardens alone out of respect and those that didn't answered to the T99s. But that didn't mean a few didn't sometimes get desperate. And people that desperate were dangerous. Matteo remembered the gun in his bag. Light footsteps approached through swishing leaves. Against the pounding in his chest, he pulled the satchel open and reached in.

"*Matteo?*" said a soft voice. Matteo hesitated. Raia stepped out of the rows, squinting in the darkness. The pounding in Matteo's chest continued, but in a different way as he removed his hand from the bag.

"Over here," Matteo said, standing up among the plants. Raia jumped a little, then placed a relieved hand to her chest. She looked so different without her skin-tight club clothes. She wore a modest, angled dress, cinched at the waist with a long, patterned scarf. The fabric fluttered softly against her curves in the hot, dry wind.

"Sorry...didn't mean to scare you," said Matteo, shying away from the curves. Something dawned on him in the anxiety. "You lookin' for me?"

Raia nodded. Even with so little light, the deep blue of her eyes flashed as she turned away in the dark.

"Doc told me you come up here at night...when everybody else is in bed. Wanted to talk without anybody seein'," she said. Matteo darkened.

"I get it," he said.

Suddenly worried, she shook her head.

"It ain't like that! If somebody saw us...if somebody *heard* me...Oki'd take me out," Raia said. Matteo waited, curiosity boiling in his head. She must have sensed it. "You gonna say 'yes' to the boss...right?"

"I..." Matteo looked down at the satchel, "I don't know, yet."

"But...I can't be your girl, if you ain't a Nine," she said, "If you was, Oki couldn't touch me *or* you..."

Matteo's head swam with a sudden rush. *She...wants me?* No one ever had. At least no one he'd ever heard of. A legion of flies buzzed in his stomach. *What the hell do I do with that...?* Raia broke off eye contact, and looked around the place.

"Why you come up here so late?" she asked. Matteo lifted inside. *Nice, I can answer that.*

"It's quiet," he said, "Calm. I feel more connected up here. Somethin' about the plants helps. Reminds me we're alive...not just dying." He snapped out of it, noticing her blank expression. Part of him dimmed. The whole thing had just sailed right over her head. He wanted her. He had always wanted her. But in his gut, Matteo knew Raia wasn't a part of the path. He didn't want to know it.

"I can't..." he forced it out. To his surprise, a grin creased Raia's full lips.

"Come on," she said, cocking her head and tilting her hips, "Every Nine needs a girl. And not every girl can get a man like you." She waited for an endless moment for him to respond. He had nothing. Raia seemed to sink then turned to leave. *Dammit—*.

"Hold up!" Matteo said. He stooped, reached into the satchel, and pulled out the gun. It didn't seem to weigh as much as he stuffed it into his waistband. "I'll... walk you home."

Together, they made their way through the eerie quiet from central to Southwest Rasalla. Despite knowing the way like the back of his hand, he found himself unsure of the allies, stairwells, and catwalks. The gun tugged on his shorts too much, so he kept it drawn. He felt her eyes on his back as they crept through the district. It was a relief when they reached the Dyer Walk. A long alley where the Blue Ladies and their girl helpers spun their own cloth, dyed it, and patterned it to be sold in Falari Market. The normally vibrant colors of the hanging wet fabrics all looked cold gray at night. Matteo and Raia started up the gradual slope of the Walk.

Matteo felt her inch closer to him, then slip smooth fingers around his arm. He was glad it was too dark to read his expression. *Just take her back to her place, then go home...take her back to her place, then go ho—*

BOOOOM! The two of them dropped into the cover of an alley on instinct. Looked up to the sky. A bright orange glow surrounded a mushroom cloud to the South. As the rumble subsided, dogs all over the Slums started barking. Followed soon after by the shouts of dwellers.

"Maybe one of the labs," Raia said, "Oki's guys ain't too smart, maybe they—" Gunshots. A few at first, then more, streaking white-hot bursts into the sky in all directions.

"We gotta go!" Matteo said, grabbing Raia by the arm. They ran down the rest of the Dyer Walk and hung a left up the stairs. Then a right up some more. The pistol grip slicked with sweat in Matteo's hands. The path ahead led to a mutated block of shacks and cinder-block apartments. *Five minutes from home.* Familiar jagged shapes loomed over them as they climbed the stairs.

Strange sounds and voices came from out of sight ahead. Matteo stopped her with his palm just shy of the top of the stairs, and they dropped low. He turned, crawled arm-over-arm, and peeked over. *EXOs...at least six.*

One of their dropships sat below on a wide, flat rooftop with its rear hatch open. *Some kinda new IG model...* Two EXOs kept watch while the others worked, picking up limp bodies and handing them down the line to the hatch. Some bodies were T99s. Others' shoulders were bare. Matteo ground his teeth and squeezed the gun grip. Remembered Jogun. Raia crawled up next to him and put a soft hand on the gun. Wide-eyed, she shook her head '*no.*' He bit hard into his lower lip. Inched back down the steps.

They took a side route back toward the Stack. Along the way, they saw one of the IG ships take-off in the distance. It rose, turned, and started its ascent when the sharp hiss of an RPG round sliced the sky. Matteo and Raia ducked as they watched the missile arc and hit the ship. It sparked, burst into flame, then listed off to the West. Crashed with a loud boom...right where it shouldn't.

"Daddy!" Raia yelled, breaking into a dead sprint. Matteo ran after her as fast as he could. Every alley and turn toward the Stack brightened with a fiery glow. *No...please, God...come on, man!*

The EXO ship had flipped sideways, plowing directly into the top three container apartments. The Stack burned as the ship's chemical blood spurted onto the flames. Two figures sat wedged in the cockpit behind a fractured glass canopy, taking pistol pot-shots at the angry dwellers who had already started to gather.

"NO!!!" Matteo sprinted through the crowd toward his toppled apartment, ignoring the gunfire. He stopped as the heat seared his front. It was already gone. His house. *The seeds...* He dropped to his knees and bowed into a tight ball. Screamed. The sound joined the chorus of screams behind him.

POP! Another shot from the cockpit...followed by wail to silence all the others. It felt like death. He turned to see Raia on the ground holding her father in her lap. A red hole gushed in the man's chest as he died by inches. The prosthetic leg jerked in the dirt, then he was gone. Raia's dad had put her through hell growing up. The fights, the binges, the bruises. Raia was hardly ever home these past years. *That what it means to have a Dad?* The question stung. Jogun had been the closest thing to one he'd ever known. As tears ached in his eyes, he turned to look at the ship. Hate washed over him like an acid bath.

Matteo strangled the pistol grip. Shaking, he lifted the weight. Aimed at the struggling pilots.

BANG! B-B-B-BANG! B-B-BANG! The pilots' bodies burst in a flurry of glass, sparks, and blood. An instant of horror passed before Matteo realized he hadn't fired. Cheers and shouts picked up as a pack of T99s flooded into the street, armed with rifles, SMGs, knives, and sheet metal machetes. Suomo ran to the center of the block, and hopped up on a smoking rubble pile.

"Brothers and sisters! This here is the day we been waitin' on!" Suomo shouted. The other T99s let out a whoop and raised their weapons.

"That's right, the War of the Righteous has started, y'all, and *they,*" Suomo pointed to the dropship, "hit *us* first! Now, I got word from my boy Oki that he's got three more of these motherfuckers caged up on Daigi's roof!" He turned and looked at Matteo. Kept his voice loud for the crowd.

"You wanna go back to ya homes and hide, good luck! Ain't nobody stoppin' you. But if you wanna *fight*, don't matter if you got the Mark on your arm or not, *you come with ME!*" Suomo turned and trotted down the pile. Quick as cats, the other T99s locked and loaded their guns, and loped after Suomo. A handful of the survivors hobbled off quickly down alleyways and side-streets. Mostly the elderly and their caretakers. Some of the husbands and wives who had children. The others looked at one another and the ruins around them. A middle-aged bald man with a rock-solid paunch knelt down and picked up a long piece of re-bar. A young woman, whose' child lay bloody and lifeless beside her, tore a strip out of her shawl and wrapped it around the end of a long metal sliver. Clutched it.

Matteo stared down at the gun. He'd never seen bodies come apart like that. As the others left to follow Suomo, he stayed still. The street grew quiet except for the roaring fire and groans of hot metal. He looked up and noticed she was staring at him. Raia still sat with her father on the ground, clutching the man's ratty, blood-soaked t-shirt. Her eyes shimmered as her face contorted in pain. It cut through him.

"Don't worry," Matteo said, tucking the gun tight in his waistband. Easier to run that way, and he had catching up to do. "I got this."

12

Courage

"JESUS CHRIST, KID, could you try to jerk my fucking shrap-torn leg any *more?* I don't think it's cut deep enough, so why don't you just go ahead and punch the wound while you're at it!" Shima clutched the collar of Vaughn's flak jacket. The rookie worked to remove the mangled Augmentor shin-plate. Charred chunks of sheet metal peppered both of Shima's armored legs, some making it through to flesh. Someone had tossed a popper-bomb into their shelter. Not enough to kill, but just enough to maim. It had been quiet since then.

"He ain't ever field dressed a wound before, Shims, let me take a look," said Mason.

"No! Stay on those windows! I want *your* eyes on the roofline, not some Red Gate—*AAH!*" The shin-plate popped free. Several blistered cuts and punctures covered the skin underneath. Vaughn set the shin-plate aside and grabbed the forceps from the med kit. One by one, he removed the remaining bits of shrapnel...some deeper than others. One was in at least four centimeters. Shima unsheathed his field knife, making Vaughn jump, but flipped it around and stuck the rubber grip in his teeth. Bit down as the forceps went in and grabbed the hot razor-sharp metal. Vaughn slid it out with little extra cutting.

"That's the last one," Vaughn said, reaching for the antiseptic spray, bandage and gauze. He sprayed the length of Shima's calf and shin, pressed on the bandage seals, and wrapped it.

"Not bad for a first try, kid," Mason said.

"Yeah, it's fantastic, now get your weapon and take a window," Shima barked as he pushed up on his good leg. Vaughn looked out his side. The long range thermal data had cut out shortly after the explosion, so they were down to personal optics. IR mode in their Neurals turned night into a cloudy day, but

77

shadows moved everywhere. The blank, black windows seemed to watch them in their sad excuse for a shelter.

It was a half-finished addition to the rooftop of a shop building. Four brick walls rose in varying heights to form a small room. The windows were open gaps with barely enough wall to stand covered on either side. Vaughn crouched beside one. *Slice the pie. Be a smaller target.* He stilled himself as he backed away from the window and pointed his SMG's iron sights along the edge. Slowly swept right. Nothing appeared in the crosshairs. Only the patchy, gray faces of chaotic buildings, silent in their stacks. Flashes and the distant report of gunshots advertised the battle raging all over the Slums. *Jesus, what the hell did we start?* He lowered his weapon an inch.

A white-hot shape bobbed into view then disappeared.

"Movement! I've got movement!" Vaughn rasped, choking the foregrip on his submachine gun.

"Great! Where? Call out the fucking location!" Shima hissed. Again, he pushed himself up on his good leg and peeked over the window ledge.

"Yeah—!—uh—it was Eas—er—North at my two o'clock...I think, sir."

"You *think?*"

"I'm pretty sure, sir. It was there, then it was gone again, sir."

"Jesus..." Shima sank back into cover and pressed his throat node. "Theta Squad to HQ: What the hell is the ETA on my evac?! I've had my beacon blinking its ass off for over five fucking minutes!"

"Be advised, Theta, all friendly aircraft are either currently engaged or flying home to re-arm. A gunship will be dispatched to your location as soon as I've got one for you," the voice hummed in each of their ear implants.

"*All* of them? The whole fleet?!" Vaughn's voice lifted a little louder than it should. Mason hissed and patted the air with a hand. The rookie groaned and leaned up to scan the roofline again.

"Over half my squad is KIA, I'm wounded and immobile, we're stuck in darkest Rasalla with hostiles closing, and you're telling me there's not *one goddamn ship?!*" Shima looked like his face would explode.

"Affirmative, Theta. Recommend you dig in, and stay quiet, we *are* coming."

Shima clenched his fists and almost punched the wall. He ripped his ammo pouch open, took out a live ammo mag, and dropped the active spur mag out of his SMG. Loaded the rounds.

"Sir? I thought we only had clearance for non-lethal." Vaughn said. Shima took out a flash suppressor and screwed it onto the barrel.

"T99s don't give a damn about spurs, but they respect bullets. If we've got any hope of holding 'em back long enough we've gotta hurt 'em," said Shima.

Mason and Vaughn changed their magazines. Vaughn finished screwing on his suppressor and looked back through the window. Just in time to be blinded by a flash between two buildings. He cringed and spun back into cover as nearby whoops and shouts broke the silence. Vaughn's eyes cleared in time to see smoking red lights arcing through the sky, over their wall, and landing in the middle of the shelter floor.

"Flares!" Shima yelled as he lunged toward them, putting weight on his bandaged shin. He landed directly on the wound, yelled, then grabbed at the flares. Threw two of them out. Three more fell in. Then two more. They heaped in a glowing pile as the first shots zipped through the walls.

"SHIT! Fire at will!" Shima screamed. The body heat signals poured out of the twilit slumscape. Vaughn couldn't hope to prioritize targets. The muzzle flashes looked like the grandstands of the Sedonia Civic Arena during the half-time show. As the brick and concrete flew apart around him, Vaughn shrank into cover, clutching his weapon. He couldn't think, let alone move.

"Wake the fuck up, kid! Kill or be killed!" Mason's voice came through low and deep in Vaughn's implant radio. Vaughn looked to the veteran EXO as the man squeezed a few three-round bursts out of the weapon, each at a specific target. Shima did the same on the opposite wall, blood pouring down his leg as he stood on it to get position.

Flip the switch, flip the switch, flip the switch. Vaughn hit himself in the helmet. His legs wouldn't budge. Concrete exploded everywhere, making their cover look more like coral. He clamped his eyes shut. Felt his heartbeat in his throat. All sound around him turned to white noise. Then something opened his eyes.

He found himself staring into the burning phosphorous light of the flares. Time slowed. In the space he felt his heart and his breath. His hands and his feet. His arms and his legs. Fear was still there, but it seemed more like another appendage. Something else to work with. The order eclipsed it: *Kill or be killed*. Gritting his teeth, he leaned out of cover and pumped half a mag into the growing mob.

Matteo sprinted across the rooftops toward the flashes ahead. He jumped over alleys, raced up and down stairs, and swung onto catwalks, movements he'd seen Jogun do a hundred times. Yet now on the way to his own battle, it felt different than he'd fantasized. Part hunter and part hunted. Righteous and terrified. Distant thoughts screamed faintly to calm down and turn back. The drive to listen gripped his chest. *No home to run to.*

The half-finished shed on the roof of Daigi's shop glowed blinding red from the inside. Dark silhouettes peeked out of the windows then darted out of sight, each time followed by a pounding hail of T99 bullets. A hazy bloodshot cloud surrounded the building. Through it, Matteo saw the dwellers climbing up the fire escape. It wouldn't be long now.

The first building to his right had a balcony on the top floor where a few T99s took cover. This close, he could see the sparks and chunks of shrapnel burst from the surrounding buildings. *Bullets, not spurs.* He crouched low behind a rooftop wall, and waited. The shape of an EXO leaned out from behind his cover and fired at the balcony. The T99s ducked. Some sprayed blind shots over the railing. The shooting stopped a second.

Matteo took his chance. Three huge strides and he pushed off on the fourth, flying down toward the balcony. He grabbed the awning and swung inside, kicking one or two gangsters in the process. They shoved him off and into the corner. His gun skittered across the floor somewhere.

"The fuck you think you doin', man?!" a voice screamed. Matteo pawed around in the dark for the pistol.

"Left window! Shoot the bitch!" another one shouted. Gunfire erupted. Matteo crumpled into a ball and clapped his hands over his ears. The noise. It felt like the shots were going off inside his skull. The sour smell of gunpowder choked him first, then someone's hand did it for real. Slammed him against the floor.

"I should kill you too!" The wild stare on Oki's face was like nothing Matteo had ever seen. A rabid Pit dog ready to rip your throat out with a crooked grin.

"Oki, chill!" Suomo shouted above the gunfire and nearby screams. The T99 Boss crouched at the open end of the balcony, leaning out to fire a burst from his brand new EXO submachine gun. Oki released the choke hold, dropping Matteo gasping to the ground. Matteo felt something shoved into his chest.

"Drop this again and I fuckin' blast you!" Oki said. Matteo fumbled at the pistol grip then took hold. Another burst from the EXOs made everyone duck again...except one of the younger Nines. The boy took a round full in the face, making a canoe out of his head. Thick wet droplets landed on Matteo's arm. The shooting stopped and something dragged him up by the hood. He choked himself on the hoodie collar as he tried to stay down.

"*Shoot*, goddammit!" Oki's voice cracked as he screamed. Matteo cringed at the gunfire pounding his eardrums. Oki slapped him in the face.

"SHOOT!"

A flash of rage set Matteo's mind on fire. He flexed his fingers around the grip as his heartbeat jackhammered over the muffled pops of pistols, rifles, and SMGs. The blood. It pooled on the ground by the T99 boy's shattered head. Raia's face appeared to him. Staring. His body trembled as he wrestled with the will to do something. Anything. The wheezing tickle in the back of his throat turned every breath into a saw blade as his knees started to buckle.

Suddenly he was lying back on that rooftop six years ago. Helpless as he watched Jogun shudder and twist with every punch, kick, knee, and elbow. For years he had dreamed of the ways he could have hurt them, should have hurt them. The thousands of things that would have saved his family. His grip on the pistol tightened. *Inhale-exhale-inhale-exhale-INHALE.* He whipped the gun up, pointed it at the glowing building. The EXOs inside moved in flickering blurs.

Matteo fired a shot and all but dropped the gun as it kicked. The sensation sent needles down his spine. He brought up his left hand to steady his aim. Two more shots. The rounds blasted dusty chunks out of the brick wall.

"That's RIGHT!" Oki slapped his back so hard it gave him a funny taste in his mouth. The others looked over at him too, all smiles. Matteo managed an insane laugh. Movement in the right window caught his eye. A pulsing shadow that seemed to turn toward him. With a sharp breath, he focused on the shape, looked down the sight, steadied the weapon, and squeezed the trigger. Since he was ready for it, the shot felt more like a little pop The shadow jerked and fell out of view.

Cheers picked up all around him. Oki grabbed him by the shoulders and shook. He tried to smile at them, but his mind struggled with the new data. *I got one. I killed an EXO.* A hail of bullets sprayed into the balcony and everyone got down. Matteo dropped with a limp thud. The sudden rush made him dizzy. He pressed himself as low as he could as dust and debris rained down from the balcony wall. It stopped. The others got up.

"One down, two to kill!" Suomo said from somewhere close-by, "Rasalla!"

"RASALLA!" the T99s shouted as they opened fire.

Between three-round bursts through his iron sights, Vaughn saw a broad, heavy shape slump and fall out of his peripheral vision. A red distress icon appeared in his Neural beside the name. *'Mason.'* He ducked into cover and turned to see the old vet clutching his left shoulder joint, struggling through wet gasps for air. The man seemed more pissed off than anything.

"Sergeant!" Vaughn screamed, lunging toward the wounded vet.

"Get the fuck back on that window!" Shima shouted as he continued to pump controlled bursts from his side of the shelter. Before Vaughn could protest, Mason planted a boot in his flak jacket and shoved him backward. Vaughn heard the sounds outside getting louder. Closer. He peeked back over his cover to see T99s crawling up the side of the building. Reflex spun his rifle up to drill the closest of the group. They tumbled backwards, knocking a few of the others off. Wild shots cracked in the air as they whizzed past close enough to graze Vaughn's helmet and visor.

"Theta Squad, this is Odin Six Four. Request sit-rep, over," said a calm voice in his inner ear. Shima stabbed two fingers into his throat mic and shouted.

"I'm wounded, we've got a man down, and about ten-thousand fucking angry locals closing! We need every goddamn thing you can give us NOW!" The pause that followed made all the screaming hell of the fight seem quiet. Vaughn dropped five more climbing bodies in the time it took for the reply to come.

"Roger Theta, Odin Six Four en route to your RFID signals for Purge and evac. ETA: 1:30 minutes." The relief washed through Vaughn to the point of feeling faint. He tensed and shoved the rifle butt deeper into his shoulder. *Pick your target. Fire. Pick the next target. Fire.* The Red Gate combat mantra returned to him as intended, but the other word the pilot had used tugged at the back of his mind.

Purge. Hope and dread came in equal parts where one of those was concerned. The new gunships were outfitted with BASE platforms. Broad Area Stun Emitters. The half-sphere shaped delivery mechanism would extend from the underbelly of the gunship, charge in a matter of seconds, then send a one hundred-foot diameter sonic blast. They'd done it to him in basic. After the initial full-body slap, it had felt like his spine turned to cotton. Every muscle fiber simultaneously lost tension and then it was lights out. A two-hour coma followed. Then the sum total of every hangover he'd ever had.

The Aug gear would dampen the shock of this one, but the thought of anything like that sensation shivered down his backbone...and there was still a chance of being knocked out. Long enough for T99 reinforcements to arrive. *Naked in the hornets' nest.* He glanced at the ETA displayed in the upper middle part of his vision. *1:14.* He had shot or killed six men since the pilot's broadcast. Eight took their place.

The noise in their shelter suddenly dropped down a layer. Enough to make them both pause and glance. Mason lay toppled on his side, weapon resting in an expanding pool of flickering blood.

"Mason! Not now, goddammit, it's time to work! MASON!" Shima screamed. The old vet didn't move.

"Reloading! *Last mag!*" Vaughn threw the spent one aside and somehow stilled the shaking enough to click the new one in place. He squeezed off two bursts before he heard it. A hundred or more voices chanting at once. Each word a hate-filled bark.

"*Ra-sa-lla, Ra-sa-lla, we-fight-for-our-home! From-scrap-and-from-ashes-and-dirt-we-are-grown! T-ninety-nine-soldiers, our-blood-for-our-own! DIE-EXO-DIE-EXO-in-pain-all-alone!*"

Matteo felt the words flow like molten metal in his veins. The fear receded, replaced with something else. All around him, the T99s shouted in one voice. Oki spat the chant, firing bursts in time with the lyrics. Suomo stopped firing to howl it in all directions. The voices lifted high above the gunfire. One full repetition later, 'Matteo had memorized the words.

"*Ra-sa-lla, Ra-sa-lla, we-fight-for-our-home! From-scrap-and-from-ashes-and-dirt-we-are-grown! T-nine-ty-nine-soldiers, our-blood-for-our-own! DIE-EXO-DIE-EXO-in-pain-all-alone!*"

This was new. Hate, fear, grief, and joy all focused into one feeling that came roaring out of his gut. He yanked himself to his feet and fired five rounds before the slide cocked back. Empty. A slap hit him in the chest. Oki's hand pinned a fresh pistol mag to it. Matteo could hardly believe this was the same guy.

"*T-nine-ty-nine-soldiers, our-blood-for-our-own!*" Oki pushed his face close to Matteo's as he yelled. Matteo took the mag. Wide eyed and smiling, he rejoined the chant as he fumbled with the weapon.

"*DIE-EXO-DIE-EXO*—!" The roar of hover-engines drowned them out and panic ripped through the crowd. Some, mostly T99s, leaned out and fired at the gunship. Others turned and ran for low ground, scrambling down ramps and stairwells, or climbing down wall ledges. A few jumped. Matteo tried. He pulled himself up onto the side railing and looked for a place to land in the alley below. The ship was on top of them, the air thick with a deafening hum and the smell of ozone. *That pile of tin. I'll get cut, but it'll break the fall.* As he lunged, Oki grabbed his hood and yanked him back into the balcony. Dazed, Matteo watched Oki's pinched face contort as he soundlessly screamed something. Matteo couldn't tell what. From his place on the balcony floor, he saw a shiny dome of metal come out of a belly panel on the gunship. Bullets plinked off of it as it started to glow...and shake. It shook so hard and fast that it blurred into a shape twice as big.

The hum gathered into a high pitched squeal over crushing vibration. Oki released Matteo as both of them pressed palms over their ears. Matteo felt like he was screaming. Couldn't be sure. It all suddenly paused in a moment of charged silence. Time enough to look up and then—

BOOOOOOOOOOooooooommmm. A pale blue wave of light burst from under the gunship, spreading instantly over the entire block. The shock of it threw Matteo back into the wall, buckling the flimsy metal. His vision flashed stark white. Then black.

13

News

"SHIT SHIT SHIT shit SHIT!" Liani pressed the yellowed elevator button half-a-hundred times, watching helplessly as the lit numbers crept toward her floor. Normally, she added some 'elevator wait time' to her morning routine, but nerves and caffeine had caused some difficulty in the outfit selection process. First the black top with the white blazer. Then the purple sport coat and white dress shirt. Then the maroon blouse with black slacks...the blouse had looked cute in the store, but in normal light it made her look like she had love handles. She had torn it off and barely fought the urge to stuff it into the incinerator chute before returning to the black top and blazer. The meltdown had taken at least a half hour.

The memory chip in her purse stayed fixed in her mind's eye. It had taken the better part of a week to work up the nerve to contact GSBC Channel 17 with the story. The 'past due' notices from her landlord spilling out of her inbox gave her the final nudge. *This whole 'doing-the-right-thing' shit had better pay off.* GSBC was already skeptical of her, and being late wouldn't help her cause.

After a long pause on the floor below her, the elevator doors slid open. She nearly barreled into an elderly man as he stepped off.

"Excuse me!" she blurted. The man, unoffended, looked her up and down and whistled. It sent a chill up her back, but was it's own kind of reassurance. She flashed a crazy grin at the man and hammered the button for the fiftieth floor lobby. He gaped at her, smiling. Thankfully the doors shut before the pervert could put whatever crossed his mind into words. She fussed with her troublesome reflection in the elevator walls for the entire thirty floors down to the lobby. *Better this than obsessing over the clock.* She did anyway.

Finally, the doors opened on the fiftieth floor. The lobby looked nicer than it had any right to, especially considering the apartments in the place. A broad arcade of windows looked out over the main landing pad and Superway terminal beyond. They'd even sprung for shrubs, pathetic though they were. Her heels clacked a furious rhythm on the linoleum floor as she sped toward the front entrance. At the front desk, the block manager's head snapped up at the sound.

"Ms. Ray! Ms. Ray!" he called after her. She pretended not to hear, entering the revolving doors. The bald squat little man pursed his lips then held a button behind the desk. The revolving doors stopped, trapping Liani inside.

"Ms. Ray," he cleared his throat loud over the intercom in the entrance, "you *are* aware that your account is fifteen days delinquent?" Liani pushed at the door. *Over 300 tenants in his block alone, and he remembers everyone's name and rent status.*

"Well aware, Mr. Korvan! I'm on my way to an interview right now so I can fix that!" She folded her arms so she couldn't yank out her carefully styled hair. In the long pause that followed, she thought about trying to break the glass with one of her heels.

"The full balance, including rent and late fees, is due by the end of the month, or eviction will follow." A buzz came over the intercom and the doors resumed spinning. They almost knocked her down. She stumbled out onto the sidewalk then stormed off toward the terminal.

The train arrived as she did. A long, snaking row of segmented cars hung from the mag-lev rail. The Superway network could take you across town in minutes, but you had to pass security, pay for entry, and catch a train first, a tricky business in this part of town. *Eff these heels!* Liani retracted them, ran flat-footed to the turnstyles, and passed her forearm over the scanner. But instead of the good beep, it screeched with the bad beep. Text flashed red in her Neural display.

"Overdraft Warning," a digital voice said in her ear, "press 'Accept' to withdraw the funds from savings with a surcharge, or 'Decline' to—" Liani punched 'Accept,' hoping that she might somehow break the simulated button. The usual tiny vibration of a button press was all she got. Liani pushed through the retracting gate, sprinted through the closing train doors, and found a seat.

She didn't have much time to enjoy the commute. Only three minutes to cross the twenty mile span from her building into downtown. All the same, she kept her eyes glued to the clear bubble canopy of the train car. To the left and right of the suspension rail, the off-white, stained buildings of her Inner Ring neighborhood passed. Liani's place would have been considered a high-rise a few decades ago. Her floor might have even been penthouse level. But as the final alley of scrapers passed in a blur, the glowing blue splendor of the midday Center Ring appeared. In its beating heart, the Trade Mesa. A gargantuan, flat-topped structure that sat lower than the thicket of shining towers around it, but dwarfed them all in scale. Only Sedonia Tower stood above and behind it in grandeur. The curves of over a hundred different superway rails converged on the Mesa, and steady streams of air traffic filed in and out of thousands of open ports.

She missed Mesa Park. The three-square-mile green preserve that stretched out from the southern base of the Mesa. Trees, shrubs, boulders, gardens, ponds, and lakes. She could almost smell the fresh air through the Plexiglas. Each day before a shift at GloboMetro, she'd been able to steal an hour to go running through the elaborately woven paths, passing Sedonia City's best and brightest as they did the same. For the first time, she had felt comfortable. Confident. At home. *And now because of that fucking stunt, I've got one last shot at it all. Then it's back to bartending...or jail.* Bitterness and nerves crept back in, spoiling the sight of blowing leaves and shimmering blue pools. She took out her compact mirror and fidgeted with her makeup for the last minute of the trip.

The Superway rail banked left and dipped out of Mesa Plaza, heading into the sweeping grid of towers. The GSBC Channel 17 headquarters appeared, twenty blocks or so from the Plaza. It's angular structure and shining windows would have made it impressive on its own, but it looked sadly average in this sector.

Another ten blocks flew by before she reached the connection station. She hoped her luck would continue and there would be at least one shuttle waiting for her to just grab and make it to the office. She waited at the door for the train to stop, glancing feverishly at her watch. *9:58 AM...come-on come-on COME-ON!* Finally, the train hummed to a halt and the hatch flashed open. She bolted out onto the platform toward the shuttles. Watched helplessly as a passenger entered the last one, closed the gull-wing door, and floated away.

She felt the second meltdown of the day boil up into her temples, but by now people were noticing her. From TV, she hoped...not because she's a crazy lady in an ugly blazer on the verge of leaping from the platform to end it all as a bloody stain a hundred meters below in the Foundation levels. The arriving troupe of shuttles yanked her from the whirlwind in her head.

"Ooh ooh OOH!" She ran as fast as heels could go to the first one in line and hopped in. *10:01 AM...maybe their clocks are slow...or mine's fast? Mine's fast. Calm down, Liani.* She sat up straight and smoothed the wrinkles from her outfit.

In front of her pounding heartbeat, Liani Ray was all charm and smiles on her way through the megalithic GSBC lobby. The morning sun streamed in through towering arches, bathing the vast flowing chamber. She felt good. Scared shitless, but good. It would be nice to finally toss off the weight of the conspiracy. *Wait 'til they see this. It'll be like a dropped a bomb on the place...this is just the beginning.* An intern almost ran her over on his way through the doors. He was gone before she could think of something passive-aggressive to say, but then she noticed the rest of them. Other interns, reporters, fact-checkers, managers, art directors, cameramen, crew-men. All ran to and fro through the lobby. Some babbled into Neural screens or to one other as they rifled through floating interface. She caught bits and pieces of conversations as she wove her way to the high front desk at the back of the room. They added up to something big.

"What the hell do you mean, it's still raw?! We need those shots cut together *five minutes ago!*"

"Are we sure about this wording?"

"If you don't have final approval, then put me on the line with someone who does!"

"No way we can air that!"

"...well figure it out! 'Massacre' doesn't exactly have the best connotation..."

Massacre? She waved off the sinking in her chest as she approached the front desk.

"Excuse me," she said. The receptionist didn't seem to hear. She almost said it again when the woman reached over and pointed to the scanner panel on the front of the desk.

"Check in here then have a seat, someone will be with you as soon as possible." The woman tapped a few icons on her Neural and started talking to a face on a screen. Liani fidgeted for a second, then rolled up her sleeve to scan her forearm. Her profile appeared on the receptionist's display followed by the text: "*4.678 minutes late.*" Liani grimaced until the receptionist shrank the profile window and stuck it into a queue of other profiles.

"Thank you," Liani said, attempting to be cheerful. She turned and strode toward the colony of circular sofas in the center of the lobby. Halfway there, everyone in the room froze at the sudden burst of intro music and soundbytes. On the high wall behind the desk, GSBC-17 anchor Garen Todd appeared on a massive physical screen. His sharp blue eyes and chisel-cut features stared solemnly down at the lobby.

"We interrupt today's broadcast of 'Inter-Lunar Freighters' to bring you this Special Report. At 5:03 SST this morning, the Sedonia Border Police Department executed what Commander Gorman of the EXOs referred to as the 'largest, most decisive strike against organized terrorism within the Rasalla District in the history of the SCPD.' The majority of the SCPD EXO division's aerial combat and infantry were mobilized in a single, organized raid to decapitate leadership structures of Slum terrorist factions plotting violence on the Border and the Outer Ring territories. Chief Gorman confirms that all major operations have concluded successfully with the capture or death of every top-ranking target. Our safety, however, has apparently come at the highest of costs, for, and it is difficult for me to share this information with you, *twenty-one* EXO officers lost their lives in the effort andthirty-six were wounded. We have correspondent Byron Youngblood coming to us live from the Southwestern Rasalla District. Byron, what is the current situation?"

★ ★ ★

Liani dropped to her knees in the middle of the floor as she stared up at the screen. No one seemed to notice or. Some even joined her in their own displays of grief, real or faked. The screen changed to show a grizzled, world-worn correspondent against a backdrop of fire and smoking debris. Gunships patrolled overhead and, to the reporter's right, EXO Cops loaded unconscious dwellers onto a carrier.

"Garen, the mood here is definitely a somber one. The official casualty report came over the Net roughly an hour ago, sending a shockwave through the men and women of the SCPD. Their friends and brothers have made the ultimate sacrifice in this morning's events, Garen, and every officer I've spoken to carries the weight of that loss. Yet there is also great relief and pride, and as you can see behind me, their mission is all but accomplished with the elimination or incarceration of over *twenty-five-hundred* individuals throughout the district, the majority of which belonged to the notorious Triumph-99 or T99 crime syndicate, a group the Sato Administration has dubbed 'a threat to civilization'—"

"Thanks Byron, but I'm going to interrupt you briefly so we can show some of the images coming to us from all over the Rasalla District. For those of you joining us, I have to issue a warning about the graphic nature of these images."

I'm....I'm too late. God, I didn't mean to— Liani's stomach turned. A slideshow of well composed, color-corrected footage appeared on screen. A ragged gash rippled through a neighborhood, collapsing its buildings into piles of smoldering debris. Women wailed in the streets as EXOs walked by with prisoners in tow. Bloody faces. Broken corpses. The last image made her turn away. On screen, a row of children stared down at the destruction from a nearby rooftop. Liani felt their eyes on her.

A touch on her shoulder made her jump. Hastily applied mascara ran down her cheeks in black streaks. She wiped it away and looked up. A thin, blond young man spoke to her between glances at the screen.

"Ms. Ray?"

"Y-yes."

"We have an editor ready to see you now. Do you have it with you?"

"Wha...? I..." Liani stood on weak knees. Buckled.

"Whoa! Taking this pretty hard, aren't you?" asked the man, reaching to help her up. She pushed his hands away and stood. Straightened her ugly blazer.

"I don't have anything... Th-thank you for your time."

Liani stumbled out of the automatic doors in a daze, drifted to the edge of the skywalk, and grabbed the railing. The GSBC building stretched what seemed like forever underneath her. Dizzy and nauseous, she swayed back from the rail and sunk down to sit on the concrete. Her purse clinked next to her. She reached in and took out the memory chip. The power to topple a government in the palm of her hand. And maybe not just a government. Murder. Kidnapping. Slavery. If the people knew, it would crush them. And if they knew she could have done something to stop it...*No.*

In a flash, Liani took the chip in both hands. Snapped it in two.

14

Crossing

MATTEO AWOKE TO thundering white-noise and a crushing pressure all over his body. Though unable to move, he felt a lead burden pulling him forward. Or was it downward? Hot blood tingled against his skin in its direction. It pressed him into something hard, crushing his collar bone, chest, and groin to the point where he thought they might crack. He fought for ragged sips of air from a plastic mask over his face.

His eyes throbbed as they darted over the space around him. Curved bars ran past his head and over his shoulders, holding him against a seat. *A harness?* His foggy mind drifted to his hands. He tried to raise them...found them pinned at his sides with thick metal cuffs.

Matteo could see flickering, blurry shapes in front of him. Violent pulses of light cast on figures that seemed to be seated and bound like him. Faint human sounds cried out against the background roar. *Gotta be engines. Big ones.* Observations struggled against the sharp pain in his temples. He pinched his eyes shut.

Then something cut the weight. A gasp filled his lungs with hot wet air and his chest trembled with each wheezing breath after. *We've stopped. Why are the engines still running?* The thought vanished, overcome by strangeness. His body felt...disconnected. As though his insides were floating around. *The stunners?* Out of nowhere, his stomach lurched. He vomited. But it didn't move right. Yellow-green liquid left his mouth and gathered into rippling blobs. They drifted out in front of him, suspended in the pale blue glow from small windows to his left and right. Scared voices in the compartment fell dead silent as they watched the liquid orbs touch, combine, and split apart.

"What...the...fuck?" said Oki, restrained opposite Matteo. The blue light faded, plunging the room into pitch black. The heads of every prisoner craned forward from their harnesses to peer out the window. Stars. Billions of them. The compartment erupted.

"Shit. SHIT! Where the hell are we, man?!"

"They can't! They didn't! They just didn't!"

"Not there! No fuckin' way! Anywhere but the goddamn *Moon!*"

Matteo heard them but didn't hear them. Where most shut their eyes or stared at the floor, Matteo stayed fixed on the porthole. On a clear night in the Slums, he could see maybe forty of the little white dots in the sky. He had counted them several nights on the roof of Utu's clinic. *So…many.* His lips parted as waves of goosebumps spread over his aching skin.

The ship rolled, giving no physical indication to the prisoners. They saw stars cascade past the portholes. Whimpering cries croaked from the T99s. Suddenly light-headed, Matteo's neck went slack.

"Never gets old," said Shima, watching the live feed from the aft prisoner compartments. He released the seal on his oxygen mask with a smirk and unbuckled his flight harness. They had removed his Augs to clean, dose, and re-bandage his wounded leg. He might walk with a limp for a few days, they told him, but on the way to the Themis Colony, no walking would be required. It felt good to have a break from gravity tugging on the recombining flesh and muscle.

"Hehe, yeah. Bunch of tough little shits 'til you shoot 'em into orbit!" The pilot chuckled.

"Fuck 'em." Shima said. The pilot started to laugh again, but saw Shima's stone expression. Shima took one last look out of the cockpit canopy. The details of the lunar surface grew bigger and sharper with each passing minute. They would soon enter the outermost ring of orbiting satellites, meaning three hours or so before touchdown at Themis. Three hours to just float and think. He couldn't take it. Shima pulled himself up over the co-pilot's seat and pushed off to the squad compartment.

The bitter reminder greeted him as he passed through the hatch. Vaughn, the rookie, was the only familiar face. The rest were replacements fresh out of Red Gate…some looked young enough to be freshmen. Vaughn sat in the rear left hand corner of the compartment, strapped snugly in his harness and typing on a virtual keypad in his Neural. Shima drifted over.

"You know, kid…typing the After-Action is the ranking officer's job. My job—eh?"

The weak-chinned replacement in the seat next to Vaughn sneezed, sending tiny particles jetting through the air. Shima dodged most of them.

"Listen, numbnuts, go…secure the lavatory or something, grown folks are talking."

"But sir, I was just in there, and it's fi—"

"Now," Shima said. The replacement paled and fiddled with the harness. Shima punched the center of it, released the shoulder bars, picked the boy up, and floated him gently down the aisle. Vaughn ignored them, rubbing at his lower lip and staring intently at the Neural display. Shima pulled himself down into the replacement's seat. As he leaned over to speak, Vaughn started typing again.

"You know my old man was an asshole?" Shima said. Vaughn furrowed his brow and shot Shima a confused look.

"Oh yeah! Total asshole. Though knowing me, that might not've surprised you." Shima grinned. Vaughn allowed a small snort of amusement. Shima gave him a brief stare-down before continuing.

"He'd come home and find me and my brothers neck deep in some kind of bullshit around the apartment or on the Beck's Run Skywalk outside and he'd just lay into us, screamin' his ass off about this and that and 'why the fuck can't you shitheads just come home from school and keep quiet?' And when I was younger, I'd get scared of him right away, I mean my old man could be like a pissed off Rottweiler when he got back from a fourteen-hour double in the Outer Ring. But if we didn't do shit that day, he'd just grumble, fall into his chair in front of the screen, and drink wine coolers till he passed out. Never understood the wine cooler thing, myself." Shima got a laugh out of Vaughn with that one.

"Right? I mean, what kind of working class hard ass chugs box-wine? Whatever, I digress. So anyway, Mom had left years earlier for some Mesa hotshot she'd met at the skin bar where she worked, so the old man was all we had left...and he got to where he didn't sweat the small shit anymore. Me and my brothers had to get *creative*," Shima tapped at the side of his head, "We'd steal chemicals from school to start fires on the Skywalk, or break all the dishes in the auto-door to our unit. One time we decided to ambush Dad in the elevators from inside the emergency hatch. I was the youngest and the only one small enough to get in there quick enough, so Hashimé helped me up into the shaft and Kaneda kept lookout to radio up when Dad got in on the commuter level. The signal came and up I went...and let me tell you, if you think those things are fast when you're in 'em, try riding *on* one. I heard the doors open and everyone file in...scared shitless. But something snapped and I flipped open the latch and dropped in on like twelve dirty, sweaty teamsters. Before I could shake it off, I felt the hand grip the back of my neck and stand me up. Nobody said a word for thirty floors. The beating didn't come until we got to the unit. Dad pushed me through the front door and gave me a good one right in the gut. I deserved it. Knew that. But I got up and just fuckin' charged *full force*. First I kicked his knee the way it wasn't supposed to go and heard a snap. Then when he went down I started in on his ribs. Then his head. The cops found me sitting on the bloody floor next to the old man. Shipped my brothers off to social services and me to Juvi. Best thing that ever happened to me."

Vaughn's attempt to hide disgust failed. The replacements had dropped all eavesdropping pretenses and leaned in to listen. Shima, punchline in his back pocket, smiled.

"Oh yeah! Turns out all I needed was structure. Discipline. I ate it up, morning, noon, and night. The drills, the PT, the chores...hell, I even liked the classes! A model inmate, all the way. So much so that by the time I came of age, some of the Ex-Mil CO's recommended me for this new special program for young adults just like me..." Shima paused and looked around the room.

"Red Gate?" One of the replacements ventured.

"Give the noob a prize!" Shima said. Vaughn had returned his attention to the report. Shima stared at him a moment.

"You did good today, kid. But don't let it go to your head, 'cuz things are just getting started. Oh I know we've 'decapitated the leadership' and all that, but do any of you kids really think that's it? Everybody retire and go home?"

No one answered.

"Believe you me, there will be more T99s and Right Hand Guards and Kangal Armies...and they won't forget what happened today," Shima projected his voice for the whole compartment to hear, "A raid like this might make everybody feel good in the short term, but the war isn't over. It'll go on. And on. And on. And on. Until somebody either gives up or gets wiped off the planet. And those who'se job it is to fight have to embrace it. Love it. I know what you're thinking, but loving it's different than wishing for it. I dread every single fight. I shake like a full blown Sway addict every time I step in that dropship, but just like when my old man's fist rammed into my gut, after the first bullet flies, everying changes. I love it. Every minute of it, even though at the same time I can't wait for it to be over! I love it because I'm a warrior. You guys need to make up your minds what you are. Wind up in the middle and you wind up dead." Shima pushed up out of the seat and drifted down the aisle for his dramatic exit.

"What about Mason? Dreivan? Babb? All the others...EXOs, T99s, average dwellers? Did they all have as much fun as you? Or were they all just in the middle?" Vaughn asked. Shima spun around and pushed off toward Vaughn. He grabbed the rookie's harness and cocked a fist back. It both felt and looked less threatening in Zero-G. As they stared at one another, the fire in Shima's face receded. The sharp features somehow looked childish...sad. Shima lowered his fist and released the harness.

"Things are just getting started, boys. Stay alert, do your jobs, and mark my fucking words." With an ounce of his recovered bravado, Shima turned to go. He bumped his leg in the maneuver, sending a knife of pain up and down his right-hand side. The offending seat paid for it with a punch to the cushion. He pushed off faster toward the cockpit.

Vaughn shook his head. He knew what Shima had meant...even agreed with him to some extent now that he'd seen Hell up close. A small part of him beneath the mission, the noise, and the terror was actually enjoying the play of it all. And that part scared him. Especially when the memory of it mingled with the sound of Mason's death rattles over the comms, and the images of the torn bodies flying apart along the roof edge. 'Duty,' 'honor,' 'protecting civilization.' All the stuff he'd bought wholesale at Red Gate still mattered, but had somehow dimmed like a childhood memory. He mourned it all.

He awoke hours later as the decel-thrusters kicked on, knocking him out of the downward spiral. At least he'd get to see the Moon. Always wanted to... even applied to be a guard on Themis, only they'd sent him a form letter about 'all positions filled, but we'll keep your information on file' or some such. The EXOs were the next best thing...or so he thought then. Not sure anymore.

Regardless, the boy inside him pressed his face to the porthole glass, trying to get a better angle to see the surface as it came up around the ship. Gray desert stretching to a sharp black horizon. He marveled at the size of some of the craters...way bigger than in the textfeeds and documentaries. Detail appeared as he squinted. *They're terraced...man made!* A turquoise explosion soundlessly rippled along the edge of one of the terrace ledges, blasting a plume of dust into orbit. Passing scows flew in and sucked up the debris with huge intake systems. Tiny dots on the surface became vehicles. Giant landcrawlers with what looked like UV spotlights scanned the ground in wide indigo swaths.

The slow pull of gravity came in a sudden wave. It was unsettling. Vaughn wasn't aware how accustomed he'd gotten to weightlessness, and this wasn't exactly like having weight again. He lifted his arm and let it fall. Shifted in his seat. Tested his feet and legs. Hopefully there would be enough time to adjust before 'cargo transfer'.

They dipped low into the mouth of a canyon and flew half-way above the ground at cruising speed. Something like a formal highway buzzed with activity below them. Industrial traffic. *All positions filled, my ass...you'd need an army to watch all these inmates.* The canyon opened wider ahead, crested around the edges by an inward-leaning rock wall some four-hundred feet tall. *Natural shelter from cosmic radiation and solar wind.*

Just as he got frustrated with being unable to see ahead, the ship turned left to skirt the rim of the canyon. Thankfully his window was on the right. The canyon floor had been gouged into a perfect circle and the Themis Facility main complex sat inside. It was a hollow cylinder, reaching down kilometers into the surface. Lights from millions of portholes and windows lined the inner cylinder walls. *The cells.* The main control hub protruded out and up from the hole in a gigantic tower, extending bridges to dock stations on the canyon walls. *No direct access from cell to dock...smart.* Inmates could access the ground level to work, but would have to get from walls-to-tower, tower-to-bridge, then bridge-to-dock to escape.

The ship slowed to a stop beside the airlock gate. Vaughn felt the bulkhead vibrate as the docking clamps slid into place and locked. Harnesses released all over the cabin, and the squad got to work. They were a bunch of kids eager to test their training...just like he had been yesterday. *Did all of it really just happen this morning?* Damn disorienting. The weird-ass gravity didn't help either. He blinked past the fuzzy feeling behind his eyes, stood, and lined up for the hatch.

PART THREE
Consequences

15

Fate

AFTER THE ENGINES cut out, the compartment fell to total stillness. The smells of sweat, piss, and shit filled the twilit cabin. Matteo couldn't be sure if it was coming from him or just everywhere. Fear was thick in the air. He'd never seen any T99 so scared in his entire life...even when they charged head-first into EXO machine-gun fire. Matteo felt himself on the brink too, but insane curiosity kept him afloat. A new kind of ship in the Pits had been enough to send him into hours-long daydreams. *Those stars...this place...what's outside that door?* If something didn't happen soon, he would scream. Or cry. Or explode. Maybe all three in that order.

A few mechanical pops broke the silence, triggering shouts and curses from the T99s. The cargo bay doors yawned open, bathing the compartment in blinding light. Matteo squinted over his restraints. Human figures appeared. Started coming into focus. He heard some of them coughing.

"Fuck *me!*"

"Yeah...takes the breath away, don't it?"

"Whatever, just stick 'em and pull 'em so we can hose the whole thing out ASAP."

Matteo saw EXO gear on a few of the figures and jumpsuits on the rest. A few details of the room beyond trickled in. A high catwalk. Stacks of crates. A hydraulic lift...then one of the figures leaning into the compartment. It opened a panel on the wall, and hit a button. A sharp pain jabbed into the small of Matteo's back. He and the others howled as their bodies went limp, but this time he didn't black out. He watched as his harness swung open and dropped him on the ground. The pain was distant and dull but enough to bring his wheezing to full tilt. Hands grabbed him under the shoulders.

"Bit sickly, this one...sure you got use for him?"

"No mark on his arm. Must be a dweller. Pit worker too, judging by the scars," the figure chuckled, "Plenty of pits on the Moon. Toss him in with the others." Matteo's body tingled as they dragged him out of the cargo doors. Totally paralyzed, he was forced to stare at the floor as they carried him through what sounded like a large room. The floors used to be white, he could tell, but had been worn to yellow-gray...stained with ruddy trails and patches here and there. Dozens of them led in the direction he was going. The pounding fear buried his curiosity. He passed out.

Consciousness came back like one of Utu's old records starting up. The floor under him had turned from stained tile to shining chrome. There were holes in it. *Cold.* His body shook as the numbness faded. He was naked, he realized, and cuffed around the wrists to a plastic-coated cable tethered to a floor track. The whole room seemed to glow with a stinging white light. He rubbed at his eyepits.

"Time to wake up, cop-killers! There's work to be done!"

Before Matteo could figure out where the voice came from, an electric current raced through the metal floor. Every fiber in his body contracted in a wrenching spasm. Once his muscles slackened, his eyes flashed wide. The blurry shapes of the others around him came into terrible focus. They looked like strangers. Suomo was much skinnier than he'd looked in all his designer clothes, and Oki... he reminded Matteo of a Pit dog. Broken and bloody after a fight over scraps.

The walls of the room were glass. On two sides, the same figures from earlier stood in darkness. Watching.

"You wanna do the honors?" said the same voice from before.

"Is that cool? Figure you guys got protocol and such for this kind of—" asked another.

"Your recommendation got me this job, remember? 'Sides, Shima, I figure after what you done for the City...you deserve a little payback."

"Heh. Well, if you insist," replied the one called Shima. A fraction of a second later, scalding hot jets of water fired down from the ceiling, pinning Matteo and the others to the floor. They writhed, pulling against their bonds as they tried to shield themselves. Matteo felt like the water would cut through him at any second. It stopped. Everyone in the chamber groaned between coughs and gasps for air.

"Hah! Just like the car wash back at base!"

"Go on, Shims, time to dry 'em off." Heavy motors thrummed under the floor. Matteo struggled to get up but a sudden blast of hot air helped him the rest of the way. It blasted out of the floor slots, rasping against raw, bare skin. The air stopped, replaced by roaring laughter

"Ho ho, *man!* Now that...that was satisfying," said Shima outside. Matteo and the others stood in line. All shaking. Noticing the track in the floor again, Matteo traced it to the end of the room. Some kind of chamber stood at the end of it. A smooth cylinder with double doors...painted solid red. *I'm third in line.*

"'What *is* that little red room for?' That's what you're all wondering isn't it?" the guard asked, "It's a...naaaah. Better if it's a surprise for each and every one of you fine gentlemen!" The red doors slid open, revealing solid darkness inside. The cables in the floor track went taut and the line lurched forward. Feet squeaked and slipped on the wet metal as they fought against the pull. Matteo fell backward, knocking into Oki.

"What the fuck, man?! Get offa me!" Oki howled and shoved. The T99 at the front of the queue screamed as the cable dragged him into the chamber. After a hiss of air, the doors snapped shut and muffled screams filled the room. Matteo and Oki paused to stare in horror. The sound. Something like the hover-engines of a gunship combined with a grinding buzz. The screaming inside stopped suddenly.

"Unknown Male. Approximately 21 years of age. 1.85 meters. 75.9 kilograms. Blood type A negative. Designating inmate number 272310-A: Scout Operator." The voice was cold and mechanical. Matteo watched as the jumpsuited guards moved around toward the rear of the red chamber.

"Ey, what the fuck did y'all do to him?!" Suomo yelled, sounding hushed and painful. Matteo swallowed past the rasping knot in his own throat.

"HEY!—-" Suomo gagged on the shout and started coughing.

"Pipe down in there, shitbird! You'll find out *directly!*" Muffled laughs followed through the glass. The red doors opened and the track started pulling again. Suomo's turn. He fought harder than the first, pulling at the cable until the shackles cut into his wrists. Drops of blood left a trail on the chrome floor.

"You motherfuckers, I'll kill you! I'll kill you all! Your families! Your friends! EVERYONE! EVERY—!" The shutting chamber doors drowned the last word. When the machine started up, Suomo pushed himself louder. The words gave Matteo chills through his already trembling body.

"*Ra-sa-lla, Ra-sa-lla, we-fight-for-our-home! From-scrap-and-from-ashes-and-dirt-we-are-grown! T-nine-ty-nine-soldiers, our-blood-for-our-own! DIE-EXO-DIE-EXO-in-pain—-*" The chant stopped. The machine wound down.

"Unknown Male. Approximately 25 years of age. 1.91 meters. 76.1 kilograms. Blood type B negative. Designating inmate number 272311-A: Crawler Technician."

Matteo's heart sank...then his eyes fixed on the track in the floor. No one now between him and the chamber. He got a head start on his bonds, tearing at the seals with bending fingernails. A heel slammed into his back.

"This is your goddamn fault, *Wheezy!* Betchu wish you could'a jumped now, huh?! I should'a shot you right then, you ain't *one of us!*" Oki sprayed spit as he shouted. He planted another kick into Matteo's side, then the doors hissed open.

"Stand up! STAND UP! Get what's comin' to you, bitch!" Oki shoved Matteo toward the blackness of the chamber.

"Get what's comin' to you! Go on! You ain't one of us! YOU AIN'T!"

Matteo stood. Maybe he did deserve it. *'No blood.'* Jogun's plea bubbled up from the past. Matteo felt hollow. Done. Whatever waited for him in the dark, it was all that was left to him now. He hung his head in tearful silence and took the final shove into the chamber. The doors clamped shut around him.

He shook in the darkness for three shallow breaths. The air was close, still, and reeking of sweat and ozone. *A small space.* Then the machine powered up. Much louder inside, instinct jerked his hands toward his ears. Couldn't reach with the cable. A blazing ring of light switched on above him, filling the chamber with red. Jagged mechanical shapes set in the walls seemed to promise pain from all directions. The ring grew brighter. Brighter. He felt the heat from it as it turned pure white. It slid down the walls, sweeping over his body to the floor and then back up again. The light died.

He furrowed his brow. *Is that it*— A sharp pain seized the back of the neck.

"Unknown Male. Approximately 18 years of age. 1.74 meters. 65.2 kilograms. Blood type AB negative. Designating inmate number 272312-A: Assistant Scout Operator." The voice sounded far away. Images pulsed through his head, bombarding all his senses. He crumpled to his knees as a set of doors slid open in front of him. The light and reaching hands were the last real things he saw before memories assaulted his awareness. At least they were like memories. The schematic of an LTS-780 scouting vessel. Its load bearing capacity and top speed. Procedures for scouting Helium-3 deposits. Titanium ore. Lunar ice caches. All so clear...at first. They started coming in fuzzy or sort of half-drawn. His own memories pushed back. The dark shape he'd shot back on the rooftops. Raia's flaming eyes. Oki laughing as he punched and kicked. Jogun lying broken on top of their shack. The first time Jogun brought home a piece of fruit...

Then...the dream. The one he'd been having off and on for years except now in full waking color. It started with a loud boom that made him cry. *Is this the dream or am I crying now?* Familiar voices spoke frantically in front of him. Their fear made him cry harder. Another boom and everything flipped... started shaking. His tiny chest fluttered at the sensation of falling. The familiar voices screamed now. The one on the left...a man...struggled with a control panel, eventually pounding it with his fists. The one on the right slumped in the seat. The man yelled back to him...something familiar about the voice. Rust-colored rooftops loomed up ahead as the man spoke. Comforting him. Then it all went black.

Matteo awoke to the jumpsuited guards bending over him. They spoke frantically, but the words mingled with the fading dream state. *Is this happening?* As his senses sharpened, he felt something press over his nose and mouth. A respirator. His eyes flashed wide open as he slapped it away from his face, and struggled to push himself away from the guards. He stopped after a boot to the stomach.

"Talk to me, Doc, what the hell happened here?!" the one they had called Shima demanded.

"I dunno! I dunno! It could've been uh...uh...shit, maybe some kind of psychotic reaction to the juice?"

"Thought you said that wasn't possible with the anti-aggro cocktail you guys mix in!"

"It shouldn't be possible..."

"Shouldn't be?! Don't tell me you've been injecting shit into an entire hostile population that *should* squash their need to kill us all!"

"I've never seen anything like this! Some of 'em just go brain dead or have a seizure, sure, but...wait a minute."

"What?"

"Counter-measures."

"Counter-measures as in neurotech? As in *top of the line* neurotech? What the hell would a mope like this need with anti-hacking hardware in his head, huh?!" Shima asked.

The medic shrugged.

"Maybe to keep us from squashing his personality and installing a new one? How the hell should I know?"

"How should you—?" Shima laughed, "Nevermind. Just do a pass with the deep local scanner."

"But the Designator already..."

"We're gonna take another look and see what's going on here, okay? Now do a pass," Shima said. The medic reached to the wall and took a device that hung from a hook there. It looked like a pistol handle with a broad, flat-nosed barrel. Matteo tensed as the man walked toward him and knelt. He grabbed Matteo's head, pressed the device to it, and pulled the trigger. A yellow-orange screen materialized off the side of the scanner. Numbers, graphs, and images flickered to life.

"Oh yeah. This kid's definitely been augged...from birth it looks like," said the medic. Matteo gaped at the man through the corner of his eye and tried to turn and see the screen. The medic wrenched Matteo's head back in place, pressing fingers hard into his skull.

"Let me see that..." Shima knelt to look, "Nah, bullshit. Had to be stolen... maybe in one of those boosted freighters last month. Check the forearm." They released Matteo's head and yanked his arm out. Turned it palm up to the scanner.

"Shit," said the medic, "Designator missed this little guy too...a full blown RFID...must've tripped the fail-safe or something after he got dosed." On the screen, Matteo saw through the flesh in his forearm. A tiny white object sat between two bones. A crosshair appeared on-screen over the object followed by an electronic beep. Text appeared on-screen.

```
Remote Frequency Identity activated...
Chip reboot confirmed...

Aden William Rindal
Male / DOB: 06-20-2062
8842 Mesa Ridge Block 2A
Sedonia City
Emergency Contacts:
    Alan and Patricia Rindal
    (8040)36.257.9816
Blood Type: AB Negative

Software Update 6.682 Available!
Querying remote servers. Please wait...
```

"Shut it down!" Shima yelled.

"That's against protocol...I can't just—"

"SHUT IT DOWN!" The medic fumbled with the buttons on the device. Matteo panicked. Glowing windows, buttons, and bits of text appeared all around him like a bad hallucination. The guards were surrounded by it too. A high-pitched squeal preceded a loud thump. Matteo felt his arm stiffen, then return to normal. Something that had brightened in his brain went suddenly dark again. The visions vanished.

"EMP?" Shima asked. The Doc nodded, "Good. Hopefully we caught it in time..." Shima said.

"Come again?"

"He's an identity thief, numbnuts. That's why they used to carry the bodies off when some poor Citizen crashed in their backyard. They call their techs 'Lifters.' These guys carve a chip out of a vic's arm, bootstrap it to a homebrew console, and hack the bio-signatures to match whoever they want. DNA syncs up and everything. So then the bastards sneak into the Net and start cleaning out accounts, or worse, try to jump the Border. Heavy shit, but we've seen it before."

"What the hell are you talkin' about, man?! I never went to no Lifter! I've never seen that thing before in my li—!" Matteo shouted, cut off as Shima backhanded him across the face. Matteo spat blood. Then started wheezing. He grasped inside for something to explain this. Anything. *I'm losin' it! That stuff they shot me with...this is still a dream!*

"Like I was sayin.' You let that update go through, and some family in town gets a message saying that their long lost loved one's not so dead after all. In fact, they're alive and well in a lunar penal colony! Imagine their surprise when they find out a cop-killing Sway addict butchered their family for the copper, silicon, and plastic in their arms," said Shima. The medic looked down at the scanner, then to Matteo.

"Maybe...but the neurotech...the RFID? Both hard as hell to get to work in tandem, and both functioning together in one guy from the Slums. What if he is this...Rindal? Like a kidnap vic or something?"

"No way. Look at him," Shima grabbed Matteo's head and jerked it to face the medic, "I've been fighting tooth and nail with these scumbags for the better part of a decade. I know how they move. I know how they think," Shima sniffed, "How they smell." He released Matteo's head, stood, then wiped his hands on his flak vest.

"This piece of shit is 100% Grade F Rasalla, and some of my best friends are in the morgue or rotting in the street because of trash like him. Toss 'em in with the others, and finish the rest without me. It's been a hell of a day, and I wanna be back planet-side before last call." Shima limped off past the silent doctor. A guard approached Matteo and stuck him with a stun baton. The familiar slackness spread through Matteo's body, but he allowed himself to sink into it this time. *I'm dreaming. I gotta be. I'll wake up soon, eat some shitty rice, and head for the Pits... Please wake up. Please...*

"Uh, Shims?" said the medic.

"What."

"Can't put him in with gen pop...if the dose didn't take, he's a security risk. Gotta send him up to Decom," said the Medic. Shima turned a grin directly at Matteo.

"Even better."

They picked Matteo up and shackled him into a harness chair pod, separate from Suomo and a long queue of others in the hall. Two by two, they filed through a plate-steel hatch door at the end. A track in the floor under the chair pod told Matteo he was headed elsewhere. He felt the dull sensation of a pat on the shoulder. A sneering voice whispered in his ear.

"Welcome to the Moon."

16

Party

THE LIMO HOVERED to a graceful stop on the landing pad of the prestigious Plateau Ballroom, one of the crown jewels of the Mesa's upper levels. Kabbard exited first into the full moonlight, wearing a jet black tux but none of the poise. He all but ripped the passenger door off its gull-wing hinges to allow Mr. and Mrs. Enota Sato to step out onto the pad. Sato touched the man on the shoulder and leaned in to an ear.

"Easy, Kabby, I don't like this any more than you do," Sato said. Kabbard seethed as he avoided eye-contact, turned, and gently shut the limo door. The craft lifted and then dipped away as the three of them walked toward the red carpeted bridge to the main entrance.

"So concerned for him? What about me? I'm the one who has to squeeze myself into this...lovely frock you say you love so much," Jada fussed with the creases over her plump hips and belly. The dress was the color of ripe plums with tiny pearls inset around the collar. Its velvet folds soft to the touch. Sato wrapped an arm around her as they walked, hiding his signature caress of her curves. It calmed him.

"You look wonderful," he told her, smiling to the security guards that stood beside each of the tall, flowing lamp posts along the path. She wrapped her gloved hand around his, tugging it to her stomach. Sato felt a pang, remembering the miscarriage. It was his public reason for the nervous breakdown six years ago, but a contributing factor all the same. Jada had kept her head held high throughout the ordeal. *The strength of this woman.*

"You sweet, sweet man...I do hope this evening won't be too painful for you," she said.

"The press and half of Congress breathing down my neck about this Rasalla business, and Finley throws a damn party. I can't wait to see the headlines..."

"You knew this was coming," Jada turned his wedding band between her thumb and forefinger, "People only like violence when the good guys don't get hurt. But the effect will be the same, and *you* need to keep Elias happy so they didn't die for nothing."

"Right..." said Sato. His eyes drifted up beyond the lamp posts to the Moon. Its historical 'face' gone, replaced by geometric patterns...like aerial photos of dead, gray farmland. He sighed. The broad, arched doorway to the ballroom loomed ahead. Above it, a one-hundred-fifty foot tall glass dome bulged up into the night sky. Its hexagonal ribs were nearly invisible due to the golden glow coming from inside.

The door guards in their foppish red tunics stepped forward to open the door. Kabbard waived them off, and took the door himself, double-checking both inside and back down the bridge as he did so. His manner refused to let Sato relax. *Maybe I shouldn't.*

The host at the podium looked like he was dressed for the Nutcracker Suite. Appropriate, considering the classical chamber music lilting in the background. He peered at the trio through stiff features.

"Ah. Governor Sato. Mrs. Sato. Welcome to the Plateau Ballroom. Stephen here will escort you to your table," he said.

"Thank you," Sato said, nodding. They walked down the central aisle toward the band.

"*Ah,*" Jada mocked. She turned to her husband, squinted, and sucked in her lower lip. A perfect impersonation. Sato elbowed her as they wove their way through the crowd to their table. Going was slow. The 'smilers' all wanted to shake hands or complement Jada or ask about some long forgotten invitation. Thankfully, Kabbard filtered them somewhat...it was both comforting and unsettling how the man checked everyone's hands.

Arriving at their table was a formality. They wouldn't be spending much time there, except for Jada to drop off her purse. *Oh, to sit down,* Sato thought. His patent leather shoes already chafed his feet. One deep breath later, he put on his best 'Governor' face and turned to the crowd. Met Finley instead.

"My friend, Enota! So good of you to come on such short notice! And Jada, such a peach..." Finley bowed. Jada curtsied.

"Plum, actually," she smiled.

"Wouldn't miss one of your shindigs, now would we, Elias? And an open bar at the Plateau? You've outdone yourself," Sato said. Finley, mid-sip in a glass of cognac, pointed at him.

"I've not yet begun to celebrate, sir," gurgled Finley, "Now. Jada, would you mind terribly if I had a word with your Statesman here?"

Sato smiled through his teeth, and started to shake his head. Jada elbowed him.

"Not at all, Elias! I have hors d'oeuvres to investigate," said Jada.

"Try the serrano ham slivers and potato purée. Out of this world. Enota? Shall we?"

Sato nodded. Followed the waddling tycoon. Kabbard kept behind at a respectable distance, scanning the room. Sato did some scanning of his own then pitched his voice for only Finley to hear.

"Is all this really wise, Elias?"

"All what?"

"Throwing a party in the most exclusive venue in town after—" Guests walked by and greeted Finley. Sato smiled and nodded to them. Finley laughed.

"After...our little arrangement? Why not? We're celebrating the crushing defeat of dangerous terrorists and exulting the prosperity to come. I should have thought even you would be happy with such a victory."

"Overjoyed," Sato said flatly, "But with twenty-one dead EXOs and their bereaved all over the news, I need to be grieving and venerating, not celebrating."

"Hmm," Finley stroked his jowels, "Quite right. One moment." He toddled to the stage and whispered to the conductor. The music faded as Finley stepped to the mic. Adjusted its height.

"Your attention everyone! I have an announcement to make!" Finley waited a few moments after the crowd settled to continue, "On behalf of Virton Energy, thank you all for coming. Tonight, the esteemed Governor Enota Sato has reminded me that we celebrate not only the safety of our Border, but the deeds of heroes. That is why I officially declare that all proceeds from tonight's event shall be donated to the EXO division of the Sedonia City Police Department, and the families of our fallen officers. Ladies and gentlemen, to the Governor— and our Heroes." Finley raised his glass.

"Heroes," echoed the crowd.

"Thank you for your attention, and please, enjoy the remainder of your evening."

Applause followed, and the music resumed with a flick of Finley's wrist. He returned to Sato's side.

"And between you and I...*to the Moon*," Finley clinked his glass to Sato's and took a sip. Sato looked down. *When did I order a drink?* It was already half empty. He shook his head and drank anyway.

"...which brings me to the point," Finley looked around and led Sato out onto the veranda. The Mesa Park fountain shone silvery blue in the center of the gardens. The City hummed softly in the distance with early evening activity. Millions of lights in millions of windows.

"We're going to need another raid," Finley said. Sato gagged on a mouthful of scotch and clapped his hand over his mouth. Swallowed hard. Kabbard's ears had perked up too...he started pacing like a caged tiger.

"Oh come off it, Enota, why else would I pour perfectly good booze money into civil service? Beyond publicly advertising your conscience of course," said

Finley with a grin. Sato leaned on the veranda railing and stared at the park fountain. Finley waddled over and leaned beside him.

"Your boys busted some heads alright, but they made a real mess of it. Out of the twenty-five hundred 'eliminated terrorists,' I got only two thousand viable workers. Don't get me wrong, now, that's a decent enough start, but we're having to push further and deeper than we ever have up there. It's dangerous work... hell, I was losing twenty units a month to radiation, solar winds, cave-ins, and all sorts of other extra-terrestrial pit-falls when we were just staying put on our *current* holdings! Now there have got to be more bad, bad men for your guys to grab in the nearly *twenty million* lurking beyond the Border."

"More bodies..." Sato shook his head, "Jesus. The public's already reeling from combat deaths on our doorstep, and you want me to send them in again? With all the coverage about 'decapitating the enemy leadership' the counter-terror angle can only be pushed so far...and if you think I'm tossing more EXOs into that—"

"You're right! You're right. The leadership *is* decapitated. Meaning there's no way they'll get any kind of a real fight the second go 'round! It'll go like the first one should have. Quick, clean, and easy."

"Easy because they'll be grabbing street vendors and Pit workers on live TV? Sedonia fears the Slums, Elias, but they'll see that for what it is."

"And what is it?" Elias asked. Sato couldn't reply. He knew what it would mean...what it had already meant. Reports coming in had said not all the prisoners had gang affiliation tattoos. Not all the dead either. Entire neighborhoods were still smoking over the horizon.

"Listen, you think it over," Finley said as he turned to leave, "But remember the clock's ticking. I'll leave you to your 'grief.' There's plenty of your favorite coping mechanism at the bar." Finley nodded toward Sato's empty glass, smirked, then walked back inside.

The one quiet moment Sato had had in recent memory was spent rolling the implications in his head. *Another raid. More blood.* And the next time, people would be watching closer. What would they see? Augmentor-bound super soldiers kicking down doors and dragging worker families into the street? Regardless of being absolute evil, the Sedonia public might just resent such a spectacle. *The jack-boot of military tyranny stomping firmly on the neck of the lowly working man.* That's how his critics would spin it anyway. He felt Kabbard approaching.

"I know! I know. I haven't said 'yes' yet, okay?" Sato said.

"Yet? Sir, with all due respect, the first time destabilized a fragile situation at the cost of *lives! Most* of which are on my head," Kabbard paused and exhaled sharply. Laughter spilled out of the doors further down the veranda. Kabbard moved closer and lowered his voice.

"It was my plan. My failure. Believe me when I say that we do not *have* the resources to pull off a second. Do this now, and things come apart...violence outside *and inside* the Border. You don't just make a call like that to ship a little more—"

"I said, *I know*, John. But without Finley...without the Helium flowing... the City suffocates.. What do you think happens to our little Utopian bubble if its lifeblood is choked off and sucked dry from every vein?" asked Sato. News footage of the devastation in the Slums and metal SCPD caskets flickered through Sato's mind. He squinted hard and pinched the bridge of his nose.

"I need another drink," Sato said, tossing the empty glass over the edge of the veranda. He attempted to straighten himself as he walked to the doors. Kabbard grunted and trotted to open the way for him.

Once inside, he wanted to go right back out again. The lights. The gaudy band. The swarming glad-handers. At least he could throw things out on the veranda. He scanned the room with aching eyes for Jada. Spotted the bar instead and set a course through the least inhabited side of the ballroom. It was there that Tycho Kirnden of Globometro News found him.

"Bourbon on the rocks?" Kirnden held up a glass with his chubby fingers. The table, one of the only ones occupied on this side of the room, pressed into Kirnden's enormous belly. He flashed a stained-tooth smile up at the Governor. Another scotch sat on the table, and the 'rocks' of both had almost completely melted. *Been planning this ambush for a while then. Fuck my life...at least he brought booze.* Sato tapped his dwindling courtesy reserves.

"Tycho! My savior," he accepted the drink. "To what do I owe this fine and, I must admit, well-timed gesture?"

"Not a thing, Mr. Sato, save to ask after your satisfaction with Globometro's coverage of the 'Scourging of the Slums.' I do hope you found all the angles approached fairly and completely..."

The scotch, albeit watered down, tasted the same. Yet it no less left disgust in Sato's mouth. Perhaps it was the man's breath wafting over. *I'm five feet away, and it still smells like death.*

"Of course, Tycho, of course! Very professional and...evocative! Now, if you'll excu—"

"Thank you, sir! I daresay the public will sleep much more soundly knowing the Border is secured. Yourself as well, I expect! Quite the master-stroke, solving so much at once—"

A pulse-tone went off in Sato's inner ear, followed by a message in his Neural. '*Incoming Call: PRG.*' Simultaneously thankful for the excuse and flushed with terror, Sato got up.

"Apologies, Tycho...I have to take this. State business," he said, turning to leave.

"Certainly, Governor...lunch next week?" Kirnden asked. Sato pretended like he didn't hear as he hurried away. Pressed 'Encrypt.' 'Answer.' Prescott appeared at her usual conference table, flanked by the Board.

"Go someplace you can talk, Enota," Prescott said immediately. A wave of anxiety crashed into the Governor. *What fresh hell is this?* He scanned the ballroom and found Kabbard. Waved the man over.

With Kabbard running interference ahead, Sato made his way to a set of pearl white doors in the corner. Opened them onto a long hall. On the left, a magnificent window wall of ribbed glass looked out on the veranda and Mesa Gardens. On the right, rows of doors to several of the Plateau's lavish conference rooms. Sato pointed to a door, and Kabbard went inside. Eventually emerged with a thumbs up. As the Governor entered, Kabbard tried to follow.

"Stay here and watch the door. I'll only be a moment," Sato said, hoping. The former Sergeant didn't seem to appreciate that. *Honest men hate secrets.* Sudden jealousy struck Sato. *Honest men...* A sad fate that duty should bind such men to liars. Kabbard scowled and shut the door, leaving Sato with his secrets.

"I am hermetically sealed and alone, Janice, now what do you—"

"Ten minutes ago, we received a flag on a person-of-interest originating from the Themis Facility. The transmission was killed before download completed, so our people dug into the corrupted data and salvaged what they could. Found one of the new 'inmates' gathered by your little smash-and-grab gambit," Janice said.

"You pulled me back here and scared the shit out of me for a POI flag from the *Slums*? Don't you have the resources to take care of whatever—"

"Aden William Rindal," was all Prescott said. The name was like a bullet through the center of Sato's brain.

"You...you're sure it's genuine? The corrupted data...it could have errors."

"Our people are the best. When they are sure, we are sure. This could be a simple ident theft, but we think you'll agree, this warrants careful and *immediate* action," said Prescott. Sato could almost taste the subtext. '*This is YOUR mess... clean it up, or else.*'

"Send me what data you have, and I'll see to it at once," said Sato.

"That would be best. If you find anyone or anything, it ceases to exist. Are we clear?" asked Prescott. Sato nodded.

"Good." The transmission went dead at Prescott's final word. '*Call Ended. Memory Block 080980_841p: Deleted.*' Sato chugged the rest of his watery bourbon, wiped his mouth, and knocked on the door. Kabbard opened it, greeting him with the signature steel glare.

"I have a job for you," said Sato.

17

Arrivals

JOGUN WATCHED THROUGH the cockpit glass as scout ships streaked soundlessly overhead. Back toward Themis. The dim light of the Crawler cockpit changed from gray to green as the 'All Clear' notification came up on his dash monitor. He tapped the screen and the Helium-3 deposit appeared on the topo-map. Not much, but spread out into several thinner, smaller deposits. The Cash Layer, untouched He3 paydirt, had been stripped clean a while ago. By someone else, judging from the pattern of the tracks.

He did his best to rub the aching behind his sunken eyes. Fifteen hours and counting behind the dash and still no quota. He'd have to scrape a huge pattern to get all the deposits in one go, taking at least two more hours...it might just be enough for a ticket back to the cells. *Those reinforcements can't come too soon.* The thought was honest, but heavy. Reinforcements would come from only one place. *Home.* Jo shook the longing from his head and laid in the course.

The Crawler rumbled to life, chewing into the rocky soil with rotating metal teeth. Once he felt the vibration smooth through the bulkhead, Jo started his pattern. A big perimeter cut to define the area, then back and forth in long strips to cover all forty-thousand square meters. Too much time to think. He wished they would have erased that part too with their mind-rape drug.

Food might help. The freeze-dried protein blocks came in three flavors. Chalk, dirt, and sand. *Sand it is. At least it's kinda salty.* Jo reached a boney arm, slid the wall panel down, and removed one of the silver pouches. He gripped the edge and pulled. It wouldn't budge. Pulled again. Still nothing. Again. The wrapper barely had a dent in it, and his forearms were throbbing. He looked at his hands. Bones and veins shrink wrapped in skin like cellophane. Making a fist hurt. Tears welled up in his eyes.

BWOOOP! BWOOOP! BWOOOP! The blaring proximity alarm filled the cockpit. A sunken crater loomed ahead, big enough to swallow three Crawlers. Jo flung the food block away, gripped the wheel, and wrenched it hard left. The Crawler's right side treads dipped down into the hole, tipping the vehicle's left toward the black sky. Not enough to flip it. It leveled out again as Jo steered past, thudding safely in a plume of gray dust. Exhaling, he throttled down and checked the topo-map.

The area showed all flat and clear according to the Scout data. Anger bubbled up inside him, but, like always, a hidden switch flipped. *They must have missed it. Too many of us out here on fumes.* He calmed, then resumed his pattern with extra care. More than a few craters dotted the landscape from there. Some he could drive over, others he couldn't. With this kind of terrain, the job would take three hours, not two. *More interesting, though.*

Pass after pass, he wove the Crawler through them and watched the Quota Bar slowly tic toward 'FULL LOAD.' Over a hill. Into a dell. Across an open stretch. Through a rocky patch. The Crawler tines ground and ground and... stopped. Screeched to a halt midway into the fourth-to-last pass.

"Warning!: Obstruction in combine system! Check immediately!" The message blinked on screen. Jo turned to look at the pressure suit in its casing on the wall. The thought of going EVA sent a chill down his spine. Even less shielding from radiation than the Crawler and a whole lot less oxygen if something happened. And something usually did, especially with combines that liked to suddenly restart when unstuck. He turned away and looked out the windshield. *Not going out there for some moon rock stuck in the gears.*

Jo flipped the Crawler into reverse and tapped on the gas. The engine protested, squealing and grinding. He let up and allowed the Crawler to settle. Tried again.

BOOM! The gray horizon outside the windshield spun as the Crawler flipped. Jo tucked himself into a ball in his harness. Screaming. His head rapped against the pantry wall panel as the Crawler crashed on its side. Moments in darkness passed. Seconds or years, Jo couldn't tell. He awoke to alarms roaring in the Crawler cockpit...and a kind of whistling hiss. As his eyes focused, they fixed on expanding cracks in the windshield.

Jogun tore at his harness with numb, boney fingers. The button wouldn't go all the way in. He pressed until he thought sure his thumbnail would rip off, and finally heard a snap. The straps released him. He clawed over the seat, wrenched open the EVA pressure suit's casing, and took out the gear. His breathing had shortened to choked gasps by the time he got it on and secured the seals. Air rushed into the helmet and filled his quivering lungs. It sounded like Matteo's wheezing as he panted. He shook his head and sat there a moment. *Okay. What. The fuck. Happened?*

The emergency release blasted the main hatch hinges and fully depressurized the cockpit. Jogun pushed the hatch off to the side and climbed out. He tried to think of things other than the suit. Difficult when he could hear every shallow breath. Luckily something caught his eye: a fresh crater in the middle of his last cut. Burns and white cracks in the lunar crust radiated out from the center. *Another landmine.* Probably one of the leftovers from the Nobidyne Company land-grab back in the 50s. Relics from the fighting were all over the expansion zones, but that shouldn't have mattered. *Just what the hell are those Scouts good for, anywa—*

The anger wilted and turned to nausea. He cringed away from the thought and fought to calm down. It worked, but the sensation turned into tears. They dripped onto the glass of his helmet, mixing with blood dropping from the head wound. *Okay...okay...* He sniffed and sat up. *The beacon.* He rotated a dial on his wrist to read 'EMERGENCY' in bright red letters, then squeezed a button on the side. A channel opened in his helmet.

"Signal received, 75508-V. What is your position and situation?"

"Sector 8709...-36A. My Crawler had a blowout. It's inoperable, but I'm unhur—"

"75508, we're sending a crew to your location, stay with your vehicle, over," said the operator. The transmission went dead.

Jo regretted not tearing into the food wrapper with his teeth. Even if he could find rations in the upturned crawler, eating would be hard to pull off through quarter-inch Plexiglas. His stomach growled against tight, shallow muscles. The constricted fit of the pressure suit seemed to call more attention to it. *Little brother, I hope you eatin' better than me.* He looked out to the Earth.

The familiar thoughts of home came to him. But after so much time, they had all turned gray. Like a half-remembered dream from years ago. Even Matteo's face took effort to remember. If the picture really looked like him at all he'd still be different now. The Moon seemed to have always been borders, crawlers, inmates, guards, rocks, and space.

Jogun suddenly felt hollow. Brittle. As if he could walk toward the horizon, crumble into dust, and finally put an end to it all. *Why eat? Why keep goin'? Could've stayed in the Crawler...gone to sleep. Finally just sleep.* Nobody would miss him. Just another casualty on the daily report. He took a floating step toward the distant Earth. Then another. Then another. He started shaking, but willed his legs onward through the drifting strides.

Three Scouts and a maintenance vessel passed over his head and hovered in front of him, blocking out the Earth. They seemed to stare for a moment. Jo stopped. Collapsed to a seat in the dust.

As the Scouts fanned out into scanning posture, the blocky, orange bulk of the maintenance vessel descended in Jo's path. A platform lowered from its underbelly and touched-down in the soil. Four pressure-suited workers stood on it beside tool kits and stacks of Crawler parts. They started unloading.

Jo squinted at them as they approached. Their movements were correct, but tight and awkward. They picked things up too fast and stumbled when they walked. Their bodies looked thick and nourished in the pressure suits. *New inmates.* Jo got to his feet.

Protocol dictated that he greet them and give a damage report. He both wanted and dreaded it. The promise of new faces was always bittersweet. He had learned to hope that they'd be total strangers, that they would all just become friends and brothers, surviving as best they could.

He sighed as he approached the first one. A stranger...but so young.

"75508-V, status report please," said the young leader. The over-stimulated glaze in his eyes and awkward shifting of his lips told that he was just Dosed. A flood of new memories, data, and programming gripped the terrified mind as it screamed in silence.

"Welcome, brother 272312-A," Jo read the boy's suit. "My unit hit some kind of obstruction on its right side, and it overloaded. No inner breach on the bulkhead, but the outer hull is shredded as you can see and the treads have been knocked off. Also, the cockpit windshield is cracked so it can't pressurize. Think you can give me a hand?" Jo asked. A bit of the boy's tension released. Initiating a new inmate could be a delicate thing. He tried to be as friendly and gentle as possible without going too personal. Even something like asking someone's real name could start a civil war in their head. It was always best to stick to the job when talking to them...so it all meant something here and now. In the real world.

The boy leader nodded and turned to his crew.

"You and you, grab a five-meter hull patch and the acetylene torch. You and I will remove the damaged tread and take a closer look at the rollers," the boy said. Jo smiled at him.

"You're doing, great, kid. Patch me up and we can—*Suomo?*" Over the boy's shoulder, the former T99 boss hefted one side of the sheet metal hull patch. His hands shook as they gripped it as though he were going to bend it in half. Jogun, realizing what he'd done, walked over to Suomo. Put a hand on his shoulder.

"This'll make a good patch," Jogun said, his voice quivering on the edge of a sob. "Be sure to—to—" Suomo's eyes flashed wide as he saw Jogun. His face tightened.

"M—M—Mat—" Suomo said. He shook violently as he fought against the Dose. He dropped the sheet metal. Grabbed Jo's arms instead. The strong, manic fingers squeezed Jo's weak muscle and bone beneath the suit.

"*M-Matteo!*" Suomo rasped. The name punched Jo in the gut. *Dead? No, come on, man, no! Don't say it...!* Jo swallowed hard, trying to keep calm enough to speak.

"Tell me," Jogun said. Suomo grit his teeth together.

"He—he—" Suomo's wide-open, bloodshot eyes stared straight into Jogun's, "Here."

18

Confidence

KABBARD RELEASED HIS throbbing right hand from the control wheel. Grumbled as he flexed the thick-knuckled fingers. Themis Traffic Control had kept him and his boys in a holding pattern for the past ten minutes and counting. Something about issues with a transport inspection in the main hangar.

"Once the bay is clear, you'll be green for docking," some silver-tongued schmuck on the other line had said. Kabbard could almost taste the bullshit. He seethed in his chair as he turned the wheel for another pass. Warden Drummond probably thought the visit to be a surprise inspection and was busy sweeping every wasteful practice and dirty secret under the rug. *A visit from Sato's personal watchdog has that effect.* He thought bitterly.

As Kabbard reached for the comms for the fifth time, the schmuck's voice slithered through his inner ear.

"Sorry for the delay, Mr. Kabbard. You and your team are cleared to dock in the Main Hangar. Do watch for debris on your way in, sir. We've stirred up quite a bit with today's excavations."

"I'm sure you have," Kabbard replied. "Tell Drummond to meet me on the deck. My employer has a...concern." *That ought to get the sloppy bastard sweating.* A sneer creased Kabbard's angular features. Before the schmuck could reply, Kabbard killed the comms, gripped the wheel, and dipped out of the holding pattern toward Themis.

Flying this thing was one of the only real perks of the job. A jet-black Zeus 12. A military class personal transport modded with a trove of aftermarket avionics, propulsion, and weaponry. Some of it, like the seventy-millimeter Manticore fleschette rockets, technically illegal. Aggressive curves ended in sharp points at the bow and stern, cradling the Geiger-12c reactor engine that spanned the underbelly. The thing maneuvered like a nuclear-powered dragonfly. Keeping that kind of power locked in a circle for ten minutes seemed to deepen the insult, but now he made his presence known. He entered the approach canyon and cleared the engine's throat with a burst of blue flame. Even with the thin lunar atmosphere, the concussion shook dust from the canyon walls. Inmates working below scurried for cover.

Andreas and Nicks followed behind him in their boxier, broad-winged Fury gunships. Nicks was a solid, loyal man, but Andreas was a different concern. Since demotion, the man had had it out for Kabbard, questioning every move and watching every step with those shifty bug-eyes. It kept Kabbard moving, guessing, thinking—the kinds of things that kept a mind sharp. Being Sato's Chief of Security was, more often than not, cushy. *Cushions make a man soft.*

The three of them braked in front of the main hangar, came about, and taxied inside as the giant airlock doors hummed to a close. The secondary hatch in front didn't open right away. It reeked of another delay meant to stall Sato's minions. Kabbard ground his teeth and tapped the control panel. Finally, the airlock gate creased open with a rush of light and air. As the squad taxied into the hangar, Kabbard spotted Warden Drummond's slouching, feeble posture among the greeting party. *Christ, this guy gets worse every time I see him. Probably hasn't been planet-side in over a year.*

The Zeus and Fury ships descended to a humming stop on the deck. Kabbard waited in the cockpit, staring at Drummond. He could see the soft bastard searching for signs of life in the opaque tinted canopy of the Zeus. Once the Warden squirmed to his liking, Kabbard flipped the release and opened the canopy. Climbed out.

"Mr. Kabbard!" Drummond blurted, "How good of you to visit. What is—er—uh...to what do we, uh, owe the pleasure?"

Kabbard ignored the slimy grin and took a quick look around. Too many eyes and ears.

"Not here," Kabbard said, removing his gloves, "your office."

Drummond's grin withered.

"Of-of course. Right this way," said Drummond. Kabbard nodded to Andreas and Nicks.

The hangar offices loomed over the deck with narrow windows that stared down like dull green eyes. The three of them followed the Warden up a flight of titanium stairs, across a long catwalk, and through a hatch just below the windows. It was painful to watch Drummond navigate the corridors that followed. The man was nervous, sure, but he seemed lost in his own prison. Kabbard was about to say something when they arrived at the Head Office door. Drummond placed a pale, trembling hand on the ident scanner and waited for the beep. The doors slid open.

Kabbard cringed at the smells of plastic out-gassings and something like rotten eggs. Yet, while dingy and yellowed, the office looked outwardly tidy. Papers in stacks, pictures on the desk, and an old-style interface panel with real-time prison stats hovering silently in the air. Drummond waddled to the chair behind the desk and sat.

"Now then, John, what is it?—"

"Four hours ago we received a POI flag from one of your acquisition chambers. Someone killed the signal and presumably disabled the RFID chip before we could get a full trace and lock. I need you to cross-reference the exact time of the flag with all new inmate tags and assignments," Kabbard said.

"But if your POI was tagged and assigned—I'm sorry, but chances are he's already been Dosed. He'll barely recollect his own name, let alone anything else you want to extract—er—*ask* him. What *is* the name, by the way?" Drummond turned to the hovering interface and opened a search prompt in the air with a circular gesture.

"August 7th, 2080. 20:08:32 SST." Kabbard stared hard-eyed at the Warden. The man shrank in his chair, brushed a wisp of stringy gray hair out of his face, and entered the information. Data ticked rapidly past until three entries appeared on screen. Two in white, one in red.

"There are three possible tags at that time," said Drummond. "Is there any other information you can provide?" Kabbard squinted at the display.

"Why is that one in red?"

"Let's see…" Drummond flicked his fingers through the interface. "Ah. Decommissioned. Looks like the Dose didn't fully take. It's rare, but it happens. The asset is usually lobotomized though, so we have to dispose of them."

"Where?"

"If he's been Decom'd, I'm afraid…"

"Where?!" Kabbard shouted. Sato had given specific orders that no one be allowed to examine the target. Drummond cringed. He tapped a few more sections of the interface, expanding the data stream.

"You might be in luck. Says here that Inmate 272312-A is in Infirmary Detention awaiting a pre-Decom examination. You should hurry though, the—" Kabbard turned to leave with Andreas and Nicks in tow. Drummond continued.

"I'll send one of my boys to escort you!" Drummond called after them, "But the technicians don't leave much behind after an exam! All that's left is sent to the crematorium!"

19

Aberrant

JOGUN'S LEG SHOOK for the entire ride back to Themis, tapping his foot on the bulkhead like he'd taken a face-full of Sway. He wrung his hands. No return flight had ever felt this slow. The lunar surface crept by outside the Scout's passenger window, one gray kilometer the same as the next. *Matteo. Here. Little brother, what happened? Will I even recognize you?* Sweat beaded on his blotchy forehead. He felt nauseous. Not unusual given his bouts with radiation sickness, but worse now. Much worse. He grabbed the pilot's seat in front of him. Leaned forward.

"How much longer?" he asked. The pilot jerked, still obviously sensitive from the Dose that had rewritten his life. Only a few hours ago if Jogun had to guess.

"Three-point-five-six minutes to Themis." The accuracy of his own statement seemed to shock the poor kid. *Matteo would be about his age.* Jogun thought about calming him, but had no calm to give. He sat back, wondering if he'd have any comforting words when he found his freshly-Dosed little brother. *If* he found him.

Finally the main facility appeared in the porthole. The pilot dropped the Scout low and set the craft to textbook approach speed. Seventy-five percent slower than they had been going. Jogun's stomach turned. He felt the retch building inside. Wiping sweat from his brow, he looked again out the window. Squinted.

He'd never seen the place so busy. Dozens of new Crawlers formed splaying lines of traffic from Themis. Every group of them escorted by five Scouts rather than the usual three. And the ground personnel. Inmates in their EVA suits swarmed along the canyon floor, carrying equipment, repairing power cables, inspecting generators, directing traffic. Thousands of them, each with the rigid control of a fresh Dose. Jogun's mouth gaped open and for the first time in six years a flicker of anger lingered inside of him.

When the Scout hatch opened, Jogun pushed his way out onto the hangar ramp. Everywhere, new inmates occupied themselves with their parts in the Helium-3 production machine. Walking down among them, Jogun could smell the faint perfume of Rasalla. The spices of the Falari Market at midday. The sweat of Sway addicts. The sour-sweet stink of a Blue Lady's blessing. All fading in place of plastic, dust, ozone, and industrial byproduct.

Jogun scanned the faces. All so young and so strong, familiar and yet still strangers. *Have I been gone that long?* A boy brushed past him, toting a duffel bag of Crawler tools. Jogun missed the face but definitely heard something. A cough, then a wheeze.

"Matteo! Little brother?!" He lunged for the boy and caught him by the shoulder. The boy dropped his duffel of tools with a crash. Turned and knelt to pick them up. *Not him.* Though fresh bruises marked his face, neck, and left arm. The EXOs had made him pay for something. Maybe nothing. Jogun turned back to the crowd.

Too many to check one-by-one. He could call out, but not without attracting attention. And Matteo might not know his name anyway. Only one thing came to mind. The employee terminals sat on the far end of the hangar in an elevated guard-shack. He pushed his way toward it through the shuffling crowd. Lifted a rivet gun from a tool palette on his way.

An A/C unit in the corner pumped fresh, filtered air up into the sealed guard-shack. Themis personnel, the legally employed kind, went through great lengths to protect themselves from the radiation and disease of gen-pop. Jogun checked to make sure nobody watched him, raised the rivet gun, and hesitated. It wasn't violence. He wasn't hurting anybody. But the specter of the Dose made him sweat as his finger felt the trigger. *Gotta find him…gotta find him…gotta—* Somewhere in the hangar, a Crawler rumbled to life. Jogun squeezed the trigger in the noise. Felt the hole-punch through the thin sheet-metal. The hiss of air followed. He repeated for the three separate chutes.

As the alarm klaxon blared, Jogun dropped the rivet gun and started walking. Above, hastily suited guards and techs retreated through a backdoor in the shack. Behind, inmates converged on the A/C unit to begin inspection. *Not much time.* Jogun picked up a tool bag, and moved upstairs to the airlock guard.

"Stop!" said the guard through a clear plastic hood. The man placed a hand on the polymer baton at his waist. Stun prongs protruded from the end.

"The airlock has been compromised, sir," said Jogun in his best robo-tone, "I need to inspect it."

The guard eyed him suspiciously. Didn't budge.

"You're a Crawler operator, not Maintenance," said the guard.

"I'm certified to assess and repair pressurized environments," Jogun said. The Themis guards liked to flex authority with the inmates, but had little fear of them.

Especially with scrawny, institutionalized 'old-timers' like Jogun. It was the new arrivals that scared them. And there were plenty around to be scared of.

"Make it quick," said the guard, buzzing the lock open, "Need to get the room scrubbed and back to operational ASAP."

Jogun entered. Heard the door shut behind him. After a feigned inspection of the airlock interior, he popped the seal on the inner hatch, walked into the shack, and shut the door. Bolted the emergency locks.

He was banking on the terminals being similar to the Crawler systems. No such luck. The wide touchscreen terminals had hundreds of icons, menus, and subsystems. *Okay...'Database'...'Assets'...'Personnel'* That led to listings of paid employee profiles. He backed out. The klaxon outside stopped. In seconds, he heard pounding on the inner hatch door. The guard struggled with the lock. He didn't look happy.

'Database'...'Assets'...'Acquisitions.' There it was. The list of every prisoner in Themis, designated by a serial number and status. Jogun touched a search prompt at the top. Had to stop and think. The Lifter had told him the name all those years ago. But that was before Themis. Before the Dose taught Jogun to read and write. The exact sound of it was a hazy memory. Jogun spoke aloud as he typed, listening for the right fit.

"Randall...Rrrringle? No. Rindahl...Rindal." That one sounded closest. He typed it in the search field and pressed enter.

"No results found," said the terminal. Jogun sank. His mind grasped for ideas that weren't there. It could take weeks to find Matteo. Maybe months. Plenty of time to die on the Moon. The hatch lock snapped open as Jogun dropped to the floor. He seized as the stun baton was shoved into his chest.

Jogun regained consciousness to the sensation of being dragged on the floor. Blinking in the fluorescence of the hangar ceiling, he recognized one of the faces dragging him. A much bigger version of the chubby little thug that used to pick on Matteo.

"Oki?" Jogun said. The kid twitched at the name, but otherwise didn't respond.

"Oki! Have you seen him? Matteo, where is he?—" They tossed Jogun's limp body to the feet of the perimeter guards.

"Whoa! Hey fellas, whatta we got here?" one of the guards sneered. His voice seemed fuzzy and distant to Jogun's throbbing ears.

"This inmate displays aberrant behavior. I am remanding him to your custody," Oki replied. The words sounded bizarre in his mouth, colored by an accent that had never once used them. The guard laughed.

"'Aberrant,' huh?" The guard looked down at Jogun. "The Moon claims another old timer." He whistled. Two more Themis guards approached, one of them carrying a pole with a looped wire on the end. Jogun tried to twist in Oki's grip, but the Earth-strong muscles held him steady as the wire slipped over his head. It pulled tight.

"Toss him in the Decom chute. But tag him for Doc Yugi first. Man's been chomping at the bit to get a peek at some of these guys," said the main guard. He turned to Oki, "Back to your post, shitbird." Oki nodded. Left without hesitation.

Jogun clawed at the wire strangling his neck as the guards pulled him away. Atrophied muscles failed. Consciousness leaked out of him as they pushed him into one of several small pods set in the wall. Everything went black as the doors slid shut.

20

Stripped

THE BLANK FLOOR was freezing in Matteo's cell. He'd awoken there about an hour ago to the muffled sounds of rambling and screaming. His new neighbors. Through the plate glass front wall of his cell, Matteo could see them. Across from him, one paced back and forth, babbling in an unending stream of terminology.

"Right pin-lock A, right pin-lock B, left pin-lock A, left pin-lock B, manifold housing, manifold carriage, primary intake manifold," and on and on and on. Matteo tried to tune him out, but couldn't help but recognize a few of the terms. From his 'new' memories or things he picked up from the Pits, he couldn't tell.

Clasping his hands over his ears helped somewhat, but sounds from another neighbor broke through. A constant thump-thump-thump. The young kid two cells down beat his head against the glass, forming a bloody patch. Matteo decided to either stare into the corner or keep his eyes shut. So exhausted. Sleep came but in restless, disorienting spurts.

Unaware he had dozed off, Matteo awoke to a hydraulic hiss across from him. A guard looped a wire around the neck of the ranting inmate and pulled him from the cell.

"CO_2 scrubber unit, O_2 converter, Recycled O_2 filter—*hurrrrkkkk!*" The guard tightened the noose. Yanked the inmate down the narrow-cell block hall. Matteo pressed his face to the glass, trying to see where they went, but they slipped out of sight. He felt guilty to be so thankful for the silence. As if on cue, the thumping resumed. His other neighbor must have woken up, too. Matteo scooted along the cold panel floor to the back corner of his cell. Tucked his head between his shivering knees. Looked at his arm. *Aden William Rindal.*

He rolled up the sleeve of his orange jumpsuit. Pushed into his forearm with a thumb, feeling again for anything under the surface. *Nothing...wait—* Through the squish of muscles over bones, something hard shifted. Too deep to tell what, even if he knew what he was looking for. A long bruise had developed there under the hours of prodding. *Aden William Rindal...Aden...William...Rindal.* The name gnawed him. Crushed every explanation that tried to form in his head. He let go of his arm. Clenched fists.

He hoped for his turn soon. Whatever lay in store for him at the end of that hall, it had to be better than waiting for it. Maybe he could pretend to be passive when the guard came for him. Give no sign of a struggle at all. Then when the moment came he would break free. Run. *Then...what?* It didn't matter. He would figure something out. There had to be a way.

Finally, footsteps approached. Matteo bristled, but forced himself to lie totally still. Like a beaten slum dog tied to a post. Closer and closer they came. He swallowed hard, imagining the wire loop tightening around his neck. *I won't fight. Not yet.* Vivid scenarios hatched in his mind. Grabbing the noose pole and ripping it from the guard's hands. Kicking the man in the kneecap or maybe punching him in the throat. All of it vanished when he heard the hydraulic hiss come from his neighbor's cell. Not his turn yet. Anger surged through him. Violent, impotent anger. He beat his fists on the floor. Hit himself in the head. Then glimpsed of the dark patch on his forearm. *Aden Rindal. Aden Rindal. Aden Rindal.* Gritting his teeth, he dug his thumbnail into the skin. A drop of blood beaded from the wound and ran down his arm. He started wheezing.

'*Breathe, my boy.*' Utu's voice drifted up with a gentle touch. He released his arm and wiped the wound. Choked on his tears.

A sudden loud din of mechanical noise shattered the calm. Matteo shrank like a frightened animal back into the rear corner of his cell. In the cell across from him, the wall slid open and revealed a hatch door. Before he could think, the door yawned open and dumped out its contents: a skinny, frail man fell into a heap on the cell floor. He didn't look like the others. Much older. Grayer. Missing hair in big patches and thin as any ascetic priest Matteo had ever seen at the Stepstones. The creature woke up with a gasp. Pushed itself up on the floor and started coughing.

Matteo saw the faded 'T99' on the old man's sinewy shoulder.

"H-hey," Matteo forced himself to speak, "Hey, can you hear me?" The old man froze. Slowly lifted his head with eyes closed. Opened them.

"Little brother?" The voice. The face. There was no mistaking Jogun in both, but they were so...broken. Matteo's throat tightened as though choked by the guard's noose. Forced himself to swallow.

"Jo..." said Matteo. It was all he could manage. The two of them sat for what felt like forever, staring at one another in the pale, silent hall. Finally, Jogun winced and crawled toward the glass. He seemed to smile but it struggled to crack the pain etching his face.

"You grew up," Jogun said, "Made yourself strong, that's-that's good. Real good." Jogun nodded with tears welling in his sunken eyes. Matteo blinked and looked away.

"Jo, I-I'm...I broke my promise,"

"No. No. Don't be sorry to me. It was my fault. Should'a been there. Should'a... should'a..." Jogun hung his head, balling his hands into fists.

"Nah, man, don't...this is on *me,*" Matteo said. Paused. "It's good to see you, bro."

"Yeah?" Jogun snorted a laugh. Looked down at his starving body, "I've been workin' out, you know...prison and all."

A brittle laugh broke out of Matteo, then utterly faded. Jogun scooted closer to the glass.

"Yo, you got a girl?" Jogun asked, grinning. Matteo went dead quiet, staring at the floor.

"N-nah... nah, man."

"Oh."

They both sat in charged silence. Quiet enough for Matteo to remember the slight throbbing in the cut on his forearm. He stared at it.

"Hey Jo? Ever hear the name 'Aden Rindal'?" Matteo asked. Jogun looked up, furrowing his brow. Shook his head.

"I...uh...Aden Rin...Rin...?"

"Aden William Rindal. They found this thing in my arm with his name stored in it."

"Don't know," said Jogun. Something had changed in his body language. Matteo saw him tense his shoulders. Shift his gaze slightly. Matteo straightened.

"You know something. What is it?"

"I—no I told you...I..."

He's hiding something. Matteo was sure of it now, but had always sensed something growing up. The way Jo would go away in his head, or the vague answers to questions. *Like he's doing now.* This had to be the heart of it.

"What. Do. You. Know?" Matteo watched the panic wash over his brother's frail body. He seemed more trapped now than the cell walls ever intended.

"Tell me!" Matteo shouted. Jogun winced. Then withered.

"When you were a kid," Jogun began, "I told you that you should be glad you never knew Dad. That was true, but I never said why. I shot him. Killed him." A long pause followed.

"Okay," Matteo said, chewing on the information, "Why? What happened?"

"He—he—" Jogun ran bony fingers through thinning hair, "He killed *you.*"

"Me? Jo, what the—"

"He killed Mom and...the baby. My baby brother...he dropped y—*him* outta the balcony, so I pulled the trigger." Jogun trembled as the words spilled out of him. Matteo stood up and spread his hands on the glass.

"More."

"I...I can't...little brother, I—"

"MORE!" Matteo pounded the glass. Jogun seemed like he would faint as he took a deep breath and struggled to his feet. Put his own hands on the glass.

"There was a crash. About a month after y—after everything happened. Me and some of the other kids, we made it there before the Cutters did. Got first pick. The others didn't wanna go in the cockpit with the bodies, they were... I went in. I went in and I found a baby in the back seat. Too sick to cry loud, so the others didn't hear. I took him and I ran. I took you."

Matteo staggered back away from the glass. His legs buckled, dropping him to the floor. Jogun fell to his knees.

"You've been my little brother ever since, man. You been my family! 'Teo, please, I wanted to tell you. Tried so many times..."

"Tried?" Matteo laughed bitterly. "Now it all makes sense. All you ever *tried* to do was keep me in the fucking dark! I never understood, thought maybe I'd be strong enough one day for you to tell me, but now...You only wanted to keep me for your damn self!"

"Little brother..." Down the hall, a door opened and footsteps approached.

"STOP CALLING ME THAT!" Matteo banged on the glass and shouted down the hall, "In here! It's my turn to go, so go ahead and fucking take me!"

"Please, Matteo. I just—I just wanted to protect you! I'm sorry man! I'm so sorry...so sorry..." Jogun rocked back and forth in his cell, clutching fistfuls of hair. Some of it tore off in his hands.

"Hurry the fuck up! 'Decom' me or whatever, but do it soon, I—" The footsteps stopped in front of Matteo's cell. In place of the guard stood the most feared EXO in the history of Rasalla. Sergeant John Kabbard. Fatter and grayer than that night on the rooftop, but it was him. Matteo felt like his head would burst. The man casually scanned the numbers on top of each cell. Pointed to Matteo's.

"This one," Kabbard said. A Themis employee crossed to a keypad by the cell and started punching commands. Gas seeped into the chamber, taking little time to slacken Matteo's muscles. His cell door slid open.

"YOU?!" Jogun's voice rasped as he screamed. He beat his fists on the glass. Kicked it. Shouldered into it. All the while shouting with a rage Matteo had never heard.

"NO! DON'T YOU FUCKING TOUCH HIM!" Blood spattered on plate glass with each wet thud. "I'll kill you, Kabbard, you got that?! I'LL FUCKING KILL YOU!"

The regular Decom guard appeared from down the hall, trotting to a stop. He looked at Jogun. Matteo. Then Kabbard.

"Friends of yours?" said the guard. Kabbard snorted a laugh as his thugs pulled Matteo's limp body from the cell. Matteo used his last bit of strength to turn his head. His eyes met Jogun's. His brother, or whoever he was, pressed bloody palms on the glass.

"Careful with that one," Kabbard said, "if he's your idea of 'pacified,' then you guys are in deeper shit than I thought."

"Never seen a conditioned unit act this way, sir, and I've been stationed here eight years. We'll get him down to the infirmary immediately and get to the bottom of the issue," said the guard. He tapped a few keys next to Jogun's cell, filling it with the same gas.

"Uh huh," said Kabbard, "Let's go." Matteo watched through tunneled vision as Jogun was pulled from his cell and down the hall. The hall seemed to warp and stretch. Kabbard's square frame loomed up beside him like a demon from a Blue Lady's story. His head felt fuzzy and dull. *Wake up.* He thought. *This ain't real. I know it's not. Wake. UP!*

21

Test

JOGUN STRAINED TO keep his neck muscles tight. He focused on the smearing red trail he left on the floor as the guard pulled him by the throat. *Where?* Each time he began to guess the thoughts jumbled into floating madness. *The blood.* Straight for a while. Then a left turn. Straight again. Then a right. Or was it left? Stopped. He heard a series of beeps then a hatch door opening behind him.

"This one's totally gonzo, can I get a hand here?" Footsteps followed. Arms scooped him up under the shoulders. Their touch was plastic. Cold.

"You kidding me with that trail of shit running from here to the cells? It's gotta be all crapped up with cosmic rads by the look of this asshole, and I sure as hell ain't gonna mop it up."

"Relax, man. Jesus! Didn't have a free hand for the mop on the way here, okay, I'll clean it up in a second. Hey, Doc! Got a special case for you here!" Jogun felt himself lifted off the ground and dumped onto a hard slab. Metal by the way the cold surface stung his skin. The blurry image of a man in a heavy gray coat seemed to materialize out of nowhere. Long white gloves spattered with red reached for Jogun's face. Grabbed his jaw, then shone a white hot light in his eyes.

"Special, you say? Doesn't look like much. Textbook radiation sickness, decrepitude, gravitational atrophy. Should be in the ovens, not on my table." The light withdrew. Jogun pinched his watering eyes shut.

"See his knuckles?" One of the guards asked. The gray-coated man said nothing. Just grabbed Jogun's torn hands and turned them over. Like he was buying meat from the market.

"Did that himself," said the Decom guard. "Beat 'em bloody on the holding cell glass screamin' something about killing us all."

The faces started coming into focus, though only from the eyes up. They wore masks of powder blue fabric.

"Really?" said the one they called 'Doc.' "That *is* special. Pass me the scanner, would you?" Jogun heard some metal clinking before having his head wrenched to the left by Doc's palm. A dragging sensation tugged at the skin on the back of his neck. Something beeped.

"Six years, two months, and thirteen days since he was Dosed. More than enough time for the conditioning to fully integrate and metabolize."

"Huh?" said the Decom guard. The Doc sighed.

"Would even a little scientific literacy kill you people? The nanotech! Long enough in the human brain and it breaks down. Passes out of the body through the blood stream. BUT!" The Doc stabbed a syringe in the direction of the guards, "Whatever changes were made become part of the brain's physical structure. For all intents and purposes: Permanent. Habits form neural physiology, gentlemen, and the life a Themis inmate...that's all about habits."

"So why'd he break his?" asked the Decom guard.

"The million dollar question! Why indeed? I imagine beating his monkey fists against the glass hurt more than just his hands. Probably set his whole brain on fire. So a few electrodes here and a bone saw there, and we might be able to shed a light on our friend here."

"Whatever, Doc. Have a ball. Hit the comms if you need anything else."

"Gentlemen," said the Doc. The guards turned to leave. One of them hesitated. He turned around, reached for the mop and wheeled bucket, then rolled it out with him through the hatch. Muttered something as he left. The door hissed shut behind them.

Without the ambient sound of the open hall, ear-ringing silence stifled the infirmary. Broken only by little metallic clinks made by the Doc as he rifled through a drawer off to the side of the slab. The man paused.

"Now that *is* too quiet..." he said. Jogun watched as the Doc swept his gloved fingers through the air, pressing invisible buttons. Jogun flexed whatever muscles he could, trying to wake them up. Nothing more than twitches answered the effort, but he jerked when a flurry of crawling notes filled the room. Music.

"Bach. Cello Suite number 1. Perfection. Please don't fight, you'll give yourself an aneurism. Very painful for you and rather inconvenient for me. Now, where to start?" The Doc prodded the skin on Jogun's neck and arm. "Ah! Let's just see how 'crapped up' you really are. Blood and tissue samples, all 'round." The Doc lifted a syringe and took Jogun's forearm in his plastic fingers. Veins bulged from the under-fed skin.

"Well that's not going to be hard, at least. Now then," said the Doc, "You may feel a little stick, here."

A point of fire seared Jogun's arm where the needle entered. He tensed.

"Well done, my boy! Now tissue...tissue, tissue, tissue. Funny word isn't it? Any word that makes a grown man purse his lips like that...sorry, I digress." The Doc took out what looked like a fat, white pistol. Tiny metal points glistened at the end of the barrel.

"We'll take one from...the foot." It felt like a starving rat took a chunk out of Jogun's flesh.

"The...thigh." Another chunk. Both wounds quickly started throbbing.

"The belly. The chest. The shoulder and the...neck. Now don't move, I'll be right back."

Jogun trembled as he felt damp warmth weeping from each ragged hole. The Doc turned away. Jogun's fingers all flexed in unison, slowly balling into a fist. His arm lifted. As sensation returned to him, he felt the cuts burn deeper and sharper. He willed his arm to the place where he'd heard the metal clinking. Fingers closed around something with a sharp tip. Jogun barely felt it cut him, but his hand jerked anyway, rattling the tray of tools.

"What are you up to over there?" said the Doc, "fumbling for a weapon, are we? Interesting, very interesting...well, come on then, let's see what you can do with it." The Doc made a window with his thumbs and forefingers, then started typing on an imaginary keyboard.

Frozen muscles started to tingle all over Jogun's body as his mind screamed at them to obey. Gradually, they twitched. His stomach tightened, lifting his chest enough to slide two arms underneath. He rested, panting harder and harder. Then he swung his right leg over the slab. The left. With one final push he sat up, bloody blade gripped in hand.

"Very impressive! Some signs of shock and obvious blood-loss, but you're fighting through both the conditioning *and* the sedative. Don't know *how* you haven't—" Jogun doubled over, falling to the floor. From hands and knees, he vomited grey liquid across the linoleum. "Ah, yes, there it is."

The world spun for a moment. He shook his head, then picked a point to stare at. The Doc. One hand slid forward on the ground. Then the other. He crawled through smeared blood toward the man's wide-eyed grin.

"That's it, closer...closer...closer.......!"

Jogun arrived at the Doc's shiny black shoes. Brought the blade forward.

"Go ahead! I stuck you, now you stick me." The Doc even crouched. Jogun lifted the weapon. It seemed to weigh fifty kilos. The old familiar aching queasiness gripped his abdomen, begging him to put the knife down. His hand dropped limp to the floor and the Doc stood. Turned to type more invisible notes.

"Nano-conditioning versus primate. Nano always wi—"

"Sh-shut the fuck up," Jogun slung the blade around, hooked the back of the Doc's foot, and yanked hard, slicing right through the tendon. Screaming followed as the Doc crumpled.

"You! You—aaaahhh! Goddammit!" The Doc tried to stand. Screamed again and fell. Jogun pushed himself up to a sitting position, then reached up for the counter next to him. He pulled his burning body up, faced the Doc, and limped toward him. The knife glistened red in the fluorescent light.

The Doc made a jagged ruddy trail as he scrambled back across the slick floor. He seemed to be aiming toward a wall panel. Jogun let him try.

"That's it. Closer. Crawl for your life," said Jogun. The Doc got to the base of the wall and stretched his arms toward the panel.

"Go ahead," said Jogun. The Doc tried to get up on his good leg as he reached. Slipped on the blood-slick floor and landed hard on his bad leg. Screamed. Jogun crouched beside him, pointing the blade at his face.

"HELP! HEL—!"

"Shhhh," Jogun brought the knife to within an inch of the man's eye. "Good. You listen like that from now on, I promise I'll let you go. You feel me?"

The Doc nodded, staring at the point.

"Is there an antidote to the Dose?" Jogun asked. The Doc paused, then shook his head.

"N-no. It's permanent."

"You're lyin', man." With the tip of the blade, Jogun drew a sharp red line down the Doc's face. "Try again."

"Aaaah! Okay, yes, yes there is! But it only works on subjects who've been Dosed less than a month, why would you—"

Jogun drew another line.

"AAAH! In those tanks over there, hooked up to the tray!" the Doc howled. Jogun turned to look. Against the wall, a battery of four plastic containers sat elevated. Hoses connected them to several tools clipped to the tray. Jogun crossed to them. Picked a tank from the shelf and disconnected the tool. A long, thick needle with several buttons on the side. Jogun looked at it a second, then crossed back to the Doc.

"N-no! What are you doing?! I told you—AAH!" Jogun stabbed the needle into the Doc's shoulder and pressed the largest button. A pneumatic hiss and a rush of liquid followed. Doc Yugi howled.

"Idiot! It won't do anything to me; I haven't been Dosed!"

"Just makin' sure it ain't lethal. Question Two: How do I open the hatch?"

"That button up there! The green one!" Doc pointed to the wall panel.

"Thanks," said Jogun. As the Doc started to relax, Jogun slashed. The knife sliced the Doc's throat from ear to collar bone. White-gloved hands locked over the wound. Blood spurted through the fingers.

"Y—! Y-y-you ssssaid—!"

"Fuck you," Jogun grabbed the antidote tank, stood, and pressed the hatch button. The door slid open. Fast as he could, Jogun limped out into the hall. A fever sweat broke out on his brow. *Where'd they take you, little brother?* He thought he'd heard the word 'hangar,' but which one? His pace quickened past the glass cells.

"Hey! Hey wait!" called a muffled voice. Jogun paused. "P-please...port pin lock B, rear feed aperture, optimal approach vector—" A new face in one of the Decom cells. He looked to be younger than Matteo, and trembling from a recent Dose. Jogun's hands gripped the needle tool and tank handle. Looked down the hall where they'd taken his brother. Looked back at the boy.

"Ah shit. Hang on, I got you kid," Jogun punched the wall plate as he'd seen the guards do. The door opened with a heavy click, and the boy spilled out of it. Jogun sat him against the wall.

"This is gonna hurt," he said. Before the boy could protest, the needle tool plunged into his thigh. The scream subsided quickly, replaced by a kind of deep silence. A twitch. Two. Then life flowed into the boy's face as Jogun braced him.

"Listen. A man in a black suit, he came through here with a slum boy and two thugs—"

"Yeah...Yeah, I saw 'em on my way in. Or, I think I did. Everything's..."

"I know, I know. Can you walk?"

"I think so." Helping one another, they stood. Struggled a few steps down the hallway, but didn't get far. Pounding on the glass of a nearby cell stopped them. Then another cell. Then ten. Everywhere, muffled cries begged for help.

22

Cargo

MATTEO FADED IN-AND-OUT to a blur of white hallways. *So it was all a dream. I must be waking up. Utu gave me something to knock me out in the Temple, and it gave me crazy nightmares.* He could almost taste the spiced incense of morning prayer. *Nightmares...that's it, that's—* A stab of pain shot through his knees as he was dragged through a hatch. The taste of incense turned to iron in his mouth and nose. His aching eyes rolled up to see the shape of a man in front of him. *Kabbard...fuck. I am awake. Then Jo... Aden Rindal...* He vomited what little he had in his stomach onto one of his captor's legs.

"Ah shit!" one of them said, wiping the spatter from his black slacks.

"Pick him up. Let's go," Kabbard grunted ahead of them. The thugs snatched Matteo under the arms again and pulled him onward.

"Shouldn't we just...*take care* of him here, boss? Sato said 'cease to exist,' right?" said the blonde, hollow-eyed goon.

"No," Kabbard nodded toward one of dozens of security camera's they'd passed on the way, "There's better, quieter places to 'cease' between here and home." Matteo did what he could to hold his head up. Saw a twisted grin curl the cheeks of the blonde man.

Faster and faster, a prickling sensation returned to his extremities. *Fear? Or the 'counter-measures'?* It didn't matter. He tried to push everything from his buzzing mind and focus on his body. Focus on the strength to jump Kabbard, tear his gray eyes out, and run.

The four of them came to a large, square hatch door with a young guard posted outside. Matteo watched the freckled, dirty-blonde boy break a sweat in his slightly oversized Themis Staff jumpsuit.

"W-where are you going with that prisoner?!" the guard blurted, "I'm going to have to see some authorization." The boy's rat claws fidgeted with the grip and foregrip of his SMG. Kabbard held up his hands.

"Easy, son. Easy." Kabbard gestured through the air, tapping buttons that weren't there. The guard tapped a few of his own then went shock-white in the face. Matteo wondered at the exchange as the guard dropped the gun to dangle by the strap, and almost tripped on the way to the door panel.

"Sorry, sir! Please excuse me, I—right this way!" The boy fumbled at the door controls, getting the combination wrong the first time. Kabbard sighed.

"Take your time," said Kabbard. Finally, the beep sounded and the hatch door rushed open. The sounds of heavy equipment, shouting voices, and hydraulic tools spilled into the hallway. Matteo smelled the bitter flavor of hover engines. *The hangar.* They dragged him inside.

All around, he saw the faces of Rasalla, or really the shells of Rasalla, busy moving like ants over garbage. Matteo felt a faint sadness in their expressions. *Probably the only thing the Dose didn't take.* A lump formed in his throat as a skinny, sixteen-year-old kid made eye contact.

Kabbard led them to a group of three ships, two of them wide and flat with beefy wingspans, the other one a sharpened, deadly curve of volcanic glass. *Two Furies...and a Zeus.* An article out of *'22nd Century Military Tech'* had shown concepts of them. Matteo never thought he'd see one, let alone be shot into orbit by it. At the push of a button, the Zeus' rear beetle-shell compartment split open.

"In there," Kabbard said. The two henchmen zip tied Matteo's wrists and ankles, heaved him into the space, and shut the hatch. Matteo couldn't see anything in the pitch black space, but could hear muffled hangar sounds between his gasping breaths. He pulled at his bonds, digging plastic into flesh. They wouldn't give.

Now what? Matteo shifted his arms behind him. Every kid in the Slums knew this trick. He stretched in the tight space of the compartment, tucked himself over his tied hands, and brought them under his legs to the front. Started feeling the door panel in front of him. His fingertips searched in the dark for any features. Almost entirely smooth except for the thin, tight seam around the edges. His heart sank. Jumped as the compartment quaked with a throaty roar. *Engines!* Any moment, the ship would lift off the deck and take him...where? *No place good.*

He made a hammer out of his fists and pounded against the hatch.

"COME! ON! COME! ON! CO—"

A piercing sound shrieked through the compartment shell. It buzzed three times then paused. Three times again. A bit of data from his new memories knew exactly what it was. *Class Four alarm... 'Prisoner Disturbance'?* Matteo felt the humming engines power back down to neutral, settling the Zeus on the deck.

Matteo's eyes flashed wide. He brailled his hands on the door again, pressing until his fingers hurt. There had to be something... *A seam!* Near the edge of the door. Too thin to get a finger into, but it was there. A dent might do the trick. He twisted himself into position and cocked back an elbow. Rammed it into the panel. *Still smooth.* Blinking back the shooting pain, he tried with the other elbow.

"AAAAAGH!" Matteo heard and felt a snap. He clutched his throbbing elbow and tried to bend it. His arm hurt like hell, but the bones were fine. The panel had buckled, making a quarter inch space. He dug the pads of his fingers into it and pulled. It popped loose in his smarting hands, showing sharp metal hardware on its underside. He sawed through the zip ties in seconds, then reached inside the hole. Felt mostly wires inside. The kind that could electrocute an amateur Cutter if the power was on...and the power was definitely on. The idling back there made everything vibrate in his hands.

He threaded a cut tie through some wires, pulled them aside, and reached in. Found it. The door latch mechanism. And a pretty standard one at that. His hand barely fit into the space, cutting his knuckles as he worked his grip on the lever. A twist. Pull. Twist again. Then a pop. The hatch creased open with the sucking pressure of air. He freed his arm from the panel and peeked through the crack. No Kabbard. No thugs. He opened the door just enough and slid out to the ground, keeping low on the deck.

No one noticed him in the chaos. His Themis issue jumpsuit helped him blend in as the other inmates worked the Class Four alarm protocol securing ships and placing them under guard, locking down the entrances, and sealing the air-locks to the outside. No one touched Kabbard's ship. *Not part of the Themis equipment manifest.* The cockpit had been left in a hurry by the look of it...and the canopy was still open. He grinned.

"No. Fucking. Way."

The inner airlock could be over-ridden. After the responsible inmate had just locked it down, Matteo trotted over. Set the lock on a timer release. He ran back to Kabbard's ship, gave a quick look around, and climbed into the cockpit. The dash controls overwhelmed him at first, but the shapes, buttons, and icons soon clicked into known patterns. *Flight stick, thrust, spatial navigation, fuel gauge.* The mental model of a Themis Scout's controls grafted on.

So much adrenaline raced through him he felt faint. A series of switches, keys, and screen commands started the launch sequence. He trembled as he wrapped clammy fingers around the flight sticks.

"I know how to fly this thing... I'M GONNA FUCKIN' FLY THIS THING!" He touched the down-thrust, lifting the Zeus from the deck. The feather-touch of the flight stick surprised him, causing the craft to tip and scrape the landing gear against the ground. It took a second for his heart to climb down out of his throat. Inmates outside turned to notice.

Matteo taxied toward the airlock door. Within seconds, it slid open on the timer. *Almost...!* Sudden tugs on the left and right wings rocked the cabin. Outside, the inmates struggled to either pull the ship down or climb the wings. Matteo tapped the throttle, throwing everyone off as he darted into the airlock. The Zeus' nose struck and dragged on the outer doors with a sickening screech. Matteo winced. *There goes the paint job.* He laughed.

Sensing the weight of the ship, the inner airlock doors shut behind the Zeus. The outer doors would be tricky. *Can't open them from outside the Zeus… can't put in a request to control…the only way would be to—* Another childlike grin creased Matteo's cheeks. He searched the dash and found it. '*Weapon Safety.*' He clicked it free on the switch marked '.75 Machine-Gun,' then gripped the flight stick. He pinched his eyes shut instead. Sucked a breath into his stomach. Squeezed the trigger.

The concussion shook the airlock. Tiny cracks formed on the canopy glass with each gigantic muzzle flash from under the wings. The outer airlock took five or six gaping holes before flying off its hinges and out into the canyon beyond. Matteo panted like a maniac. Shook it off.

"HA HA HAAA!" He punched the thrust controls the craft shot out of the air-lock. "WHOA!" The ship darted directly toward the opposite canyon wall. He throttled back and pulled up hard, shooting straight up and out of the canyon. Smoothed. Through the glass, a field of shimmering lights spread across endless night. He'd glimpsed them through the porthole of the prisoner transport, but now found himself lost among them.

Awe, excitement, terror, nausea…time seemed to stop entirely, dangling him over the edge of some bottomless pit he had no way of imagining. It was too much. He looked back at the controls and tried to breathe past the spinning in his gut. A display showed him on a flat grid with a handful of stars highlighted and labeled. The highlights changed as he moved the flight stick. *Reference points.* Scouts used them to reorient themselves if they were knocked out of orbit by a blast or outgassing. He leaned the stick hard left, trying to ignore the dizzying rush of the Universe above the canopy.

The lunar surface appeared below and the Earth beyond. The sight seized him. A lonely blue and white ball floating in an ocean of sparkling black. *Home.* He felt tears coming and he smiled. Pushed the flight stick forward. The craft dipped toward the lunar surface and strafed the fields of craters. Matteo rolled left. Rolled right. Wove through mountain ranges and cliff-sides. He pulled up, pointed the nose at the blue planet, and punched the throttle to maximum.

23

Mission

Minutes Earlier

KABBARD, ANDREAS, AND Nicks waded through the crush of Themis employees in the corridor to the Control Room. The alarms along the hall screeched in triplets, stoking fevered panic in the filtered air. Kabbard felt it too, but it underscored the next thing to do. *Get to command. Get a sit rep. Organize all these bodies.* They were out of shape. Slow. Drummond especially. All used to dealing with a completely pacified population of drones. But a real Class Four alarm? An insurrection? That meant that at least a handful of Rasalla's hardest and fastest had somehow bucked the conditioning and gotten loose. The match in the gas tank. People were going to die.

Pushing past a few engineers, Kabbard entered the Control Room. Switched on his government Neural override and surveyed the scene. Technicians worked at several surveillance stations, searching through CCTV feeds on hovering Neural screens. Some of the servers had been cannibalized for parts or weren't functioning at all. Desperate teams struggled in tangles of wire to get them back to limping. On the wall-sized screen at the head of the room, an overall picture emerged. Flashing red dots spread from section to section, radiating outward from the infirmary. The skeletal slum rat with the bloody fists flashed through Kabbard's memory. He dismissed it.

Drummond hobbled from station to station at the call of his name. A tech would give a report or ask for orders and, before Drummond could answer, another shouted for him. The nervous breakdown was written on his sunken face. Worse, it was spreading.

"Everybody calm the fuck down!" Kabbard shouted. The force of the command seemed to hit everyone in their chests. Stunned, they listened like guilty children. Kabbard paused, allowed the moment to settle, and pitched his voice clearly.

"Drummond. Sit rep, please."

"I—uh...We—There's been an incident in the Infirmary. Details are fuzzy, but a few—er—uh—a few assets have deviated from their programming. We are containing the disturbance now," said Drummond. Andreas let out a chuckle. Swallowed it when Kabbard shot him a look.

"'Assets'...'Deviated from programming'...You've got T99s running amok in this corporate park you call a penal colony, and they're waking up to the fact that they've been taken from their homes, shot into space, and turned into slaves. Call it what it is and deal with what it is. Now, I'm seeing movement in sectors Five, Six, and Seven. Are all those areas locked down?"

Drummond stiffened.

"Of—of course they are! Triggered by the Class Four as per standard operating procedu—"

"Sir," a technician's voice cracked as he interrupted, "I've been trying to tell you, sir, the doors in Sector Five weren't triggered and won't respond to direct commands!"

"Sector Five..." Drummond turned and looked at the big screen. Red dots spread into the corridors surrounding the sector. Kabbard bristled.

"There's a direct path leading from Sector Five to this Control Room. Andreas! Nicks!" barked Kabbard. The two of them stepped forward in silence. They weren't EXOs and they weren't military, but scheming killers were more useful than stuffed shirts and new-hires.

"Move to intercept the inmates in the main corridor, and recruit any guard you find along the way, particularly those with stun batons or spurs. I'll dispatch more to you over the Comms. Go." The two of them hesitated. Looked at one another.

"I dunno, sir...going off mission?" asked Nicks.

"Yeah...Sato sent us here for the kid, not to go play hero. I'm not trying to get myself killed off the clock," Andreas said. It took every ounce of Kabbard's iron discipline to not knife-hand Andreas' throat. A little extra when the bastard shrugged.

"Sato sent you here to follow my orders. You've heard them. Now go."

They backed slowly toward the door. Technicians around the room nervously gestured to refresh their Neural keyboards. One of them shot up from his seat.

"Mr. Kabbard?! Mr. Drummond?!" the tech blurted, waiting to be called on like a school boy. Both men turned their version of a cold stare on the frail man too young to look this old. The words tumbled out of his trembling lips.

"P-perimeter breach...Main Hangar, Airlock Four," said the tech.

"What?!" said Drummond. "That's impossible. The disturbance is contain—"

"Full Screen, NOW!" shouted Kabbard. It seemed to blast the boy back down in his chair and flip him to face his station. A few keystrokes and the live feed appeared on the big screen. Kabbard squinted at it. Beyond the chaos of

SON OF SEDONIA

the scrambling workers, the Hangar looked fine. Except...*Where's the Zeus?* The Furies sat parked where they'd left them. But Kabbard's prize office perk and the cargo therein were missing. Andreas cocked his head.

"Where's the—"

"Roll back the feed! Five minutes!" Kabbard commanded. The Tech scrubbed the feed backward. Eventually, Airlock Four opened and the Zeus emerged. It taxied in reverse to where Kabbard had left it. The canopy opened.

"No. Fucking. Shit," said Andreas, almost laughing, as their prisoner crawled backward out of the cockpit and backtracked to the rear compartment.

"Freeze it there," said Drummond. The low-res image of the Rasalla boy paused him mid-stride on his way around the rear of the craft. Kabbard gritted teeth behind tight lips.

"There is your culprit, Mr. Kabbard. Thank you for offering your services, but you have my leave to pursue your vessel," a wry grin tugged at Drummond's corpse-like face. "Rest assured, we have the situation well in hand," he turned his back. Kabbard dug his fingernails into the meat of his palms.

"Let's go, boss. His funeral," said Nicks. Kabbard felt like he could breathe fire.

"It could be all of ours," Kabbard said, taking one last glimpse of the panicked faces throughout the control room. He turned away. The three of them trotted off to the door as the buzz of activity resumed in the Control Room. Kabbard tried to ignore Drummond's nauseating voice rising above the din.

"Organize what personnel we have to push the inmates back into Sector Five! Have some engineers accompany them to manually lock down the doors, then perform a gas purge on Five, Six, and Seven."

"Vent the O2? Some of our own people are stuck in those sectors, we can't—"

"Just long enough to stun, not enough to kill. Moron." Hearing Drummond say that, Kabbard hesitated in the doorway. Kept walking.

"Sounds like they got a plan. What's ours?" asked Andreas. Kabbard wanted to smash the man's smug, mercenary teeth down his throat. Instead, he pointed the white hot rage at the end of the hall. Beyond.

"Get the Zeus, rip that little piece of Rasalla shit out of it, and burn him alive."

143

24

Voice

JOGUN'S ENTIRE BODY shook with fatigue as he stared the captured Themis guard in the face, clutching Doc Yugi's bloody scalpel. Two of the new inmates, Kolpa and Rusaam, held the man down with the toned, cable-fiber muscles of Pit-hardened Cutters. They were the first Jogun had released and "healed". He had tried to explain it to them, but Kolpa...his mother was a Blue Lady back home. The hand of God was in everything. *Even this?* The wet blade flashed in the blinking red light of the alarm.

The guard was nothing special. Mid-forties, expanding gut, and a brand new uniform soiled at the crotch. He hadn't stopped babbling about his 'first week on the job' the entire time. Between that and the blaring alarm, Jogun could barely get a word in.

"Where—. Whe—WHERE IS THE—Goddammit! Rusaam will you slap him, please?" Jogun said, face-in-palm. Rusaam punched the fat man across the jaw, knocking him out cold. *Just a Pit worker.* Jogun thought, seeing the pain flood Rusaam's scarred, narrow face. *A worker ripped away from his family.* Rusaam cracked the knuckles on his calloused, trembling hands. Spat on the guard.

"Get another one," said Jogun. He rubbed at the ice—pick pain in his temples. Somewhere beyond those doors Kabbard had his little brother. *But...he's not... not for real. Oh Christ, Matteo...*All these years, Jogun had almost allowed himself to forget. He shook his head, frowning. *The love is real. He's family. I'll find him.*

Kolpa, solemn, stocky, and silent, brought the next guard. The gaunt man seemed half-dead already, staring through sunken eye sockets at no place in particular on the floor. In the blinking red light of the alarm, Jogun almost didn't notice the dark stain soaking through the uniform. The smell of blood followed. Jogun winced as he got up, hobbled closer, then clutched the guard by his sallow cheeks.

145

"Hear me?" said Jogun. The guard's glazed eyes rolled. Eventually settled on Jogun. He nodded slowly.

"Good! Now. How do we open these doors?! Is there any other way outta Sector Six?!" Jogun pointed to the massive plate steel doors that had cut his group off from those that ran ahead. Too weak to keep up, he had lagged behind with Kolpa and Rusaam helping him carefully along. Then everything slammed shut. As far as they could tell, there was no way out. Other inmates beat against the doors with anything they could find. Mostly their shoulders and fists.

"No..." said the wounded guard, "Can't open...closed from the Con—Control Room."

Rusaam balled up a fist and cocked it back. Jogun stopped him.

"Gotta pray," said Kolpa, "Pray for the way to open!" Kolpa knelt on the ground and started muttering in the thickest Riverspeak Jogun had ever heard. Suddenly, it was drowned out by a new sound. It started low, then rose. Started over again. Again. BowwwWOOOOOP. BowwwWOOOOOP. BowwwWOOOOOP.

"Purge!" the wounded guard rasped, "Have to get out! Have to—" A sharp hissing sound followed. Within seconds, everyone in the room started gasping. Men broke their hands and arms pounding on the plated doors. Collapsed. Kolpa's wide-set eyes turned bloodshot as his prayers withered into ragged croaks.

The guard wrenched free from Rusaam and started crawling. Jogun crawled after him. After reaching a panel in the floor, the guard tore a lariat out of his uniform collar. A small silver key dangled at the end. Jogun watched as the guard took it in clumsy fingers and tried to insert it in a space on the floor panel. Failed. Passed out.

One last breath. Jogun took it in deep as he could, then pulled himself to the panel. He felt consciousness fade as he fumbled with the key. *Calm. Focus.* It slid into the hole. Clicked when he turned it. The panel popped open. He shot a hand inside and felt some kind of handle. *Pull. Twist. Push.*

A seam creased the floor and a blast of visible air sliced through it. The purge alarm stopped as the seam slid wide open, revealing stairs leading down.

"Sector 6 breached. Purge overridden. Sector 6 breached. Purge overridden," the electronic voice repeated. Around the room, chests began rising and falling. Rusaam and Kolpa crawled to Jogun and looked down into the opening.

"Hidden service tunnel?" asked Rusaam.

"Our miracle..." said Kolpa, his voice choked and rasping.

"Somethin' like that," said Jogun. He turned his flicked eyes upward. *Was that you? If it was, I could use some more. Give me the strength.* "Hey y'all! Over here!"

They traveled through the tight passages for what seemed like hours. In the soft copper glow of the floor lights, they chose a left. Then a right. Another right. Jogun longed to find stairs leading up, but every turn led them further down. Away from the hope of finding Matteo. *Where are you takin' me?*

It was a while before Jogun noticed the silence in the others. No one asked where they were going or what the plan was. It made him nervous, more so as he felt the eyes on his back. They were following him. He balled his hands into tight fists, clutching his faith as it tried to vanish. Years of unanswered prayers and desperate nights had worn it paper thin. As conditioned as the training from the Dose. God, if he was there, had been deaf, blind, and dumb since that day on the balcony. *Why now?* T-junction looming ahead, his last shred of faith tugged him left.

Dead end. It felt like the wind was knocked out of him. His knees buckled, collapsing him backward into the alert arms of Kolpa. *I'm just a dumbass cripple gettin' everybody lost in the dark.*

"Need to get 'im some water," Kolpa said.

"Sure, hold up, lemme just turn on the faucet," Rusaam said, "Where the hell we s'posed to find a drink in here?" Voices behind them were getting restless. Kolpa strained to look through the amber darkness.

"Maybe those pipes on the wall," said Kolpa.

"Pipes?" Rusaam walked to the dead end wall and felt around, "Motherfucker, these ain't no pipes! It's hatch coaming! We got us a maintenance hatch right here!" Rusaam grunted as he pulled the handle. It wouldn't budge.

"I'm fine," Jogun said, "Help him." Kolpa gently propped Jogun up on the railing, then trotted to Rusaam. They counted to three then put all their weight on the handle. It popped open. White light spilled into the narrow hall, striking Jogun in the face. He blinked at the shock of it. As his eyes adjusted, the light seemed to fill him. Things beyond took shape.

"Ground Level. The Motor Pool..." Jogun said. He crawled past Kolpa and Rusaam to the door, then peered through. Business as usual for the start of the day. The cells were emptied to take advantage of the low-daylight part of the month, putting all hands on deck. Only a week or two until Full-Day, cooking the surface up to two-hundred-sixty degrees Fahrenheit. Jogun climbed through the hatch and stood on a catwalk overlooking the facility. Kolpa and Rusaam joined him. Then the rest.

"Kolpa," said Jogun in a voice that felt like someone else's, "How much antidote we got left?"

"We'll make it enough," said Kolpa, nodding. One-by-one, every inmate they encountered across the motor pool was injected, then embraced by the Healed as muscles seized. In most, the antidote did its work. Life flickered back into their eyes. Souls to their faces. In others, the seizing stopped with dead silence and a trickle of blood from the nose. It ripped Jogun apart, watching the young, healthy brothers get carried off.

He felt strange. His heart searched every face for Matteo. A searing frustration that burned him from the inside-out. And yet an unshakable certainty that he was right where he should be. Right now. Brother by brother, he helped all he could. Escorting the Healed from their confusion and terror. Comforting the dying with whatever came to mind.

The last one they dosed, a Rasalla boy of fifteen with a fresh 'T99' on his shoulder, passed away slowly. Painfully. The convulsions wrenched tendons and dislocated joints. Blood poured from his flared nostrils.

"It'll end soon. Don't be afraid. Don't be afraid. We're with you, brother. Your family's got you. It'll stop, your pain'll be gone, and you'll walk with God. Go on and sleep." Jogun felt him seize in a final choking breath, then relax. Peace seemed to come over the boy's tear and blood-streaked face. Jogun touched the eye-lids. Closed them gently.

He got up to find the next one. Found instead a crowd of silent onlookers. Hundreds of them. As he met their eyes, each of them touched their foreheads. Then their lips. Then their chests. *The Mind to see the Righteous Path. The Voice to find the words. The Heart for the courage to walk the Path.* A blessing every Rasalla boy learned on his first visit to the Stepstones. It had never made much sense to Jogun. Yet now his veined hands trembled as he returned the gesture.

"The Righteous Path," he said to himself. Though hoarse and faint, his voice carried far in the Motor Pool. Like it or not, the Healed waited to hear him.

"I-I'm not. Ah shit, the 'Voice to find the words' would do me good right now," he said smiling. A laugh rippled over the crowd. The long lost feeling almost brought him to tears. As the room settled, he found his Voice.

"But the Mind to see, the Heart to walk—*that's* what we got, y'all! And it's damn clear to me: our path leads *home!*" Jogun shouted as hard as his vocal chords would let him. The crowd roared. Rusaam pushed to Jogun's side.

"Hot shit," Rusaam said, "Where do we start?" Jogun looked around the Motor Pool. *Scouts, Crawlers, Loaders, pressure suits, hydraulic tools, detonators, core charges, fuel cells.* All the mining equipment he'd known for years is just that, mining equipment. Very different uses began popping up in his head.

"Here. We'll start right here," Jogun smiled.

25

Assets

"SIGNAL LOST–CHECK INPUT Device" had been blinking on every screen in the Control Room since the Purge. From his post, Kruger could only watch the chaos unfold. It was his first week on the job. One of the dozens of new hires, he was nowhere near qualified to debug, hack, or otherwise duct tape the servers into working again. That was left to his trainer, a fat, pale, red-bearded tech named Scotty. And Scotty looked like he was about to keel over. Sweat poured down his stretched gray jumpsuit. Each burst of his rapid staccato key-strokes ended with a critical error. Again. And again. And again.

Drummond dashed from console to console, yelling frantic nonsense at each tech. Though things looked pretty well screwed, Kruger couldn't help but feel relieved that matters were out of his hands. He took advantage of his short stature and bean-pole frame, tucking himself behind Scotty's seated bulk.

"Somebody give me a fucking visual!" Drummond shrieked, "Something! ANYTHING!" No one spoke up. Only the sounds of clicking, typing, and the buzz of error messages.

"It's simple! THINK!" said Drummond, "What would cause the Purge to trigger a server crash? How are those systems connected? Didn't I pay one of you useless slobs to write the system to begin with?!" Scotty stopped typing in his Neural. Froze. Kruger stared at the floor, waiting for the axe to drop.

"Scotty," said Drummond through his teeth. The Warden's attempt to look threatening as he stomped to the desk was more of a preteen girl's tantrum. Still, Kruger saw Scotty gulp behind the bearded neck-rolls.

"I-it's some kind of weird edge-case," Scotty blurted, "I'm doing all I can to track it down but the debugger———"

"But nothing! You'll find it and you'll fix it, or you'll be looking for a new job with a big, fat, black mark on your RFID Profile! That's *if* I don't have you arrested, locked up, and driving a Crawler for the rest of your pathetic life. You—Do you hear me!?" Scotty lurched forward in his distressed office chair. It creaked and snapped as he winced, rubbed his chest, then fell out. The wet smack he made when his body hit the tile made Kruger cringe. Scotty's shared Neural image above the desk disappeared. *That's…not a good sign.*

"No no no no no, don't do this to me you fat bastard!" Drummond crouched beside Scotty's beached mass and tried to roll him over. Scotty wouldn't budge.

"Get up and fix this!" Drummond gave one last feeble push, then plopped back on the floor. Grabbed the thick wrist and felt for a pulse. Dropped it. He lolled his head backward and stared at the ceiling. Kruger leaned out to steal a look at his late trainer. A mistake.

"You!" said Drummond, "Yes, you, come here!" Drummond circled around the desk and grabbed Hendrik by the arm. He dragged him to the terminal, righted the broken chair, and pushed him into it.

"Sit! Type! Do something!" Drummond said.

"Sir, I—I'm just a trainee," Hendrik said, his own heart thumping in his chest.

"You didn't lie on your resumé, did you? You *can* program, can you not?" said Drummond. Kruger, light-headed, sat at the desk. He pressed a finger to his temple to summon his own Neural, then searched his history. Found Scotty's last shared data cache, then opened it. Miles upon miles of debug scripts materialized in front of him. The language looked familiar enough, but the system itself would be like reverse-engineering a fusion reactor with a screwdriver and a pair of pliers. *How the hell do I even start?*

The squeal of interference on Drummond's radio pierced the moment. Everyone jumped. Kruger almost pissed himself, half as much from relief as from shock.

"Sir, this is Officer Rigby at the doors to Sector Five, requesting orders," said a voice over the radio. Drummond fumbled with his transmission display, then pressed his throat mic.

"Offic—Officer—Officer Rigby, what is your situation?! A report, give me a report!" Seconds passed in static filled silence. Finally a click at the other end.

"We pushed the inmates back into Sector Five and successfully sealed the doors before the Purge. Killed four of theirs," Rigby paused, "Lost two of ours." Drummond paced the floor, tapping his chin. Touched his throat.

"Rigby, I need you and your people to open those doors, and—"

"Open them?! Are you insane!? I just sacrificed two men, and y—"

"Open the doors, assess the situation inside, and report back to me immediately, or find yourself out of work and facing a congressional hearing! 'Non-fulfillment of contractual duties resulting in a catastrophic loss or damage to Virton Energy property and personnel.' I don't want that. You don't want that. Do. Your. Job."

"Sir, this…" Rigby sighed over the radio, "Yes sir. But it's gonna take some time. Only got one Engineer after the last fight."

BOOOOOM! The entire Control Room shook, knocking Kruger out of the broken chair. Dust and debris fell from the ceiling, some of it into Kruger's bloodshot eyes. He spat and rubbed at them. Tried to blink through the pain to see what was happening. The blurry shape of Drummond sat sprawled next to Scotty's corpse. Speechless, the Warden stared at the ceiling. Kruger had seen his son Josh do the same thing when he'd skinned a knee falling out of a Superway train. The unstoppable tears bubbling up behind a childish need to be tough. *Josh.* Kruger wiped what he could from his eyes, refreshed the Neural screens, and started typing.

"What the hell was that?!" said Rigby over the radio. Focus descended slowly over Drummond as he felt around for the transmit button.

"Rigby," Drummond said, "I want you and your men to report back to Control at once. We—"

BOOOOOM! The Control Room swayed as if it were perched on the San Andreas during the LA Quake. Drummond crashed to the tile floor, cracking his hip. Kruger's chair snapped in half and dropped him onto Scotty's soaked back. *No time!* He rolled off the dead man, pushed up to his knees, and kept typing. As the fuzz faded from his ears, he heard Drummond screaming.

"Lock us down! Blast doors!"

Kruger had learned that much. With a few keystrokes and swipes he found the directory. *primaryControl>security>perimeter>doors>alertProtocol_lvl5.* Sheets of blast steel and reinforced titanium dropped down into place in the two entryways. From there, Kruger expanded other directories and rifled through their contents. A picture started to form.

"Call the Hub! Tell them to send more guards…mercenaries…hell, paramilitary! Anyone!" Kruger dug through and found the Comms directory. Tried to connect. *No signal.*

"Sir," said Kruger, "That last explosion…was the Comms Tower. We're cut off."

"Cut off…" said Drummond. The entire room fell dead silent. Quiet enough to hear the distant pops of secondary explosions and hull breaches high above where the Comms Tower had been. Then, suddenly, closer pops. No. More like footsteps. Movement in the ring of skylights high above caught Kruger's attention.

Figures in pressure suits walked on the hull outside. For a moment Kruger lifted. *Maintenance crews! The damage report must have gone through and triggered a work order.* Except these men lingered around the skylights. Drummond squinted up at them.

"What are they doing…?" The suited EVA workers divided themselves one to each skylight, and mounted long, bulky devices to their hip harnesses. *Laser Drills?*

"Shit, close the shutters! Do it now!" yelled Drummond. Kruger shook as his hands flitted through menus and subdirectories. Above, white-hot beams of light powered on in unison. Slowly boring molten holes through the six-inch plate glass. *primaryControl>security>perimeter>skylights>alertProtocol_lvl5, ENTER!* The titanium shutters snapped closed. Everyone breathed a sigh of relief until glowing red hotspots appeared in the center of each shutter. Panic erupted. Techs burst from their chairs and scurried to the walls. They clawed open the emergency supply lockers and pulled out the pressure suits inside, most of which were torn apart in the struggle. Kruger navigated to the door control again. *If I could open them, then set them on a timer...*

Too late. White beams streaked into the Control Room, melting limbs off of a few of the Techs. *Josh...I—* Air roared out of the room through the glowing holes, taking the contents of the room with it. Kruger clung to the edge of the desk. One-by-one his fingers failed his grip. He blacked out as he flew through the escaping air.

26

Fish

INMATE 272313-A TRIED to keep his eyes off the laser drill's beam as it sliced its way through the double hatch doors. All that stood between his group of over two-hundred Healed from the hangar wing. *Freedom. Home.* The words tasted sweet against the otherwise acidic pressure in his skull. Though the pain seemed to be fading. Not a moment too soon.

"Oki," said a shaky voice next to him, "might be some guards on the other side of that, huh?"

"Might be," said Inmate 272313-A. *Oki.* The name was like an old shirt he hadn't worn in years. He slipped it on and savored its memories. Its power. He grinned.

"Better be. All this runnin' around…" Oki twisted his grip on the giant Crawler wrench he'd grabbed from the Motor Pool, "High fuckin' time to go to war." Remnants of the anti-aggro put a sting into the words like the curried pepper kebabs of Falari Market. He glanced at the doors and caught a side-glimpse of the laser's ice-blue beam. Snapped his head away. *Almost through.*

"Get ready, y'all!" Oki shouted with eyes pinched shut.

"RA-SA-LLA! RA-SA-LLA! RA-SA-LLA!" the chant began all at once. It melted through the pain in Oki's head, just as the final inch of the hatch doors was cut. He and three others rushed the doors. They shouldered into the reinforced titanium slabs, pushing until the molten seam split apart and opened. Wide enough for two to squeeze through.

He and a thick-necked Nine named Tolai were the first. They brushed against the ragged, torch-cut edges as they passed, marking their T99 tattoos with raking burns. There were guards on the other side, but far down the hall. Running for their lives. Oki, Tolai, and the two-hundred Healed poured down the corridor after them. Yelling curses through wild laughter.

They caught up in no time at all. Oki raised the wrench and brought it down on the exhausted guard, crunching into the man's shoulder and neck with a force that flung the body into the wall. Another caught Tolai's three-foot crowbar in the small of the back. The tide of the Healed rolled over the rest of the guards in seconds.

The rest of the way was marked with signs. Oki read them several times before he realized. *I can read.* Bittersweet. The ability came from the end of a needle shoved into the base of his neck. *But this is what it's like.* He crumpled the thought, threw it in the corner of his mind, and led the charge on through the halls.

Other groups emerged from doorways along the route. Their numbers swelled to three-hundred. Five-hundred. Twelve-hundred. Before long, the wide halls were choked with them. Some in the crowd embraced and cried out when they saw each other. Their cheers rippled through the throng as they surged toward the Hangar Wing.

Oki peeked above the ocean of heads to see the hall open up into the Wing. A huge, circular chamber with industrial doors around the rim and a radial front desk in the middle. The crowd split up. Inmates each picked a door and ran to it. *Which one?...Hell yeah.* He turned to number Nine.

Waiting in line was torture. Half from the wonder of what he'd find. Half from suffocating crush of the others. Slowly, he inched through the doorway and took it all in. Ships of all shapes and sizes loomed over their heads. Like one of those auto-shows he'd seen when Suomo had a TV. Three bulk prisoner transports. Four high-occupancy commuter shuttles. And at least eight private craft. There was a sleek, sporty red vessel with soft edges and a flat nose. A silver luxury four-door with sixty-four point flight control. And even a glossy black ShadowBird with its muscular body and quad-core fusion engine.

Oki let the others beeline for those, picking a commuter shuttle instead. Something about it reminded him of the long, straight Copperfish his uncle used to hand-catch in the Rasalla River. They'd soaked up too many chemicals to be safe to eat, but when reminded his uncle would smile and say, "It's nice to fish." *Back when there were fish, anyway. This one's mine.*

He stepped onto the ramp leading inside, and the mob suddenly hushed. Oki turned. Rusaam and Kolpa had entered the hangar. Without a word, everyone parted in front of them to make way. Then in walked the Healer. Cheers. Laughter. Shouting. Crying. All of it exploded in an instant. Oki let out a whoop.

"Rasalla!" he called out, waving. Jogun waved back to the room then gestured to Rusaam who bent to listen. Rusaam straightened and raised his arms. The noise died in seconds.

"Listen up y'all! Pick a ship, get inside! Pilots, turn your comms to Channel Three! We're blowing the doors when the 'Moon is Low'! LET'S GO HOME!" The noise erupted again, louder and higher than before. Oki yelled himself red in the face and still couldn't hear his own voice. It felt amazing. The love people had in their faces when they saw each other, even for him. *Not fear...love.* Hands trembling, Oki climbed into the Copperfish, joining roughly fifty brothers.

As a hangar foreman, he had all the basic vehicle packages jacked into his brain. Crawlers. Loaders. And Scouts. *Guess that makes me a pilot too!* He rubbed his hands together. Inside the cockpit, two sixteen-year-old, bottom level T99 soldiers bickered in the flight seats.

"Cuz you don't know shit! That's why. Cuz you. Don't know. Shit! Intra-atmospheric avionics just ain't the fuckin' same as low-atmo maneuvering, and if you think I'm trustin' yo ass with the flight stick, you crazy!"

"The thing with the motorcycle? That what this is about? We were *twelve*, man!"

"And you was drunk, yeah yeah, don't matter! I ain't never forgave you for that shit, and I ain't about to trust you now with my life and the lives of every other sumbitch in this boat—AH, hey what the fuck?!"

Oki grabbed the kid by the neck and picked him up out of the seat. The kid went passive once he recognized a senior enforcer.

"Run along back there with the rest of the 'sumbitches.' Me and little man here got this," said Oki. The kid nodded and took off for the upper passenger cabin. His friend, Little Man, tried to bite back a shit-eating grin as Oki sat down and strapped in.

"Now this ain't no damn motorcycle," said Oki, "You got this?"

"Y-yeah. Yeah I think—"

"Cool. What's your name, little Nine?"

"Kiosu."

"Kiosu," Oki put on his headset, took quick stock of the flight controls, then started flipping switches. "You know the song right?"

"Yeah," Kiosu ran through the co-pilot startup protocol, "Pop used to sing it to me."

"My man..." Oki toggled the intercom, "We full up?!" Replies came over the headset all at once.

"Yeah!"

"Fuck yeah, good to go!"

"Rasalla!"

"Aight brothers, get ready to sing! 'When the Moon is low,' we go!" Oki closed the main hatch, pressurized the cabins, then punched the ignition.

"Kiosu, flip us to Channel Three and patch it through to the cabin," said Oki. Kiosu nodded and dialed the comms. Four minutes passed in static before it started. Many voices as one. Clear and strong.

My ladies of my family, don't worry don't cry
Don't stay awake all night for me, I'm not gonna die
I live to bring your bread to you, I fight to survive
My tools: a brain, a heart, a soul, and edge of a knife

No doubt the fear will follow me but I'm not afraid
A Nine-ty Nine is strongest when his brothers are brave
Rasalla Soldiers, God's own soldiers, no one a slave
And for you, my people, nothin's gonna stand in my way

So shut the doors and cut the lights right after I go
Lay your head and close your eyes, you know I'll be home
Rasalla waits, I'm on my way, one thing you should know
Tonight my eyes won't need more light

"*Be back before the moon is low*," over three thousand voices said in unison through the intercom. The hangar doors along the wall burst in a shower of sparks and were sucked out into the canyon. The rush of escaping air pulled at the ships on their pads, scraping landing gear across the deck.

"Gear up! Engines to Idle-Three," said Oki. Kiosu did his part. The ship dipped all at once, then stabilized with a low-frequency vibration felt through the bulkhead.

"Main thrusters?" asked Kiosu, his hand poised on the throttle. Oki nodded. Chuckled.

"Moon's *risin'* tonight!"

PART FOUR
Civilization

27

Sacrifice

SATO STOOD EXACTLY where he least wanted to be: at the front of a legion of grieving families. From the elevated stage in the Mesa Park Amphitheater, he waited for the Anthem of the Fallen to play its final notes. He had learned to dread that song. Played at every EXO officer's funeral since the founding of the Border, it meant that he would have to look the bereaved in the eyes, and tell them their lost loved ones were heroes. The men and women of the EXOs certainly were. But every word of Sato's rehearsed justifications made him feel ever more like a fraud. Thankfully it was almost over.

As the final somber note died in the choir, the mother of Officer Dreivan, one of the KIA Red Gate conscripts, stepped up to the podium. The short, husky woman, red-faced and dressed in a knock-off brand black dresscoat, shakily adjusted the microphone. Another working-class woman 'whose son had probably joined the EXOs to pay for school. She removed a piece of paper from her purse. Unfolded it. *She took the time to write it down...on paper.* Sato swallowed in a dry throat. The woman's voice trembled as she spoke.

"Uhmm...I..." she lowered her head. Raised it. "There's nothing I can say... to express what we're going through. The loss... The loss of a child is devastating. Our boy...our *man*, Dreivan was more precious to us than life itself." Naked grief flowed out of her in stepped, forced words. The momentum was the only thing keeping her going. In the middle of it, Sato felt Jada let go of his hand. When he looked, his wife had it clasped over her mouth. Tears streamed down her cheeks. When Sato went to touch her, she broke down and quickly excused herself from the stage. As the speaker continued, Sato realized everyone was watching him.

"But Dreivan believed in his City. He wanted to make a difference, and that's what he did. He died...he died to protect us all," the mother finished and stepped down to thunderous applause. Sato joined in as he wrestled with what to do. *If I go after my wife, it could look like I'm abandoning these people...but...if I don't go after her, I'll be slammed for being insensitive.* Like most decisions these days, he was fucked either way. He chose Jada. Felt the cameras watch him leave.

Sato found her by the pools, sitting alone on a curving park bench. She sat totally still, watching kids and families glide in circles over the water. Gentle ripples moved the surface as the patrons each banked and swayed on rented hover-domes. Some held hands as they went around, or waved to their younger siblings playing in the sand on shore.

The miscarriage. Sato realized. It would be six years ago this week. He turned to the Secret Service agents who had followed him, and gave the signal to hang back. Sato crossed to the front of the bench and sat down next to Jada. She sniffled.

"I'm sorry," Jada said, "I didn't mean to make you leave, I just...All those *families*...talking about losing sons and daughters, I...it's like I was in the hospital all over again. Our baby..." Jada choked as Enota put his arm around her and pulled her close. After a string of heavy sobs, she tensed. Sat up.

"Oh God, I'm so *fucking* selfish! Those people watched their kids grow up. *Sacrificed* for them. My pain is nothing compared to theirs."

Sato felt a vice grip squeeze his chest. *What have I done?* He looked away from her. Hung his head.

"No...*I'm* sorry," said Sato. Jada turned and wiped her eyes. Furrowed her brow at him.

"Enota, you haven't done *anything* wrong," she reached out and grasped his hand, "Why be sorry?"

"I—" he paused, "I shouldn't have asked you to come with me today. I was so preoccupied with the politics and decorum that I didn't take the time to consider *your* feelings," said Sato. The best lies contained partial truths. *I'm doing this for my family!* The justification was flimsy, but it held.

"You sweet, sweet man," she said, "You have forty million people to think about, and you consider my feelings just fine. Pretty sure that makes you extraordinary." She smiled and wiggled closer to him on the bench. Laid her head on his shoulder. The sounds of laughing and splashing came from the skating pool as a father and son banked their hover-domes, spraying clear water on a mother and baby on the shore. The mother laughed, picked up a clod of sand, and threw it. The baby tried, but just grabbed gritty fistfuls. Sato realized he had relaxed. For the first time in years, it seemed. He ran a hand on the black silk of Jada's funeral dress, remembering her curves.

"What if we...revived the adoption discussion?" he asked. Jada pushed up abruptly.

"What? You wanna buy me a new kid to cheer me up? Real smooth," she said. Sato bristled a moment, fearing some fresh trouble. But Jada's poker face had never been worth a damn. The grin cracked the corners of her mouth in seconds. Both of them burst out laughing.

"Uh oh! Careful that the cameras don't see you. You're supposed to be *sad!*" Jada added, hysterical. Sato doubled over, breathless. His face hurt by the time it died down. They both sat back and sighed. After the calm settled over them again, Sato laced his fingers in hers.

"Seriously, though," he said, looking directly into her emerald eyes. She had blushed from laughing, but now the color seemed to deepen. Brushing her graying hair aside, she nodded slowly. Smiled.

"Yeah...okay. Let's talk more about that," Jada said. Sato smiled back, but a sudden pulse in his ear warned of an incoming call. He raised a hand to dismiss it when the heads-up message appeared. *'Andreas Calling,'* it read. Sato darkened. Stood.

"I have to take this. Are you gonna be—"

"I'm fine," Jada said, smiling, "I think I'll stay here a little while. Go be the Governor."

Sato leaned in, planted a kiss on her, then turned away. He tapped 'Answer' and kept his voice hushed as he trotted to the main path.

"Andreas...? Where's Kabbard? What's your situation?"

"That's just it, sir. The situation has...escalated. I gave my recommendation to Mr. Kabbard that we call you for a sit-rep, but he refused."

"What the fuck do you mean, 'escalated'?!" Sato hissed.

"The POI evaded capture, but we're in pursuit and closing fast."

"Well what kind of *pursuit* are we talking about here?" Sato spoke through his teeth, "A foot chase there on Themis? Because you don't sound winded, Andy."

"No sir...we're...two hours from Earth orbit. Nicks and Mr. Kabbard are in the other Fury, and I'm following. The target stole the Zeus." Andreas' tone had changed rapidly from lap-dog into a sheep. Sato felt himself start to lose it as the spineless climber continued.

"There was a situation at the prison that Mr. Kabbard ordered us to investigate, a riot or disturbance of some kind near the prison sic-bay. The target got away in that time."

"Put me on with Kabbard. Right now," Sato said. Andreas started the connection as the Governor stepped into a wide tunnel along the park path. He pressed himself against the wall and waited as the ringtone pulsed once. Twice. Three times.

"Sir," Kabbard finally answered. *Bastard. He knows he's in for an ass-chewing and he's still playing the Cop.* It put Sato off-balance as he pressed his throat mic.

"John. I just got some shit news from Andreas that I should have gotten from you. Explain."

"Focused on the job, Mr. Sato. We'll have the package in hand for you shortly."

Always to the point. Sato had never known John Kabbard to make a mistake. Sounded like the man took it personally. And if John took it personally... *May*

God have mercy on anyone who gets in his way. Though there was no reason not to poke the bear.

"Glad to hear it! But please be aware, John, we cannot afford any more mistakes on your end. In the future, I *do* expect to be kept informed of any developments by *you*. Not one of your subordinates."

"Understood," Kabbard said.

"Good," Sato said. Paused. "The boy...he was a match?"

"Yes, sir."

"Ah..." Sato's mind swam with the implication. *Alan's son. His flesh and blood.* Sato braced himself on the cold concrete wall. Shook his head as if it would clear the descending fog. "...and this 'disturbance' on Themis...anything I should be worried about?" he asked. Silence followed the question. Sato felt the hope for a casual *'No, sir, it's all okay'* crumble.

"That's—Warden Drummond assured me that everything's under control."

"And do you believe him?"

"Lost comms with 'em two hours ago. Could be nothing, but I suggest you get your friends on the horn and send whatever you can up there ASAP," said Kabbard.

Sato pinched his eyes shut and rubbed at the bridge of his nose.

"Thank you, John," Sato said, "I expect *good* news the next time you call."

"Yes, sir. Kabbard out," he hung up.

Sato felt more dismissed than reassured, but it was Kabbard or no one. He groped through his mind for comfort, trying to recall the finer points of the former Sergeant's extensive resumé and character references. *Twenty years in the EXOs. Fourteen of those in a command role. Decorated veteran of the Summer Siege, Falari Market Standoff, and the Doco Uprising. Wounded twelve times in the line of duty...he'll get it done.* Turning to leave his alcove, 'Incoming Call: PRG' appeared in front of him. *God dammit.*

"Hello Enota," Janice Prescott's dried wrinkles creased the edges of her smile.

"Janice! Speak of the devil, I was just about to call you..."

"Yes, we know. Mr. Kabbard's appraisal of the developing situation on Themis is understandable, if a touch dramatic. We are looking into it and will make a judgment soon," said Janice. Sato felt the imagined fingers around his throat loosen. He breathed a sigh.

"But the Moon isn't what concerns us, Enota. The Rindal boy, and your failure to apprehend him, is," Janice said as her thin lips flattened. The spectral fingers tightened again on Sato's neck. Thankfully, the Neural augments that had served him so well in public debate did their job. *Minimize.*

"A momentary setback. The boy's chip may have been disabled, but the Zeus has an integrated tracking system. Wherever he goes, John Kabbard will find him."

"You're sure of this? The man has an impeccable record, yes, but we understand that he's not as sympathetic to our aims as you are, Enota. Let us know if we can provide assistance in resolving this issue," said Prescott. Sato kept his face frozen still. *And prove me totally incompetent to the Board. Obsolete.* The Raid debacle had no doubt already hurt his standing. This would push it over a cliff.

"John Kabbard is driven, loyal, and now very, *very* pissed off. He'll get it done. Sending company assets would complicate things, risking a bigger splash than we can afford."

"We agree…for now. The impact of the boy's exposure to the public is an unknown quantity that we *do not* want to risk. Even if he remembers nothing about his father, his name alone could cause significant, untimely waves. A dangerous possibility for *all* concerned, we think you'll agree," Prescott leaned back in her chair. Sato brooded over the phrase. *'All concerned.'* The conspiracy theorists had calmed down with their Rindal ideas over the years, and it had taken that long for Sato's damage control to do its work. *If Aden shows up alive? With even a shred of proof?* It could make Alan a martyr, validating everything that the man had said to the press. *Ruinous.*

"We expect good news the next time we call," said Prescott.

The feed cut out, leaving Sato alone in the shadowed tunnel. *'Call Ended. Memory Block 081080_1210p: Deleted.'* He patted himself down, searching for his flask. Winced when he realized Jada had made him leave it at home.

"Enota?" Jada's voice called down the tunnel. He must have looked like death because she withered at the sight of his face. *I don't deserve you.* The thought occurred to him out of the fog as she embraced him

"Let's go home," she said, rubbing his back, "I'll help draft a statement saying I got sick, and you took me back to the house."

"*You* go," said Sato, "I'll be fine…just have to go make another appearance at the ceremony then take care of some things at the office. I'd feel better knowing you're home safe."

"Okay, but later you're telling me what's going on. I'm your wife, not your constituency."

He kissed her.

"I promise," Sato said. He'd think of a suitable lie before then. One small addition to the list of reasons to hate himself.

28

Dreams

"14,400 KILOMETERS TO Earth orbit. Please input destination." The voice from the console scared the hell out of Matteo, lifting him up out of his seat. His head hit the bubble canopy. He had closed his eyes for only a moment, overwhelmed by the ocean of stars surrounding him. The chance his body was looking for to power down for a while. His muscles ached as he rubbed the rising knot on his scalp, and squinted at the display projected in the canopy glass. The message awaited with a blinking cursor. A keyboard panel of black glass ppeared on the dash. He cracked his knuckles and dug through his memory for a name. Any name. Only one came to mind.

"R-A-S-A-L-," he stopped typing as the matches flew out on screen with names, descriptions, distances, and looping video footage of spots throughout the Rasalla District. Falari Market, Temple of the Wheel, Ninetown, Stepstones, Pits. *Home.* He reached for the screen. Stopped. He knew it would be safer. Knew that he could just disappear and forget about the Moon, Kabbard...and Jo. He'd ditch the Zeus in the Pits, hike to Utu's, and sleep for a week. *And then...what?*

The rush of a new idea crept up his back. His heart thrummed in his chest. *No...it's stupid...it's so stupid.* The thoughts snapped under the weight of the idea. Matteo held down the delete key. The rust-colored images of Rasalla disappeared. His outstretched finger hunted for new letters.

"S-E-D-O-," hundreds of matches filled the screen, all of them with the same heading. *Sedonia City.* They waited for him. Mesa Park, Sedonia Civic Arena, The Plateau Convention Center, and...

The Kuwahara Commons! Nerve center of the Inner Ring. You could buy anything there. Food, clothes, medicine, cars, drinks, and any kind of entertainment you wanted. Some of his favorite buildings in the skyline were rooted in the Commons. The Hotel Equinox with its gigantic, tilted glass dome glistening in the afternoon sun. DAGA Technical College pouring legions of students from its gentle high arch into the surrounding plaza. And Seraphim Station. One of the four main superway hubs in the City, connecting the Outer, Inner, and Center Rings with a webbed network of rails.

Enough people around to keep hidden, and the rest of the City's just a train-ride away.

He tapped the button. The Zeus puffed its attitude jets and changed course in a tilting zero-G roll. Matteo went cross-eyed for a second, watching the Earth flip underneath him. A 3D projection in the canopy drew a glowing path over the curve of the planet. The Zeus locked into it. Fired thrusters. In seconds, the smooth ride became a shaky one. And as the star-filled black gave way to blue, long fingers of flame started to lap at the nose and canopy. Everything outside disappeared behind a shroud of red heat.

His body slicked with sweat beneath the Themis jumpsuit as he gripped the flight sticks and focused on the brightened bubble display. Barely readable in the chaos. And on top of it all, the wheezing. He hadn't noticed it start. Each breath heaved from his chest as though he were pinned under a concrete slab. He took each dry gasp slower than the last. It smoothed as the fire vanished and the shaking stopped, replaced by the high-pitch drone of the engines. Deep blue sky.

He'd passed through hell and into heaven. Soaring over violet clouds in a sunset sea. *Like a bird.* He licked his lips and hit the icon on screen marked "Manual". The Zeus lurched. He tilted the flight stick to the left and the ship rocked hard, shoving him against the side of the cockpit. He corrected quickly and laughed like a lunatic, triggering a few more throaty coughs. A completely different game than flying in zero-G. Throat cleared, he took a deep breath. Pushed the stick hard to the right.

"OOOHHHHHHH SHIIIIIIIIIIT—HAHAHAHAHAAA!"

The force buried him in the seat, pulling his skin tight over his lanky frame. He almost lost his grip on the controls. Absolute terror and pure joy exploded in his brain. The Zeus dipped and banked with the slightest bit of steering. Matteo punched through pink and orange cloud towers hundreds of miles high. Strafed through the cotton rifts and valleys. Spiraled down until he thought he'd blackout, then pulled up, accelerating out in a huge arc.

"Recalculating," said a digital woman's voice. He finally noticed the blinking message on-screen. Hesitated, sighed, then tapped "Resume Auto". It was over too soon, though forever wouldn't have been enough. The Zeus locked into the descent and hit the throttle. Matteo looked up through the canopy, said a final goodbye, then plunged into gray. Clouds enveloped the Zeus. Something else wrapped tight around his insides.

"Here we go," he said in a breath. Water drops streaked over the glass as he peered into the darkening yellow fog. Moments passed. A multicolored glimpse appeared ahead of him before falling back in the polluted shroud. Too quick to see anything. Then all at once it was all there. Sedonia City. The skyline gathered low near the edges by the Border, then swept up in the center like a crystal mountain. All shining in the copper glow of the setting sun. The rush washed over him like an electrified current from his temples down to his toes. Tears welled up in his eyes.

"Entering Sedonia airspace. Reducing speed to 50 kph and descending to Traffic Altitude: Beta," the message appeared on screen. *I...um...ok...* The flight sticks turned by themselves and set a course for a flowing line of headlights below. The Zeus dipped for the queue of cars, found a space, and drifted gently in. Matteo, wide-eyed, puffed a lung-full of relief.

He noticed that his cruising speed was actually damn fast. The Slums appeared beneath him, and rushed by like a giant ant colony. He watched the garbage scows drop their payloads into the Pits. Saw the first lights of Ninetown nightlife. Then millions of little smoke columns all over the rusty jagged landscape. Some cookfires. Some still smoldering from the raid. He soared above and apart from it all. Goosebumps washed across his skin as he passed over the Border.

The Outer Ring passed underneath, wider than he'd ever thought it would be. Miles of short factory buildings, shipyards, and freighter ports stretched on for miles. He could make out tiny ground vehicles as they drove along the circuit-like access roads.

Past the dirty foothill apartments and offices of the Outer Ring edge, the Zeus flew deeper. Buildings took on the familiar angles and beautiful curves he'd studied on faded pages. They lived and breathed in front of him. He could see swarms of people gathering on skywalks, hanging plazas, and balcony tiers. Vehicles dropped from the queue and joined criss-crossing lanes of traffic through the structures. Matteo's hungry eyes darted everywhere, filling his chest with what felt like white light.

"Arriving at: Kuwahara Commons." The Zeus dipped down for one of the radial parking pads on the edge of the main plaza. Hovered to a gentle stop. Matteo engaged the landing gear, killed the engine, and tore at the harness buckles. As he popped the release, the canopy slid back. He climbed out on wobbling, half-asleep legs and stepped down the ladder onto the pavement.

Matteo took one last look at the Zeus. Sighed, then turned. He walked briskly toward the plaza steps at the end of the pad. Others around him, dressed in tight-fitting patterns of bizarre clothes, shot glances his way. The bright orange jumpsuit probably got their attention. He unzipped his collar and spread it out, covering the Themis insignia on his chest. Then he ripped at the shoulder seams, tearing off both long sleeves. Whether or not it worked, at least it was more comfortable. He shoved his hands in the pockets, tucked his chin, and walked into the Plaza.

"...for that, Governor Sato, we *do* hold you accountable!" a loud female voice barked through a megaphone on a raised platform. A crowd of people gathered around her, shouting and waving signs. Matteo squinted to read them. *'21 EXOs Dead! For what?' 'No blood for Corporate Profits!' 'Governor Sato: Killer of Children'* This didn't make any sense. People from the City didn't get angry about things in the Slums. *Do they? Why?* He took five steps toward them, then heard heavy engines behind him.

The two Fury Class ships from the Themis hangar descended to the parking pad beside the Zeus. Landed in front of it with their wing guns spooled up. People on the pad scattered, then went about their business like nothing had happened. One of the Fury hatches opened. Kabbard stepped out. Matteo whirled away and pushed past a group of gawking onlookers and into the Plaza.

In the middle of another backward glance, Matteo almost bumped into someone. A skinny, shaggy haired guy had stepped in his path. Handed Matteo a piece of bright red paper.

"Join the Future. Empower yourself," was all the young man said before turning with a flip of his shiny scarf. Matteo looked at the paper as he sped on through the Plaza. Big, bold letters at the top said: *'Utopia is an Illusion.'* Matteo swept a glance over the surrounding skyscrapers. *Looks real enough to me.* A commotion of angry shouts picked up behind him. The three black-suited forms of Kabbard and his men stormed into the crowd, sifting through the angry protestors. A thicket of screaming bodies and swinging signs blocked them.

Matteo ran, sprinting through ramps, stairwells, and clustered kiosks. He almost tripped through a mound of trash in the street. Leaped to one side. Two concrete tiers above, a massive block of escalators led up to a skywalk. He jumped, kicked off a wall, and lunged through the air. Grabbed curved railing at the top and pulled himself up. A homeless man, dressed in rags and lying on a cardboard sheet, lunged at him. Matteo rolled away and stood up, shocked at the face that could have been pulled straight out of a Falari Market gutter.

He ran to the base of an escalator, got on, and wove as far as he could through the crush of sweet-smelling citizens. All around him, people made strange hand and finger gestures in the air. Swiping, twisting, pinching, tapping. Most talked to themselves. Few to each other. Sure that he was being ignored, Matteo caught his breath and looked back down into the shrinking Plaza. Kabbard and his guys had stopped by a kiosk. One of them, Matteo couldn't tell who, kicked the pile of trash.

Matteo hung his head and took a deep breath in the belly. Exhaled.

29

Welcome

THROUGH HIS PORTHOLE window, Jogun watched the flashlights, torch-flames, and lanterns of Pit workers gather like a swarm of fireflies on the barren plain. Most had probably been on their way back home for the day when they saw the landing fleet of Themis ships and came running. Even exhausted from sixteen hours of work, a payday this big would be hard for any Cutter to pass up. More waste to be cut, carted away, and sold off to the City Seedmaster, maybe buying an extra day's rice. Seeing them made his chest flutter.

Six years in lunar gravity meant one thing. Atrophy. His limbs were in agony, filling with acid moments after the fleet broke atmo. It was like being under twenty tons of water and on fire at the same time. And now he would be expected to be...what? A hero? A prophet? A savior? He did his best to lay still in the sticky, sweaty upholstery of his cabin seat, trying desperately to enjoy what might be the last peaceful moment left to him. *'All you ever tried to do was keep me in the fucking dark!'*

He felt the titanic feet of the landing gear flex beneath him and the whole cabin sagged to a full stop. Cheering erupted in the compartments behind him. He and the other old-timers looked around at one another in their forward compartment. Most exchanged tearful nods or held hands with the interlacing of feeble fingers. But the weight. Jogun could feel it in the others as much as himself. Heavier than the gravity dragging down on their bodies, the weight of a long forgotten home suddenly there again...and feeling foreign. Totally alien. He wished he was happier.

Jogun flinched as the compartment door popped then hissed open. Cheering, singing T99s flowed in. Two by two, they lifted each of the old-timers and bore them to the exit ramp. Rusaam and Kolpa were the last two in. They approached with the care of Rasalla River priests, stopping beside Jogun in his private front seat.

"Hey y'all," said Jogun, "How was your flight?" A brittle smile creased the lines of his sunken cheeks. The two of them exchanged confused looks, each of them searching for just the right thing to say to the almighty 'Healer.' Jogun sighed. Nodded. Russam unhooked him from his harness, like a parent does a child, then raised the arm rest. Jogun took a deep breath as the two of them scooped under his legs and supported his back. He winced.

"You okay, Brother? If we're hurtin' you, let us know," said Rusaam.

"I'm fine, but...just call me Jo."

Rusaam nodded, though Jogun noted the man's wounded silence. Jogun took a deep breath into his heavy, aching chest.

"Slow and easy, y'all. Let's go."

The sounds of the celebration outside wafted up the exit ramp as they walked down. Laughing, crying, shouting, and singing filled the warm, dust-laden sweat of the sunset air. The long forgotten smells of Rasalla filled Jogun's nostrils, squeezing his throat with the threat of tears.

Ten young T99s in Themis jumpsuits flanked the center path of the ramp, holding fluorescent lanterns to light the way. They had been waiting for the last passenger. As Jogun appeared in the arms of his attendants, the hush spread like a wave in front of him. He fought down the seizing panic, closed his eyes, and breathed deep. Astonished whispers surrounded him as he felt Rusaam and Kolpa step off the angled platform onto the flat desert ground. More voices than he could count. Against every urge to keep them shut, he opened his eyes.

In the fading violet bath of the setting sun, thousands of silent faces watched him. Rusaam and Kolpa stopped.

"Stand me up," Jogun heard himself say. His caretakers obeyed with delicate care, lowering him to touch first his right foot, then his left. The coarse shipyard soil ground into the soles of his work boots under his gathering weight. Legs trembling, he willed himself to stand. The electricity of the moment coursed from his fingertips to his toes and to his ears. His head felt light, as though it would carry him away. The lights across the Pits trembled at first in the gathering twilight, then seemed to rise into streaks of charged color.

Cold with sweat and shaking, he reached up to shield his eyes. The streaks bled together into a blinding aurora. The last shape he saw was the ocean of people holding their hands up in unison. Jumping. Dancing. Everything went white and Jogun swooned. He felt the dull impact of the earth beneath him before everything just stopped.

Jogun's eyes fluttered open and awareness flickered on to the sensation of violent, shaking movement. The dull orange sky of dusk hung above, or rather in front of him. The tops of slum buildings passed to his left and his right. *I'm on my back.* His hand drifted to his face to touch something warm and wet. Red smeared fingers. *My fingers...my blood...* The stabbing pain above and behind his ears mounted in a single, sharp pulse. He winced as it subsided. Then it came again.

More sensation switched on throughout his body. He lay on something hard. *A wood cart.* He spread his livening fingers over the rough planks. The roaring noise in his ears became the familiar rhythm of wheels on a packed dirt road. He lifted his head and peered through the dissipating fog.

The familiar shapes of Rusaam and Kolpa loomed ahead. They had their backs to him, pulling the cart handles as they ran at a fever pitch. Jogun tried to speak, but the sound came out as a cut-off croak.

"Brothe—Jo! Can you hear me?!" Rusaam glanced back with wide, angled eyes. Jogun gnashed his teeth for another knife surge in his skull. Nodded. His head fell back onto the wood with a thud and his eyes clenched shut. After a never-ending instant, the pain melted away again. He spoke.

"W-where?" was all he could get out.

"Don't worry, Jo, we takin' you to the Temple. Gonna see Doc Utu," said Kolpa. The name was warm in Jogun's ears. He felt a teardrop stream down his cheek, then drifted back to blackness.

Jogun awoke again as the cart stopped underneath him. The sudden stillness, after the constant rhythm of movement, vibrated in his bones and slackened muscles. *Night now...* The far-away dotted stream of headlights crawled across the dim clouds above him. To his left and right, gas torches flickered playfully along the Temple walls. The headache still pressed deep into his head, but was somehow less important here. *Footsteps coming this way...fast.* He lifted his head and saw the blurry forms of Rusaam and Kolpa. They came into focus as a third joined them. *Utu.*

The relief of seeing this man slipped away before Jogun was ready to let it go. The laugh-creased, rich brown face of the family friend turned into a look of shock and deep sadness.

"Hi, Doc," Jogun rasped.

"Jo..." said Utu. The man who always had a word and a smile for any situation was speechless. Jogun looked down at himself, remembering his busted body.

"You uh..." Jogun coughed a dry breath, "I don't guess I could get some water, could I?" The flanking jab of the question staggered Utu. His wrinkles accepted the familiar, squinting smile like the embrace of an old friend. He laughed. The sound washed over Jogun and spilled throughout the Temple alley.

"Of course, my friend, of course!" Utu shouted, scrambling to grab a hold of the hollow gourd canteen that hung from his shoulder. He rushed to Jogun's side and set the mouth of the canteen to Jogun's lips. Tipped up slowly. The cool, earthy liquid flowed down Jogun's dry throat and landed cold in his gut. He raised his trembling hands to take the canteen as though it were a holy relic. Drank deeply. Utu withdrew it at the proper moment, then started prodding. The Doc felt Jogun's forehead with a palm, then the back of the hand. Took Jogun's wrist in his fingertips and waited, counting seconds on a wristwatch. Utu spoke as he worked.

"Where have you been?" he asked, gently lifting Jogun's leg at the knee. Jogun gritted his teeth as the throbbing in his muscles seemed to squeeze tight to the bone.

"Get ready, my friend. It's a long story," said Jogun. He felt Utu suddenly stop the examination. The pulse of distant voices caught in the air. Three shouts then a pause. Three shouts then a pause. As it got louder, the sounds came into focus.

"RA-SA-LLA! RA-SA-LLA! RA-SA-LLA!" they chanted in unison. Soon, the tromp of hundreds of feet underscored the chanting. They rounded the corner. T99s, house-wives, old men, old women, children. The beating heart of the Slums filled the temple, then stopped at the sight of Jogun and Utu. All lowered their heads.

"Of that," Utu said, "I have no doubt."

30

Flavors

SURROUNDED BY THESE people, Matteo never felt more alone. But at least alone could be safe for now. Time enough to try and absorb the sensory overload. Up close, the City moved differently. In the shadow of giants, the Sedonia citizens and their world had real color and texture. Lights of juicy bronze, aqua, red, gold, and emerald danced everywhere, transforming the buildings into collages of colored animation. People in the street walked past wearing intricate circuit-like patterns all over their clothes. Some glowed slightly, pulsing to the rhythm of their heartbeats. *So much power, they wear it...* He thought of all the cold nights when he couldn't afford fuel for his tin lantern. Most people in the crowd were so distracted with their weird hand gestures that they didn't notice the puddles and trash they walked through.

Tints of the smells wafting through the air were familiar, but rotated into things entirely new to his nose. Freshly baked bread mixed with a bite of something salty-sweet. A slightly fishy smell tinged with a distant cousin of Utu's garden spinach. A pale, spikey-haired couple passed him holding skewers of something that smelled like pork. *Where the hell did you get that?* He picked up the pace in the direction from which they'd come.

At the end of the bridge, a block of neon storefronts hugged the base of a massive, tiered neighborhood of buildings. The pulsing beats of several stereo systems overlapped. Matteo felt like every step took him out of one song and into another. He saw more people holding skewers. They were centered around a semi-circular counter that jutted out in neon yellow from the wall. A gigantic cartoon pig ran, did backflips, and faced the crowd over and over above the counter. Going near it was out of the question.

"It's kinda over-cooked this time; must have the B team on the grill tonight," a voice said as it walked by him. A milk-faced teenager ran fingers through a fountain of hair and tossed a full skewer into a round can on the street. Matteo pounced, reached into the can, and pulled out the meal. He sank his teeth in and tore at the juicy, brown flesh, swallowing chunks before they were fully chewed. His eyes teared as they rolled back into his skull.

Digging into the last morsel, the rest of his senses trickled back to him. The crowd kept its distance. A group of exotic, mouse-like girls crinkled their noses at him through their multi-colored hair. Shame-faced, he stuffed the last bite in his mouth.

A hard knock to the shoulder almost sent it flying back out. He whirled, ready to fight, but froze when he saw her.

"Ah shit, *sorry!*" said the voice from behind a flowing mass of red curls. She stooped to fix her shoe that had popped off in the impact.

"Sorry, sorry, sorry, sorry," she said as she stood up and brushed her hair out of her face. Cute, pursed features with sharp, green eyes and pouting lips. Matteo had turned into a wide-eyed statue with a lump in his cheek. She snorted a laugh and started jogging.

"Have a good one, buddy. Don't choke!" she called back to him. Matteo swallowed, tossed the skewer, and walked after her. The smells of food faded, giving way to the familiar cocktail of cigarettes, alcohol, and vomit. Lines formed around corners to get into structures clothed in other-worldly displays of light and color. In glimpses, Matteo saw the redhead break from traffic, skip to the front of one of the lines, and slip past a door-man about the size of Oki. *The Sing—u...Sing-u-lar... 'Singularity.'* The name of the place hummed over him in brilliant, aquamarine script.

He wiped his mouth, cracked his neck, and shimmied through the crowd to the door. Stopped dead in his tracks. The hotdog-sized fingertips of the doorman's giant paw jabbed into Matteo's chest, holding him there.

"Uh-uh, chief. End of the line's back there." He pointed down the block over about a hundred heads. Matteo looked down the line, hesitated.

"O-kay..." said the doorman as he leaned into Matteo, pushed him aside, and beckoned the next person in line. Matteo noted the looks he was getting, hung his head, and walked down the row of psychedelic bodies in search of the end. Anger chewed at him the whole time. Clever, manly things to say to the doorman materialized in his head by the dozens, but nothing cleared the shame of just taking it and walking away. *'Don't ever fucking touch me.'* *"No way, 'chief,' the end is right HERE!"*

Once The Singularity was nowhere in sight, he found the end of the line. People clumped together in groups, talking with one another in familiar words and sounds, but in patterns he didn't understand.

"Yeah, I was blurred the fuck beyond focus at that spot! Utterly blurry."

"I'm not texting him back after that shit-show..."

"Oh, tag me when you check in! Besties!"

All the while, they flitted and swept their hands through the air at the same imaginary shapes. Every time the line inched forward his legs begged him to just walk on and leave. His eyes wandered. The wall to the right was embellished with small blocks that stuck out, forming a kind of overall wave pattern. The ends of each block pulsed with bits of a giant video feed. He reached out and touched one. *Sturdy.* Looking up, the wall of blocks stopped some fifteen feet above to a ledge. He glanced back at the oblivious club kids and grinned. *Good thing I'm invisible.*

It felt good to climb. Hand over hand, he scaled the wall in seconds and crouched into the recess at the top. He crept along the edge above the queue until he reached a gap. The roof ledge ahead would take a bit of a jump to reach, but easier if he used the sign that stuck out just underneath. Matteo leaped toward the sign, planted his right foot, and then launched himself toward the ledge. Climbed up and over.

A battery of angled vent shafts lined the short roof of the club. He'd hoped for a door, but one of them would do. Matteo popped the slatted covering on one and lowered himself inside. After a minute of squeezing through the cramped shaft, he hit a drop-off in the path. Looked down. Women's voices drifted up to him, laughing, shouting, and squealing above the thumping bass. He grinned, carefully removed the vent cover, and lowered himself down.

He landed in a tiny, dark room with a black door ahead of him. A dim, blue light filled the space from glass tiles in the floor, and dainty, clicking footsteps approached outside the door, followed by a rapid *knock-knock-knock-knock.* Before he could say anything, the door opened.

"Oh my god, you *sleaze!*" The pointed claws of a skinny, rope-haired girl grabbed him by the collar and yanked him out. Wide-eyed, he found himself surrounded by a pack of shrieking women. In a circular room of curved mirrors and shock-white lights, they shielded themselves from his gawking eyes. Gorgeous women of all shapes and sizes, dressed in clothes that shrink-wrapped their bodies in electric colors.

"Get out! Get the fuck out, perv!"

"Are you serious with this shit?! Somebody go get Trey!"

"Haha! Hey, wait! He's kinda cute!" Against the several pairs of hands shoving him toward the exit, Matteo turned and smiled wide. The door caught him in the face and swung hard open, spilling him onto the cold glass floor outside. A couple of passers-by jumped aside to dodge him.

"Sorry! Sorry, sorry, sorry!" He said, coughing. The strangers seemed to understand, if not appreciate it that much. They continued on their way down the black hallway, walking the path of the same glowing tiles. The floor, walls, and air hummed with a throbbing current of music. *I'm in!* He excused himself from the screaming ladies behind him and followed the others.

The hall opened up into a gigantic, perfectly circular chamber with the same black walls and indigo-lit floor. Silhouetted bodies danced in dramatic, curving sweeps and primal rhythms on the largest segment of the floor rings. People in wall-set booths crowded around tables of exotic drinks. And along the perimeter were the bars. Towers of neon bottles loomed behind each of the curved counters. Matteo licked his dry lips.

It took some doing to get anywhere close to the bar through the layers of people, but he finally found a hole. Leaning forward and waving seemed to work for the others. He pushed in and raised his hand higher than everyone else. A familiar laugh answered him.

"And you, sir! What is your question?" In the twilight of the room, Matteo made out a head of curly hair and a familiar, arresting face. His stomach flipped.

"You...can put your hand down now," she laughed. Matteo obeyed. She sank a scoop into the ice bin and spread her hands on the bar. Cocked her head at Matteo.

"Do you...have an order open or something? 'Cause if we didn't get it, you didn't send it. Probably gotta reboot." She tapped a shiny red fingernail on her temple. Matteo raised a hand and mimicked her, tapping twice on the side of his head.

"Ummm...gotta hold it down, bud." She raised a perfect, thin eyebrow at him. He bunched two fingers together. Pushed hard. A beep sounded in his inner ear, making him jump. Then a patch on his forearm vibrated under the bruise. *'A System shutdown occurred to prevent damage to your RFID Platform. Continue reboot?'* The message in his mind was clear and crisp. *Umm...'Yes?'* He answered in thought. A gold square flickered to life on his arm.

"Whoa! Well *hello*, your majesty," the redhead said with a mocking bow, "Good of you to come down from your ivory tower to hang out with us Low Folk."

"What's that supposed to mea—," the entire room around Matteo brightened and somehow seemed to bend, squeezing in on itself. BoooooooOOOOOOP! The black walls of the club came alive in twisting, imploding patterns of bright gold and jade. Vibrant blooms of mathematical shapes moved in perfect time with the music, cascading over the ceiling and floor toward the DJ booth, then rushing back out as the beat changed. The floor tiles seemed to react on the dance floor to the feet of each person in the crowd. Chills prickled up through Matteo's fingers and toes, up his arms and legs, and into his core. He parted his lips in a breathless gasp.

"Working now, I take it? Your Goldi-box software's probably a few versions ahead of this place. Try ordering again," said the redhead. Matteo rubbed his eyes, shook his head, and turned back to her. A floating band of light had appeared in the center of his vision. Focusing on it, he made out a string of words. *'Update Available! Do you want to proceed? Yes. No.'* He reached for the lights and touched *'Yes,'* feeling a slight vibration in his finger. Another rush of blinding brightness later, and interface appeared everywhere. *Everywhere.* The meaningless gestures of the others around him suddenly made sense as he saw them interacting with hovering screens that flitted back and forth, up and down, in and out. Information about each of them poured out in front of Matteo. Their names, interests, social status... *'Relationship Status?'*

Next to him at the bar, a woman drank blue, smoking liquid from a fragile, long-stemmed glass. As Matteo focused on the drink, a highlight appeared around it and summoned a block of information in his periphery. Something called a 'Blue Motherfucker.' A button reading 'Buy' appeared underneath the profile. He laughed, shrugged, and tapped it.

"Really?" The bartender smirked. Matteo nodded. "Coming right up." Moments later, she returned with the drink, spilling the strange smoke on the bar.

"One BMF for his Highness," she said.

"That's not my name," Matteo said, gently taking the drink from her. "It's Mat—It's... Aden. My name is Aden." Alien as it was, the sound coming out of his mouth seemed to click into place somewhere deep inside him. She offered him her hand.

"I'm Liani," she said with a wicked smile. Her silky fingers wrapped around his weathered palm. Heart racing, he released her hand. Raised the drink to his lips. The cool, tart sweetness hit his jaw first, followed by a slight burn. He felt it warm his insides as it traveled down his throat and splashed in his stomach. The glass was empty in seconds. A horrible pounding vice-grip squeezed his temples. He winced. Liani threw her head back and laughed hysterically.

"You know what, kid, you're alright! Careful with that brain freeze, though, you'll blow a fuse. Another?"

"Hell—," he coughed, "Hell yeah!"

31

Warnings

IN THE SQUAD leader's shotgun seat of the IG-6 dropship, Shima began to regret giving up his medical leave. The patched bullet-wound underneath his leg Augmentors was, for all intents and purposes, healed. But the phantom ache left behind by the nano-fuse stitches got worse in the dropship's rigid bucket seats. His eyes compulsively focused on the medication timer in his head's-up display. *"-30:09 minutes until next dose."* He winced, then leaned forward to look out the cockpit windshield. The Border drifted underneath them as they entered Slum airspace. The heaped landscape of tangled hovels, bridges, and rooflines seemed asleep below them in gentle, corroded twilight. Shima knew better.

"I could walk faster than this," he muttered. The pilot ignored the remark and maintained regulation speed. Shima dug his palm into the side of his Augmentors. A walk would probably work out some of the stiffness. And the idea of taking a stroll in a war zone was strangely sweet to him. He gnashed his teeth.

This recon op was a milk run. All that HQ would give him until his leg was a hundred percent. Better than being laid up on his shitty couch at home, but still "'on the bench,'" so to speak. Confined to the cockpit for the duration of the mission. *Better make myself useful.* He swept his gloved hand in front of him, pulling the mission details into center focus. Not much to it. He played the audio from the initial civilian report.

"Uhh...Randyll Jackson," said the recorded voice, "Class B Operator for FTL Shipping & Freight LLC. I wanna report a near miss—naw, reckless 'dangerment and criminal negligence on the part of them Junker boys. A whole fleet of the bastards nearly knocked me outta my lane on their way down to them Pits! No warning lights, no approach communique, nothin'! I know

179

these fellas got quotas for this garbage, but they don't have to junk *me* in the process! Y'all better hit 'em with more than just a pussy-ass fine this time, too. I want 'em arreste—"

Shima scrubbed back in the audio.

"No warning lights, no approach communique, nothin'!" the recording repeated. The official wrecker logs showed only two deliveries made during the day. Two tankers. Nothing out of the ordinary. Shima sucked his teeth.

"Whaddya think, sir?" asked the Pilot. "Another Dust Swap?" *No doubt.* City thugs couldn't get enough of the stuff, and Rasalla chefs cooked the best. Millions of credits-worth of Sway traded for a few hundred-worth of seeds. Too good for some to pass up. SCPD had been breathing down the department's neck for months to keep the shit on the right side of the Border. Something about Sway addiction making implanted citizens feel invincible. Even homicidal. *Just like the SCPD to bitch about real work.*

"Sir?" the pilot prodded.

"Sorry, son, I was ignoring you," Shima said, staring off in the opposite direction. In the following quiet, the pilot's bruised pride throbbed in Shima's ear. He rolled his eyes.

"Yeah, probably a Dust Swap," Shima sat up and squinted at the live satellite feed streaming in his Neural. A few random thermal readings showed up across the Pits, but nothing out of the ordinary.

"Long done now, though. Looks like another rousing night of lifting serial numbers and pushing pixels for me. Hell *yeah*," Shima drew a circle in the air with his index finger. The white heat from their afterburners appeared on the sat-feed. Shima touched a section of the terrain next to the beached ships, dropping a digital waypoint.

"Bring us down there," Shima said.

"Yes, sir." The braking thrusters kicked on and the IG-6 banked into its descent. Shima hissed at the shooting pain in his leg as he stood up.

"You okay, sir?"

"Fuck off, son." Shima swung from the ceiling rails to the rest of his squad, "Alright boys and girls, let's go see if we can find a serial number that hasn't been filed off." The IG-6 lurched as its heavy legs pressed down into the packed dirt.

"Mount up!" Shima shouted. Buckles clicked and straps retracted as the team stood. The IG-6 ramp yawned open, spilling the pale blue light of the cabin out onto the dirt. Shima and the others stormed down the ramp with submachine guns drawn. All quiet. Shima touched his throat mic.

"Delta-Three is on the ground. Button up and climb to observation altitude."

"Roger," said the Pilot over comms. The ramp hummed shut and the IG-6 engines belched blue fire. Soon the ship was nothing more than a pair of glowing specs against the night sky. Shima turned to his squad.

"Eyes on, legs off," he said. Each EXO touched his temple and blinked three times. Shima watched the Pits flash to pale gray-green daylight. A few bright blooms of sparks burst out of the distant haze, showering down at intervals. *Dumbasses.* Cutting during the day was bad enough, but doing it at night was usually a death sentence. Only the most desperate ever dared, but there were always a few. None worked on the so-called 'fleet' from the esteemed Mr. Jackson's incident report.

"Let's hit that fat fucker over there first," said Shima, nodding toward the over-sized, fish-shaped personnel carrier. "And stay *sharp*, dammit! We may have clipped the T99 hierarchy, but that doesn't make this a casual stroll."

The five of them started walking. Shima pushed out in front to hide his grimacing from the others, but there was little he could do about the limp. He focused on the small, blurry lettering on the side of the ship's nose. Too hard to make out at 1-X view. Tracing a light circle on his temple, the image jumped to 10-X. *'Virton Energy.'*

Walking in 10-X, his left foot tagged a bent chunk of rebar on the ground, sending him into a painful stumble. He winced, dialed back to 1-X, and limped onward.

"Virton," said Ackley, one of the smarter rookies in the squad, "Not like them to dump gear off the books...is it?"

"With a greaseball like Finley running it, who knows," said Shima. It didn't help him shake the same feeling. An itch up and down his spine. They came to the base of the ship and fanned out. Ackley came through moments later.

"Got one! 'Alpha-Tango-Alpha 37859-8842,'" said Ackley over the comms.

"Run it," said Shima. He sauntered up to the door and wrapped a gloved hand around the latch. *Locked.* He grumbled, looking over his shoulder at the glowing green Pits behind him. A small light flashed on a few klicks East, bobbing toward them at a gentle pace. *A lantern.* Shima pressed his throat mic.

"Hold fast, we've got a local headed our way. I'm moving to intercept." Shima crouched and flanked wide around the bobbing light like a stalking cat. It was just a kid. Looked to be a Cutter with his torch and blanket-covered wagon in tow. Six feet behind the boy, Shima's thigh decided to bind up, dragging his feet through the dirt in the process. The kid whirled, greeted by a limping EXO with machine-gun drawn. Not the most badass ambush, but the kid still looked like he would shit himself at any moment.

"Shhhhhh," Shima said, "Over there. Nice and easy. Bring your gear."

The kid obeyed, one hand raised and the other pulling the wagon. They greeted Ackley at the carrier's main personnel hatch.

"Sir, the ship's last stated destination was the Themis Facility. Logs for that serial stop there. I sent a query to Themis, but haven't heard anything back yet. Want me to try and hail Virton corporate?"

"No...not just yet," Shima said, "Hey kid, what do you know about all this new merch, huh?" The Cutter boy stood rock still, eyes fixed on his toes.

"Nothin', huh? Not a damn thing? No fancy dressed guys waiting to take a few kilos of the Red Stuff off your friends?" No answer. Shima looked down at the kid's cutting gear. Grinned.

"Well, you're here to cut, so cut! Get that door open for me and I'll give your skinny ass half a protein bar."

The kid looked at his torch and wagon, then back at Shima.

"Fine," said Shima, "I'll just borrow this." He snatched the torch from the wagon. The boy lunged for it, but an Augmentor boot caught him in the chest. Kicked him into the dirt.

"Let's take a look," Shima tapped his temple to cut off IR mode, then dropped his visor. The glass went solid black as he sparked the torch, adjusted the flame, and focused it on the latch. The metal started to glow.

"Boy, I tell you, this thing is a piece of shi—" The hatch door swung open, cold-cocking Shima in the shoulder and face, knocking him to the side. Orange-jumpsuited figures stepped into the doorway. Opened fire. Ackley and two of the others, blinded by the sudden flood of light, were cut down, taking high-velocity rounds through their armor plates. Explosions of blood and twisted metal sprayed over the red-orange soil. The cutter boy yanked the cloth off his wagon and took a pistol from the heap of Slum guns piled there. Shot Shima's remaining squad member through the neck, and put a bullet through Shima's bad thigh.

The Sergeant crawled through the bloody dirt to cover behind the man-atee's landing gear. His weapon sat eight feet away, harmless in the stark white light coming from inside the ship. Swallowing hard, Shima bit his lower lip and pressed his throat node.

"Call Headqua—AAAHH!" A hail of metal punched into the landing gear, flinging a chunk of shrapnel into his back.

"Calling John Kabbard," said the status window in his Neural. Footsteps and clicking weapons approached from behind him. He waited. *'Beeeeep. Beeeeep. Beeeeep. Beeeeep. Click!'*

"You have reached the voicemail of Johnathan Kabbard, please leave your message after the tone."

"Fuck! John! They're hiding in the Pits! Something big, John, you gotta—ULLLGHHH!"

32

Report

"SHIMA CALLING" THE text flashed in the lower-left corner of Kabbard's vision along with a four-year-old profile picture of Shima. Wasted drunk at the annual EXO Christmas party, shirtless and flexing by the indoor pool. Kabbard reached up, dragged the 'Ignore' slider to the left, and resumed watch on the location trace. Despite cruising in the enforcement lane through the Kuwahara Commons, the digits on his ETA ticked down painfully slow. A crime now that he was back at the Zeus' controls.

"Fuck the speed cap," said Kabbard into his throat mic, "both of you hit your strobes and follow me." He squeezed the flight sticks and pressed his foot down, accelerating past the speed cap.

BEEP! The new voicemail tone shrieked in his ear, making him miss the days of handheld communication. At least back then you had something you could tomahawk into a wall.

"Sir, with all due respect, isn't racing through the Commons with government strobes a little 'above-board'?" asked Nicks over the comms.

"Follow. Me." Kabbard said as he flicked his strobes on and pressed faster through the lane. SCPD patrol cars and ambulances made way for him. He glanced at the meandering gold dot in the trace display. It had registered about a half-hour ago in downtown Shibuya, and stayed pretty much still in some chip-trash dump called The Singularity. As the Furies flicked on their blue and whites and throttled up beside him, Kabbard watched his ETA adjust. '*Sato calling…*'

Kabbard wrapped his thick-knuckled fingers around a phantom device in his hand. Releasing it, he dragged the "Answer" slider to the right. The congressman's wide-set eyes greeted him with a flat scowl.

"I've been waiting by the phone, John. I hate waiting by the phone," said Sato, his silver-tongued voice cracking. *The phone's in your head, asshole. You're always waiting by it.*

"Uh yes, sir, we're closing on the subject now and will have him in custody within the hour. Now if you'll excuse me," Kabbard did his best to not talk through his teeth. Reached for 'Disconnect.'

"Within the hour?! It's been *four* since you assured me this would be taken care of!"

Kabbard wasn't scared of this little man. Sato had impressed him once, but now that the bullshit had been screened away, the visionary Governor was just another bureaucrat who decided on things he didn't understand, delegated all the real work, and threw a fit if the results didn't taste right. *Useless prick.* But this wasn't Sato's fault. The recognition flickered somewhere in the back of Kabbard's awareness, doing nothing to calm him. It twisted in his intestines.

"We've got a solid location trace, and we—"

"What?! You mean you're tracking an *active chip?!* In the goddamn CITY?!" Sato roared. Even through the color fluctuation of Kabbard's Neural display, he saw the Governor's oaken skin pale.

"Won't be active for long, sir. Nicks is talking to the central server right now installing an intercept algorithm on the trace," said Kabbard. But he knew Sato's reaction before it left the man's lips.

"Meaning...Christ. It's active and available for anyone to see right now, including the fucking Rindal estate," said Sato. The Zeus and the Fury ships arrived at the nearest open pad in downtown Shibuya, away from the larger crowds. Kabbard, Nicks, and Andreas stepped out, checked their weapons, then holstered them under their coats. Kabbard kept talking.

"We've got no indication that there's been any transmission to the estate."

"Actually, sir," Andreas said, joining the call stream, "the target has accessed—"

"Gotta deal with what's in front of us. Let me do my job and we'll have him within the hour, sir. Kabbard out," Kabbard swiped across the call, ending it. He set his status to '*Busy: Try again later*' then lunged at Andreas, grabbing the snake by the silk tie. Cocked back a shaking fist.

"Undermine me again. Please," Kabbard growled, inches from Andreas' crooked, wide-eyed face. Kabbard stared until a bead of sweat rolled down the kid's brow, then released him.

"I was just going to say," said Andreas readjusting the suit, "the estate has already been pinged. Nicks managed to tag it as a hacking violation, but it looks like the kid has charged over *fifteen-hundred* credits and counting to the trust fund," Andreas smiled, revealing his crowded teeth. "One hell of a bar tab."

33

Wasted

"WOOOOOOOO!" MATTEO HOWLED.

"WOOOOOOOOOOOOOO!" replied the pumping throng of dancers around him. The room spun to the savage, rushing beat of the music. Or was that his head? It didn't matter. In the center of the dance floor, surrounded by beautiful sweating bodies, Matteo writhed to the beat. His muscles twisting in the rhythms and shapes of Ninetown fire dancers. The moves spread through the crowd like a sweet infection. Closing his eyes, the vibrant explosions of The Singularity's Neural display still seemed to be there. The music, the people, the colors. All of it throbbed in his blurred senses.

Opening his eyes again, a clear circle had formed around him. Everyone clapping to the beat. Matteo smiled wide and raised his arms toward the ceiling, stomping the heel of his foot. *One. Two. Three. FOUR!* He exploded into a staggered trot around the edge of the circle, leaned into the center, planted a hand, and spun both legs into a windmill. The cheers swelled in his chest. He realized suddenly that he was laughing like a maniac then collapsed back on the floor, holding his stomach. Dozens of hands reached down to help him up.

On his feet, the head rush narrowed the neon chamber and smiling faces into a dark tunnel. He shook his head. The cotton-stuffed heartbeat in his head slowly opened back to the full primal sound of the dance floor.

"More drinks!" He slam-dunked a hand through the air toward the bar. A short, feline brunette and a barely clothed blonde wriggled under his arms. Smells of sugary jasmine and alcoholic strawberries wafted from their tight, smooth bodies. The three of them led the charge to the bar. Customers waiting four-deep in line parted to make a space for them. Matteo released an arm and the blonde raised it high.

"I have a question!" he shouted.

A black, flame-haired guy in a dark blue vest came over. Matteo frowned. Lowered his arm.

"Yes sir! What can I get you?" asked the man. Matteo slumped forward on the bar, glaring at the man's inability to stay in focus.

"Where'sss...where's Liaaani?"

"Out back on her break, talking to a visitor. She'll be right back, now what can I get you?"

"Nooo," Matteo said as he pushed himself away and released the brunette. He turned around in a carousel of light to look for 'the back.' Braced himself on a stool for a moment. The door to the back parking bay swayed and multiplied on the opposite end of the room.

"I'm taking a break!" Matteo announced to the crowd. A few chuckled, but they seemed to forget him instantly. He wiped sweat from his eyes, then focused on the door. Each step was a prevented fall as he blundered through the psychedelic dance floor, pushing and barreling into people along the way.

"Watch it, asshole!"

"Hey fuck you, kid!"

The voices seemed to shout from half inside a dream. Shoving hands passed him back and forth like a soccer ball. Somehow he kept the door in sight. Finally getting there, he shouldered into the handle and flung the door wide. The sound of it hitting the concrete wall echoed off the curved walls of the space.

Rows of candy-colored hover cars lined the deck, their backs turned to the panoramic exit at the far end of the bay. A widescreen movie of the nocturnal City glistened beyond, silhouetting Liani and her visitor. A puff of smoke wafted up and away from the curly headed shadow. Against the ringing in his ears, their voices carried to him over the cool cement platform.

"So you just *broke it in half?!* Li, I realize you felt guilty, but it would have *buried* those responsible! Justice!" the male voice said. Matteo decided he didn't like the tone. He took a couple steps toward them. The whole platform seemed to tip underneath his feet, turning his knees to noodles. He buckled at the waist and grabbed onto his thighs. The conversation continued.

"Yes! I did it! I helped them cover it up. You think I feel *good* about that?! No! I feel like shit! I haven't *stopped* feeling like shit since I heard about the Raid! If that story broke *now*, what do you think would happen?"

"Revolution," Corey said.

"You mean war," said Liani, "Maybe a *civil* one. I thought it would save more lives if people didn't know." After that, there was a long silence between them.

"That's not our job as journalists, Li. We give people the information, and they make up their minds. We don't do it for them. I know you think you deserve to be back here in this shithole, but—"—

"It was a nice dream, Corey, but the reality...I can't live with that kind of shit on my conscience anymore. At least here, I know what to expect," Liani said.

'Raid.' 'Revolution.' 'Civil War.' The words echoed in sync with Matteo's thumping heartbeat. Images of Rasalla materialized in front of him in fleeting but extremely sharp detail. Like watching a floating movie screen. The picture morphed and shifted to his glass cell on Themis. And as a familiar face appeared in countless ages and situations, another word rolled in his mind. *Jogun. Jogun. Jogun.* A flood bubbled up from his stomach and into his throat. Splashed onto the concrete.

Rapid footsteps approached Matteo like an EXO on the warpath. He rolled onto his back and stared up at the two blurry figures above him.

"What the hell are *you* doing back here?" asked Liani, stooping to help him. He wrenched his arm away.

"I'm okay! I'm okay, I can do it," he planted his palm on the ground and crouched. The man Liani called Corey grabbed him under the shoulders and stood him up. Matteo swung a wild fist, nicking against Corey's cheekbone.

"Whoa, chill the hell out, bro!" Corey dropped him back on the concrete as the door opened behind them. Matteo craned his neck. Caught an upside-down view of two bouncers coming toward him.

"I'm...not your brother..." Matteo muttered as the bouncers scooped him up, "I'm *nobody's* brother!"

Minutes later, he landed on the front sidewalk like a sack of rotten garbage. People in the queue outside laughed like a pack of stray dogs. He crawled for a few feet before making the attempt to stand. An invisible metal shard jabbed him in the temple when he finally did. *Motherfuckers...Blue ones.* He drooled a little as he snickered. The smile faded. *The Raid...Jogun...What does she know about them? She's beautiful...*

He stumbled down the line, pushed through the people there, and started back up the video block wall. People shouted up at him this time, pointing, laughing, and recording. *Whatever.* The wall-kick to the roof vents proved harder than the first time. His foot slipped during the plant and he caught the ledge by inches on his fingertips. Arms shaking, he heaved himself up and over the ledge, fell flat on the roof, then commando crawled all the way to the vent.

Someone was in the bathroom stall when he came crashing through the ceiling. Shrill screams pierced his eardrums as the stiletto heels threatened to pierce his skull. The cat-like brunette shoved Matteo to the side then stormed out of the stall. He crawled out like an old dog.

"AAAH! What the fuck are you doing in here! Out! Get out," a familiar voice screamed. Matteo turned his bloodshot eyes to look.

"Liani? Liani!" he croaked, coughing as the recent injuries seized his lungs.

"Listen, buddy, you don't belong here, you—"

"I know, I KNOW! '*Look at that wall*,' right?! I should've...should've stayed on my side of the wall..." He heaved up to his feet. Braced himself against the stall bracket. Liani squinted her shining green eyes at him. In an instant, a pack of girls pushed through the door. Liani lunged for the opening and slipped through, leaving Matteo pawing at empty air. He followed her out.

The club had turned on him since he left. Jagged green vines and blooms surrounded him in step with a flurry of electronic notes. He felt his head loll back a few times. Everything was moving too damn fast. He focused on the curly red hair as it bounced away from him. Stopped. He grabbed her by the shoulders.

"The Raid!" Matteo screamed with tears in his eyes, "Whaddyu know 'bout the Raid!? Can y-y-you take me home?"

She answered him with a frozen, wide-eyed stare. He let her go and hung his head, sobbing heavily. Liani didn't move.

"Hey, here he is!" One of the bouncers appeared behind her and pointed at Matteo. Liani looked behind the bouncer toward the door. Matteo stood on tiptoes to see, then felt the blood drain from his face. *Kabbard!*

"Kabbard? What would somebody like him want with—," she stopped. Matteo plowed through the dance floor, dodging punches, elbows, and flying glassware on the way. Bursting through the back door, he found Corey talking to someone on a glowing display. Almost ran him over.

"What the—! Fuck, man, you don't know when to give up!" Corey said. Before the door could snap shut, Liani swung it wide, knocking Matteo across the platform. Out cold.

"Oooh...I uh," she glanced to the door behind her then back to Matteo, "Grab him," she said, "We're getting him outta here!"

"What?! Why?"

"Something's up with him," Liani said.

"No shit! What does that have to do with us?"

"I—just shut up and help me get him to your van!" Liani threw one of Matteo's limp arms over her shoulder.

"*My* van?!" Corey gaped at Liani. Meeting her angry matron stare, he groaned and stooped under Matteo's opposite shoulder.

"Fine," Corey said, "but since this is your change of heart and your idea we're taking him to *your* place!"

34

Resurrection

JOGUN'S STOMACH AND back had ached for the past eight hours. He just wanted to sleep. To lay down and not wake up for at least a full night. But it was still dark when the nausea had roused him. Still dark when he decided to go up to the roof and let the others sleep. Morning had crested over the Sedonia City skyline by the time his feeble legs made it up the gnarled concrete steps. They throbbed with the sensation of a thousand pricking needles.

Two heaves came up dry, then his stomach went dormant. He collapsed back in the aluminum folding chair, staring up at the yellow ripples of dawn. The cheap-shit anti-radiation meds they had rationed to him on Themis had run dry in his veins before they even left. It took this long for his body to realize it was poisoned. Shivering in the morning haze, he pulled the moth-eaten fleece blanket up to his chin and tucked his arms underneath. Tried to breathe deeply. Into the belly like he'd told Matteo so many times.

"Maybe we understand each other better now, little brother," he said, wheezing into the wind. Sighed a breathless sigh.

It was nice, at least, to be among growing things again. The rooftop garden hadn't changed much in six years. If anything, it looked healthier. Happier. A strange island of life in a twisted metal ocean of smoking rubble. And the water was about to rise. He could feel it everywhere. Anger, madness, grief, and now... hope. *They think I'm that hope.* And there would be no stopping the war. Jogun heard Suomo and the others planning it in the rooms around him. Plans that depended on him. Another dry wretch gripped his stomach.

Padded footsteps came up the steps with a swishing of loose fabric. A low-humming tune lilted in the air as the sounds got closer. The corners of Jogun's mouth creased in an attempted smile.

"I've always been a morning person," said Utu in his half-laughing way. Jogun craned his neck to watch the man weave a path through the rows of leafy fronds. They seemed to nod as he passed carrying a steaming terra cotta bowl. The spiced fragrance of Utu's chicken broth arrived before the broth itself, triggering a flicker of an appetite. Jogun's nausea rolled right over it. He slouched back into the chair under the blanket as the doctor stopped next to him. After a waiting a few silent moments, Utu gave a little shrug.

"Hm," Utu grunted. Placed the soup to the side on a stack of plastic crates. Jogun tried closing his eyes to calm his stomach, but felt a backward spinning sensation. The kind like he'd had after drinking his ass off then smoking up for initiation. An inability to hold onto the floor. He flashed his eyes open, focusing on the first thing he saw. The Border. As his tunnel vision cleared, the anxiety trickled back in. Became a deluge. *I can't do this! I can't!*

"Open up," Utu said, holding out a pinched finger-full of ground leaf pulp. The fire died a little inside as Jogun focused on the green-black mush. Comprehension came slowly. He wrinkled his nose as he parted his lips only to have them instantly stuffed with pulp. Utu met his shocked glare with a deep, piercing look.

"Chew," said Utu. The stuff was bitter as hell both on his tongue and in his nose. Cool menthol juice flooded his mouth as he bit down. Utu watched quietly. Jogun bit again. And again. Very slowly, the first effects did their work, calming the shaking in his belly. Utu walked to the roof ledge, interlaced his fingers, and twisted his arms up in a grand stretch. Relaxing, the doctor looked out to the Border. Beyond it.

"Did you know we come from the stars?" Utu asked without turning. Although Jogun just shook his head, Utu seemed to hear him. Continued.

"Not so long ago, some very bright men discovered this. Through study and observation, they traced the smallest pieces of our bodies to the deaths of faraway suns. And not just pieces of *us*, but of *all* things. The earth, the sky, the moon," Utu faced the sky, then back down to earth. "...and the Border. Like us and the suns, nothing made of this...Stuff...seems to last forever. Through time, or the will of other Stuff, it all dies so that new Stuff can be born. Over and over."

Jogun didn't follow much of it, but the words had a kind of ring to them. He couldn't place it.

"That supposed to help me?" Jogun asked, forgetting the numbing mouthful of pulp. A bit of dark green drool dripped on the blanket. Ashamed, he wiped his mouth.

"Nope," said Utu, "That's just what is. Keep chewing."

The two of them waited there in the humid dawn as the sounds of the waking Slums drifted up to them. A distant echo of boards dropping. A baby crying. A dirt bike motor choking and sputtering to life. Then the morning metal-drum song of the Stepstones...the call to prayer for those who wished to pray. Hollow metallic tones bounced gently through the jagged streets and debris mounds.

"Can you feel it?" Utu asked. Jogun breathed a deep, mixed lungful of menthol vapor and the dusty Rasalla perfume. Nodded as he slowly chewed.

"No, fool, the caffeine! It should be coursing through those atrophied muscles of yours by now," Utu said. Jogun snapped alert. Moving under the blanket, he realized he did feel stronger.

"We've got to get you moving as much as possible if we're going to rebuild," Utu said. Before Jogun could think about what 'rebuild' meant Utu clapped his hands together.

"Try to stand," said the doctor, yanking Jogun's blanket away. He folded it as Jogun leaned forward in the chair and flexed his toes. The roof felt rough and solid. Pushing with his arms and legs, Jogun began to rise. Utu braced him gently with a hand on the back. Every muscle tensed with the effort, pushing and pulling him into shape. Finally, he was upright. He lifted an arm for Utu to enter as a crutch.

They took one step together. Rising tremors in Jogun's thighs quivered up his waist, into his core, and up his spine. He gritted his teeth. Took another step. Then another. And another. Acid pain tightened the vice on his limbs. Chanting rose above the Slums behind him, faint at first. As his heart pounded blood into his failing legs, the voices got louder. Though his will could have flipped a shuttle, his body was done. He went limp in Utu's arms.

"I—I can't," Jogun said, "How the hell can I climb the Border if I can't walk..." He stopped as the words of a rising chant took shape in the streets.

"Die EXO, Die EXO, In pain all alone! Die EXO, Die EXO, In pain all alone!" A crowd of dwellers, Healed, and T99 soldiers massed in the Temple below, led by a wagon carrying a corpse. The EXO's body laid face up and sprawled on the wood in full uniform. Ragged, bloody gouges marred the signature urban camo and flak jacket. Kolpa and Oki emerged from the group.

"Healer!" they called out. On the roof, Utu lowered Jogun back to the chair and covered his feeble legs with the blanket. Returned to the roof ledge.

"Jogun!" they called again.

"He's up here with me," said Utu, "Bring the EXO."

Oki and Kolpa exchanged glances, looked up at Utu, then lifted the corpse off the wagon. Carried it upstairs.

"Here! Here," Utu said as they reached the top. He cleared a space among the heavy burlap sacks. They dropped the EXO in a bloody heap at the foot of Jogun's chair.

"In the Pits last night," Oki panted, "caught us stockin' one of the ships."

Jogun looked down at the EXO's face, it's expression stretched in a sort of disgust. The eyelids sagged heavy and still, but just barely open. As if the man's hate made him hang on for every last drop of life. A fever chill rushed through

Jogun. Utu crouched beside the body and closed its eyes, soundlessly murmuring to the dead man. He paused, breathing deeply.

"Now," Utu said, brightening, "Send for a Lifter."

"What would I need a Lifter fo—" Jogun stopped, realizing.

Within fifteen minutes, Yasin, one of the Black Hoods, followed Rusaam up the stairs to the garden with a blanket-roll under his massive arm. He stopped and looked at Jogun. The giant's dark eyes glittered in the shadow of his hood.

"This him?" asked Yasin.

"It is," Utu answered. Yasin stooped, put the blanket-roll on the ground, and got down on his knees. Bowed until his forehead touched the ground.

"Nah, man...stand up. I ain't the son of God, just a busted ass Nine," said Jogun. Yasin looked up, paused, then stood as commanded. He unrolled his tools on a crate beside Jogun. Tiny, delicate surgical tools beside bits of tech. Circuits, wires, Wi-Fi cards, all cobbled together and connected to a tiny rectangular screen. One of the 'phones' from before the Border. After turning all of it on, Yasin crossed to the EXO.

The giant's hands were shockingly fast with the tools. A few cuts, pulls, and tugs in the officer's forearm, and the RFID chip was torn free. He cleaned it gently, mounted it to the device, and keyed a flurry of buttons on the screen.

"It's ready," Yasin said, "DNA and BioSigs are wiped. Go ahead an' get the Augs."

Utu stooped by the EXO and popped each of the seals on the smooth, urban camo panels. Jogun watched as his forearm was cleaned. Stared as the razor blade cut into his flesh. It burned like a son-of-a-bitch. He jerked when tiny jets of vapor puffed out of the Aug rig sections. Piece by piece they took it off.

"Aight," said Yasin, pulling the last stitch closed, "Check this out." He tapped a button on the screen and rocked Jogun's world. Nanotech coursed from the chip into his body, introducing itself as it reached his brain. He felt the nausea disappear. The headache vanished. Yasin seemed to know. The stoic Black Hood nodded to Rusaam and Kolpa. With reverent care, the two of them fitted the gear onto Jogun's withered body.

It came online all at once. A million pinpricks of fire rippled through him then faded to a low, steady hum. *They're a part of me now.* The fact came to him. He lifted one leg, then the other. Panels and joints shifted with his muscles underneath, obeying his commands with the soft buzzing of servo-motors. He stood up, quick as a soldier. Laughed out loud.

"What was taken, let it thus be restored," Utu intoned, "through this joining of flesh and invention."

Jogun grinned, taking a few solid steps on the roof. Yasin smiled.

"That ain't shit," said Yasin, "It's still in Neutral."

"Yeah," Oki said, turning to Kolpa, "'*Legs On.*'" Anyone who'd ever fought the EXOs and escaped knew the phrase. It usually meant it was time to run.

192

"Time to run," Jogun said. He crouched, turned the dial on the right hip. The high-pitched whine that all of Rasalla learned to fear sliced through the dense morning air. Jogun stood, walked to the edge of the roof, and jumped.

Maybe too high. He hadn't expected a ten meter leap from flat feet. The animal fear in his brain faded as all focus shifted to full body awareness. Midair, he pitched himself perfectly to land in the street below. In the center of a group of T99s. They staggered back. As they recognized him and cheered, Jogun jumped again, planted his foot on a ship's hull wall, then pushed off to the nearest roofline. *Step-step-step-step-JUMP-step-step-JUMP-step-JUMP*. He sprinted like a demon over concrete, gravel, shingle, fiberglass, and tin.

Soon, Utu's green island was a tiny patch in the haze. Jogun ran a giant circle around it across the rooftops, streets, and bridges. All of Rasalla spun around him.

He landed like a cat on the edge of the Temple roof, and stepped carefully into the swaying rows of spinach and kale. Yasin, Oki, Rusaam, and Kolpa waited at the end of the row, kneeling with heads bowed. Utu stood behind them smiling. He simply nodded.

"Those should do," Utu said, "Now what?" Jogun flexed each muscle in his legs one after the other. He grabbed the steaming bowl of chicken broth. Chugged it.

"Now," he said, clearing his throat, "Storehouses, safe houses, bunkers, dead drops, personal collections. Empty 'em all. Weapons for anyone old enough and willing to hold 'em. Same goes for supplies, so spread the word down in the Market. Bring all they can spare to the Pits."

35
History

SATO AWOKE TO the feeling of falling. He gasped and shot glances around the room, scrambling through the foggy panic for a point of reference. The curving surface of his ashwood desk felt smooth and cold. A glass cup with a splash of bourbon backwash sat in front of a picture frame...Jada in her twenties, mid-swing on the Mesa Park swingsets. He squinted at the sunlight cascading through the thirty-foot-tall windows of his top floor executive office.

How long have I been out? Pre-lunch traffic drifted silently outside through the ivory pillars of the Center Ring. He leaned back in his leather chair and impulsively pressed his finger to his temple. The gold square under the skin of his forearm blinked three times then the Neural home-screen shimmered to life in front of him. He blinked at the familiar vibration behind his eyes.

"Good God..." he said, grabbing the side of his head. '*Thirty-two New Messages*'... The little envelope icon seemed to blink in sync with the pounding in his skull. He expanded his settings menu. Told his implants to dull the sensation.

Most of the messages complained at length about the same things they had for the last twenty-four hours: Helium-3 shipments have ceased, Virton is unresponsive, and supplies are running out. Fast. The super fuel could run the entire early twenty-first century United States for a year on a single shuttle load. Sedonia City torched through at least half that every day. Utopia on the outside. Insatiable monster inside. Or rather a swarm of locusts.

For the hundredth time, he hit the shortcut tab for Elias Finley's direct line. The call tone beeped eight times then clicked over.

"Hello, Enota Sato, and thank you for calling Virton Energy Industries. How may I assist you today?" The clipped female speech of the AI answering program buzzed in Sato's ear as it had the previous ninety-nine attempts. Sato hung up, snatched up the bourbon glass, and chucked it across the lavish office. It bounced once then skittered to a soundless, pathetic stop on the Sixteenth Century Spanish rug. Sato bit his teeth together until it hurt. Calmed.

Finley had always been ready with some sort of tailored political response. Didn't matter how catastrophic the situation, the almighty Bottom Line kept the man in check. But now. To hear nothing at all. It had to mean the bastard was in the wind. That left only one other number to try.

"Call Janice Prescott," Sato said, holding the command key. It rang the characteristic three times before her spider silk voice answered.

"Hello, Enota. Good news? —Christ...you look like hell," she said, leaning forward in the video feed. A tickle on Sato's scalp told him his thinning hair must be an abomination. He smoothed down the cow lick as best he could then straightened in his chair.

"Considering the Devil has skipped town on our deal and left me to manage Hell, I should think so," Sato said.

"Yes. Finley. He's emptied his accounts and fled the country. Wise, considering Virton Energy is ruined," she said like it was gossip at a lunch meeting. Sato blinked.

"Ruined..." Sato's heart flopped in his chest.

"Oh yes," she said, "Themis is quite inoperable. Most of the staff dead, equipment destroyed or missing. Literally ruined."

The news punched Sato in the throat.

"An attack. One of the hostile firms: Qin Industrial or the Alhaka Group," said Sato. It had to be. *Who else could?* Prescott coughed a dry laugh.

"I'm afraid it was your little army of, shall we say, 'civil servants.' We're not sure how they reversed Finley's illegal mind-jacking operation, but they did, and they're coming," she said. Sato felt like his legs had been cut off underneath him.

"Oh, don't look so terrified," Janice scolded, "Something like this was always on the horizon and it fits the program, so you can rest assured that intervention will occur when it needs to. As for the fuel, our people have established a foothold and are restoring basic function to the Themis facility. It will be a while before it's back to production strength again, but it's at least a viable bargaining chip."

The pieces of their plan floated in Sato's awareness and settled into shape, but the blatant gaps defied him. He formed pointed questions, grasping for some semblance of control.

"When does Nobidyne take over?" he asked.

"Once their check clears, they should start retrofitting Themis within the week. We've purchased a quantity of product for immediate distribution, but Sato, there isn't much and it isn't cheap. Austerity measures and rationing will have to be put into effect," Janice sighed, "Your constituents will have their lifeblood, but they'll want their pound of flesh too. Yours, I'm afraid."

You fucking bitch. The hangover made it hard to hide the shaking in his hands. He curled his fingers into fists.

"*Austerity* measures?! You know full well that there is more than enough available fuel—"

"No," Janice said, sunken eyes glittering, "There is not. Not for *this* purpose. There will be no further debate on the subject."

Sato fell silent, shamefully swallowing the unspeakable secret. *But the blame... more unemployment, more food riots, ruinous fuel prices, another inevitable market crash, and a pack of angry T99's whereabouts unknown...all on MY head? For all history?* That he refused to swallow.

"I should have been kept in the loop, Janice. The City is breathing down my neck for a workable solution, and I have *not* given up on them! My head on a platter won't fix this!"

"Oh, but it will, insofar as we need it to be fixed moving forward. This is too delicate a game to balk at strategic sacrifice. *Personal* sacrifice. It's for the survival of humanity, Enota, you know that," she nodded, drawing her thin lips in a matronly frown. Sato snapped.

"You mean 'Stay of Execution,' don't you?"

"Wait *right* there!" her words whipped at him, "The bourbon is driving again and you're headed for a cliff. You made a desperate call with the Raid and now that it's backfired. It's up to *you* to take the blows and beg for the people's forgiveness. There is no other way forward."

Sato felt the vice lock on his balls.

"Fine. I'll draft my crucifixion speech at once," Sato moved to hang up.

"One more thing before you go," Janice said.

"More?!"

"Yes. More. The Rindal matter has continued long enough. Let's be clear about something that has been, until now, implicit. Yours, Jada's, and your extended family's seats onboard the Narayana are officially contingent upon your success. Right here. Right now. Your *last* chance. Wrap this up, Sato, and chalk the rest to early retirement." A twisted cousin of pity showed on Prescott's waxen face. The video feed closed with a beep and his Neural displayed the message '*Call Ended. Memory Block 081280_1130a: Deleted.*'

Sato slumped back in his chair. The air in the office hovered, still as a sealed tomb. From the silence, a dead man's words rang crystal clear in Sato's memory. As though a program embedded deep within him had been set to go off at the precise moment. '*They'll come after you one day.*'

A sickening chill ran up his spine. He clasped his hands together and squeezed as the voice of Alan Rindal set his guts on fire. Furious tears stung his eyes. *I'm sorry Alan...I should have helped...really helped...should have listened. Not—*

A bolt of lightning struck his brain. He swept his hand through the air to refresh the Neural home screen then hit the icon marked 'History'. Before him, in a vast grid, lay folders for every year since he was implanted as a teen. He hadn't touched the one folder in eighteen years, but never forgot its place on the grid. It was the recording. The one he'd brought to Prescott's desk. The one that had buried Alan Rindal...and the family. Discovering the boy's existence had been bittersweet.

Sato studied it, feeling his hand and arm tingle as they waited for him to give the order. He pressed and expanded the folder. Found the month, then the day, then the time. '*Loading Memory Block 072262_645p.*' The task bar stuttered as it hunted for the data.

All at once, he was in the old kitchen of his executive block apartment, back on the lower Mesa. He was just a PRG lobbyist back then, working his way up the corporate ladder. Alan faced him with a pleading stare, leaning forward on the marble island. Rindal had been a hard man for years, masquerading as a lackey for the PRG. His thin, wiry-athletic frame never fit his clothes right, giving him the look of a college student wearing hand-me-downs. His wide eyes burned bright next to his light-brown complexion. The sharp jaw and cheekbones had a way of underscoring his fanaticism.

Sato shuddered inside his aloof observer brain. The 'Play' icon in his periphery blinked three times, froze, and faded away, breathing life into the remembered room.

"—can't do this! They hold all the strings! You go in with a machete, and it all comes crashing down: you, me, everybody!" Sato heard and felt himself hiss in the whispers of a younger voice, yet could only watch the scene unfold like some shameful rerun.

"Are you really that blind? All of it *is* crashing down! The environment, industry, economy, *society!* The Narayana isn't some 'just-in-case' backup plan; it's the *main event* for these people! They spent the past fifty years squeezing every drop out of this planet so they can just cut and run and leave everybody else in the lurch!" Alan said, pushing himself from the island to pace the slate tile floor.

"You really should hear yourself right now," Sato said, laughing, "You sound like some crazy-ass blogger with a doomsday conspiracy. They don't want to abandon Earth; they're working on the next logical step for all of us! Twelve billion people on the planet and counting...I'm glad *someone* is working on spreading us out a little!"

"Spreading us..." Rindal breathed a humorless laugh. "A fleet of fifty generational starships under secret construction worldwide. Trillions of credits bled from a suffering public *in secret*. And a war of attrition against the Slums waged to provide an Evil Enemy to blame. That sound like a group who holds humanity's 'best interests' at heart? They built the Border twelve years ago to protect themselves. Not society, *themselves*. And they're ramping up to do it again. There is *no* wall like Deep Space."

Alan was right. No denying it. The powerful had deemed themselves worthy to survive and the rest undeserving. *Triage of the Species.* He wanted to tell Alan everything. The seats he had earned for himself, Jada, and her family. The agendas he had helped the Prescott Group draft into policy. Instead, Sato kept silent, waiting for his best friend to bury himself. *For the greater good.* Alan pressed on.

"If you help them with this...hell...even turn a *blind eye* and they'll come after you, too one day. One day when it's convenient for them, they'll take you and everyone you love and toss your lives into the incinerator without a second thought. You are an *asset,* a tool with limited use. That's how they see people, Enota. That's how they own the world. I won't just sit by and let my son grow up an unwitting slave."

Sato looked down and away from Alan's flashing glare. Inside his observing mind he did the same.

"Okay," he heard himself begin the lie, "I hear you. What do you need from me?"

"Your voice. Everything you know about the back-room deals, cooked books, propaganda campaigns, and, of course, the *convenient* disappearances within the opposition. All of it in written in a sworn affidavit and mailed to my office," Rindal said. Sato paused and rubbed his chin to make a show of the decision. Alan had a reputation for smelling lies.

"Then you'll have it. But it *will* take more than the misgivings of an ex—collaborator to bring them down. You don't have any proof. They'll discredit me and shoot down my story befo—"

"I have blueprints, construction sites, and a current passenger manifest for the Narayana, leeched from the PRG's internal files. Share-holders, bureaucrats, and other company men mixed with an as-yet *uninformed* contingent of doctors, scientists, and cultural figures. Unimpeachable," Alan said.

"So why do you need my—"

"Your name is on the list. Harder to deny if it comes from you," said Alan. That gave Sato pause. *He knows? Why trust me?* Alan seemed to read the question. "You're my best friend, Enota. The brother I never had. I trust you. I need you. *Humanity* needs you."

"I said 'Okay,' didn't I? Where is this list?" asked Sato, realizing that he hadn't even seen it. His observing self watched the next agonizing moments unfold.

"It's safe," said Alan.

"*Safe?*"

"Hidden."

Stop playback and Close. Sato gave the internal command and Alan vanished along with that hideous kitchen, dumping Sato back in his stale three-hundredth-floor office. All these years he had wondered what 'Hidden' had meant. Now he had a pretty good idea.

"I'll finish it," he said with a knot in his throat, "I'll find Aden and finish what you started and the whole fucking lot of it will come crashing down around them! Like it has to." *To hell with their 'seats.'* He reached forward and held down the Neural command key.

"Call John Kabbard."

36

Accomplice

LIANI HAD BEEN tossing and turning under her cotton sheets since dawn. She would burrow into one position, stay still with her eyes closed, and flip over ten minutes later. It had taken them until four in the morning to get settled, depositing the passed-out stranger on her floral print futon. Since then, her half-sleeping brain swam with paranoid dreams.

Rolling over again, she compulsively tapped her temple for the millionth time. *'Net connection interrupted. Tower Signal lost.'* Her Neu Feed, news tickers, email, and UptOwn resource management game sat cached in the same state they had been for hours. Her pack of robo-dogs in her UptOwn villa were probably starving by now, tearing the penguin butlers apart. *That actually upsets me.* Serious 'real-time withdrawal' had officially set in.

"Unnngh! Hell with it," Liani said. She swiped the Neural home screen closed and sat up. The heavy, black ring on her finger glinted through the slatted light of the blinds. She turned it on her finger. An RFID signal jammer. The reason she couldn't connect, but also the only reason Kabbard wasn't banging down her front door. It was one of three Corey had handed out in the van. *Just whipped them out of his backpack like they* wouldn't *get us all thrown in jail!*

Although, it had been her idea to cross the line in the first place. For what, she still wasn't sure. Her gut had said 'sleep on it.' But half-dreams of being paraded naked through Mesa Park en route to execution didn't clarify much. *Ass-naked except for my running shoes...screw you, subconsciousness.* She swung her long, bare legs out of bed and began the hunt for a clean-ish pair of jeans.

Liani heard snoring as she peeked her head out into the tiny living room. Her special guest's feet dangled motionless over the edge of the futon armrest and to the right, facing the front door, Corey sat slouched in the flimsy kitchen chair. His chin rested on his collar bone, and he held a curtain rod in his lap. Each time his chest rose it sounded like a motorcycle from one of those old action movies he'd insisted on lending to her.

"My hero," she whispered with a grin. The fossil fuel engine in Corey's sinuses stalled as his eyes flickered open.

"Huh? What? Everything okay?" he asked, rubbing sleep from his eyes to scan the room.

"Down boy," she teased, then yawned, "It's been quiet all morning. Coffee?" Corey nodded and reflected the yawn as she turned into the kitchen. She picked up the coffee pot from the sink, sniffed it, and then shrugged. Stuck it in the maker.

"Uh oh," Corey said from his chair. Liani tensed.

"What?!"

"Seems like your new friend left a chunky, blue puddle on your rug," he said, snickering. Liani scurried out of the kitchen. The boy who'd called himself Aden had a thin line of drool running from his mouth to the sickly sweet mess on her microfiber carpet.

"Ahhhh, really? Really? So much for the members of the ruling elite," said Liani, dipping back into the kitchen for a roll of paper towels.

"What do you mean, 'ruling elite'?" Corey asked.

"Kid comes in last night and drops the better part of two G's on drinks for the whole bar," Liani said, "His chip came up Gold."

"Could explain why Kabbard was after him...pissed off somebody up top. Probably a good thing I'm so 'paranoid' and had those rings handy." Corey got up and squinted at Aden, "Dresses kinda weird for a Mesa Brat, doesn't he?"

"I thought so, too," Liani said, emerging with the paper towels and crossed to the futon, "No hex-mesh skinny pants or bad hair." She knelt beside the puddle and dropped the whole wad on it. As it soaked, she studied her unconscious guest. This 'Aden' hardly had any body fat on him at all, drawing the lines of his tight, lanky muscles into sharp creases. His rough skin was slashed and pock-marked all over with dark, ashen scars. A big one on his shoulder. The ghostly forms of the Rasalla raid victims entered her mind. *'Can you take me home,'* he'd said in the garage last night. *Where's home?*

A twinkle of silver thread flickered under his jumpsuit's lapel. Gently, she lifted the fabric.

"Themis," she read aloud. Aden's eyes snapped open.

"AHH!" both Aden and Liani screamed at the same time. He leapt back to climb over the futon and flipped it over, landing with a crashing thud on the faux hardwood.

"WHOA! Whoa, whoa, hey, buddy, you remember me," said Liani, "Nice lady who fed you too many drinks last night?"

The terror on Aden's face dimmed a little when he saw her, though he studied the room like some kind of feral child.

"Yeah," Liani said, "Aden, right? Your name is Aden?"

"I—call me Matteo," he said, wincing. "Where am I? And why's my head hurt?" Liani laughed, making him smile shyly.

"You're at my place," she said, "My apartment. And your head hurts because you had more girly drinks than I've ever seen *anyone* order in a single evening."

"Liani, stay back," Corey said flatly, gripping the curtain rod like a club.

"What? Why?" she asked.

"He's an escaped convict from the Themis Colony, that's why, now stay back!" said Corey. Liani furrowed her manicured brows at him.

"Chipped with a gold RFID? They don't exactly hand those out in the Rasalla District from Red Cross food trucks, Corey, now put the battle axe down."

Corey hesitated, then obeyed. Matteo looked down at his hand. The ring Corey had fastened there flashed in the kitchen light.

"That's so they can't track you," Liani said, holding up her hand to show hers, "Blocks your signal. Corey, where did you get these anyway?"

"Friends," he said. Liani rolled her eyes. Matteo scratched around the device and straightened.

"*Why* am I here? What happened?" He dug his palm into his forehead, wobbled, then sat on the toppled futon. Liani and Corey exchanged glances. They walked slowly around the upturned wooden frame, and peered down at him.

"Corey, get him some water," she said. Corey frowned and started to say something. Liani shot him the obligatory death stare, sending him pouting on his way to the kitchen. Matteo slouched and stared at the floor through his knees.

"Ade—mm—Matteo. Hi. Ummm, you were really, really drunk, got kicked out, climbed back in, then John Kabbard showed up," Liani remarked, noting Matteo's face when she mentioned the name. "And then you freaked out and tried to run. I kind of accidentally knocked you out with the door, so we got you outta there. Brought you...*here!*" Liani presented her apartment with an awkward flourish. Matteo gave it another cursory look, then tried to stand, stumbling a little on the crooked futon pad. Corey met him at the top with the water.

Matteo looked, nodded, and hesitated, staring at the glass.

"Here, take it," Corey insisted. Matteo carefully accepted the water, then knocked it back, drinking deeply. Done, he licked his lips, savoring the taste of it. Liani furrowed her brow. *Jeez kid, never seen a glass of water before?*

"Thanks," Matteo said, wiping his mouth.

"You're welcome," said Corey.

"No...for everything," Matteo stepped off of the futon, then stooped. He picked up the wood frame and turned it right-side-up.

"Our pleasure. So...what did he want with you? Kabbard," Liani asked, feeling brave. Matteo froze and seemed to go away in his head. The journalist inside Liani stirred. *Ooooh, that is a sensitive subject.*

"That man hates us. Always has. My brother used to tell m—" Matteo's breath sputtered out, choking. He tried to hide it.

"What did your brother say," Liani asked. Corey put his hand on her shoulder. "Li..."

"Shh!" She pushed his hand away.

"Doesn't matter now," Matteo answered, "Everything's different." He noticed the light from the window, then turned. Step by step, he inched toward it as though it might hurt him, then parted a crack in the blinds. She couldn't see what he was looking at, but whatever it was captivated him.

"You...really are from Rasalla, aren't you?" she asked.

"I grew up there," Matteo said without turning from the glass, "Lived there my whole life. But my brothe—I was told I was born *here*." The words hung in the room. From the silence, Corey gasped.

"Li, what did you call him before?!"

"At the bar he said it was Aden. His credit account came up under that name too: Aden Rin...Aden Rin-something."

"*Aden Rindal?*" The color drained out of Corey's face. Matteo whirled.

"Jesus, yeah...good guess," Liani said, cocking an eyebrow at Corey.

"Around eighteen years ago, a well-liked district attorney and his family crashed their transport in the heart of the Slums, killing all three of them. It was chalked up to mechanical failure, but never confirmed since all possible evidence was cut up, carried away, and scattered immediately by the locals. That far out, the first responders barely had time to dispatch, let alone find anything once they got there."

"Oh my god, are you talking about *Alan* Rindal?! The freakin' conspiracy theory? Tell me you're joking," Liani said, hoping he was. But out the corner of her eye, she noticed Matteo facing them. Quiet, focused, and still as ice. Her comforting doubt slipped through her fingers.

"Keep going," Matteo said, staring a hole through Corey.

"Right...um...Rindal was saying some pretty radical things to the press in the days leading up to the crash. Basically went from hard-line party man to whistleblower overnight, going after corruption in every tier of the state. Company man gets a conscience." Corey shook his head. "It wasn't a secret he'd made some damn powerful enemies in the process: the Prescott Group, Virton, shit, even the World Bank wanted to shut him up. Most of *us*, to this day, think someone did. Murdered him, his wife, and newborn son. Alan, Patricia, and...*Aden*," Corey finished, looking squarely at Matteo. Shaking now, Matteo lowered himself to the floor. The poor kid looked like he was about to short circuit. Though, something Corey had said itched in Liani's ears.

"Wait, what do you mean '*us*?' These shadowy 'friends' of yours?" Liani asked.

"It's a movement, Li, and it's been building for years. Doesn't exactly pay the bills so I never got in too deep...but I know a guy. He's connected. Kind of a weird cat, but he used to feed me leads all the time when I was still just an indy blogger. I think he can help us out." Corey stepped around the coffee table and reached for his backpack.

"How?" blurted Matteo. Corey stopped and grinned at him.

"You want answers, buddy? They're all in your head. You've been set to record since the day you got that chip."

37

Answers

MATTEO FELT RIDICULOUS in the new clothes they'd given to him. The long-sleeve, shiny, mesh shirt-thing shrink wrapped his upper body and chafed his joints pretty badly. Over that, they stuffed him in a thick, puffy vest with an equally puffy collar that almost buried his head. Probably a good thing he had trouble seeing his legs over the collar. Whatever kind of boots they'd strapped him into made him feel like he'd jumped calf-deep into wet concrete. Sitting in the backseat of Corey's bulky hover-van, he scratched at the bunched fabric in his arm pits and retreated back into his mind.

Matteo was still trying to make sense of what Corey had said. He knew you had to have a chip to get into the City, but the rest had been a mystery.

"They're like little computers," Corey explained simply for Matteo to under-stand, "and everyone has a color based on their class. Mine and Liani's are blue because we're from Inner Ring, a few levels out from the Mesa. Yours is gold. Either the chip or you, or both are from the Mesa itself. Some call it Center Ring, and it's the tippee-top. Home to the richest, most powerful bastards in Sedonia City...no offense. Anyway, that chip combined with the top-shelf nan-otech you were injected with at birth made you just a little more than human. You're sharper, more observant, quicker to react, and you have a memory like a steel trap, all thanks to these microscopic gadgets hooked onto your neurons." He saw Matteo's blank stare. "The building blocks of your brain. Now, we all have the same kind of memory storage in us, but it's illegal to access it directly without a court order...it's not exactly productive for society if everyone can live in the past *for real*, right? But if you commit a crime, out comes the memory to convict you. If you're killed, your memory is your witness." Corey's friend, Illyk, was the man to see about 'getting access.'

Matteo blinked and shook his head. He realized all of it was true. The entire conversation had just played back in his head. In detail. He'd always been able to do that. Jo would frown at him when he'd recite the exact words of a broken promise Utu would give him shopping lists without writing them down, and laugh deeply when Matteo came back with every last item. And in the Pits he'd had a mental catalog of which objects were valuable, which were useful, and which were dangerous. There had to be thousands.

Growing up, it had been just one more thing to get him called a freak.

Sweat poured from his forehead as heat radiated up from inside the vest. He tugged at the collar. *Illyk can get 'access.'* The thought of digging up every fucked up detail of his life for all to see made him ache. Liani turned and faced him from the passenger seat.

"Nervous?" she asked. Her feline-green eyes glistened at him as she smiled. Matteo's pulse raced. The mop of shiny red curls draped over her shoulders, just hiding the curves of her chest.

"Nah..." he said, shaking his head, "Nah."

"Good, good. New outfit's cute on you! Cuter than it was on my ex anyway... you like it?" Matteo wiped his forehead then rubbed the sweat on his mesh pant leg. Nodded.

"Yeah, it's great," he said, puffing his chest, "Great outfit."

"He looks like a marshmallow in combat boots," Corey scoffed. Liani punched his arm.

"Ahh! Shit, Liani, I'm driving!" said Corey. Matteo smiled, escaping the quicksand of his thoughts. He pulled the vest collar down further to get a better look out of the half-canopy window.

The buildings had gotten shorter. Blockier. Where the downtown ones were sleek and beautiful, these wore their guts on the outside. Complex networks of pipes and bits of worn machinery seemed to both decorate and entangle the neighborhood. Not so much flying traffic out this way either. There were a few transports and freighters humming in their aerial lanes, but most of the movement happened on the hanging train system. *The Superway.* There had been a blurb about it in one of Utu's magazines. The tracks wove through the City like veins and arteries in a massive body. Train cars slipped along the rails at ridiculous speeds, stopped for passengers, then took off again like a gunshot. Matteo instantly wanted to ride one. Yet the further they went, even the train stops seemed fewer and further between.

"Jesus, Corey," said Liani, "How deep in the sticks are we going?"

"These guys live as far on the edge of the grid as they can, Li. They don't exactly want to be found," said Corey.

"And you *have* found them before...right?"

"I...um...not exactly."

"Oh this should be good," said Liani, leveling a stare at him.

"I managed to trace my contact's IP back through a couple dummy servers he'd set up. Rather badass of me considering these guys don't fuck around with security," he grinned at Liani as she rolled her eyes. "Naturally, the signal dead-ended before a specific location came up, so all I could get was a district tag."

"Meaning?"

"We've gotta stop in the neighborhood and ask around."

"Perfect," Liani said.

The squat apartments and dingy storefronts finally gave way to the Outer Ring, a skeletal, tangled landscape of power plants, towering steam vents, loading docks, shipyards, and warehouses. As a kid he'd assumed the smoke rising from just beyond the Border was some sort of curtain, meant to stop him and his kind from looking in. Maybe the City kept monsters there.

Corey flew the van over the belly of the beast and dipped down into one of its gaping mouths. They landed on a round, concrete clearing amidst all kinds of other parked vehicles. Most had wheels though. Cars, trucks, vans, even bikes. Matteo fiddled with his harness, excited for a closer look but more eager to get the hell out of the van. Flying had been more fun when he wasn't hungover.

"Okay, here we go," Corey said as he popped the seal on the van doors. "We'll start in that power station over there. My guess is they use the interference given off by the transformers to help block incoming Wi-Fi."

"We're guessing now. Awesome," said Liani.

The complex felt unfriendly right away. Workers with tattered jumpsuits, dirt-streaked skin, and suspicious eyes kept their distance. They milled through the maze-like facility with exhausted, silent purpose. Grating metallic sounds of sparks and heavy tools rang out, underscored by a low electric hum. Matteo's palms started sweating. For a moment he thought himself back in the twisted stomach of some wrecked sky-freighter in the Pits.

Corey had a hard time approaching the workers, let alone talking to one. Either they ignored him completely or pretended not to hear him over the noise. After half an hour of this, he finally dropped the excuse-me's.

"We're looking for Illyk!" Corey shouted above the din. Several men stopped what they were doing and glared. Liani grabbed Corey's arm and clung tight. A stocky, brick house of a worker stepped toward them. Seemed like out of nowhere.

"We don't know who that is, bud. You guys ain't safe in here without gear. You should leave before some kind of accident happens." The man nodded to the way they came in, then turned his back on them.

"We, uh,—" Corey coughed, "We have something he'd be interested in. Worth his while."

"You?" the worker asked, laughing the question.

"Yeah, me. He used to help me run a blog back in the day," Corey gulped and glanced at Liani, "'Engine of Vengeance?'" The worker squinted at him.

"Nerd," Liani snickered under her breath. A booming laugh from the worker startled all three of them. The spectators all around seemed to relax.

"Shit yeah! I used to check out EoV all the time! So...you must be Truth-Hammer! You're a real wise-ass, bro," the man chuckled as if remembering an example. Liani laughed out loud.

"TruthHammer?!"

"Told you, I'm a badass," Corey said sheepishly. Matteo heard the click, saw the handgun.

"Whoa—" Corey started.

"Sorry, T.H., just a precaution. EoV went dead five years ago, and that's plenty of time to turn Fed. Give me the rings and show me the arms." Corey frowned, then took his off. Nodded to Matteo and Liani who both followed suit. Matteo watched as his two new friends held out their left forearms. The worker took out a local profile scanner and touched it over their chips, triggering a quick beep.

"Hm," the man said, reading as he stepped to Matteo. Matteo turned his arm over and hesitated, looking at the skin. He remembered Themis. Being pinned to the ground and forced to submit to a similar device. He looked at Liani.

"It's okay," she said, "It doesn't hurt."

Matteo nodded. Stretched the arm out for the worker. Reading the profile, the worker's eyes went wide.

"Yeah. He's what's worth your while," Corey said, "calls himself Matteo, but, as you can see, the chip's got a different name."

"He follows me. You two stay here," he said, turning away.

"Wait, what?! No, man, we're—"

"You're Media, or at least you were. We can't risk you leaking anything that we'd rather keep tight," the worker tapped a finger on the side of the gun, "No arguments."

Matteo stole himself, putting on the toughest scowl he could. But truth was, every inch further into the complex they went, his nerves screamed. He buried the thousands of questions for the moment and refocused his mind on their route. A long forgotten lesson from Jogun surfaced right on cue. *'When in doubt, know the way out.'* The voice was so vivid in his head. Heard through the new knowledge of his hidden talents, it dropped a lead weight on his shoulders. Still, he did his best to take the advice.

He found the pattern in their path. Thick black cables hung bracketed to the metal frame walls. Some kind of hard line setup for both power and networking, not all that different from some of the rigs used around Rasalla. The EXOs could tap into Wi-Fi signals too easily. The cops had to find a local hard line before they could hack in. *Why would anybody on this side of the Border need to hide like this?* The people of the City were all supposed to be rich, fat, and comfortable, living in beautiful apartments that look down on the rest of the world. *Do the EXOs raid here too? In their own City?*

Another turn and the two of them arrived at a small clearing in the structure. In the center of the cylindrical chamber squatted an older model IG-6 military transport. Matteo flinched as years of programming begged his legs to run. But this one was rusted. Sleeping under a camouflage net to hide it from open sky. A ring of dried mold surrounded its base and crept up the hull, showing him it hadn't moved in a long time. The black cables wormed their way up to modified ports all over and around the ship, spread over the platform like thick noodles. The worker stepped over the cables toward the ship. Matteo hesitated. Heard the familiar click.

"No turning back now, I'm afraid," said the worker, holding the gun for Matteo to see, "C'mon." With every step, the decaying ship grew. It loomed over the two of them as they approached the hatch door under the nose. A surveillance camera next to the hatch buzzed as it focused on the two of them. The worker grinned up at it, showing his crooked stained teeth.

"It's Simon, open up," he called up to the camera, "Got a special guest who'd like to...uh...reminisce." The hatch bolts popped and the door squealed open on rusty hinges.

It took a moment for Matteo's eyes to adjust in the dim blue glow of the inside. Flickering monitors lined the stripped bulkheads, outlining seated figures. They swiveled in their chairs to look at him, then turned back to their work. Whatever that might be. A thin figure descended from a ladder in the ceiling and jumped down, landing with a thud on the metal floor. The hot cherry of a lit cigarette swayed from side to side in the twilight as the figure walked over to greet them. A monitor brightened, lighting the mystery man's face. *Just a kid?*

He had to be between Matteo and Jogun's age. Sunken eyes studied Matteo in the dark, set in a gaunt, scruffy face. He was thin except for a slight gut and dressed in a filthy undershirt and baggy sweatpants. They watched each other in silence for a moment.

"Well?" asked the raspy, young voice, "What's up Inner Ring? How can I be of service?"

"You're Illyk?" Matteo asked. The strange kid spread his arms and bowed.

"A votre plaisir," Illyk intoned, "Now, I'm busy so get to your fucking point." Matteo had just about enough.

"I'm not 'Inner Ring.' I'm not any 'Ring.' My name's Matteo and I grew up in Rasalla. Scrap, ashes, and dirt, but *this*," Matteo held up his left arm, "This says my name is Aden Rindal." Illyk sucked on the filter of the cigarette, staring. The others in the room stopped typing and turned in their seats. Matteo felt hard, expectant eyes on him. The air hung dead as Illyk exhaled a curling plume of smoke.

"That's...a heavy story...'Aden,'" Illyk said, "'Long lost son of the fallen hero.' Not sure I believe it, although trust me...I'd like to. That'd get some serious cloudtime, and way beyond just the forums. Dad, prep the Chair for our guest here." Simon crossed the room, opened an inner hatch door, and dipped out of sight. Illyk stepped closer to Matteo, his sour breath seeping out as he spoke.

"To reiterate, I'd like to believe you. But I don't. My time and services are not only valuable, they are very, very risky and, as I'm sure you know, very, very illegal. We'll take a look for you, but it comes with a price. Whatever I find, I copy and keep, got it?"

Matteo didn't. He squinted at Illyk.

"TM Data, bro. Your worst, most traumatic memories. Don't ask me why, but people pay max credits to live through someone else's pain and anguish. Not exactly pretty, but it's how we keep the lights on and fight the good fight, so I'll repeat: Whatever I find, I copy and keep. Got it?"

Matteo clinched his fists. Looking around the room, the others were still seated in front of their screens. Illyk looked pale. Underfed. He could take him. A quick punch to the jaw or throat, then he'd flip around to deal with...

Matteo felt the gun barrel dig into the small of his back. Simon. Father to the grinning rat boy in front of him.

"Sorry, kid, it's for the cause," said Simon, "Think of it as your contribution. Now let's go have a seat."

It was a reclining chair bolted into a platform in a small separate chamber. A headdress of electrodes and wires sprouted from the headrest like some kind of techno jellyfish. Open shackles waited for his limbs on the arm and leg rests, each blinking inside with strange technology. Where the main cabin had been for prisoner transport, this room was for something else. *Interrogation.* Matteo had heard rumors around the market about it. The EXOs would strap you down in this chair, hook you up to machines, and put the screws on you. A few T99s would try to brag that they got put in the chair and never gave up a thing. But the ones that really went through it...they never came back the same. Most spent the rest of their lives as permanent patients in the Temple. Matteo prayed a silent prayer that the hardware in his head made him different. *Corey said I was recording...maybe they'll just hit 'Play'?*

No choice. Matteo tried to imagine he was sitting in Utu's healing chair back in the Temple, waiting for a check-up. He regained focus as he sat down.

"What 'Cause' is this for again?" Matteo asked, "All I see is a buncha guys sittin' on their asses in a rusted out dropship."

Illyk turned his forearm over in the humming blueish light. A long, ragged scar ran the length of his pale flesh where the chip should be. It rippled as Illyk closed a fist.

"To show people that their paradise is a prison. Death Row for the human race," Illyk said as he stepped to the chair control panel and punched a few buttons. The shackles clamped shut, trapping Matteo's forearms and ankles. The tentacles of the headdress grasped his skull and squeezed. He felt the electrodes arrange themselves with little ice-cold snaps. Illyk tapped a few more buttons then inserted a smooth, rectangular cartridge into the panel.

"Brace yourself," Illyk said.

The comforting memory of Utu's office dissolved as bits of blinding light streaked toward him from the room. They gathered faster and faster, blotting out his vision. Before leaving the present moment entirely, he heard Illyk's grinding voice.

"This isn't gonna be fun."

The scenes came on fast. Racing through settings and times and people and emotions at a thousand miles-an-hour. All from his living point of view. Every bit of it was as vivid and detailed as though the moments were happening. And somehow his mind kept up, tasting every breath and feeling, every hurt. The hurts seemed to slow things down closer to real time. Somewhere in his current awareness, he could almost feel Illyk watching.

Matteo felt the cold floor of his cell back in Themis, watching himself pound the glass as Jogun explained the truth. His past mind swam with confusion. Waves of anger crashed against denial and pain as the answers rolled out of his broken brother, destroying the world and his place in it. Then came Kabbard. Then the gas. Darkness. Fading to Jogun's screams.

He blinked then winced as the cinder block wall above him was cratered by rifle rounds, raining hot debris down on his head. Suomo and the T99s huddled around him, popping up to take quick shots at the stranded EXOs. A boy beside him, no older than sixteen, took a bullet in the brain. Warm, red wetness splashed his ear and shoulder. Bits of gray in it.

Rewind through six years in the Pits. A chunk of falling fiberglass nearly took off his arm at the shoulder, crippling him for weeks as he healed.

Lying awake and starving to death on more nights than he cared to remember.

Jogun appeared, lying bloody and limp on the grooved metal roof of their old house. Kabbard and the EXOs had beaten him almost to death, and they kept at it. The sickening impact of each strike shook Matteo's tiny body. His throat burned with wheezing, choked sobs as he shrieked for them to stop. Jogun smiled. '*You got this.*'

Then he was in the Dream. The same one he'd had off-and-on since he was a kid. Yet as the scene slowed to real time, it came into waking focus. He looked at his hands. Small, chubby fingers wiggled and flexed. The feeling made him curious. He waved the little hands in front of him, then squealed. *So happy.* A white bandage wrapped tightly around his left forearm, tugging the soft skin as he wriggled.

Two people sat in the front seats, talking. A man and a woman. Beyond them, bright white clouds and blue sky shone through glass, moving gently over them. The two familiar voices warmed him as they spoke, but his observing, adult mind understood words that the young mind did not.

"Dammit, Alan, would it kill you to look on the bright side?" the woman asked. "I know this is important to you, I really do, but it's been eating you alive for years now. It's been eating *all of us* lately with all the long nights, press conferences...cameras in our faces. We all need some time away, and this—"

"There is no 'time away' anymore, Patty! We're not taking a break, going to visit old friends, we're running for our lives...and I'm not sure I can live with what I'm leaving behind," the man said. Somewhere in time, the icy tingle of recognition worked its way up Matteo's spine. The voices...his real mother and real father, continued.

"Are you so goddamn preoccupied with that that you can't see what you're taking *with* you?!" The painful tone in his mother's voice tightened Matteo's small, weak chest. Tiny, wheezing sobs chirped out of him. His parents turned in their seats. The looks on their faces filled him, both then and now. The corners of his mother's hesitating smile...he'd seen them thousands of times since in the mirror. Her opal eyes trembled as they looked down at him. *Mama?* He'd always wondered what she looked like. Dark, almost black skin, smooth like still water. Short black hair kept neat in gentle waves, the longer strands in the front draping across her forehead.

Then there was his father. The man Jogun told him he didn't want to know, except this was a different man. *My real dad...* Love radiated from the man's gaunt, brown features, but through a mask of desperation. Matteo had seen that face in the mirror too. His parents turned back to each other.

"That's *all* I can see now," his dad said, "I look at you and Aden, and I just—I don't just want us to be safe, I want us to be *free*. I'd do anything to find a place where he could grow up to be his own person and not a slave. To choose a life rather than it be chosen for him, but that's not the world we live in now." His dad held up the left hand. A thick black ring coiled around his middle finger.

"Like hell it's not," his mom said. She reached over and snatched off the ring.

"Patty, no!" he screamed, lunging for the device. She recoiled in her seat, holding the ring out of reach. Matteo...Aden started to cry. After several moments, the cabin stilled.

"You see? Nothing's happened. Nobody's chasing us, your brain wasn't hijacked. It's not the end of civiliza—" she stopped as a loud bang erupted from the reactor compartment. The ship's smooth glide dipped into violent, shaking free fall.

"Alan?! ALAN!" his mother screamed, clawing at her arm-rests. She fainted, rapping her head on the dash.

Though his dad's hands were firmly locked to the flight sticks, trying to pull up, the man could still speak. Matteo strained to listen past his own piercing screams.

"You've seen what's happened, Aden! You can't understand it yet, but if you survive this, someday you will! Others have to see what you've seen, and they need the truth you carry! Five-seven-echo-alpha-zero-zero-one-two-one! Remember it! Remember forever...we'll always love you!"

The roar outside the ship drowned out any other sound as they plunged. Matteo could still feel his cries stinging his soft throat. The dust-colored streets of Rasalla quaked in a blur below them. Closer and closer until...Black.

Then he was alone. Wheezing sobs reflected back to him in the tiny chamber of his child seat. It was hot. Smells from his wet pants choked him as he struggled to breathe. His sips for air grew smaller and smaller.

Muffled sounds came from outside his bubble. Yelling voices, heavy thuds, screeching metal...and a scraping. A chunk of foam broke away, spilling light into his car seat. A shadowy face appeared in the hole. More scraping. A series of pops released the bubble, and rough young hands scooped him up.

"Stay quiet, little brother," the young voice whispered, "I got'chu."

Jo.

The sunlit halo around his brother spread until all was white. As the blindness faded from his weeping eyes, Matteo found himself back in Illyk's chair. The shackles clicked open and the head-tentacles retracted. Illyk, Simon, and all of the technicians in the room gathered around the chamber, staring at him. He wanted to hide. To shrink into a deep, dark hole somewhere and come out maybe five years later.

Suddenly, strange text files, blueprints, and photographs appeared on screens around the room. *Some kind of ship...* Beyond massive in the half glow of the curved Earth beneath it, the body looked almost whale-shaped. Miles of solar panels lined its broad, flat wing arrays. Giant glass domes punctuated both the back and the underbelly, housing every biosphere on the planet. And millions of pin-point windows covered the hull.

Without reading the screens, fresh memories bubbled up into Matteo's awareness. *'The Narayana.' Total Occupancy: 2.8 million persons. Top speed: 99.9992% SOL. Destination: Gliese 581g. Distance to Target: 20.26 LY. Projected Launch Date: 09-2090AD.*

"My God..." Simon said, "They're gonna—"

"Leave us all to *rot*! Ho-ly SHIT!" Illyk shouted, "We got 'em! Dead to fuckin' rights, *we got 'em!*" Excited laughter broke out all over the room. Matteo willed himself to sit up, but his head rolled into a mat of fuzz. He almost passed out.

"Whoa, whoa, buddy! I bet that was rough...but don't worry man, 'cause everything's about to change! We're gonna put this out on every channel we can think of. Hell, we'll project it on the sky over Mesa-fucking-Park!"

Matteo heaved his throbbing head up and saw the control panel. The memory cartridge.

"No..." Matteo muttered. He yanked the head-tentacles off, killing the streaming data. Then, in one quick move, his hand shot out and grabbed the memory cartridge from its port. The laughter died in an instant, replaced by the click of Simon's pistol.

"Now, you got what you came for, Aden," Illyk said, "You've seen more truth about yourself than most people ever should, but we had a deal. Give us the stick, and you can walk away. Don't, and...well..."

They'd never let him walk away. They would parade him through the streets for their 'cause,' and plaster his name all over the Net. A rallying cry that would destroy the City of his dreams, replacing it with...what? *These people?* His palm sweated as it gripped the digital sum total of his life, and the secret stored within.

BOOOOOM!

The entire cabin shook, throwing Illyk and his people off balance. Lights flickered and several monitors fell off of their mounts and smashed on the bulkhead. Matteo stumbled, but seized the moment. He launched his shoulder into Simon's chest, wrenched the gun out of the man's thick hands, and rolled out of the way. The group lunged for him then stopped, facing the barrel of the gun. Matteo kept it trained on them as he crept backward to the hatch door.

"This is my life," Matteo said, holding up the cartridge, "Use your own for your 'Cause.'" He opened the hatch. Sounds of chaos spilled inside.

"Kid, you're making a mistake! Didn't you hear your old man, he said—"

Matteo interrupted Illyk with a warning shot.

"Don't follow me!" He jumped outside, slammed the hatch shut, and twisted the lever as hard as he could. As he got his bearings, he saw a column of ink-black smoke rising toward the sky. Sirens, screams, and shouting filled the air.

Spotting the opening in the path, he sprinted for it, bounding over the thick cables in the dirt. He'd almost made it to the opening when he heard the IG-6 hatch door slam open behind him. The familiar near-miss shriek of speeding bullets surrounded him. He tucked his arms and head toward his chest, then dove through the opening as rounds tore shrapnel off its metal frame.

Following the cables out was harder than he'd thought coming in. They curved down paths he hadn't seen, split into several directions. He turned a right he thought he remembered. It dead-ended into a transformer box. With the violent shouts growing louder, he looked up into the hollow framework of the facility. Started climbing.

The labyrinth of multicolored supports, braces, and beams made picking a clear direction impossible. *Gotta get distance.* The same advice the vets would give young Nines for being chased into a strange district. '*Don't worry about where you're going. Just go.*' He wove through the columns and swung over gaps. Climbed around generator hubs and over groups of sprinting workers. Before long, he realized that no one nearby was concerned about him anymore. They all ran in one direction. Matteo paused to breathe the acid out of his lungs, then climbed through to the top of the super structure.

Half of the sky toward the Border had turned black with smoke, filling his nose with the smell of burned synthetics. Then, eyes drifting downward, he saw it. No more than five miles away, a jagged, freighter-wide wound gouged through the Border in a giant 'V' shape. Glimpses of the Rasalla District beyond peeked through the billowing smoke. Matteo's jaw dropped. Paralysis gripped his body, locking him in a blank stare. *They did it. It's happening.*

"Corey! Corey, get the fuck down here, let's go!" said a female voice carried by the wind. Matteo blinked. Others had emerged all over the rooftops, towers, and landing pads of the Outer Ring. Everyone faced the Border.

"Corey!" screamed the voice that had to be Liani. Matteo scanned nearby and saw Corey's chunky silhouette climb clumsily over a catwalk ledge. The man struggled to his feet and lifted a handheld camera. But the wind carried another sound to Matteo. A kind of low background noise that got louder. And louder. And louder. Then it was a roar. Thousands of voices chanting in unison.

The wave of shock dissolved into needle-flesh all over Matteo's skin, waking his throbbing limbs. He sprang up, picked his route to Corey, and took off across the complex.

"Corey RUN!" He waived his arms then leaped to catch the next ledge. Pulled himself up to face Corey. Still filming. Matteo grabbed the camera and stared his new, dumbfounded friend in the face.

"*Rasalla is coming!*" said Matteo. As Corey opened his mouth to speak, a shockwave slammed into both of them.

BOOOOM! BOOOOM! B-BOOOOOOM!

Knocked flat on the catwalk, Corey pushed Matteo off of him. Both sat up. Columns of smoke and giant boulders of falling concrete rained down throughout the Outer Ring. Three fresh fractures had punched through the Border to join the first. Corey shouted above the ringing in Matteo's ears.

"Okay, we can go!"

As they turned for the climb down, Corey's van sidled up to the ledge, blasting them backward with exhaust. Liani at the wheel. The rear passenger hatch hissed open.

"You have five fucking seconds to get the fuck in the fucking van!" Liani shouted through the PA.

"Jesus..." Corey said.

"NOW!" she shouted. The two of them fell over each other to climb inside. Matteo barely got his foot through the door before the hatch snapped closed. The van bobbed hard and lurched up into the sky.

"About time," Liani said, "Now quit dicking around back there and get a shot of *that!*" She pointed out the window. Matteo handed the camera back to Corey, and the two of them clung to the seats to take a look.

Streaks of gunfire waived through the smoke in sweeping curves. Thousands of muzzle flashes crept along the ground in front of four smoldering gaps in the Border. Fresh explosions popped off throughout the Outer Ring. Flames licked up toward the van. Then, from the ashen plumes emerged ships. A fleet of them...all shapes and sizes. Matteo recognized names spray-painted on their hulls in giant red letters.

'Falari.'

'Alati.'

'Temple.'

'Rasalla.'

'Jogun.'

'Matteo.'

PART FIVE
Destiny

38

Calling

10 minutes earlier

THE TRAIL WENT cold at the apartment. Without the kid's RFID signal, it was a miracle they'd even tracked them this far. Especially true given the state of the nightclub manager's staff records and his 'not without a court order' attitude toward sharing them with a 'Fed.' It had taken till morning to wake up a judge to sign off on it.

The background check on the girl was another kick in Kabbard's nuts. Liani Ray. Ex-reporter for Globometro. The possibility of fulfilling his quick and quiet mandate was getting more screwed by the minute. He surveyed the craphole one-bedroom studio with exhausted eyes. Coffee left to cool in the pot. Tousled sheets and laundry scattered around the floor. Dishes crusted with red-orange food matter and glasses with cheap pink wine dried to the bottom. *Amazing that a woman lives here.* The thought made him feel old. Older.

Andreas crouched next to a sticky blue puddle on the carpet, gathering a sample with a metal pipette. The attached machine beeped.

"Got a match," Andreas said. *More great news. Here and gone again.* Kabbard was beyond tired. Like a reanimated corpse begging to go back to the void. *Chasing some kid all over the City…for what?* So Sato could suddenly grow a conscience? An old, familiar thought floated back to the surface. *'None of it means a damn thing.'* Six years down the drain.

"Any ideas about the third guy?" Kabbard asked as Nicks came out of the bedroom.

"Third guy?" Nicks asked. Kabbard wondered if these two clowns had any kind of conventional training whatsoever. Beyond online searches or friend posts on Neu.

"Ms. Ray does not own a vehicle, correct?"

"According to her file, no she doesn't," answered Andreas, "Meaning she either took the Superway home or someone gave her a ride. Had she scanned her RFID on the superway, we would have picked up the trace, so there has to be at least a third accomplice. If not more."

Smart ass.

"Contact Globometro," Kabbard said, "See if anyone quit or was fired the same time as her termination. Kirnden's a lap dog, he'll be more than happy to help."

BOOOOM! The unmistakable sound of a distant explosion cut the air. Plates and glasses throughout the apartment clinked softly together from the vibration as Kabbard felt the building sway around him. He bolted for the door.

Throughout the cramped halls, people emerged from their doors with confused looks. They started rifling through their Neural feeds, searching for any late-breaking explanation. Kabbard sprinted past them to the nearest landing deck access. Outside on the platform, several residents stood motionless, recording the images on the horizon and gabbing amongst themselves. The pale stripe of the Border wall, barely visible from this deep in the City, had been split. Divided now by a column of burning smoke. A chorus of sirens rose from the eerie, whispering quiet, echoing throughout every sector in every direction.

Kabbard scanned the deck for the Zeus. His body flushed with long-forgotten purpose as he took off running for it.

BOOOOM! BOOOOM! B-BOOOOOOM!

"Everyone back inside! BACK INSIDE!" He shouted at the top of his lungs. The people around him flinched at the voice and scurried away. With three lunging strides, he arrived at the Zeus, leaped onto the landing gear steps, and yanked the canopy release open. Andreas and Nicks caught up to him, panting with their hands on their knees.

"You guys comin'?" asked Kabbard. He dropped himself in the cockpit, strapped in, and ran through the start-up procedure, flicking switches and pulling levers in a speeding blur.

"No, sir, we can't!" shouted Andreas, "*You* can't! Sato needs us to—"

"Didn't think so! Now I have absolute faith in you Andreas, vicious little cunt that you are, to do everything Mr. Sato requires! In fact, for your first act as the new Chief of Security, pass the man a message for me!" Kabbard extended his middle finger as hard as he could as the hatch door closed and sealed. He fired the engines, grinning as he saw the blast of hot air blow Andreas and Nicks back on the deck.

The grin faded. Through the windshield, he saw tracer rounds and anti-aircraft fire streak through the sky against a backdrop of solid smoke. He couldn't believe it. He always knew it. As he squeezed the throttle to maximum, his teeth clenched. *The War...My War...* A very real pang of fear struck him, then soaked in. He had almost forgotten the taste of it. But this was different. *This is it.*

39

Hell

THE AIR WAS on fire, full of hot ash and dust. In his dulled ears, Jogun heard his choked, ragged breaths in between the thumps of cannon fire and artillery. Gun shots and whizzing near-misses sounded soft against the fuzz. The vibration of his EXO rig fell into a super-human rhythm as he leaped over concrete and twisted rebar. It was hard to trust the gear, especially since it was launching him deeper into Hell.

The flagship 'Matteo' had taken an EXO stunner blast from one of the IG-8s, sending it fishtailing into the side of a warehouse when half the crew went unconscious. The whole thing had crashed like the fist of God. They lost nineteen soldiers to the crash. Eight wounded or stunned. Eleven killed. Beaten and bloody, Jogun and the forty-three survivors had crawled out of the wreck and joined in the ground assault. He felt better with his feet on solid ground. But not much.

Kolpa, who had kept pace with Jogun's EXO rig since the crash, took a round in the face. It blew the man's skull in half. Jogun felt warm drops skitter across his arm as he planted a crushing boot on a concrete slab, pushed off, and fired three bursts from his Themis security-issue assault rifle into a pack of shooters covered behind a truck. They popped in plumes of red mist. Fighting with the Augs at full tilt felt like being trapped in a machine with a mind of its own. Good thing the machine knew what the hell it was doing..

They fought against a mix of Border Patrol, EXO first responders, and several others he didn't recognize. Crazy men in hardhats firing rivet guns, throwing explosives, and even swinging wrenches. But the T99s and Healed were organized. The top fleet pushed up into the skyline to spot and take down any party crashers, forming a perimeter in the air. The mid fleet protected the boots on the ground with its smaller carriers and Scouts making firing runs, bombing runs, and evac. And then there were the Soldiers. They had filled every fleet ship to the brim, and still thousands more streamed through the burning canyons carved through the Border. Some wore full Themis loader rigs, spraying chemical jets of fire. Others armored themselves in t-shirts, shorts, and rotten sneakers. Their roar gripped Jogun by the bones.

With the EXO Gunships locked in dogfights above, their BASE stunners wouldn't be a problem. Jogun and his battalion pressed through the streets at break-neck pace, washing over the shocked, disorganized enemy. The loader troops helped with that. Jogun saw a squad of five EXO's melt in a blast of a loader's liquid fire. A few T99s passed, laughing like stray dogs.

Jogun paused, Augmented knees suddenly weak. There were civilians everywhere, too. Cowering in alleys. Defending small shops with broom-handles and pistols. Running toward the City with their children. Jogun saw a young Nine dragging a pretty girl through a broken store window. Cut, bleeding, and screaming, she clawed at the Soldier. Jogun clenched his teeth and took two bounding strides toward them. Stumbled when a hand grabbed his shoulder.

"JO!" a voice screamed, "Get DOWN!" Rusaam pulled him into cover behind a truck, then pointed up at the sky. The 'Alati' cruised to a stop over the Outer Ring and swung its cannon around. As its rear engines heated for the counter-push, the cannon fired, burying a Scorcher round in a domed, metal hangar. The shockwave blew away what wasn't vaporized, leaving a white-hot mushroom cloud in its wake. As the rolling thunder faded to echoes, cheers filled the streets, buildings, and rooftops. Rusaam stood up, raised his rifle, let out a whoop, and ran on.

Jogun stepped back out in the street, light-headed. He searched the storefront and nearby alleys. Nothing. The girl and the T99 were gone. Sweat poured down his face as gasped for air in his scorched throat. He clenched his eyes shut and raised his face to the sun. Panic gripped his chest. *What the fuck are we doing here?!*

"Healer," said a nervous voice. Jogun's eyes flashed open. The young T99 instantly looked away despite his obvious size and strength. Under the soot and drying blood, Jogun put the squashed face to a name.

"Oki," said Jogun, "You're Oki, right?" That seemed to hook the kid up to a wall socket. Jogun sighed, remembering the younger, pinker version of this soldier that last day on the rooftops. A long time ago.

"Yeah...yeah, that's me. Doc Utu's lookin' for you. Said he got somethin' you need to see..." Oki said. Jogun looked once more at the shattered storefront, shoved the memory somewhere deep, and nodded to the boy.

"Lead the way," Jogun said, nodding. Oki made glancing eye contact. Grinned.

More joined them on the way, following behind Jogun with hard looks on young faces. The growing posse bristled with weapons as they marched over the enemy corpses littering the streets. Again, the awareness of his bizarre, growing legend tugged at him. *They'll remember this forever. If we survive.*

Finally, Oki stopped and pointed to a small cluster of soldiers grouped in a bombed out parking deck. They quickly noticed the Healer's presence, and made a space. Utu sat among them on an upturned bucket, leaning forward on his palm. Talking. A skinny, rat-like kid sat across from him. The boy wore the same kind of jumpsuit a few of the strange soldiers had worn, unzipped to the waist with a dingy undershirt plastered to his pale skin. A smearing of dark blood gathered underneath his nose. Utu turned on the bucket.

"My boy," Utu beamed as he stood up. He looked so different without his airy temple robes, clothed instead in a flak vest, canvas pants, heavy boots, and two ammo bandoliers. Somehow smaller. The doctor crossed to Jogun and wrapped his arms around him. "Come! Come! I've met someone rather interesting. Um, Illk? Illyk? I'm saying the name right, aren't I?"

Only the Doc could make friends in a war zone. The boy on the bucket nodded, careful not to move too much with so many gun barrels trained on him.

"Yes, sir, that's right."

"Very good. Illyk, I'd like you to meet Jogun. Would you be so kind as to tell him what you just told me?" Utu asked. Illyk rubbed his palms on his pant legs and cleared his throat.

"We can help you," Illyk said, "Our group."

"Help us?" Jogun asked, "A lot of your people just died tryin' to *kill* us."

"Y-your attack caught us completely by surprise," said Illyk, "We live here. We work here. After the bombs went off, we were just trying to defend ourselves, but now... Now we realize what you're trying to do."

"And what're we tryin' to do?" Jogun really wanted to hear the answer to this question. Any answer. Every spare moment to think had been consumed by it. Illyk blinked and shook his head.

"Well...Revolution...right?" Illyk said, "That's what we want, too."

Jogun squinted. Illyk had to be lying to save his skin. No one on this side of the Border could possibly want that. They lived in Utopia. The promised land. *They built the Border to keep us out. Why help tear it down?*

"Listen, the entire City runs twenty-four hours a day on the power that we kill ourselves to pump out. You'd think they'd be more grateful, but we're practically slaves, barely able to feed ourselves or our families. Tried petitioning in the beginning, but we were ignored. Tried striking, then Sato dissolved the unions. Now we Hack. Dig up every dirty secret we can get our hands on and rip it out for all to see. It helped us organize and pool our resources, but it's pretty much stopped there. No one wants to hear that their government's corrupt or that they're enslaved, and even fewer want to do something about it. Now we all have to."

This kid was hopped up on something, that was for sure. Jogun kept staring, waiting for the punchline. Illyk deflated a little.

"You need us. Cut off the City's power supply, network connections, satellite connectivity, and imports, and they're at your mercy. Then you'll need information. City layout, target selection...places to raid, buildings to hit...EXO stations...EXO *Headquarters!*"

A ripple of excitement swept through the Soldiers. A few whispered to each other. Laughed. Jogun rubbed the stubble on his chin, considering.

"And you speak for your people?"

"I do."

"We take your help, we get theirs?"

"You will."

Jogun stepped toward Illyk. The sound of the EXO servos made the kid flinch. Jogun extended his Augged hand. Cautiously, Illyk stood and accepted it.

"Put the word out," Jogun projected his voice to the Soldiers, "The workers are with us. Any of 'em try to attack, tell 'em Illyk sent you. Take care of their wounded like you'd take care of ours."

The soldiers muttered in agreement, then dispersed, running out in every direction across the debris field.

"One more thing," Illyk said after they'd gone. For some reason that Jogun didn't know, the hairs on the back of his neck stood up. "This is gonna take more than brute force. Forty million people live in Sedonia City, and right now most of 'em aren't exactly *happy* to see you guys. You go in guns blazing, trying to occupy every apartment and skyscraper you come across, then you're gonna lose. Without the people, this is pointless. We need to convince 'em we're on their side."

Jogun felt a cold finger of panic. The scope of the whole thing had just jumped by forty million. He buried the terror. Listened.

"I recently came across this story, and man, I guarantee you it's the perfect knife to shove between the administration's ribs: first-hand mem data of an assassination carried out by the state, and *proof* that a fleet of ships is being built for the rich and powerful to *ditch Earth!* Grab the best talent, suck up all the resources they can, then leave the rest of us behind to just die out!"

Jogun furrowed his brow. This guy was sounding more and more Swayed by the second. "You gonna have to forgive me if I think you're full of shit." The soldiers around him chambered rounds in their guns and pressed closer.

"C'mon, man, it's the truth! The government hacked this whistleblower guy Rindal's transport while he was trying to escape with his wife and kid! Crashed him in the Slums, and covered the whole thing up, but the kid *survived!* Recorded the whole thing on his implant! He showed up out of the blue this morning, and asked me to dig it up, but—"

"Where is he?! Is he alright?!" Jogun realized he had two clenched fistfuls of Illyk's undershirt. The kid went ghost white.

"Uh! Y-yeah man, yeah he's alright! He's not here though...ran off with the mem-stick right after you guys hit."

Jogun pulled Illyk closer with a buzzing jerk of servos.

"D–don't worry!" Illyk continued, "I'm in contact with a guy who's with him! Says we should have the kid and the data in an hour or so."

40

Evacuation

LIANI STRUGGLED TO get a grip. She had jumped in feet first and couldn't remember why...especially now that everything was on fire. Something to do with owing it to him? To everyone? All Corey's bullshit about being a conscientious objector must have gotten under her skin pretty deep. She thought she'd successfully ignored him this whole time. Her shot at making a difference had come and gone once, and she had hated herself for it ever since.

Out of the panic crept the most intense anxiety Liani had ever felt. Not helped by Sato's official declaration of a state of emergency and martial law. She tried to focus on flying Corey's clunky-ass van in a straight line. Bumper to bumper, three-level traffic snaked its way forward for miles through Sedonia's main avenues, and everywhere, SCPD cruisers patrolled the airspace. Their shiny, unused cannon attachments glinted in the sun, begging to unleash violence.

Corey may or may not have suggested several times that they switch places, but his voice was far away. Remote against the noise of her brain as it tried to make sense of everything. They hadn't flown far into the fringe districts of the Inner Ring when the emergency broadcast message appeared in her Neural.

'*ALERT: All civilian traffic is hereby grounded until further notice. Evacuations to the eastern zones will be coordinated via Superway. Any civilian vehicles in violation of the No-Fly Mandate will be considered enemy combatants.*'

"They're not screwing around..." Liani said. Corey didn't seem to hear her, absorbed in some messaging window in his Neural. He had it set in privacy mode. *So shady.*

"Hey!" she shouted, slugging Corey in the arm, "*Help me*, would you? I'm kinda freaking out here! Where do I park this thing so we don't get blown up?"

"Oh, right, uhh," he swiped the conversation away, and pulled up the local GPS, "Set it down over...there. Wellington Plaza. There's a station within walking distance."

"Great! Wellington! Whatever!" Liani pushed down on the flight sticks. The harsh, lurching dive of the van made her stomach jump into her throat. Matteo and Corey both grasped frantically for the safety handles.

"Just...take it easy, okay? We'll be fine," said Corey. Normally his caretaker act was kind of dopey and sweet. Right now she wanted to bury her fist in his face. *It's really not my fault this thing handles like a giant ham with humming bird wings! Asshole.*

"Okay," was all she said. Liani brought the van to a stuttering stop among the other randomly parked transports in the plaza.

"Not bad, Li-Li," Corey said, "thanks for not wrecking her." This time, his shit-eating grin managed to loosen some of her tangled nerves. She still shot him a dirty look. As the cockpit and passenger doors squeaked open, the three of them got a first-hand look at the chaos on the ground.

Wellington was a nowhere place on the map. Just another strip mall tier with attached housing complexes and low-rent office space. Certain kinds of people lived their whole lives in these neighborhoods. Today, all kinds clogged the sidewalks and bridges. Wealthy celebutantes on their way back to the Mesa from vacation had to carry their designer bags alongside waiters, shop owners, and cart retrieval kids from the grocery store. Even the homeless. Some had their families with them. Most others weren't so lucky, trying to dial their loved ones through jammed bandwidth in their Neurals.

Liani, Corey, and Matteo walked to the end of the queue for Wellington Station, and started the wait. Seeing everybody glued to their Neu feeds, Liani reached to touch her temple. Stopped. *Right. No unnecessary signals.* They didn't have the rings anymore, and couldn't risk any waves. She hadn't even realized she was about to turn it on. Matteo was the only one around who didn't have some kind of window up. *Now you* know *he's not from around here.*

The crash of a storefront window sent a shock through the crowd, interrupting their idle Neu browsing. Looters climbed through the broken glass, and came out with electronics, sack-fulls of credit sticks, and anything else that wasn't nailed down. The owners soon gave up trying to stop them. To her disgust, Liani saw a cop standing oblivious beside the crowd, directing traffic to the station. As she came up with the particulars of her rant, she got a better look at his face. Blond and fat-faced with an outbreak of freckles on his cheeks.

"Jesus, he can't be over eighteen!" she said.

"Early graduation from the Academy," said Corey, "Must've just dumped 'em onto the streets; all the real cops either off fighting or patrolling the skyline."

The young officer, crestfallen, seemed to hear him. Matteo scanned the crowd and surrounding sky for any sign of trouble. Liani sighed. *Poor kid.* She felt the need to say something to him. Though, she had little comfort of her own to give.

"Hey Matteo," she said as they shuffled forward with the thickening queue. Hearing his name, the boy brightened a little. "You know much about the East Side?"

He shook his head, 'No.'

"I think you'll like it. A lot of public green zones, cute little privately owned cafes and coffee shops, all kinds of theaters and museums. With so many of us going there, a lot of it will probably be open for us to check out," Liani said.

"If they let us out of whatever refugee camp the stick us in...*and if* we're not caught and branded traitors in the meantime," Corey added.

"Not helping," said Liani. Corey pressed his lips together and darkened. She rolled her eyes, feeling the dead air effect he always got when he had something else to say. Usually a lot.

"We shouldn't go East," Corey said, finally bursting.

"And there it is. Why shouldn't we go East, Corey?" It had been a long night and an even longer day. Her hands still trembled from their near-death experience in the Outer Ring. She wanted to go further than East, she wanted to head out past the coastline and Sedonia Bay to one of the outlying island chains and hide under a martini bar. But here she was. Saving the boy from out of town. Doing the 'right thing.' *Whatever the hell that means.* Liani braced herself.

"Matteo's memories. The *files*. They tie all this together," Corey dialed his voice to a whisper, "The City, the Slums, Rindal, the Revolution, everything! We have to get back to Illyk and his people. Spread the story and—"

Liani cut him off, straining to keep her voice low at a hoarse whisper.

"That's suicide! Even if it *were* possible...*Jesus!* You don't even know *what* they found in his head, you just have theories!" People around them began taking notice with sideways glances. Information drifted together in Liani's head and her green eyes went wide. "You've been talking to them...?"

"It *is* possible, Li. And we have to. This City's time has been coming for decades. You can't have so few people with so much and so many with so little. The many will always realize that they hold the real power. It's started with the Slums and it's continuing into the Outer Ring. It'll all be for nothing if we don't wake people up to the truth!"

"Truth," Matteo said, as though the word punched a fresh bruise. He hadn't said one word since the escape, seemingly lost in some corner of his brain. Liani had heard that enhanced, clear memory was a side effect of popping the Neural firewall, lasting a good while after. Like vivid, waking dreams.

"What happened to him belongs to *him*, you asshole," said Liani, "We can't force him to hand over the worst parts of his life for your crazy ideals!"

"Crazy, Liani? Really? After all we've seen? All *you've* seen?" Corey said.

"What is the truth?" asked Matteo.

"I knew it! I knew before this is over, you'd rub that in my face! I hate that I didn't act in time! I'll never forgive myself! But that doesn't change the fact that Matteo—"

"This is bigger than him, Li! Bigger than all of us!"

"*What. Is. The. TRUTH?!*" Matteo yelled into Corey's face, locking on with bloodshot eyes. The murmur of the refugees died around them. Liani took it upon herself to run damage control.

"His cousin," Liani pointed to Corey, then shouted to the crowd, "Asking if there really is a twelve-story skate park on the East Side. Move along!"

The shell-shocked throng turned back into the march as they approached the broad mouth of Wellington Station's front gates. Corey leaned to Matteo's ear. Spoke slowly.

"The Truth: your family died because a few of the highest players in the City thought your dad talked too much. He tried to warn people of what was happening to them. The price hikes. The food shortages. The fuel stoppages. The constant raids on the Slums. The congressional votes that allowed district by district to be sucked dry and left to rot. Building the Border was supposed to stop the spread of poverty, but many of us know why they *really* built it. To make people feel safe enough to die slow from debt and self-consumption. Put them to sleep to keep the money train rolling as long as possible until the wheels came off, and then bail on humanity! Look around and see it now! The wheels are *definitely* coming off."

A few in the crowd eavesdropped. Others clasped their hands over their children's ears and pushed away through the crush. Liani felt for Matteo's reaction. The boy was hard to read.

Ahead of them, armed rookie police stood in sparse guard at the turnstiles. Progress crawled along as each and every citizen was instructed to stop, scan their chip, and pass through. Liani stopped and looked at her forearm.

"Scan your chip and move along!" One of the young officers held his SMG at the hip, pointing it at them. Liani and Corey froze with Matteo watching behind them.

"NOW!" screamed the officer, glaring at them down the sight of the gun. Corey stepped in front of Liani and rolled up his sleeve. He looked at her as he scanned in. She read his face. '*No choice.*'. Liani took a deep breath and rolled up her sleeve. *It's over.*

"'Others have to see,'" Matteo intoned. Liani looked back, seeing him examine the crowd. The turnstiles. The guards. Out of nowhere, Matteo leaped up onto the scanner and hopped down on the other side. The business end of a SCPD rifle greeted him in seconds.

"Back in line and scan!" The same cop screamed in the voice of a nervous teenager trying to sound bigger and older. Matteo was a hard-eyed statue. People in the crowd noticed and started recording.

"Back in line, NOW!" Calm as water, Matteo took a step forward. Then another. And another. The shot never came. Liani's lips parted as the scene unfolded before her. She started her own recording. Down the row, a square-shouldered young man with a shock of white hair planted a foot on his turnstile and stepped over. He turned and helped a cleaning lady over the bars. Few became many. Many became all. The refugees swept over the entrance in an orderly, silent deluge. As she walked across the tile floor of the vaulted station hall, Liani saw a few of the cops shoulder their guns, join the crowd, and press toward the platform.

The previous Superway cars sped away as the empty ones arrived. The doors hissed open, and bodies piled in. They filled the seats, squeezed into corners, pressed together in the aisles, and sat on the laps of strangers. Damp, still air tensed as the far-off thump of an explosion reminded them to be afraid. Liani rested her cheek on Corey's chest. The lack of space didn't give her much of a choice, but the warm, steady throb of his heart eased the pounding jackhammer in her own. Corey's heavy paw rested on her back as the cabin chime sounded. The doors closed.

Matteo turned and caught a glimpse of the two of them as the train started to move. He quickly shied away and stared out the window at the clouds of smoke shrinking into the West. Liani sighed. *Sorry, buddy.* She lifted herself back up from Corey's embrace and reached forward to stroke the thickening stubble growing on Matteo's head. The shrug told her to stop.

"You said gettin' back to...your friends was possible. If it is," Matteo pulled a rectangular memory drive out of his vest pocket, "I wanna help."

Corey nodded, took a look around, accepted the drive, and quickly slipped it into his jacket. No one else saw.

"We don't have to go the way we came," Corey lowered his voice, "Three stops from here, there's an Inner City municipal building with a direct line down to the Foundations. Under it, too. Should have railcars down there that they use to check the grid. If we get our hands on one, Illyk's people can meet us halfway."

"Shit," Liani said, the gravity of it pressing on her, "Couldn't you just send it as an attachment or something?"

"Can't. The Net's overwhelmed. The transfer would take too long, and we'd get nailed before it even hit ten percent. A giant upload into a war zone would send up more than a few flags. Illyk has the gear and the connections, Li. They know what to do with it. We have to go."

Liani groaned to herself.

"So let's go," she said. The words weren't one second past her lips when she saw it through the window. A Fury Class transport dipped down at the rear of the train and accelerated along the curve of the connected cars. Scanning. Panic vibrated through the crowded train car as people turned to notice it. Tightly packed bodies surged in place. *Payback for rushing the gates?* The same thought seemed to occur to everyone as the train powered down to a dangling halt on the tracks.

"No, no, no, no, NO!" Matteo said as the Fury slowed, then hovered beside their train car. He squirmed in place, but couldn't budge in the crowd.

"The cops?!" Liani asked.

"Kabbard!" Matteo shouted as the doors slid open behind him. A middle-aged food vendor howled as he fell back through the open door. Liani's hand shot out, catching Matteo by the wrist before he could slip. The side hatch to the Fury swung open, revealing a suited man with a submachine gun. Against the blaring noise of the engines, a cold, clear voice spoke over the PA.

"Please remain calm. The train will resume shortly. We apologize for the inconvenience." The suited man aimed his weapon at Matteo's back and fired. Screams filled the tight compartment. Liani added her own as she watched Matteo slump forward.

"Spurs! They're just spurs!" Corey shouted to an unhearing crowd.

"Please remain calm," The voice repeated over the PA. With a blast of air, the Fury sidled in closer to the exit door. The man in the suit reached and grabbed Matteo with the gun trained on the crowd. Liani struggled to keep her grip on the boy.

"Li, you have to let him go! Li! There's nothing you can—LIANI, LET GO!" Corey shouted, wrapping a powerful arm around her stomach. Liani felt Matteo's clammy skin slip through her fingers as he was pulled from the train and onto the Fury. The suited man zip-tied Matteo's limp arms as the hatch clamped shut. The train door slid smoothly to close.

"Thank you for your cooperation," said the PA. The hum of the train rose as they ramped back up to top speed. The Fury lifted, turned, then sped off North and East. A blue, shimmering wake faded in the air behind it.

Coming to her senses in Corey's arms, Liani jerked free, spun around, and slapped him across the jaw. Corey took it without a word. His sullen gaze drifted to the floor.

"*Why?*" said Liani.

"They would have opened fire...those guys—"

Liani slapped him again.

"He trusted us! Trusted *me*! How could we just give up on him like that?"

"We haven't," Corey said meekly. He pulled the memory drive partway out of his pocket, then stowed it, "*We've* gotta finish this."

Liani turned to the window and wiped her tears away.

"It's my fault," she said, "All of this...if I had just fucking *done* something when I had the chance, it—" The sob choked her. As Corey placed a hand on her shoulder, she wrenched away. She couldn't look at him anymore.

41

Crucifixion

"NO! ABSOLUTELY NOT!" said Sato, standing behind his desk surrounded by open Neural windows. GloboMetro news feeds, scattered police reports, live satellite feeds, and several calls-waiting demanded his attention at once. And now, his assistants begged him to listen too.

"Sir, it's protocol!" his interim chief of security pleaded. With everyone else dispatched to the Inner and Outer Rings, the best Sato could find for the job was little more than a rent-a-cop receptionist. *Where the fuck is Kabbard?!*

"I'm not going down in that bunker, and that's final!" Sato roared, "I won't hide from something that isn't a threat! If you want to be useful, go find my wife and bring her here!"

The kid actually saluted then scurried out of the penthouse office into the hall. Sato's own lie rang in his ears. *Not a threat?* His subordinates needed to hear it. His strategists listening over the Neural channel needed to believe it. If they lost confidence in him, he was finished. And, as far as he could tell, the City would be too. Prescott's promise of a timely intervention was nowhere in sight.

Liquid-hot panic started to boil in his brain. He did his best to contain it.

"Apologies for the interruption, Commander, please continue," Sato said.

"Right, well...as you can see on the map, there are five passable breaches in the Border with a sixth only partially opened. We're tracking ground movement with satellite, but data is limited given that most of the insurgents aren't chipped with RFID. Estimates put their numbers at five thousand and growing, not including their Themis issue and Slum-built aircraft. We never saw 'em coming," said Commander Gorman. The graying man should have retired a decade ago, but had no savings to do so. Firing him would have caused...complications with the rank and file, so Commander he remained.

"Yes, yes, a surprise attack, I believe we're all crystal clear on that part, Commander! What is the situation on the *ground?* What's our status on a counter-attack?" Sato asked. His tongue was dry, but not for water. Several times, he put down the itch to dig the flask out of his jacket pocket. *Right…it's at home.*

"The attack totally decimated our first response EXO and Border Patrol forces, but scattered units are holding fast at the edge of the Outer Ring for now. But the perimeter is so full of gaps that… sir, my men believe that the insurgents are waiting," said Gorman.

"Are they? For what?" Sato asked.

"Don't know, but we're not sitting around to find out. We're rallying all EXO forces and any Red Gate grad who knows how to shoot for a counter-offensive within the next hour."

"SCPD on-board with this?"

"Yes, sir, we've coordinated with their HQ, and each of the precincts is arming up best they can," said Gorman. Sato's Neural called out hesitation in the Commander's wrinkled stone face. Pained hesitation.

"But…?"

"But none of them have combat experience anything *close* to this. My vets do, but they can only do so much with an army of rookies against a hostile army of seasoned killers! We need Federal help, and we need it fast," said the Commander. *No kidding.* Sato had been on the horn since the attack began, begging Congress to approve military support. After some posturing and grandstanding, the only real answer he got was 'Soon.' That meant that they would likely intervene, but the bureaucratic process would make it a trek through the mud. Off the record, his representative told him the subtext. Not many were strictly comfortable with ordering shock troops to crush an impoverished, domestic group of people. Rebels or not. The poor in their own cities might take it as a rallying cry. *All the more reason to publicly put them down!* Sato fumed. Prescott's influence would have been valuable here, but she was conspicuously absent. 'Unreachable' according to her office. Sato guessed that her Group's influence was already at work. And had been for some time.

"I've been given assurances, Commander, so that's all I can give you for now. Make do with what we have, and keep them at bay in the Outer Ring. I'll make it happen on my end," said Sato. Gorman puffed, then swallowed whatever he really wanted to say.

"Understood, sir. Now if you'll excuse me…"

"Good luck, Commander. We're counting on you," Sato said, hoping it would prod the man's sense of duty. Gorman's grim, straight mouth and hollow glare told Sato otherwise. The transmission ended.

"The rest of you, I expect strict rationing of food, water, and power in your zones. Whatever it takes," Sato said. A chorus of complaining voices filled his cochlear implant until one overpowered them all. It was Tycho Kirnden's idiot older brother, Jeffrey. The Chief Magistrate of Inner Ring Zone 5: Whitlatch.

"Rationing?!" the Magistrate's elderly jowls quivered, "It's not as if they control the *entire* Outer Ring! We're on scant supply and fuel rations as it is, and you want us to cut deeper?! Nevermind the Border, we'll have rioting in the *streets!*"

Sato flexed his fingers into claws beneath his desk, strangling the phantom of Jeffrey Kirnden's bulging throat. Z5 was upper-middle class suburbia. Its grocery stores overflowed with imported food and supplies that could last for months. Their 'scant' rations were little more than shortages of fresh produce and meat due to rising shipping costs. Sato had his doubts that the desperate housewives and self-entitled yuppies would break windows or set fire to anything anytime soon.

"I understand your concern, Jeff, but I assure you it's necessary. We don't yet know the full impact of the attack, and—"

Sato stopped, finding himself alone in the dark with his Neural screens. They hovered in space before him, but all of the feeds had dropped, leaving question mark 'Standby' icons in their place. He tapped the holo-keys and tried to reconnect. Nothing. Just a triangular sign with an exclamation point and text below it reading: '*Net Connection interrupted. Tower Signal lost.*' Sato dismissed the Neural display with a swipe of the hand, leaving him in the lavish, twilit office surrounded by dumbstruck assistants. They shuffled over to the windows. Sato followed.

The shining, day-glow brilliance of Sedonia City at dusk had been replaced by a dead landscape of shadowy monoliths. A few pairs of tiny headlights drifted silently through the structures like bioluminescent fish in the City Aquarium.

Boom. A plume of fire erupted near the Outer Ring, shining molten light on the nearby buildings. Boom—BOOM! Two more plumes burst through the dark...but these weren't at ground level. The curling clouds of red-orange rose from places up high. Amongst the skyline. *EXO headquarters?* It was off in that direction, but Sato couldn't be sure. A rock dropped in his stomach.

The whirring of turbines telegraphed the back-up generators' start-up protocol. Emergency track-lighting flickered on, filling the room with a pale orange glow. A few floors of certain buildings outside the window came to life as well. Sad, pathetic echoes of the full nighttime City. Sato pulled up his Neural display and tried to connect. *Yes!* He had a signal. As various services and apps came online, a new message notification appeared for his private line. His heart stopped. *Jada...* He exhaled slowly, then pressed the notification.

'*Andreas: Kabbard has abandoned his post, leaving me in charge. We have secured the package. En route to deliver.*'

42

Stand

AS SOON AS the lights went dark, shrieking hot rounds cut the stillness that had descended on Officer Vaughn's outpost. Two of them gouged long, deep channels in his helmet as he dropped behind cover and ducked under a shower of department store window glass. Looking to his left and right, some of his other squad-mates had gotten down in time. Others hadn't. Sergeant Keyes lay flat on his back, convulsing in an expanding pool of dark blood. Not the way Vaughn had imagined being promoted to squad leader.

Flip the switch. The thought pushed through his screaming nerves, begging him to take control. Same as it had done for each assault since the invasion started.

"We're cut off!" shouted Officer Reeve, veins popping out of his bulging, footballer neck, "Got no comms, no sat-nav, nothin'!"

Vaughn rifled through his Neural, verifying. His satellite uplink: Disconnected. Real-time battlefield intel: Gone. Soldier to soldier comms: Unavailable. *Net Connection interrupted. Tower Signal lost.* Whatever triggered the blackout also managed to screw every piece of modern communication equipment he had been trained to rely on since day one at Red Gate. Flying blind along with every EXO holed up in the pitted, cratered ruin of Dynex Valley Mall.

He raked his hand across the Neural display to close it and gripped his assault rifle. It took a few seconds to work up the courage.

"Ok-Okay!" Vaughn shouted to his squad, "On my count, pop up and let em have it! Keep small! One! Two! THREE!"

The six of them pushed themselves up to just above their cover, and opened fire. To Vaughn, it felt like they might as well be shooting paintballs at a tidal wave. Hundreds of T99s roared in the flashing darkness, sprinting through the parking lot toward the mall's first tier. *The food court...* From Vaughn's elevated position on the second tier, he knew instantly that the squads below were screwed. He shouted down to them anyway.

"FALL BACK! FALL! BACK!" He screamed at the peak of his vocal chords. Miraculously, a few soldiers seemed to obey, turning and hauling ass for the left and right escalators to the second tier.

"Reeve! Williams! Get in position and blow the escalators on my signal!" The two of them nodded and sprinted off with the thump-whine-thump-whine of their Augmentors. The food court EXOs scrambled up the steps, but few made it more than halfway before they were ripped apart by focused T99 fire. Desperate, scalding anger boiled in Vaughn's chest as he watched the last soldier burst into a cloud of red. He toggled to the flare attachment on his rifle and popped a round into the air. It shot up, then drifted down like a smoking emerald star. In the hollow seconds before the explosion, he allowed a small hope to creep in. *Maybe the good guys'll see it.* He plugged his ears and curled into a ball.

BOOM! BOOM! The detonations were small in comparison to some of their heavier ordinance, but they still shook all four tiers of the cheaply constructed strip mall. As the tremors settled, Vaughn peeked out from the shadows. The blasts had done their job, both destroying the only access routes up and spraying shrapnel and debris into the enemy. A chorus of blood-curdling agony filled the aftermath.

Sergeant Keyes had really known his stuff. In the lull before the blackout he'd had them destroy all the stairwells and elevators within the complex stores, turning each set of plaza escalators into choke-points. Some of the guys had taken to calling the place "Fort Macy's." The few ad-hoc squads they'd managed to assemble here might hold the position for some time, shooting any T99 dumb enough to climb the storefronts. It could even give reinforcements the time they needed to assemble and dispatch from HQ.

If HQ's still there.

Men from the upper tiers double-timed it down to the second, and assembled in firing teams along the perimeter wall. It was the order Vaughn would have given over the comms. Seeing them do it by themselves made him proud. As the T99s shook off the shock and charged, they ran head-long into a solid field of EXO bullets.

Even with his Neural marking targets and set to infrared, Vaughn could hardly see what he was shooting at between the muzzle flashes. A body would go down here. Another there. Entire rows of them crumpled and folded up to die. Gradually, the tsunami receded. Insane laughter and cheers picked up from the haggard band of EXOs.

"Yeah, motherfuckers! We got more where that came from!" Reeve bellowed.

"Crawl back to your mud huts, SlumFucks!"

"Alright, lock that shit up!" Vaughn shouted above them, surprised at his own voice, "Keep it tight, they're not done yet!" He almost regretted saying it when he heard the approaching hum of engines. Mid-range Scouts judging by the wasp-like undertone.

"Ours?" Reeve asked.

"COVER!" Vaughn barely had time to say. The Scout ships came in low and fast, spraying parallel lines of fifty-cal ammunition into the second tier plaza. Ten EXOs burst apart. The rest scrambled to the department store, shot out the windows, and dove through the broken glass. Bloody, beaten, and exhausted, they crouched together amongst bullet-riddled mannequins and display cases. The latest fall fashions ripped to colorful shreds.

Vaughn watched his men sink as the rhythmic pulse of chanting wafted through the store windows. Without suppressing fire, the T99s would climb the rubble in no time. He did a quick head count. *Only fourteen of us.* Fourteen against thousands. They needed a plan and they needed it now.

"On your feet and *Legs On!*" Vaughn said, "We've got about twenty seconds to get to the third tier and blow the escalators, now MOVE!" He leaped through the door first. Hesitated when he saw the Scouts accelerate out of their turns, straightening for another run. Reeve grabbed him by the collar of his flak jacket.

"Come on!" Reeve shouted. Vaughn stumbled, then matched pace to Reeve's five meter strides. The squads bounded up the escalators just as a wave of T99s climbed onto the second tier. Through blurry vision, Vaughn thought he saw the last of the EXOs make it to the third. He popped another flare.

"BLOW IT! BLOW IT!"

BOOM! The left escalator exploded, knocking Vaughn and most of the others off their feet. The right one stayed quiet. Ignored tears streamed down Vaughn's cheeks as he pushed his aching body up. Over the ringing in his ears, the screech of the incoming Scouts bore down on them. Their gatling guns spooled up. Started blasting. Ragged ditches shot through the concrete toward Vaughn. He crouched, then pushed his Augs harder than he ever had. Harder than it was safe to do. He hurtled through the window a millisecond before the ground exploded.

Waking from blackness, he found himself on a broken bed. The force of his impact must have snapped it in half. He looked around.

"HAH! You've gotta be fuckin' kidding me!" Vaughn said.

"Way to kamikaze into a Mattress Hut, you lucky bastard!" Reeve called back to him, firing from the windows with eight others. Vaughn rolled off the fractured bed. Dove into cover by the window. Peeking outside, he saw the Scouts fly off toward the horizon.

"Okay," he croaked, "Their guns are dry! Everybody up to the fourth tier!"

"Are you fucking crazy?!" one of the officers said, "There's no air cover up there, another strafing run and we'll be torn apart!"

"Won't even last *that* long if we stay here!" Vaughn pointed to right-hand escalator. T99s shoved single-file through the bodies choking the space. Others climbed the face of the third tier. Several EXOs fired into them, clogging the path with bodies. "Besides, we'll blast 'em one last time after we make it up!"

"Sounds good to me!" said Reeve, tossing aside a smoking, empty magazine then loading a fresh one.

The third tier flooded with T99s as Vaughn and his men made it to the top.

"FIRE AT WILL!" Vaughn called out as he raced for the detonators beneath a garden oak tree. The EXOs backpedaled into the top tier plaza as they fired into the escalator openings. One by one, their ammo ran out. Vaughn slid through a patch of gardenias and scooped up the detonators.

"FIRE IN THE HOLE!" He shouted as he clicked the trigger. Nothing. Tried again. Nothing. Then the sound of engines rose from the distance. *Jesus...* His weapon felt suddenly heavy in his hands as he aimed it at the T99s. He maintained discipline, firing one shot at a time, aiming for the center mass. As though it mattered now.

But as the sound approached, he knew it wasn't a Scout. Too throaty and sharp. *A Fury? No...a Zeus...* It was. There was no mistaking the knife-edged silhouette as it barreled down on the top tier. The T99s seemed to recognize it too, high-tailing it on top of each other back down the escalators. The Zeus opened fire into the enemy, cutting a red swath through their ranks. Vaughn and the EXOs lifted their guns in the air and howled.

"Okay, pick your targets, guys! Push 'em all the way back!" The group went to semi-auto, cleaning up what the Zeus missed on its first pass. But as they reached the edge of the top tier and looked down, they saw the rest of the horde. T99 soldiers supported by Outer Ring workers in weaponized loader rigs. Steel plate armored trucks with mounted machine-guns. And a mobile, deep-core laser drill platform.

The Zeus' sensors didn't register it as a weapon right away, reading only the gathering heat source at the front lines. It cost Kabbard valuable microseconds in reaction time. He sucked in a breath, held it, and rolled left to avoid the initial path of the beam as it bore a blinding hole through the night. The Zeus was fast, but not faster than light. The beam swung to follow Kabbard as he struggled to stay ahead and come about for another run.

"Arm salvo!" he shouted to the Zeus console. Four red lights appeared on the Zeus diagram in the canopy glass, followed by the 'Armed' message. As the heat of the laser drill distorted the canopy glass, Kabbard screamed.

"FIRE!"

The payload fell away just as the laser clipped the Zeus' right wing, sending Kabbard into a slow spin. He felt the shock of the explosions beneath him. Through the whirling chaos, he caught blurred glimpses of the top tier of Dynex Valley

Mall, and pulled against the spin with all the strength his ill-fitting Augs could muster. Pops rippled through the cockpit moments before impact.

FwwooooOOOOOP! BANG! The Zeus' impact foam dulled the crash, but it still felt like absolute shit. The undercarriage ground to a stop in the concrete beneath him as he struggled to dig out. Finally, the canopy blasted off the frame, deflating the foam around him. Aching from head to toe in his old, tight-fitting Augs, Kabbard climbed out to the sound of cheering.

A group of what looked like kids in EXO kit rushed over to him, jumping up and down. Kabbard noticed the glow below to his right. The salvo had found its mark, decimating the T99 ranks. He allowed a half-smile to cross his face before straightening.

"Who's in command?!" he barked.

"I-I am, sir!" said one of the rookies. *No...not rookies anymore.* These guys had really been through the ringer. Augs torn to hell, blood and dirt all over. A few had holes through them, leaving arms dangling limp. Kabbard squinted at the commanding officer. Recognized him.

"You're the 'sir,' Officer Vaughn, I'm a civilian," said Kabbard, saluting. He turned and trotted to the wreck of the Zeus. Yanked open the rear hatch.

"Weapons! Ammo! Grenades! Take what you can, sir, it's gonna be a long night!" Kabbard hefted two crates out and slid them across the ground where the EXOs tore them open. For himself, he took his favorite out of the hatch. A belt-fed fifty cal SAW. Even with his Augs on, the thing weighed more than he remembered.

"Sir—uhh...Mr. Kabbard," said Officer Vaughn, limping over, "Is HQ gone?" Kabbard chambered the first round of the ammo belt and paused. Nodded. "Saw it go up right after I left the armory."

"So that's it? There's no one else coming?"

"Governor Sato will call in the Feds, but who knows when they'll mobilize." Kabbard saw the young officer sink. *Sato probably can't even get that much done.* He cleared his throat. Spoke to Vaughn loud enough for the other men to hear. "What are your orders, sir?"

Vaughn looked back at the men. All waited, weapons at the ready.

"Okay...I want claymores set up in stages at each escalator! You six, set up along the front line! You three—" Vaughn stopped as he saw something over Kabbard's shoulder. Kabbard turned in time to see the RPG smoke trail streak toward the fourth tier.

"INCOMI—"

BOOOOM! Kabbard woke up in mid-air, just in time to feel himself crunch down into a flower bed. The Zeus had gone up in flames, and EXOs lay scattered across the tier. Only four were moving. The rest lay still in smoking heaps.

"VAUGHN!" Kabbard yelled. It sounded like he'd shouted the kid's name into a pillow. He winced at the pounding in his skull as he rolled on the gutted flower bed. Against the firey backdrop at the tier's edge, shadows climbed up.

Kabbard scanned the ground around him. Found the SAW. In an agonizing lunge, he dove for the weapon, scooped it up, and opened fire.

The shadows screamed as they fell back, but more shadows replaced them. An endless wave of devils cascading over the edge. Kabbard's Neural readout beeped at seventy-five percent ammo. Then fifty. Then twenty-five. It ran dry as they closed on him.

"COME ON!" Kabbard screamed, losing his voice. He tossed the SAW aside, and reached behind his back. Detached the two-and-a-half foot carbon steel short sword from his back panel.

"YOU WANT THIS CITY?!" Kabbard sprinted toward the gathering crowd with Augs at full tilt. "COME BLEED FOR IT!"

The honed, vibrating edge of the blade sailed through bodies as the horde converged on him. He cut one from neck to armpit. Lopped another open at the waist. Kabbard's Augs screeched with every desperate, swing, kick, elbow, and punch. Until finally a shot shattered his knee. Kabbard howled and doubled over onto his side. Hands reached in for him. He writhed, hacking a few off until he caught another round in the forearm, and a final one through the other knee. The blade dropped to the ground as the rabid throng reached underneath the former Sergeant. Heaved him up over their heads.

Kabbard screamed a curse, silencing the crowd for the briefest instant. It roared from his throat in no language and yet all languages. As the blood loss took him, it stopped.

43
Underground

WHAT LITTLE LIGHT there had been in the cavernous service tunnels suddenly vanished, leaving Corey and Liani surrounded by darkness. The tiny flood lights from their rail car kept Liani from totally freaking out, but the echoing void ahead swallowed all light after a few feet. Corey assured her they were going the right way. Their rail car was a Department of Energy personnel shuttle, designed to move freely on independent power to damaged points on the Grid. Input the Grid location you needed to access, and the uncomfortable bucket whisks you off along the edge rails. Liani shifted in the oversized harness of her hardened plastic seat.

They didn't seem to be going anywhere. Straight for a while, then a gentle curve right, then straight again, intersected at regular intervals by crossing tunnels of the same gargantuan size. The 'walls' were a jumble of wires, jutting machinery, and massive pipes. The guts of Sedonia City. *Power goes in. Shit goes out.* They passed one of the giant garbage scows, frozen in the process of being loaded for a run to the Pits. The rotting stench of it stung her sinuses.

"We're almost there," Corey said, raising his voice above the noise of the engine and rail wheels. Liani nodded without looking. She'd barely said three words to him since Matteo, but here in the dark on the way to God-knows-where...her shell cracked. The thought of opening her mouth in the sour, rushing air made her choke, but she felt the words coming anyway.

"Listen," Corey said after another turn, "Liani, I'm sorry. I wanted to save the kid too, but..."

"It's okay!" Liani blurted, "I mean...it's not 'okay,' but...I understand."

"You do?"

"Yeah, I mean it's like you said...this is bigger than us and him. We need to play our parts, and it wouldn't have done any good for us to get killed on the train...I just—" She felt his thick, warm fingers wrap around her left hand. A split second told her to pull away, but she hesitated, lingering in the moment as it dawned on her.

"Oh," she said. Her heart raced, pumping her skin with tingling blood. Her mind left, taken over by the sensation. It rippled down her arm. As she squeezed his hand she felt a spot of rolling wetness creep down her cheek. His thumb caressed a soft patch on her index finger. *Oh boy...*

"We do this last thing, and that's it," Corey said, "We go back up, head East, and wait this out."

"What if it works?" Liani asked. The question seemed to blow through him. He rubbed the sweat-laced stubble collecting on his cheeks.

"No way to know how it'll land," Corey said. The billions of possibilities rushed through Liani's head as she asked herself. *Would everything just collapse?* The City, stripped of its dysfunctional but staggeringly complex government...would everything just die? Or would people fight just as hard as the rebels to ignore it? Desperate to keep their lives the same.

"But we're journalists," a smile crossed Corey's face, "We report the truth as best we can. People make up their own minds."

The final truth of it snapped together inside her like a puzzle piece. She smiled and took a deep breath. Gave Corey's hand another squeeze. *I'm going to explode.*

Then both of them noticed it at the same time. The tunnel ahead turned left, but they could see the walls better than usual...and from farther off. A pale light shone on the networked piping and conduits on the wall, coming from an unseen source around the corner. The faint, echoing murmur of moving machinery bounced and clinked through the metal cavern.

"Must be them," Corey said, "Grid's all run by Outer Ringers, nobody else comes down here." He pushed up against his harness, arched his back, and reached behind him. Before she could ask, he pulled out a gun. A shiny pistol with a snub nose and a short handle. Corey couldn't even fit four fingers around the grip. He popped the tiny magazine out and checked the bullets.

"Uh, whoa, what the fuck are you doing? I thought you said it was *them!*" Liani said.

"It is," said Corey as he reloaded the mag and pulled back the slide, "Probably. But there *is* a war going on...I figure that makes us war correspondents. Morris Locke carried one the whole time during his coverage of the Mumbai Siege—"

"Jesus, Corey, put it away! Have you ever even fired that thing?"

Corey inspected it for the safety switch, clicked it, then put it back in his waistband.

"I...No."

"Great."

Their railcar rounded the corner, immersing them in the shocking brightness of a battery of flood lights. Two massive, flat platforms sat side-by-side on the tunnel's main center rails. *Construction and maintenance platforms...* Mechanical arms craned up thirty stories to the ceiling and walls, frozen in half-completed tasks. A Grid Station sat adjacent to the gargantuan equipment, recessed into the tunnel wall. A group of figures waited at the rail dock.

Whoever they were, they soon noticed the approaching rail car. It seemed to make them nervous. Three of the figures ducked down while two other ones stood ahead. Liani squinted.

"Corey," she said, "they have *real* guns."

"This *is* a real gun!"

"Shh!" she planted a jab in his hip. Corey composed himself and lifted his hands in the air. Liani did the same as their rail car jerked to a stop, docking at the station. Clamps snapped shut on the track, trapping them there.

"Who the hell are you?! What are you doing here!" shouted one of the two gunmen. They looked to be wearing black at first, but Liani's heart stopped as she recognized SCPD blue. *Cops.*

"We—uh...we..." Corey stammered.

"...missed the trains headed East!" Liani finished, "My...husband and I...we missed the trains and had no place else to run..."

"It's true!" Corey followed her lead, "I worked for GloboMetro News and we did a piece on Grid worker conditions a few months back...figured the tunnels would give us a shot at getting someplace safe."

The cops looked ragged. Terrified. They kept their guns trained on Liani and Corey.

"Bullshit! That were true, you'd be headed *away* from the fighting, not toward it!" said one of the cops. His dark black skin poured sweat.

"*Toward* the fighting?!" Liani shrieked at Corey without skipping a beat, "Babe, are you fucking *kidding* me?!"

"I—must have misread the map controls, excuse the shit outta me! I *am* trying to save our asses, you know! It's your fault we missed the goddamn train!" Corey fired back.

"*My* fault?!"

"SHUT UP! Both of you!" yelled the other cop. One of the other three behind the officers peeked out. A slightly chubby woman in her mid-forties, she trembled like a cornered mouse.

"Excuse me?" she said, "I think they're telling the truth."

"What?" the cop's gruff question made the woman cringe.

"I-I saw that young lady on the news last week...doing a story from our Central Hub. She was covering the ongoing negotiations between Governor Sato and Mr. Finley." Slowly, the cops lowered their weapons. Everyone relaxed as the woman continued.

"Sorry about that...Li...Liani is it? I'm Connie Dreivan, City Municipal Supervisor for this Grid sector. Governor Sato sent down everyone he could to investigate the blackout...the officers just wanted to keep us safe. I hope they didn't scare you too badly."

"That's alright," Corey said, "We'll turn around and leave you to—"

The towering mechanical arms burst into animation on the main platforms behind them. Liani felt like she leaped out of her skin. The arms retracted with a hiss of hydraulics and buzzing of servos, folding neatly into their designated places on the platforms. Liani spotted the incoming headlights first. The Virton employees and SCPD officers had no time to react.

Rapid shots echoed through the tunnel as the five citizens burst in sprays of neon blood. The flood lights underscored every detail, throwing highlights on Connie Dreivan's beaded necklace as it flew apart. Corey and Liani scrambled to click out of their harnesses and drop behind cover in the rail car. Corey took out his gun. The shooting stopped, replaced by whooping laughter.

"Hoho *man!* If I had a credit for all the times I wanted to plug one of those big city supervisor fucks!"

Liani heard the sounds of heavy boots walking on a metal platform. She tried to make herself smaller behind the fore-console of the railcar.

"Mr. Corey Burrows! Ms. Liani Ray! Come out. Come out. Wherever you are!" said one of the voices. Corey shifted to stand up, but Liani grabbed his wrist. Shook her head, 'No.'

"Let me rephrase," said the voice, "Stand up from behind that fore-console, please. Nice and slow with hands where we can see 'em."

Corey quietly put the pistol down on the floor panel of the railcar. Showed his hands. Liani did the same. Both stood gradually, careful to make no sudden moves. Facing them from the oncoming rail were three men in Virton jumpsuits and hard hats, brandishing assault rifles strapped around their shoulders. Their apparent leader was shorter and thinner than the other two. Faded tattoos curled and twisted out from the cuffs of his sleeves and the collar at his neck. He grinned as they sidled their car beside Liani and Corey's. Got a full up-and-down look at Liani.

"Ah, *there* you are...or there two of you are, at least. Where's the kid?"

"Got away from us," said Corey, "Ran off at the evacuation checkpoint when he saw SCPD guarding the place."

"SCPD..." the leader stepped out of their car and crouched beside one of the officer's bodies, "Shame to have to kill 'em. Got a brother applying to the police academy talkin' about wantin' to serve and protect. But that was before all...*this*." He rolled the body over, unclipped the officer's weapon from its strap, and picked it up. Handed it to one of the other workers.

"I've got the mem-stick in my pocket," Corey said, "I'm just gonna reach my hand in and take it out, okay?" The leader stood, pointed his weapon at Corey, then nodded. Corey held his opposite hand up as he carefully went into the pocket. Removed the memory stick. One of the workers leaned forward, took it from him, then stepped back. Used some kind of Neural interface to scan it.

"We're good," said the worker.

Loud clinking machinery broke the tension as the construction platforms undocked themselves and started moving along the main center rails. Their floodlights cut off as they crept away into the darkness of the tunnel where Liani and Corey had come from. Other lights appeared down the tunnel to the West, accompanied by the sounds of countless voices.

Two new platforms emerged from the darkness. Each carried a small army. Some of the figures wore the same kind of Virton jumpsuits or operated hulking Virton repair mechs. Others were clearly T99s to Liani's eyes, but there was something different about them. *They're wearing EXO gear!* Both platforms passed then turned around the bend in the track, disappearing. Corey and Liani looked at each other, wide-eyed.

"Hmmm," the leader said, scratching his pitted face, "I'd say that complicates things. See, we might have sent you on your way, but now...you've seen a little more than you should've. Can't have you running back East telling stories about that, now can we? Kill the guy. Take the girl."

One of the men reached into their railcar for Liani and grabbed her under the arm.

"Hey, fucking let go of me!" she shouted. Thick fingernails gouged her skin as she tried to pull away. Corey lunged to push him off, but caught a heavy elbow to the temple, knocking him to the floor of the rail car.

"Easy, lover boy," said the leader, "we'll take real good care of your pretty little Inner Ring lady-friend here—"

POP! POP! Corey got two shots off before the pistol jammed. One tore through the cheekbone of Liani's attacker and the other pierced the leader's tattooed throat. As they collapsed, the third gunman turned on Corey.

"NO!" Liani grabbed her attacker's sub-machine gun, turned it on the third man, and sprayed until he collapsed in a heap. The tunnel fell to hollow silence. She dropped the gun and rushed to Corey. He had slumped on the floor of the rail car. Three weeping holes crossed from his shoulder to his hip. Corey opened his mouth to speak. No sound came out. Liani pressed her hands and forearms down on the wounds.

"We'll get you some help...we'll take the rail car and...and..."

Corey raised his shaking hand and interlaced his fingers with hers. The look in his eyes told her a simple 'no.'

"You *brat!*" she said, laugh-crying, "You just *had* to play hero and save the girl, didn't you?" That same goofy grin crossed his red lips.

"Love y-you...Li-Li..." it barely came out a whisper, but she heard it. Corey's grin faded. His muscles slackened.

"No! Uh-uh!" Liani howled, echoing through the tunnel. She took him under the arms and pulled with everything she had. More than she had. Corey groaned at the pressure on his shoulder wound, but didn't budge as she put him in the rail car seat and closed the harness. *The docking clamps!* She stepped over the bodies in the workers' rail car, hopped up on the deck, and rushed to the console. Hit the big green button marked 'Release.' The clamps clinked loudly as they folded away. She hopped back in the workers' rail car. Shrieked when a hand grabbed her foot.

"P-p-leassse—" the man hissed. It was the one shot through the cheek. The bullet must have gone through his sinuses. Liani snatched up an SMG and aimed the barrel at his broken face. Started to squeeze the trigger.

"Nguh—Ngd—Ndoctor," he said, coughing blood. She lowered the weapon and scanned the floor. Beside the dead worker, she found the memory stick and snatched it up. Climbed back into her rail car beside Corey. He wasn't moving. Wasn't breathing. A trickle of blood dripped down the side of his seat. Liani pinched her eyes shut, letting the tears roll down her cheeks.

"Hell yes, we're gonna find a doctor," she said, her heart gone from the words, "And you're gonna tell me where to find one."

44

Enemies

"ABOUT FOUR DAYS," said the chief engineer. *Four days?* Jogun could hardly believe it. The tanks in the fusion plant were over twenty stories high...and there were hundreds of them. The City must have been running week-to-week on shipments from Themis. *How could they let things get this bad?* All his life he'd watched the City glowing silently beyond the Border. The exact same brilliance each and every night. Powerful. Ever-lasting. It had looked as if it were made by God to light Heaven and Earth. *'Like us and the suns, nothing lasts forever.'*

He had tried to look hard and calculating during his tour of the plant, but fear churned in his gut. The place was huge...huge and crazy complicated. The container-lined walls reached up forty stories to the domed ceiling, and groups of big, round 'reactor chambers' sat in the center of the floor. The engineer rattled on about deuter-something-reactions this and neutron-something-damage that. Jogun hated feeling so stupid. His Themis programming as a Crawler tech had been so specific, limiting him to geology, lunar physics, and basic maintenance. *If only Matteo was here...he'd have all this stuff on lock.*

"If four days is what we got, then that's what we work with," Jogun said, "Just gotta be careful where we use it. The teams'll be in place by midday tomorrow, so we gotta get movin' on prep for the main push." He looked up at the tanks as though he were deep in thought. Really, he just meant to hide the fear. He had enough of his own to deal with, no sense in spreading it around.

"And after, sir? How do you plan to occupy a modern MegaCity without power?" asked the engineer. *Good question, asshole.* The answer in his heart told him that they would just leave. With their enemy crippled, they would go back to Rasalla and live in peace. But the hunger in his soldiers' eyes told him the truth. Same as Matteo, they had wanted the City and its treasures for their whole lives. They'd never leave willingly.

"Oh, we *got* power. All that the Righteous need. The Power of God, my friend," Jogun said, loud enough for his T99 escorts to hear. It didn't feel right coming out of his mouth. Shouts from the entrance bounced through the warehouse, along with the sounds of rattling ammo belts and thumping footsteps. Jogun tensed as his men turned on the noise with their rifles ready. They stood in front of him.

Just a group of T99 runners. They were smiling...laughing. Jogun's men lowered their weapons as the runners trotted to a stop.

"Oki..." Jogun said, "Man, you gotta stop haulin' ass into places unannounced!"

"Jo—!" Oki panted as he tried to talk, "Whe—We got 'im!"

Cold goosebumps rippled down Jogun's neck, shoulders, arms, and back. *Matteo?*

"Whoa, calm down man, got who?" Jogun asked, trying to keep calm himself.

"K-Kabbard! Sergeant motherfuckin' *Kabbard*, the Robo-Pig Himself! Got him trussed up in a bodega down the street!" said Oki. Jogun sank a little. Then, from a dark place deep inside, the rage eclipsed everything.

"Show me."

Jogun had to use his Augs to keep up with the young Nine. The ape-like soldier bounded ahead through the technological maze of Outer Ring streets and alleys, calling out the news to anybody nearby. By the time they reached the ruined shopping center, they had gathered an army.

The crowd parted in the ground-floor mall plaza to allow the Healer and his men to pass. Jogun ignored the whispers as he walked uncomfortably through ashen burns and dried blood on the concrete. His fingers twitched as he imagined wrapping them around Kabbard's throat. But the man had to answer a question first.

Armed T99 Black Hoods stood in front of a glass doorway with sign above it reading 'Utopi-Mart.' The guards stood aside as the door slid open for Oki and Jogun. A chirping electronic chime greeted them.

Oki led him past the freshly emptied shelves to the back storeroom. They had turned its reinforced concrete walls and cold laminated floors into a cell. Bodies of EXOs and SCPD lined the edges of the room, facing Black Hoods in the center as they were tended by the Blue Ladies. All were wounded. Some had died. The EXOs' legs were bare, tugging at Jogun's memory. Outside, he'd seen, but not noticed, several Nines with shiny new Augs on their legs. He flexed his own, feeling the new familiarity of the servos' soft hum.

Then there he was. Sergeant Kabbard...or at least some withered shell of him. He sat flat-legged in the corner with two reddish black lumps of stained, twisted fabric at his knees. Arms tied behind his back. A wrinkled old Blue Lady knelt beside him, dabbing the wounds. Kabbard's head drooped forward, his tightly groomed hair matted and stained. Something foul dripped from it to his soaked suit pants. *They pissed on him.* The urge to choke, let alone touch this broken creature dimmed a little. Still, the question burned. Jogun dismissed the Blue Ladies with a wave, then a bow. Spoke once they'd gone.

"Douse him," Jogun said. One of the Black Hoods picked up a metal bucket of water and flung the contents at Kabbard. The man jerked back and coughed. Shook his head. Jogun stood over him, clutching a pistol.

"Where is he?" asked Jogun. Kabbard blinked in the cold, buzzing light of the storeroom and looked up at him. Started laughing. A deep chuckle at first that grew sharper and louder, empty of any real humor.

"*You* again..." Kabbard said, stopping as he saw the Augmentors. Jogun didn't move a muscle.

"Everyone out," said Jogun. The Black Hoods nodded and obeyed. Oki lingered.

"Hey man, you sure you want to—"

"OUT!"

Oki sucked his teeth and walked to the door, kicking an EXO's bloody stump of a foot on the way. The man yelled in pain as Oki stepped out. Jogun crouched beside the Sergeant.

"Where did you take him?" Jogun asked. Kabbard stared into him. Gray eyes as still as a dead man's.

"Take who?"

Jogun sucked in a breath and swung the pistol hard, cracking Kabbard across the jaw. Blood spattered the smooth concrete wall.

"WHERE?!"

Kabbard winced, worked his tongue against his inner cheek, then spat a glob of red on the floor at Jogun's feet. Said nothing. A moan from beside them answered instead. A young EXO stirred on the floor. Burns and char marks covered much of his body. Black blood seeped from both his nose and a gash in his forehead.

"Sir...?" the officer squinted and tried to push his way up. Like some kind of old blind man back in the Temple. Jogun glared at Kabbard.

"Maybe I'll ask *him*. 'Scuse me, officer..." he read the name stitched into the blackened uniform, "'Vaughn!' Do *you* know where this man right here took my baby brother?" Jogun trained his gun barrel on Vaughn's exposed right knee. Only pitiful moans escaped the officer's lips. Jogun kept his eyes locked on Kabbard's.

"Do you. Know where. *This* man. Took my baby brother...?" Jogun gnashed his teeth together as tears welled in his eyes.

"Wha—?" Vaughn said.

BANG! Vaughn's kneecap shattered in a spray of bone and blood. The man screamed, then passed out. Kabbard lunged forward, forgetting his own knees. Added his own scream. Jogun slapped him in the face. Fighting down the urge to retch, Jogun pointed the gun at Vaughn's other leg.

"*Where.*"

Kabbard panted in ragged gasps through his teeth. He wasn't laughing any-more. He glared up at Jogun again. Squinted.

"Son of a bitch...I remember you...You're the Slum-Fuck I put away for murdering Kathy Roland. Mousey little house-wife type. Real pretty. Didn't deserve to go out like that, but *you* motherfuckers," Kabbard glanced at Vaughn's leg wound, "You put her down like a dog. And *now* you want your '*baby brother.*' Just what in the *hell* makes you think you deserve something like family?"

It felt like a shotgun blast to the gut. Stitches that closed the long hidden wound ripped apart, spilling the terrible memory inside. The night of the storm. The cold, wet dark of the apartment. Mama dead and bloody on the floor. *And him. Dad.* The man who was supposed to love and protect them. The man who ordered Mama not to have any more kids, but still raped her when he felt like it. Standing out on the rain-soaked balcony with a baby in his arms. Jogun felt the gun in his hand now as he did then. Heavy. Slippery from sweat. The tug of his finger against the trigger, helpless as his father dropped the baby over the side.

But Matteo...*The Gift.* His second chance. Even though he didn't deserve it. That meant it was a gift of grace...not a reward. *A gift from God.* He would do right by God and protect his gift. Didn't matter what it cost. He stood, walked over to Vaughn, and pressed the gun barrel to the officer's forehead. Watched as Kabbard seethed in the corner.

"You son of a bitch...SON OF A BITCH!" Kabbard howled. Jogun lifted the gun and chambered a round. Inhaled sharply as he pushed the barrel harder into Vaughn's head.

"NO! Stop..." Kabbard said, gathering the will to say it, "*Fuck* Sato..."

Jogun waited, feeling the terrible moment. Fear of the answer suddenly choked him.

"They've probably got him by now. Top floor of the tallest building in the City. Can't miss it," said Kabbard. Jogun stood, holstered the pistol, and stormed to the door.

"Probably dead now though," Kabbard snickered. Jogun paused. Took the gun back out.

"At least...I hope he is," said Kabbard. Jogun crossed to him in a heartbeat and jammed the pistol barrel into the man's sneering skull. Kabbard pushed into it.

"Go ahead, go on, DO IT! Do it, you fucking piece of shit, this is what you are, this is what you do, DO IT!"

The trigger squeaked as Jogun squeezed harder and harder, waiting for the pop.

"You tell Governor Sato, I'll see him in Hell," said Kabbard.

In the space of three breaths, Jogun stopped. He jerked the gun to the side and buried three rounds in the wall. Kabbard looked up, confused.

"Maybe that *is* where you're goin'," Jogun said, standing up, "Or maybe that's where you are." He holstered the gun. The Black Hoods rushed in, having heard the shots. Jogun turned and pushed through them.

"Prep one of the Scouts," he said.

45

Birthright

MATTEO DROWNED IN the space between sleep and consciousness. The memories of his life whipped through him with no sense of order or time. His capture on the Superway replayed in front of him, teasing his sense of the present enough to pull him awake. Harness straps held him in a hard plastic seat. Two figures sat with their backs to him in the cockpit ahead. The image blurred as the stern, suited men morphed into Alan and Patricia. *Mom and Dad.*

Everything snapped to high-detail. The smell of plastic and his mother's orange-cream perfume in the transport cabin. The sound of their voices murmuring to one another...getting louder. He felt his soft blanket brush smoothly over his delicate skin. Then it all went wrong. *So loud.* His entire world started shaking as he cried from the car-seat. Mom's body went limp. His Dad's face reflected in the glass. '*...remember forever...we'll always love you!*'

The hatch opened beside him and, for a moment, Jogun stood there. But as his young older brother climbed in to take him home, it transformed into one of Kabbard's men. The bug-eyed blonde one with the cold straight face.

This is real! He jumped away inside, then realized his body didn't follow. Fuzzy dullness buried all his limbs in thousand-ton cotton. The blonde went to work on the strap buckles, tossed them aside, then pulled Matteo out of the seat by the arms.

"At fuckin' last!" one of them said.

"Seriously," said the other.

Matteo could only watch as his body flopped to the ground. Pain shot through him, giving his limbs a sickening jolt. They woke up in waves. Suddenly he could move his head. His legs and feet dragged on some kind of landing pad. As he looked around, he realized something was off. No buildings anywhere to the left or right. Not behind him either. Only the dead, navy sky of pre-dawn, stretching on forever, and a thin tower poking up into the sky from the pad. A tiny red dot blinked at its peak. The same light that had lulled him to sleep on more nights than he could count. *Sedonia Tower!* The only building tall enough to stand above all the others.

They dragged his waking body down a curving ramp to a steel plated door, and buzzed their way in. Matteo put weight on his feet, but they were kicked out from under him.

"No sir, no more running for you," said the blonde. The two flights of stairs beat his feet and shins so badly that he let himself go limp at the bottom. *Better if they think I can't move, anyway...*

He was brought to a wide open room off the hallway. High, bright ceilings. Men and women wearing what had once been neat, rigid clothes paced through the arrangements of sleek furniture, babbling into their Neurals. Panic hung rotten in the air as Matteo listened and kept still.

"Well can you confirm or can't you? I've already got reports of three Inner Ring attacks in Shibuya, Montos, and The Primaeum, I need to know if you're telling me about one of those, or a new one! You're in *Whitlatch...?*—Hey, we got another sighting in Whitlatch! Insurgents coming up from the municipal buildings!"

"...flyby has verified, EXO HQ has been destroyed, and our assets on the ground are dropping fast!"

"This is Governor Sato! All patrol birds in the air, deviate to intercept the Inner City targets, repeat, deviate to intercept Inner City targets!— Christ, where are the fucking Feds?! Somebody try Prescott agai—" The man stopped as Matteo was deposited in front of the broad, crescent moon desk. The rest of the room stopped with him. Stared.

Matteo looked up wearily and squinted to study the man's expression. It read like a leather-bound book. Wide-eyed. Thin mouth gaped. Thick chin quivering slightly. *But why?* Even with his fine-tuned memory, Matteo had never seen this person before. But this 'Governor Sato' looked like he'd seen a ghost.

"Sir?" said one of Matteo's handlers.

"Uhh...umm...Nicks, Andreas...great job guys...lock him down in the suite for now, I—my City is burning," Sato said.

"Yes sir." Matteo heard them groan as they turned around.

"Alright, time to walk," said the squat, short-haired one called Nicks, "Tired of carrying your ass."

They picked Matteo up and set him down on stinging feet. He could carry his weight again. The office revved back to life with phone calls and voice commands as he was escorted to the door. But a woman entered before they could leave. Middle-aged, full-figured, and beautiful, with smoke-colored hair flowing over the back of her summer dress.

"Enota!" she called into the room. The Governor raced around the edge of his desk, pushed past a few assistants, and took her in his arms.

"Oh thank God, Jada!" Sato said, "When I heard about Shibuya—"

"Shhh...I'm here. I'm safe. And you need to get back to—Who is this?" she asked, looking Matteo over. Something warm and reassuring about her face...the concern written there. Sato seemed to tip off balance.

"Oh—this...this is—"

"Aden," Matteo said, "My name is Aden." He felt Nicks and Andreas tighten their grip, but they stopped short of showing it.

"Aden..." said Jada. The sweet cream color drained from her expression as she turned to Sato, "...Rindal?"

Sato's stunned silence seemed to be enough of an answer for her. She touched her fingers to her lips as tears welled in her eyes.

"My poor baby!" she said, leaning in to embrace him. Andreas stopped her with a firm hand. Shook his head.

"Wha—? What's going on here...Enota?" Jada asked. Matteo looked for an answer too, starving for the pieces he was clearly missing.

"Jada I...I can't right now," Sato said.

"You'd damn well better *try!*" said Jada, unmoved. Sounds of distant combat chattered in the stillness.

"I—we found him—"

One of Sato's aides jumped out of his seat.

"Sir! Just got a line from Prescott, the military is mobilizing!"

A cheer ripped through the office. People hugged each other. Some kissed. Sato drooped, puffing a leaden sigh.

"Package our intel and set up the Feed! I want them patched through to commanding officers on the ground ASAP!" His smile dimmed as he turned back to Jada, "I'm sorry, there's—"

"Go," she said, "The City needs you...but we're far from finished here."

Jada followed behind with her escort as Andreas and Nicks pulled Matteo down the arched corridor. Dim, yellow light fixtures glowed on the walls, casting strange reflections as they walked. Matteo twisted his head back to steal another glimpse of Jada, but a sharp tug from Andreas and a hidden gun barrel in his ribs told him to try again later. *They won't do much while she's around...* The main threads of a plan wove together in his mind as he got to the elevators.

"Where are you taking him?" Jada asked. Andreas punched a button on the wall panel and stared at the closed metal doors. "Uh huh, okay..." said Jada as she squeezed in between them and the doors. They opened behind her, "Think about laying hands on me again. Think real hard."

"The Exec Suite," Andreas finally said.

"Thank you," Jada said. She nodded and stepped aside. Matteo watched her disappear behind the closing metal slabs, along with his flickering hope for escape.

When the elevator opened again, Andreas pushed Matteo out into a small, circular room with three carved wooden doors. High-backed chairs with curving animal legs stood guard next to each of them. Matteo's boots clomped loudly on the marble floor as he stumbled to right himself.

"So he gets locked up in one of *these?* Really?" asked Nicks.

"That's what the man said," Andreas crossed to the center door and scanned his forearm on the side panel. It beeped. The door jarred with a soft click and Nicks pushed it open. He whistled as the lights came on inside.

The room was enormous. Big enough to house at least twelve Rasalla families and their relatives. The floor stepped down in plush carpeted terraces to a central area where high arched windows pushed up the ceiling. Couches, recliners, foot rests, and all other kinds of inviting, obese furniture sat waiting throughout the room in pleasing, flowing patterns. Matteo recognized a bar off in one corner with an array of handsome stools and back-lit bottles of liquor on the wall. A kitchen in another with pristine, high-end versions of appliances he'd seen dropped from Pit Scows. And there were other doors set in the perimeter walls. *MORE rooms...?* No fantasy he'd had on the roof of the rusted family apartment ever came close to this.

A fist rammed into his stomach, knocking the breath out of him. Matteo doubled over on the floor, coughing. His hands sank into the silky, fat threads of the carpet.

"Don't get too comfortable, shithead," said Nicks, cracking meaty knuckles. Matteo fought for breath as the two goons walked out of the room and slammed the door. His airway winked open with each sucking gasp, gradually making the familiar sound. He gnashed his teeth together. Forced himself to sit back on his heels.

The room was dead quiet. Against the ringing in his ears and wheezing in his throat, his every move made some kind of god awful noise. The City clothes chafed him. He tore his puffy white vest off and flung it aside, followed by each of his skin-tight long sleeves. The boots weighed heavy on his legs. He clawed at the buckles and yanked them off one by one, freeing his calloused bare feet. *Better.* He winced as he rocked forward to stand.

The thought of looking for a weapon crossed his mind. There had to be one somewhere. A knife from the kitchen, maybe, to sink into Nicks' skull. But as he looked around, feeling the carpet caress his toes, his body begged him to relax. To take it in. He limped down the carpeted terraces to the common area and ran his rough fingers over the supple fabric of a couch. The cushion swallowed his hand as he pressed into it. On the low glass coffee table, a colorful mutant plant reached out of a silver vase. He took one of its velvet red and yellow petals between his thumb and forefinger. Smelled the sweet, heady fragrance. It gave him a fleeting buzz.

Boom. The low thud vibrated the still, clean air. Matteo looked to the arched bay window and saw a burst of hot orange rise into the twilit sky. As it faded, another rose. Fainter and further away to the left. Boom. The distant sound caught up with it. Matteo felt sick as he took a step toward the window, the floral perfume still in his nose.

Boom. B-boom...

He reached his reflection in the crystal glass, cupped his hands against it, and looked through. Fires. Great twisting columns of blackening fire swirled up to the sky from places throughout the dark, vertical landscape of Sedonia City. The tiny point-lights of ships darted through the structures, firing bursts of white streaks. A few ships popped in flashes of light as they crashed into glass and steel. Matteo staggered away from the window. The reflection of his heavenly prison surrounded him, broken by the molten clouds rising in the distance. His hands balled into fists.

He picked up the silver vase, dashed the flowers over the couches, and threw it crashing through the coffee table. Shards of glass dug into the soles of his feet as he grabbed the legs of a plush white chair. Flipped it over backwards.

"It's not real!" he screamed as he picked up a slender standing lamp, "*None* of it's *fucking real!*" He turned and threw it at the bay window. It bounced harmlessly off, leaving a pathetic scuff mark on the safety glass. In midstep to try and use the lamp as a club, Matteo heard voices from outside. Shouting.

Matteo sprang up and sprinted to the kitchen, tracking bloody footprints behind him. As the main door beeped open he spotted a wooden block of knives, yanked out the biggest one, and ducked behind the counter, slipping in his own wet tracks. The wheezing betrayed his struggle to keep quiet.

"Aden?" a woman's voice called out. *Jada...* His grip on the knife handle loosened, but he stayed down, listening in breathless silence.

"Oh my God," she said.

"Tried to tell you, ma'am, the kid's dangerous! You shouldn't—"

"Get out. Both of you."

"Ma'am, your safety is—"

"You would have to drag me out," she said, "Making my safety a moot point. So I'll repeat. Get. Out."

A silent moment passed. Then the door shut.

"It's just you and me now," said Jada, "I brought some food...unless you've found something in the kitchen."

Matteo tensed, seeing the bloody trail he'd left on the floor. He leaned slowly out from behind the counter. Saw Jada with her back turned, setting a steaming tray on a long, glass table. Rich smells of sweet meat and exotic spices drifted over to him. He got up, hesitated, then set the knife down on the counter.

"Come. Have a seat with me," she said, pulling out a chair for him. The tray made his mouth water. A slab of thick, brown meat sat in its juices on a square plate, flanked by steaming green veggies and a soft, fluffy pile of something he'd never seen.

"Catering leftovers, I'm afraid...but I've brought them back to life as best I could. Hanger steak, green beans, and mashed potatoes."

When he didn't move, she sat in the chair adjacent and began cutting the steak into bite-size chunks. She stuck a fork in one and took a bite.

"See?" she said, smiling with her mouth full, "Delicious."

Matteo couldn't help but smile back. He slowly crossed to the table. Sat down. His eyes darted between Jada and the plate of food.

"Go ahead," said Jada. He reached forward and picked up a piece of steak with his fingers. Brought it slowly to his lips. As he bit down, salty-sweet juice flooded his mouth. Hunger took over everything. He dug in. Jada smiled wide as his cheeks filled to bursting.

"Not much to eat in Rasalla, is there?" she asked. He froze mid-mouthful. Swallowed hard.

"No—" he coughed, "No, ma'am..." She handed him a glass of pure clear water. He gulped it down.

"I can't begin to imagine what it was like for you. All those years...I'm so sorry, baby," she said, "We searched everywhere after the crash. Even after they told us all three of your family's chips had been disabled by the...by the people who found you."

Feeling the ghost of the alien object under the flesh of his forearm, Matteo put down the empty glass. His hands retreated from the table to his lap.

"Why?" he asked, looking up into the strange woman's eyes. The blue-green circles trembled as they looked back at him. Drops filled and crept down her cheeks.

"Sweety, I'm your Godmother. Enota, the man you met upstairs, he's your Godfather. Your parents... When your mother, Patty, was pregnant with you, she and your father asked us to be your Godparents. To take care of you if anything should ever happen to them."

Boom. Boom. The far off explosions rippled gently through the windows. Jada saw his glance shift to the skyline. She reached forward and placed her soft, smooth hand on his.

"It's okay," she said, "This'll all be over when the military gets here. In the meantime, you're safe here with us...safe for the rest of your *life*... If you want."

His heart ached as the words rolled in his head. He shifted his gaze around the room. This palace in the sky. From it, he would never have to look up again. He could read every magazine, every book. Ride the Superway...hell...buy his own flying car. Date beautiful women and drink at the most exclusive clubs. Eat the best food in the world at any time of day and never go to bed hungry again. *And leave it all behind one day. Flyin' to the stars on the Narayana.*

Then there was the blood on the floor. A stark red path leading to the rich meal in front of him...leading to the woman who would be his mother. The dark memories rushed in like tear gas, flipping the hot meal in his belly. He jerked his hand away from Jada's and stood up. Jada sighed.

"Aden..."

BOOM! Sedonia Tower shook beneath their feet. Spiderweb cracks shocked through the massive bay windows as Jada screamed. Matteo dropped to the floor, then scrambled to cover behind the kitchen counter. There, he remembered Jada. Before he could get up to help her, the door swung open and Andreas and Nicks ran inside.

"Mrs. Sato!" Andreas shouted.

"We're here!" Jada answered. Andreas scanned the room with his gun drawn as Nicks collected her.

"Come with us, ma'am, we've gotta get you down to the bunker with the others!" said Nicks.

Jada pulled away.

"Not without Aden! He's family, he's coming too!" she yelled in Nicks' face.

"Forgive me, ma'am," Nicks stooped then picked Jada up over his shoulder. She screamed. Cried. Spat curses as she buried her fists and elbows into his back. Nicks cringed, but kept moving to the door. Andreas covered their exit, pointing his pistol wherever he looked.

"ADEN! ADE—!" The door slammed shut behind them. Matteo grabbed the knife and leaned out of cover. Andreas stalked the room.

"Come on out, you piece of shit," Andreas said, "I'm not gonna hurt you..."

Matteo heard lying curl in the man's voice. He stayed put.

"Mr. Sato says he needs you...told us to keep you...SAFE!" Andreas darted around the counter where the blood trail stopped. Matteo had crawled to the opposite side.

"You know what? I say fuck that. You're one of *them!* Bullshit Rasalla garbage...you deserve to burn like all the rest of them. With Sato on the way out, I made a little call...and Ms. Prescott's gonna pay me a *fortune* to kill you. Maybe even a couple seats on the—-AAHHHH!"

Matteo slashed the back of Andreas' leg, sending the man crashing to the floor. A quick elbow to the goon's outstretched arm released the gun. Matteo grabbed it. Pointed it right between Andreas' shifty, terrified eyes. Rasalla burned white-hot in Matteo's heart.

"H-hey man...you know I didn't mean all that, right?"

"Men like you deserve to die for what you do to us," said Matteo, leaning in close to Andreas, "But I already broke my promise once." Matteo lifted the gun and brought the butt down on Andreas' temple, knocking him out cold.

"I won't break it again."

Matteo got to his feet and limped through the door to the elevator. No buttons. Just some kind of flat scanner panel. He tried pressing his thumb to it as Andreas had done, but it flashed red instead of green. *Dead end.* He raced back into the room and looked around. They wouldn't have locked him in if there were another exit. *But maybe I could make one...* He remembered the cracked

windows and ran over to one. Looked down. Not far below this floor, there was
a landing. Some kind of a garden patio with tables and chairs.

He found his boots, slipped them over his stinging feet, then found the
knife. The smooth underskin of his forearm looked up at him. He probed it
with a finger. The edges of the thing underneath blurred through the skin and
muscle. It carried the truth. All that he was meant to be, all that was stolen from
him, and and all that he became. But so long as it was there, he would be hunted.
People around him would die. There could be no life in the clouds or the stars,
no matter how much he had dreamed about it. He blinked back tears.

But here he felt the familiar pull. The deep Knowing that had always stayed
with him, even when hope had gone.. Utu's lesson drifted up from his childhood.
'It is up to you to follow it or not.'

Okay...

Matteo aimed the knife-tip to the left of the veins he could see. He took
a deep breath. Pushed the point in. Fire shot up his arm to his shoulder as he
widened the cut. Stopped. He almost blacked out as he reached in. Blood gushed
out onto his fingers and hand and ran down his elbow, dripping to form a puddle
on the floor. Slowly, he pressed the buried square of plastic toward the wound.

He felt an electric shudder ripple through him as the chip popped out in
his fingers. It was a clear blue square with gold circuitry crawling over its surface
in minute, maze-like patterns. *Like a Falari jewel...* Staring deep into it, Matteo
swooned. His entire arm glistened red in the clean white lights of the suite. He
picked up one of his black discarded sleeves and wrapped it around his arm,
pulling tight. The blood soaked through, but the fabric seemed to hold.

Matteo raised his light head and looked at the cracked bay window. Breathing
deep into his belly, he took out the gun. Aimed. Exhaled. Fired. The glass shattered in an explosion of shards and dust, sucked out into the high, thin air. He
walked to the opening. Took out the chip.

"I'll always remember," Matteo promised. He stretched his arm over the
edge and dropped the chip. Watched it plummet out of sight.

Without the glass, the drop to the landing looked a lot further. But the
side of the tower sloped down to the garden, and the windows looked smooth
enough. He ran to the couch, grabbed a fat cushion, and returned to the edge. His
heart pounded in his chest.

One. Two. THREE!

46

Judgement

Moments Earlier

THE EXO IG-8 came out of nowhere, screaming between the smoky, sleeping buildings like a fusion-powered nightmare. It locked onto Jogun's hover-wake and gained on him in a matter of seconds. He knew the ride in had been too smooth. He had seen shadows and fire moving in every hellish alley and opening. It was almost a relief to see one come to life.

As he punched the throttle, Jogun's modded Scout shot through a lane between skyscrapers and came out over the Center Ring. 'The Mesa,' Illyk's people called it. Jogun's sweat-slick hands quivered on the flight controls as the sheer size of the place surrounded him. A barrage of sixty cal rounds smacked into his hull. He dodged right. Swerved left and down. The black, beetle-shaped IG-8 kept on him, taking its toll on the Scout's makeshift armor plating. Jogun looked up at the shining, golden tower top piercing the morning sky. *Gotta get crazy...*

He faked right then yanked the wheel back, launching the Scout skyward as hard as it would go. His vision turned red as immense pressure drove him into the seat. He held on through the loop. Gravity shifted and suddenly he was looking down at the IG-8 and the sprawling Mesa below it. Approaching way too fast. *Fire! FIRE!* His thumbs fumbled at the safety release, then found the buttons. His guns spooled up then belched fire. The stream of bullets missed the IG-8 then swept closer. Closer. *HIT!*

Yet as it came apart below him, the enemy ship launched heatseekers. One made it out of the flames. Jogun plunged through the separating fireball, then pulled up for the tower. The missile's thrusters burst on as he passed, locking onto his red hot engines.

"Proximity Warning: Collision Imminent," said the electronic voice of the console. Jogun tried to shake the blip on the radar, twisting, banking, and turning.

It stayed on his tail like it was reeling him in. Throttle to the floor, Jogun stared up at the tower, the red light at the top another ten seconds away. Seconds he didn't have. *I tried...* He turned the wheel to the side, pointing the ship at open sky. Away from the tower.

"Emergency Eject Initiated!" The Scout's canopy blasted off of the frame. "Wha—?"

FWOOSH! The seat launched and Jogun blacked out for a split second. BOOM! He awoke screaming inside an O2 mask. Wind roared in his ears as an intense heat churned below him. His vision cleared, and he looked down. A swirling fireball blackened beneath him as he drifted helpless above it. Sedonia Tower had been slapped with the shockwave, but still stood. The wind pushed him straight toward it. *I can still do this!* The roof landing pad loomed ahead, but the closer he got, the more the seat's weight pulled against the parachute. *NO! Coming in too low!* He struggled in his harness. Managed only to turn it as he crashed through the top floor windows.

Screams, his own and others, stirred together in the crashing chaos. The ejector seat chassis dug into the floor and ground to a screeching halt. People got up from the floor, dazed and bloody. Ears ringing and nose bleeding, Jogun's senses gathered out of the fog. He twisted the release on his harness and took out his uzi. Stood up with a sharp whirr of his augmented legs. More screams.

"Everybody down to the bunkers, NOW!" shouted a man's voice from somewhere. *Must be the man in charge.* Jogun focused through the blinding headache, raised his uzi, and fired a long burst into the ceiling. Everyone around him froze as he turned the weapon on them. Their faces. Downcast like beaten dogs. Their whimpers stung Jogun in the chest as his finger faltered on the trigger.

"N-Nobody—" he ripped the oxygen mask off, "NOBODY MOVE!". Wind howled through the window as wires sparked and papers fluttered. Jogun's heart throbbed in his neck, his mind drowning in panic. No Matteo. Only terrified men and women dressed up like black and white statues.

"What do you want?" said the same voice from before. Jogun whirled, pointing the gun squarely at the source. A graying man stood behind a desk, his olive skin glistening with sweat in the flickering amber lights. He held his hands up.

"You in charge?" asked Jogun.

"I...I'm Governor Sato. Anything you want, I'm the one to get it for you. Please let them go...you don't need them," said the man. Jogun looked around the room at all the expectant faces. Nodded, keeping the uzi barrel trained on Sato.

"Get the fuck out! All of you!" Jogun said. The group quietly shuffled to their feet. Ducked low as they scurried out of the room. Jogun stepped over shattered glass and torn furniture as he walked toward the desk. Stuck the gun in the Governor's somber face.

"Thank you..." Sato said, "Now...what do you want?"

Jogun darkened. Clenched his teeth.

"The brother you stole from me."

"Brother?" asked Sato. Jogun yanked the bolt on the uzi with a sharp click. Pressed the gun to Sato's wrinkled forehead. Sato blinked. Swallowed.

"I don't know about any brother," he said quietly, "What makes you think I have him?"

"Kabbard." Jogun watched the understanding slowly dawn in Sato's eyes. A storming silence hung in the scorched air.

"Okay," Sato finally said.

Sato led the way down to a round room with three doors. Never looking back, he walked to the center door. Opened it with a beep. The man stopped dead in his tracks as he saw the inside.

"Move!" Jogun shoved him. Sato stumbled and fell to the carpeted floor as Jogun took in the room. An empty wreck. Furniture flipped, table smashed, windows broken...and blood. A pool of it next to a bloody knife. Footprints of it smeared across the floor leading to—

Jogun clasped his head in his hands and dropped to his knees. The blood in his veins turned to liquid fire. His hands. His feet. His ears. His face. All of it went numb as the fact ripped his soul apart from the inside.

"Listen," Sato said, "We don't know wha—"

BRRRAPP! Jogun buried a three-round burst in the middle of Sato's chest. The Governor parted his jacket and looked down. The pressed white shirt turned quietly red as he dropped to his knees. Jogun stood up with the buzz of servos. Turned a dial on his hip. As the familiar thump-whine-thump-whine pierced the air, Sato closed his eyes and waited.

The kick landed center mass, buckled the ribcage, and launched the Governor limp through the big bay window into the creeping edge of dawn. Fine, red droplets settled on the carpet. On Jogun as he flicked the dial off and let his arms hang. He looked out at the yellowing sky. Took a step toward it. Then another. A humming gathered over the ringing in his ears as he approached the high-arched window.

He stood on the edge and watched the first of the ships pass overhead and all around him. Gigantic gray-green war platforms escorted by tight squadrons of fighters. Other ships zoomed past them, hurtling toward the burning West. Explosions popped off in the distance. First among the pillars of the Inner Ring. Then throughout the Outer.

Jogun felt hollow. Blown through by the violent winds whipping into the room. *It's all gone. There's nothing left. I'm nothing...* He leaned forward, trying not to look down first. Did anyway. His chest heaved as the tower stretched forever below him in a sickening slope. But a landing just a few floors down caught his attention. It jutted out from the sheer glass surface like a garden oasis. The faint outline of a body lay still next to a patch of bushes. It wasn't the Governor.

"MATTEO!" Jogun called out, hoping. The body didn't move. He followed the bloody tracks on the carpet to the smaller open window.

"MATTEO!"

Jogun whirled at movement in the corner of his eye. Soldiers roped down through the windows of the suite, landing hard on the floor. They stood in unison, each armored from head to foot in bulky, gray-and-white camouflaged Augmentor gear. Ammo mags the size of cinder blocks stuck out of their giant weapons. They turned to Jogun, staring through blank, eyeless masks.

"Engage!" croaked one of their filtered voices. Jogun planted a boot on the edge of the window and dove as a deafening barrage of slugs tore the room apart.

Hurtling downward, Jogun kicked his legs underneath him. As the landing rushed up ahead, the soles of his boots started vibrating.

"OhhhHHHH SHIIIIITTT!"

His heels bit the concrete and punched through, driving his legs deep into the landing. A shockwave blasted the material out from around him in a deep, round crater. He doubled over, pain shooting through the rest of his body. But it subsided. The fall hadn't broken him. He winced as he climbed out of the crater. Hobbled through elegant cafe tables and chairs to the body on the ground.

His brother lay unconscious with a raw gash seeping blood above the eyebrow and a soaked bit of cloth tied around the arm. A torn, bloody couch cushion sat off to the side. Jogun crouched beside Matteo. Hands shaking, he grabbed him by the shoulders. Shook gently.

"Matteo! Ahh God...MATTEO! Come on, little man, *wake up!*"

47

Redemption

THE VOICE REACHED in and pulled Matteo out of a pitch-black dream. He expected to open his eyes in their Slum apartment, staring up at the posters and magazine clippings he'd pasted to the container ceiling. Jogun's fuzzy image gazed down at him, coming gradually into focus.

"Jo...?" Matteo said, lifting his head. He felt Jogun's thin, aug-covered arms scoop underneath him and squeeze. Tears dropped on his shoulder. Matteo's arms heaved up. Embraced his brother. Behind him, the blinking red light of Sedonia Tower came into focus, followed by the shapes of tank-like men jumping from the window above. Firing.

"JO!" Matteo yelled, pushing his brother to the side. Jogun rolled and staggered to his feet with Matteo close behind him as the concrete exploded in a hail of sparking debris. They sprinted toward the overhang in the side of the building. As Jogun kicked open the double doors, five armored soldiers slammed down behind them, shattering patio furniture in bursting shockwaves.

Inside was some sort of eating hall. The two of them wove between the white plastic tables and chairs that lined the tile floor. Jogun reached cover first behind a marble fountain set in the back of the hall. A craning sculpture of a beautiful winged woman reached up out of the fountain, covered in ivy. She blew to pieces as Matteo slid in next to Jogun.

"Any ideas?!" Jogun shouted above the gunfire. Bits of dust and rock rained down on them.

"How the hell should I know?!" said Matteo.

"Man, you've had your nose in those damn books since Utu taught you to read! You gotta know *somethin'* about this place!" Jogun reached out of cover and sprayed with the uzi.

"Looked a little different in the pictures, Jo!"

"THINK!"

Images of Sedonia Tower drifted in and out of Matteo's mind as panic begged him to stay present. *Okay…escape! Travel. Uhhh, elevators. Superway. Landing pads. Parking Garages.* "Parking garages!" Matteo shouted, "Should be one every thirty floors!"

"Sounds good!…Which floor are we on?!"

"Uh…fifteenth from the top, I think! Elevator should be further in…up those steps!" Matteo pointed. At the end of the dining hall, two curving staircases swept around a crystal replica of Sedonia Tower. Tall, silver elevator doors shone above it on a thick marble balcony.

"Keep low and move!" Jogun said. The two of them took off toward it as the shock troops bore down on the fountain. The hailing gunfire dug melon-sized pits out of the replica tower and stairs, missing the brothers by inches. Jogun went left. Matteo right. Matteo bounded up the exploding steps, vaulted over the block marble railing, and punched the button on the elevator. A tiny blue light started moving along a line above the doors, creeping closer to the enlarged number '285' etched in the metal. The two of them took cover behind the marble railing as it chipped away in flying chunks.

"It's takin' too long! We gotta go!" said Jogun, checking the ammo left in his uzi mag. He reached over the wall and sprayed down toward the soldiers. Recoiled instantly. The barrage didn't skip a beat.

"Stairs!" Matteo said. On either side of their balcony, modest hinge doors were set into the walls.

"On my back!" Jogun shouted. Keeping low, Matteo climbed on and wrapped around his brother's torso. A ridiculous smile crossed his lips. Jo had carried him like this all the time when he was little, dashing across the Rasalla rooftops to run errands. It had always felt like freedom. He squeezed Jogun's chest tight as the high-pitch whine keyed on. Jogun launched through the air, swung his legs forward, and drop-kicked the door flat off its hinges.

"Holy shit!" Matteo laughed. Jogun sprang up without effort, Matteo and all.

"I know, right?!" said Jogun, "These things are balls-out crazy!" The distorted voices of the soldiers closed in behind them, barking orders. Matteo and Jogun looked down the spiraling staircase. The floors stretched to infinity, fading out of sight into blackness.

"Fifteen down from here?" Jogun asked.

"Yeah!"

"Aight then, hang on!" Jogun cleared the first flight in a single jump, then the second, then the third. Matteo struggled to hold on and keep watch behind them. They got a floor and a half down before the soldiers filed into the stair-well. All five jumped across the center gap in unison and turned their guns.

Jogun planted a boot on the railing and launched across the gap. Matteo's stomach dropped as Jo's feet almost missed the railing on the other side. Landed safely. Again and again they jumped across the bottomless pit, matched step for step by the descending soldiers. On each landing, Matteo scanned for numbers. '280.' '279.' '278.' Missed three or four. '273...'

"Next one!" Matteo shouted in Jogun's ear. After landing, Jogun spotted the door across the pit. He leaped hands first, planted them on the railing, tucked his knees, and shot forward. The door broke off with a snap. But they didn't land. They fell through empty space. The concrete deck rushed up to meet them. Jo took the first impact with the boots, but the two of them bounced. Flipped. Matteo lost his grip. Smashed back-first into a rear windshield.

The safety glass saved him when it didn't shatter. It buckled, cradling his ragdoll body. He groaned as he forced himself up. Shook his head. Jogun, stirring slightly, lay face down on the deck as the troops came through the door and marched down the side-facing stairs. Matteo leaped off the car and sprinted to Jogun's side. Picked him up under the shoulder.

"Come on, man, almost there! I'm not losin' you this time!" said Matteo, dragging Jo up as the first of the bullets flew. Jogun groaned and clutched his side. They limped behind a concrete pillar. Matteo quickly took in the surroundings. It was a wide, single-level deck with a panoramic opening to the sky at the end. The relaxed, elegant shapes of Sedonia City leaned toward it. *The way out.*

"You go find a car...I'll hold 'em off," Jogun said.

"I ain't leavin' you here! You don't have to save me anymore!" said Matteo. Jogun reached into a cargo pocket, took out a high-velocity ammo mag, and clicked it into the uzi.

"Who saved who?" Jogun said, smiling sadly. Chunks of cement exploded from their column.

"I'm crap at hot-wiring anyway, *go* man!" shouted Jo, "Pick a fast one!" Jogun rolled to his stomach and stretched out with the uzi. He fired controlled bursts at the soldiers' blank masks. They barely left a mark, but it seemed to at least stagger them. Matteo looked at his brother one last time. Breathed into his belly. Breathed out. Turned to scan the garage.

Not much to choose from. Most people must have bugged out after the attack and headed east. What was left, though, didn't disappoint. There were two or three government-issue sport-utility transports, the bulky kind people could take over-land, underwater, wherever. *Bulletproof too, but slow.* There was a Pulsar Carbon, a luxury sedan with real leather seats and a galaxy of convenient gadgets, but again...*Slow.* Then there it was. The Solari F5. It crouched at the far edge of the garage like a stalking cat, shining orange and sleek with sharp black accents. *Zero to 100 kph in 2.8 seconds...*

"You still here?!" Jo yelled. Matteo snapped out of analysis and took off, weaving through the pillars and sculpted dividers. He slid around the edge of one of the SUTs. Whatever ammo the military used, it punched right through the bullet-proofed windows. Matteo heard shots detonate close behind him as he reached the Solari. A chunk of rebar served to smash the window and set off the wailing alarm.

He crawled inside and yanked open the panel under the wheel. It looked like techno gibberish inside. Stacks of circuits and wire intestines. *Hell of a lot easier to just unhook it and sell it...* But as he stared wide-eyed into it, the patterns emerged. Wires leading to the ignition sensor, interfacing with pin connectors. His hands darted to work, stripping wires, finding leads, and rerouting connectors. The Solari's alarm clicked off. *Okay, close!* He tapped a couple contacts together. Nothing. Switched a few out. Nothing. Switched again. *YES!* The Solari hummed to life with a cascading vibration.

"YES! YES! YES!" he hammered the ceiling with his fist. Stilled himself as his hands drifted down. One to the wheel. One to the gears. *Jo...* His sweaty palms slipped the Solari into reverse and he gunned it out of the space. A few bullets punched the rear body as he turned to face the exit, shifted to drive, and darted out into the Sedonia sky. The shooting stopped.

"Okay," he said, puffing the air from his lungs. He air-braked into a one-eighty degree turn then laid on the gas. The shock troops had no time to react. Matteo flew straight at them, banked hard right, and flashed them with a full blast from the hover engines. Parked facing the exit.

He punched a button on the center console and watched as the passenger door hissed up and open. Jogun, head slumped, sat back against the ruined column. Blood trickled from a gouge in his side.

"JO!" Matteo called out. Jogun heaved his head to look. His mouth moved but the voice failed against the storming hum of engines. Matteo threw open the driver door and scrambled around the front end. Behind them, the soldiers started to rise. As he reached his brother, Matteo squatted, scooped under Jogun's knees and back, and lifted him like a half ration of rice.

"Never *could* tell you anything..." Jogun rasped. Heartbeat drumming in his ears, Matteo carried Jogun to the seat and set him down. As the door slammed shut, high-pitched whines sounded off. The first shots fired as he dove away onto the hood, swung his legs around, tucked through the driver's side door, and dropped in the seat. He rammed the throttle to maximum.

They fired out of Sedonia Tower like a cannon shot, shoving them both deep into the upholstery. The Tower shrank in the rear-view, fading to a silhouette in the hazy dawn. No one followed. *If they even could...* The pressure stopped as the Solari cabin adjusted to the speed. The ride smoothed, sailing over the Center Ring like a knife through water. Jogun gasped and coughed, clutching his torn flank. His breathing stuttered and heaved.

"Come on, man, into the belly," Matteo said, "Told me to do it enough times, you think you'd remember..."

Jogun shivered as he pressed his lips together, taking slow, bumpy breaths one by one. Jo rolled his head to the side. Looked down out the window.

"I-it's over…" Jogun said. They crossed above the City skyline at blinding speed, passing from Center to Inner Ring in seconds. Fires raged everywhere, stippled throughout the monumental angles, platforms, and curves. Heavy gunships took crowds of prisoners some places. Fought fever-pitch battles in others. Giant Federal command ships hovered amongst the clouds like angry Gods. Through the windshield, Matteo saw stray rounds streak up to the sky, most disappearing into the dawn drenched fog of smoke. The quiet rang in his ears.

"Matteo…" Jo cringed in pain. Continued. "You did good…on your own… just like you always said you would."

"Jo, I never meant—" Matteo stopped as Jo kept talking.

"I think I was scared you were right. That you didn't need me. That—that—I was alone… That I should be," Jogun stared out of the window, "I never told you the truth because I knew you'd leave…but you deserved to know, you *always* deserved to know…"

"Quit talking like this, man, we're gonna find Utu!" Matteo ground the ball of his foot into the accelerator. The Solari shuddered as it reached top speed. The first squat apartments of the Outer Ring appeared under the horizon. Matteo poured sweat as he forced the wheel steady. He felt Jogun's hand gently rest on his shoulder.

"It's-o-okay," Jo said, sucking short breaths, "It's okay…you're strong. You can choose for yourself now. You got this…" The hand slipped off Matteo's shoulder.

"No, no, no, no, NO! Come on, Jo, I need you, man, *I need you!*" Matteo clutched Jo's hand, "I've always needed you, you're my— You *are* my brother. Rasalla's our home. I can't do this without you, now please just…just stay…stay—." The sadness settled over him as the Solari boomed over the Outer Ring. Past the ruined Border.

Tracing due East from the Rasalla River, Matteo recognized the Healing Quarter. The Temple of the Wheel sat at the far end of it with strings of prayer flags blowing in the scorched air. Scores of the wounded, dying, and dead lined the grounds, tended by fluttering blue shapes. Matteo brought the Solari down in the only open patch he could find, feeling a twinge as those who could walk scattered to hide. He powered off the engines and released the doors.

"I'm one of you! Scrap! Ashes! Dirt!" Matteo shouted, waving his arms, "Get Utu!". He ran around to the passenger side, took Jogun's body from the car, and turned. Stopped. Jogun's eyes gazed at the sky, unblinking as ash-colored raindrops wet his face. Before the tears could come, Matteo looked around him. The Blue Ladies, wounded dwellers, T99s, others strange to Matteo…they crowded together, heads bowed. All at once, they dropped to their knees. Bowed. An old woman stepped forward with two young helpers. Dressed in temple blue, bits of copper and tin rattled on long necklaces around her thin neck and shoulders. She lifted a withered hand to Jogun's forehead.

"The Healer has gone home," she said aloud, "We will take the machine from his flesh and send his body to the Earth as it came. Place him here." The two helpers laid a blanket of heavy Rasalla cloth on the rain-dappled ground. Matteo stepped forward and knelt. Lowered Jogun's broken body to the blanket. Reaching forward, he closed his brother's eyes. The old woman placed her hands over her heart. Raised her tiny voice to the crowd.

"When the hour is dark, do not despair.

For He is with us.

Begging his children to find their path.

Blessed are those who do, following unto its end.

Blessed are those who find faith, not only in God, but in themselves.

Blessed are those who show the way of Love, of Sacrifice, and of Peace.

Do not despair."

Matteo blinked back tears. His path was clouded. City. Slums. *The world?* Who knew what it would mean from here. He looked one last time at the peace on Jogun's face. Over the swirling chaos in his mind, Matteo heard his brother's clear voice. *'You got this.'*

48

Stepstones

Weeks later

LIANI FIDGETED WITH her kevlar Press helmet. She wished she would have tried a few more on before stealing this particular one from the GloboMetro field HQ. The pinching straps worked at her frayed nerves as she approached the City-side checkpoint to the Outer Ring. Kilometers of razor-wire fence had been rolled out to form a new Border, thirty meters high, guarded by legions of government troops and patrolling aircraft. Liani glanced up. The Federal command ships hadn't moved since the 'Intervention,' hovering high above Sedonia City with an ever-present hum. Liani felt tiny. Exposed. *The Narayana's supposed to be twelve times the size of one of those...* She wondered where it might be.

The Aug-troops at Access Point Charlie each stood taller than an average gigantic human, decked out head to foot in heavy Augmentor rigs. She felt their eyes glaring at her from behind those smooth, blank masks as she walked up to the gate. Thankfully, a regular size officer in a helmet and fatigues seemed to be in charge of clearance, checking a cargo manifest of a ground truck. He waved them through and turned to Liani.

Okay...showtime. Liani threw on her cutest smile and batted eyelashes over her brown, color-corrective contacts.

"Hello," she said with a sly pitch. She rolled up her sleeve, gulped a lump in her throat, and held out her upturned arm.

"Evening, ma'am," said the officer as he took her hand and waved a scanner baton over her arm. Concealer cream covered the tiny scar on her smooth skin. He didn't seem to notice it. *This better work...* The technician working with Doc Utu had called it a 'Bounce Chip.' It would detect the scan, block communication with the main City server, then reroute the query to their server back in Rasalla. New picture, name, date of birth, social security number, current employer, political affiliations, and detailed family history. All of it had to gel, or she'd go away for identity theft. Not a healthy idea in the Post-Intervention world. The scanner beeped, stopping her heart. Liani watched as the officer read through the information on his private Neural display.

"Thank you, Ms. Deckard...Sorry if we make you nervous," the officer released her hand, "I know it looks like some kind of alien invasion around here."

Liani laughed, bleeding the pressure.

"Yeah," she said, "At least they give us a human face to talk to, Officer...?"

"*Corporal* Schilling...and I gotta say, *your* face is a sight for sore eyes," he said with a smile. A loud throat clearing behind her made Liani jump. She whipped around and scowled.

"What?" Corey said, "This thing's heavy." He set the blocky gray case down in the dirt then rose to stretch in his white medical Augs. She could kill him all over again. That 'thing' happened to be a stolen Hi-Band Broadcast Unit.

"You crew with her?" asked Schilling.

"Obviously," said Corey. Liani made no secret of punching him in the shoulder...forgetting about the healing gunshot wound there. Corey yelped. The Corporal tensed and rested a casual hand on his sidearm.

"There a problem?" asked Schilling.

"No!" Liani and Corey said in unison.

"I got shot...in the...Whitlatch attack," said Corey, rolling up his left sleeve. Schilling studied the bandage as he stepped forward with the scan baton. Swept it over Corey's forearm.

"Heard about that...we should've been there. Damn bureaucratic—-wait, says here you live in Shibuya."

"I do, uh..." said Corey, stumbling, "*She* lives in Whitlatch..."

The Corporal lowered his head and turned away. He pressed his throat mic. Murmured something. Corey and Liani exchanged looks.

"Okay, you guys are good," said the Officer, "But if you're headed into the Hostile Zone, you'll need to get an escort. Look for Sergeant Yeighman at the border tent, he'll set you up."

"Thank you very much, Corporal Schilling," said Liani sweetly. Corey picked up the case with a grunt and forged ahead, pushing Liani through the open gate.

"Hey!" the Corporal called out, freezing the two of them in their tracks. *Shit!* Liani turned wearing her best innocent face.

"You guys be safe out there, okay? Media likes to paint Dwellers as 'just people,' but they're desperate people. Desperate people do crazy things."

"We'll be careful," Corey said flatly. They turned and walked briskly toward the rift in the Border. Tanks, armored trucks, and squads of soldiers crowded the central avenue. Through brute force, they occupied the war-torn Outer Ring, pumping power rations into the City like life support. Fenced-in tent villages had also cropped up. The news didn't have much to say about them. Watching a wounded plant worker get dragged from his tent kicking and screaming, Liani realized why.

They skipped the border tent and Sergeant Yeighman, tagging along instead behind another group of press and their three-man Aug-troop escort. After a quick scan, Corey and Liani were part of the group.

"Okay folks!" shouted one of the soldiers through his mask, "Please walk two-by-two! Please keep between me and my associates *at all times!* Do not deviate from this little tour of ours...the enemy would be more than happy to get their hands on a couple City reporters! Let's go!"

Just like that, they walked through the Border. The charred canyon stretched a hundred meters above them on either side. Corey, following suit with the others, snapped pictures rapid-fire.

"Hard to believe..." Corey said.

"No kidding." Liani looked out over the Slums. Utu had described them to her, but she'd never seen them in person. The rusting towers, the stacked containers, the criss-crossing catwalks and bridges, the shanties in the street...all of it full of hidden people. Few dared show themselves with the Aug-troops around.

"Okay, there it is," Corey whispered. The road bent ahead. Several alleys, stairwells, and pathways radiated out from it. One path dipped down and out of sight. A blue prayer flag flapped in the breeze, tied to a pipe on the corner.

"Ready?" Corey asked.

"As I'll ever be," said Liani. When the convoy turned right, Liani took off her helmet, spilling her red curls over her shoulders. She sucked in a breath. Gunfire erupted from the surrounding buildings. As the soldiers scrambled to react, Liani and Corey bolted for the alley. It changed direction several times inside, forking in ways Liani didn't remember from the instructions. Behind, a savage thump-whine-thump-whine-thump-whine of military Augmentors bore down on them.

"There!" Liani shouted as she saw another flag dangling from a clothesline. A door beside it opened and a little woman in blue robes leaned out. Waved them in. There were three women in all, old, tiny, and frail. But fast. In a series of deft moves, they slipped jammer-rings on Liani and Corey's fingers and wrapped the two of them in earth-colored cloaks.

"Come!" said one of the ladies, waddling to another door. She swung it open and shuffled everyone out. *The Falari Market.* The bustle of evening activity quickly swallowed them up between the tents, stands, and blankets full of items. Liani chanced a backward look. Saw one of her escorts perched on the roof, scanning the crowd. Not finding them.

"We're good," said Liani.

"Are we?" asked Corey, "Gonna have a chat later about flirting with Corporals and punching bullet wounds."

"Crybaby."

They reached the Temple of the Wheel within the hour, crossing through its round metal gate. Liani loved the place instantly. It was dirty, tarnished, and made from God-knows how many bits of scrap...but the space calmed her. She could see it was built with love. One of the ladies took Liani by the hand.

"Oh! So soft!" the little woman said, "You betta' tell me your secret!" Liani laughed as she and Corey were led to one of the metal containers. They passed through the hanging bead curtain into a makeshift broadcast room. Wires snaked over the floor like black pasta, hooked up to old-style consoles and monitors. Utu greeted them.

"Fantastic!" he said, "You made it! Did you get what you needed?"

"Right here," said Corey, panting. He put down the case with a thud and opened it. Illyk stood up from behind a console, cigarette in mouth.

"Perfect, help me hook it up over here to the mem-data ports," Illyk said. Liani shot the sketchy kid a look that made him cringe. Illyk avoided her eyes as he turned and crossed the room. He had said his men acted alone that night. *But he picked the men.* She didn't like trusting him now, but bigger things were moving.

Corey grunted as he lifted the HBBU out of the case and followed. Liani pulled her hood off and ran her fingers through her hair. Her heart still hadn't calmed down. Utu walked over with a small ceramic bowl of water. Handed it to her.

"You and your friend have done a brave thing, Liani," said Utu, smiling that smile she'd already learned to love, "We thank you. Would you like me to show you to a bedroll for some rest?" Liani drank deeply from the bowl then withdrew it from her lips. Stared down into the rippling water.

"Thank you," she said, "But...if he's ready, I'd like to see him."

"Of course. This way."

Utu led her cloaked through streets and alleys to the West. The Slums were rebuilding, little by little. Scorched gouges, collapsed dwellings, and tumbled walls grew new structure, fed and shaped by scores of Dwellers. They sang as they worked. Liani eventually heard the sound of flowing water echo through the neighborhoods. Flowers and incense masked the pungent smell of the Rasalla River as she and Utu walked out onto the concrete-stepped shore.

"There he is," Utu said, pointing through the crowd. Matteo stood at the water's edge, cradling something in his hands. Liani followed the Doctor to his side.

"We got it," she said to Matteo, "Corey should have everything working soon. You sure you want to do this?" Matteo knelt by the muddy water. A metal flower with a small lit candle in its center drifted from his hands, joining a flickering current of flowers. He stood, turned, and looked at her, rubbing his fingers tightly against his palms. After a deep breath, he nodded. Looked back out at the water.

"Thousands of people are about to watch my life...They should know what I think about it," Matteo said.

"They should, indeed," said Utu. Matteo shook the nerves out of his arms and squared himself to Liani.

"Okay," he said. Liani pressed a finger to her temple, calling up her Neural's camera mode.

"Remember, you're just talking to me...tell me what you want to say," she said, framing him in the floating interface. She tapped the record button and held up her hand.

"Okay...five, four, three," Liani held up two fingers. Then one. Pointed at Matteo. He lowered his head. Took three long breaths into his belly, and looked up into Liani's eyes.

"My name is Matteo. But I was born Aden Rindal. Son of Alan and Patricia Rindal. I've lost family on both sides of the Border. My City mother and father when I was a baby. My Rasalla brother who raised me, to the War. You're about to see events in my life that...that changed yours. All of ours. And you're about to see the plans of the people who think they own the world. I won't tell you what to think about all this. Your life is up to you. But after you've seen this story, take a look around. Ask how you'd change things if you could. Then *know* that you can. I am a Son of Sedonia, from both City and Slums. We're in this together."

EPILOGUE

THE SLIGHT COLD, burning sensation in Janice Prescott's veins grated at her last nerve. Each one of these yearly treatments felt worse than the last. *Probably because these sadists keep upping the dosage.* A cadre of the world's best doctors and nurses buzzed around the pristine infirmary, monitoring Janice's vitals, taking samples, and fine-tuning the fresh nanotech as it settled into her decaying cells. Hooked up to wires and tubes, she felt like the TVs of her twentieth century childhood. All the irritations that came with immortality.

The Narayana progress reports didn't help. Documents in her Neural showed that fuel was frozen at eighty-two percent capacity. Not near enough for launch. Leave alone the fact that entire sections of the hull were still open to Space. It was comfortable progress for their pre-Intervention timetable, but the 'Son of Sedonia' broadcasts stuck a fork in those plans.

A thousand needles suddenly raked Janice's chest. *Ugh, god dammit, just stick a fork in ME!*

"Please, Mrs. Prescott, try to relax," said the doctor through his clean-mask, "A spike in your cortisol production could complicate the exchange.".'"

"Relax. That's your advice, Lucius? Just *relax?* Have you even been *conscious* for the past month?! Do *you* have a planet's worth of damage control to manage?" Prescott's anger cooled to a sour distress as she saw the Doctor's reaction. The anti-aggro dose had made the man bloody sensitive. The nurses cowered too as they monitored and adjusted the state-of-the-art equipment.

"We're done here," Prescott said, swinging her frail, Augged legs out of bed, "I have far too much on my agenda right now to—"

The door to the hall whispered open, revealing a familiar face at the door.

"Marcus, my savior! Take me away from all this," said Janice. Marcus, second on the PRG board, stepped into the room with the soft clack of his lambskin shoes. Hands folded behind his back. The usual charming humor she'd come to admire was gone from his tanned, weathered features.

"Nobidyne has called a meeting. We've assembled on the Veranda," said Marcus.

"Right..." Janice sighed. She straightened her neck through a stab of pain, "Give me a moment to 'detach' and dress. I'll meet you in the hall."

The nurses around her quietly got to work removing the tubes from Janice's taut, dry skin. Fire shot up her arm as one of the IVs slipped out of a vein.

"Enough!" Janice waved them off and did the rest herself.

With brittle posture forced upright by the Augs under her pantsuit, Janice met Marcus in the vaulted hall and from there they walked to the tram entrance. Together, they entered the open car and sat facing each other. She studied his grim, wrinkled expression as they coasted to top speed.

"How bad is it?" asked Prescott.

"Bad," said Marcus, "They want to clip our time-table by another six months."

"*Six months?!* That's—"

"Impossible, yes. But Alhaka, Qin, and Seelatek are all on track to launch their fleets before that. The trip to Gliese may take twenty dull years of travel time, but months are going to count in the first land-grab," said Marcus. "Territories will be claimed."

"New nations founded on prime real estate, yes. But if we launch prematurely, we won't make the fucking *trip!*" said Janice.

"And if we don't accelerate, Nobidyne *will* leave without us. Taking the lion's share of the supplies, personnel, and equipment with them. Three G-ships to our one," Marcus, short of breath, tapped a few buttons in his Neural. Took in a smooth, even breath with the sudden release. "They need to be reassured."

"Reassured," Janice repeated to herself. She looked, with weary eyes, out of the tram's clear canopy. The sprawling green preserve below them was coming along, to be sure, but the workers were still in the planting stages. Full crop rotation was at least another 'season' away, and there would be a lot of debugging to do. Both on the facility and the personnel.

"We *had* their consent to let the Themis riots escalate into a rebellion. The Invasion, the Intervention, martial law...all of it right on schedule. Now they want what? For me to fall on my sword because of this...*externality?*"

"Letting Sato handle it was *your* call, Janice," said Marcus.

Prescott couldn't argue with that. Not without sounding like a pathetic child, especially to Marcus. *How the hell was I supposed to know what Alan Rindal hid inside his own son?!* She pursed her thin lips and scowled. Through the tram canopy and the Preserve's colossal geo-dome, the curvature of the Earth pressed down on her. Amongst the sprawling grid-webs of light on the planet's surface, tiny explosions winked in the dark. A few glowing strands and branches faded to black with each blast.

"Regardless," Marcus continued, "We have to convince them to wait. By any means."

Janice sighed.

"Agreed."

Their tram car arrived at the marble pillared terminal, and they both stepped out. Climbed the spiral stairs to the Preserve Veranda. Janice had helped design the modest finery of the circular Veranda platform. Granite tiles, green topiaries around the edges, upholstered wicker furniture... It could have been part of the family's Mediterranean villa she'd visited as a girl.

The entire board had assembled there, some seated and comfortable, with others standing and shiftless. Janice spotted an extra face among them. Nathan, her eldest nephew, sat on the end of a couch. He took a glass of brandy from one of the uniformed server's trays. Sniffed it with his surgically straightened nose. *What is that idiot doing here?*

"It looks like we're all here. Are we ready to proceed?" asked Prescott. A general mutter of consent answered her. Everyone tapped their temples, revealing a shared Neural display hovering above the coffee table.

"Call Kuwahara," Prescott said, "Authorization: Janice Prescott. Encrypt and Connect." The display shifted and pulsed in mid-air as they waited for an answer. Prescott used each ring as a call to composure. *Confidence. Strength. Control.* She repeated her mantra over and over until the connection went through. Akira Kuwahara materialized before them.

"Hello Aki," Janice said, "How are you doing?"

"Not well, Jan, not well. Demonstrations in our Cities are on the rise, and the local governments are restless. Regardless of our promises and reassurances, it appears no one wants to be the next Enota Sato," Kuwahara said.

"Restless is not rebellious. At least not yet. I have several strategies in mind that can buy us the appropriate 'padding' with regards to our timetable, and—" a tickle in Janice's throat stopped her mid-sentence. Marcus stepped into the silence without hesitation.

"We understand the complications the Intervention and this 'Son of Sedonia' have produced. We want to express our deepest apologies for this lapse in judgment, Kuwahara-san, but the timing of this was never going to be comfortable or convenient. That's the simple reality of the challenges humanity now faces. We want to assure you that our partnership remains not only strong, but essential to maintain our collective advantage moving forward to Gliese 581g." Marcus finished and relinquished the floor as Nathan Prescott stood.

"Wha—" Janice choked on the breath. Realized her throat was closing. She clawed at her neck with one hand and pawed at the Neural with the other. No help or relief came. *The treatment...!*

"It is in that spirit," Nathan said, keying a few buttons, "that we offer atonement for the error, and thus guarantee that insightful, *fresh* leadership prevents any future missteps." He pressed 'Enter.' Janice's Augmentors switched off simultaneously, dropping her ninety-six year old body to the granite tile. Her throat closed completely as her chest seized. She reached for Nathan. The spoiled ingrate just turned and cracked a smarmy grin.

"I will assume control of the Prescott family assets, and take my Aunt's place on the board. But as a senior shareholder only. My friend Marcus Rindal, who has endured *personal* sacrifice time and time again for this venture, is our unanimous choice for the role of Chief Executive Officer."

Vision tunneling, Janice Prescott turned her gaze on the Rindal grand-patriarch. Her friend and confidant of so many years didn't even look at her as she slipped away. Heart-rate slowing and thoughts drifting, Janice stared at his face. The cheekbones. The skin tone. The hard eyes under heavy brow. *So much like the grandson...so much alike...so much alike.*

Her world faded to the sound of polite applause.

ACKNOWLEDGMENTS

It almost seems unfair that so many people did so much to help this book come to be, yet my name is the only one on the cover. Although if I did justice to everyone, taking the three days to paint the cover illustration might then have been a moot point. Still, none of this would have happened without the encouraging, inspiring, selfless people I've had the good fortune to know.

My teachers Mrs. Garland, Lora Stager, Mark Schultz, Paul Hudson, Jay Hawkins, Michael Nolan, Michaela Roessner, and countless others who taught me lessons both complex and simple. So many of you did so over the internet or TV, and we've never met. I hope that changes one day.

My past employers Redstorm Entertainment, Epic Games, Schell Games, Radioactive Software, and Villain LLC. May your fantastic games be fruitful and multiply.

My friends. Many of you feel like family to me, regardless of how long we've known each other. Thanks and love to Ryan Johnson, Jack McAlpin, Jonathan Krug, Kari Barry, Dave Yeaman, John Washington, Mike Schaefer, Oliver Burling, Kevin Altman, John Gabbard, Kris Grace, the Rockers, Danny Green, Roger Collum, Lindsay Edwards, Ben Namie, Shaun Smith, Dwayne Brown, Willie Smith, Byron Youngblood, Rachel Acquaviva, Evan Miller, Lauren Holt, John DeRiggi, Nicole Epps, Jared Mason, Kwamé Babb, Reagan Heller, Sam Polglase, Suzanne Kafantaris (whatever the end result, she saved this book), my Brent-hood neighbors, and the countless others I wish I had more space to list.

My editors, designers, and compositors at TIPS Technical Publishing in Carrboro, NC. I apologize for the post-period double-spaces on every sentence in the manuscript. Old habits die hard, but consider the lesson well learned.

As you can probably tell, I've saved the best for last. My family. Thanks to Uncle Jim, Aunt Sandra, Foster, and Aunt Jan (both of them). Thanks to Jacob for playing video games, watching movies, and spending time with a little brother thirteen years younger than you. Thanks to Meagan for all of your heart-to-hearts, sisterly advice, and for making time to read the book while being an awesome mother to my two nephews Cooper and Fletcher.

Mom and Dad. Patty and Les Chaney. Two people who sat me on their shoulders so that I could reach as high as I dared. They struggled, saved, and sacrificed to support whatever I chose to do, all the while repeating "we're so proud of you." Mom, Papa...you are my light in the world.

Ben Chaney grew up with a passion for SciFi and Fantasy that led him to study visual storytelling and illustration at the Savannah College of Art and Design. After graduation, he worked his way up through the video game industry: QA testing at Epic Games and Redstorm Entertainment; game art production at Schell Games in Pittsburgh, Pennsylvania; then art direction at Villain LLC in Cary, North Carolina.

But storytelling had taken a hold of him at SCAD, and manifested in a pet writing project. Often neglected or pushed aside for other things, Son of Sedonia grew slowly over six years. Somehow, the image of the boy on the slum rooftop endured. As Ben honed his craft, the world changed. America plunged into recession, political discord, and uncertainty, triggering a desire for information the likes of which Ben hadn't before experienced. His writing, and this book, matured as he did.

Video game development had given Ben the confidence in his abilities. What to do with those abilities became impossible to ignore. That and the ceaseless, loving voices around him, all saying the same thing: "Follow your heart." In June 2012, Ben quit his successful job in game development to do just that.

The book you hold in your hands is the result.

www.ingramcontent.com/pod-product-compliance
Lightning Source LLC
Chambersburg PA
CBHW060539180626
46817CB00002B/637